BRAIN TRUST

Mercy Watts Mysteries Book Eight

A.W. HARTOIN

ALSO BY A.W. HARTOIN

Historical

The Paris Package (Stella Bled Book One)

Strangers in Venice (Stella Bled Book Two)

One Child in Berlin (Stella Bled Book Three)

Young Adult fantasy

Flare-up (An Away From Whipplethorn Short)

A Fairy's Guide To Disaster (Away From Whipplethorn Book One)

Fierce Creatures (Away From Whipplethorn Book Two)

A Monster's Paradise (Away From Whipplethorn Book Three)

A Wicked Chill (Away From Whipplethorn Book Four)

To the Eternal (Away From Whipplethorn Book Five)

Away From Whipplethorn Box Set (Books 1-3, plus bonus short)

Mercy Watts Mysteries

Novels

A Good Man Gone (Mercy Watts Mysteries Book One)

Diver Down (Mercy Watts Mysteries Book Two)

Double Black Diamond (Mercy Watts Mysteries Book Three)

Drop Dead Red (Mercy Watts Mysteries Book Four)

In the Worst Way (Mercy Watts Mysteries Book Five)

The Wife of Riley (Mercy Watts Mysteries Book Six)

My Bad Grandad (Mercy Watts Mysteries Book Seven)

Brain Trust (Mercy Watts Mysteries Book Eight)

Down and Dirty (Mercy Watts Mysteries Book Nine)

Small Time Crime (Mercy Watts Mysteries Book Ten)

Bottle Blonde (Mercy Watts Mysteries Book Eleven)

Mercy Watts Mysteries Book Set (Books 1-3, plus bonus short)

<u>Short stories</u>

Coke with a Twist

Touch and Go

Nowhere Fast

Dry Spell

A Sin and a Shame

Paranormal

It Started with a Whisper (Sons of Witches

For the staff of Penrose Hospital, who saved my brain in October 2015 and for my husband who, as always, knew exactly what to do.

http://www.stroke.org

The truck came to a halt, but I didn't open my eyes. I was too warm and comfortable to face what came next. There was definitely something coming. I could feel it. Usually, I was fairly optimistic about *next*, but this time there was every reason to dread it.

The window crank squeaked as someone forced it to move and I snuggled into my grandad's bony shoulder, trying to get a few more seconds of shuteye before I had to drag myself up the three flights to my apartment and an angry feline. Mr. Cervantes had been watching my cat and probably feeding him pork fifty different ways. It'd be hell getting my boy back on the dry food, but Skanky was the least of my worries.

Humidity flooded into the truck and I breathed deep the smell of impending rain, fully expecting my friend and partner, Aaron, to shake me awake. Instead I heard a familiar voice say, "Aaron, my man, you remembered."

My eyes popped open and I saw Mr. Knox, the Hawthorne Avenue gate guard, accepting a black bag imprinted with the Sturgis Motorcycle Rally emblem. He grinned and shook Aaron's hand. My partner stared at the windscreen through smudged glasses circa 1983. His hair stood on end and the Sturgis tee he wore was rumpled and stained with sausage grease and coffee, but he smelled mostly of hotdogs. Not for the first time, I wondered how he was *still* my partner. My father assigned Aaron to me *once* when I investigated Gavin Flouder's murder and he seemed to take it as a lifetime appointment like the Supreme Court, although he didn't say so. He never said much of anything. That we should spend so much time together didn't seem any more likely than Aaron being a fabulous chef, but he was and we did.

Mr. Knox rummaged through the bag, exclaiming with joy before glancing in the truck. "Miss Mercy, did I wake you?"

I sat up and stretched. "It's okay. I had to wake up in a minute anyway."

He held up the bag. "Look what Aaron brought me. Quite a guy, your partner."

"Yes, he is," I said with a twinge of guilt. I should've thought of bringing Mr. Knox a swag bag from Sturgis. He was a biker and went to the rally every couple of years. In my defense, I'd been a bit busy. Grandad's reunion with his Vietnam buddies had turned into a week of poisonings, murders, and a couple of stabbings. Grandad was one of the victims with a slash across his back that took multiple stitches to close. But that wasn't the worst of it. An unknown suspect had incited Cheryl Morris to start her murder spree, but she hadn't followed his intentions. It looked like her target was supposed to be Grandad and when Cheryl didn't do as she was told, a shadowy figure started stalking Grandad and me himself.

We'd left Sturgis at the crack of dawn when the cops figured out what was going on and we'd driven back to Missouri in hopes of outrunning him. So far, so good, but I had no faith that our luck would hold.

Mr. Knox leaned on the door and said, "You deserve a good rest after the week you've had."

"She doesn't need rest," said Grandad, reaching over and shaking Mr. Knox's hand. "She's a Watts. We keep on ticking."

His movement woke up Wallace, the pug I was watching for my ex-boyfriend. She yipped a couple times and went back to snoring.

"Wallace the Wonder Dog. Who knew pugs could be so useful." said Mr. Knox.

I glanced at Wallace's wrinkly snout. "I guess she's useful."

"I'd say so. I'm glad she's on your team. What would you have done without her?"

I wouldn't have been peed on quite so much.

"I have no idea," I said.

He smiled at me and stepped back. "Speaking of your team, I'm glad you're back, Mercy."

Oh, no.

"Why?" I said slowly.

"Well, it seems your mother has taken to jogging again," said Mr. Knox.

"Accidents?"

"A couple of minor fender benders. Nothing serious."

"I'm sorry. Dad got her a treadmill."

"I know, but she hasn't accepted that you can't have Marilyn Monroe running around in spandex without having heads turn. Men can't help it. Your mother..."

I nodded. My mother. The woman was incorrigible. If Mr. Knox thought I had any pull with her, he was dead wrong. Carolina Watts didn't listen to me. My dad and Great Aunt Miriam had some pull but not me, her only child. Even with Dad's influence, Mom went outside to jog when he was out of town. Mr. Knox was right. Seeing my mom, a Marilyn Monroe look-a-like, jogging had and always would cause accidents. We'd be sued again, probably for reckless endangerment. I had to admit they had a point. Mom knew what could happen and she jogged anyway. Since I was the spitting image of my mother, Dad banned me from jogging, too. Unlike Mom, I had no problem with not exercising outdoors or indoors, for that matter.

"Talk to her for me, will you?" asked Mr. Knox.

"I'll try," I said with a groan and he smiled. "Thanks again, Aaron."

My partner cranked up the window, peering through the windscreen without a response. That was so Aaron and Mr. Knox wasn't bothered. If you knew Aaron, you knew he had a good heart buried somewhere beneath the weird.

"That was nice," I said.

"Huh?"

"Giving Mr. Knox that stuff."

"Yeah." Aaron put the truck in gear but not in reverse.

Mr. Knox waved from the gate house pagoda and the enormous wrought iron gate opened.

"Wait," I said. "Where are we going?"

"You wanted to see your mother," said Grandad.

"*Want* is putting it a bit strong. I'll just go home."

Grandad frowned. "You'll go see your mother and make up."

"We're not really fighting."

"She knows that you've done something."

"I haven't done anything."

"If you didn't want your mother to know about Hunt, you shouldn't have called the director."

I crossed my arms and stared at the roof as we drove past the stately homes on the most exclusive street in St. Louis. Maybe I shouldn't have called Hunt Hospital for the Criminally Insane, but I was trying to get information about a visitor Kent Blankenship had. He was a mass murderer that Dad sent me to interview. And I kept interviewing him in a mostly pointless attempt to ingratiate myself with the psycho. Dad and the cops were certain Blankenship had information on other murders, but he wasn't giving it up. He just liked to torment me. His visitor was interesting though. Other than me, only his lawyer got in. Blankenship wouldn't even see his own poor parents and this visitor asked about me. It had to have something to do with the events in Sturgis, so I called Wilson Cleves, the director of Hunt. Huge mistake. Cleves immediately called my mom and she was pissed. I should've known. Cleves' loyalty would be to my parents. Everyone in the law enforcement community knew them. My dad had been a renowned police detective. He'd since retired and opened up his own shop, consulting for the FBI and anyone else who had the funds to pay his hefty price tag.

Mom didn't want me to have anything to do with Blankenship and it was one of the few things my parents disagreed on. She'd tried to tell me off, but cell reception on the drive back from South Dakota was spotty at best.

The truck rolled to a stop and Aaron poked me. I looked up at the house. There was no sign of Mom, but she was in there. I could feel it. Anger radiated off the hundred-year-old Tudor.

"Come in with me," I said.

"Not a chance, sweetheart," said Grandad. "Carolina will weigh me if I go in there and you know I haven't had time to bulk up."

Bulking up wasn't a realistic option for my grandfather. His width had been compared unfavorably to swizzle sticks, turkey jerky, and someone named Twiggy. Grandad took offense at the last one, but I had no idea why.

Grandad was supposed to be on a weight-gaining diet and my job was to make him stick to it. We'd fallen off the wagon hard, what with all the murdering going on. If my mother and grandmother found out, there'd be hell to pay, mostly for me. I was in charge of my grandad, a concept I still couldn't get my head around.

"I should go home first," I said.

"You don't want to go home first."

I chewed on my lower lip and then said, "No, I don't. Why is that?"

"Because you're a good daughter."

"That doesn't sound right."

"True. You're only a medium daughter, but you're a great grand-daughter."

"Thanks." I got out and kissed him on his sallow, bristly cheek. "Get some rest."

Wallace woke up and began barking her fool head off. Grandad held her out to me. "Here you go."

"You keep her," I said.

"She pees."

"You don't say?"

"Mercy." Grandad gave her a tiny shake. "She's your dog."

"She's not my dog. I'm a cat person. Cats."

Grr.

Wallace eyed me and I could see the wheels turning in her pea-sized brain. She was working out how many pairs of shoes I had left to ruin. Not many, I can tell you that.

"Go ahead and growl. I like cats," I said.

Grandad looked past me. "What about those cats?"

I turned and squinted. To my ultimate dismay, Mom's evil Siamese were lurking in the front window. They'd spotted me and probably already had their claws out.

"Those aren't really cats," I said. "If they were human, the FBI would have profiles on them."

Grandad pushed Wallace into my arms. "I couldn't agree more. I've arrested murderers with better dispositions, but if that dog pees in my house, Grandma will beat me with a stick."

"My life sucks."

"You'll be fine."

"If the Siamese eat Wallace, it's on you," I said.

"That's fair. Now talk to Carolina and tell her I'm practically porky."

I rolled my eyes before dragging my stinky army bag out of the back of the truck.

Aaron pulled away and I stumbled up the long brick walk under heavy low-lying clouds. The three tall stories cast a long shadow and a hot breeze wafted through the old oaks, inviting me to climb up into their broad branches the way I used to do when Mom was angry. But I was too tired to climb and Mom was better at it than me anyway. I expected her to fling open the door and glare at me, hands on hips. She didn't, but her cats were still in the window, acting like homicidal maniacs. I could hear them yowling through the glass. They clawed at the window, their lithe bodies stretching to surprising lengths.

Wallace saw them and dug her heels in. Despite her tiny size, she was really hard to drag. "Come on, Wallace. I won't let them get you."

Bark. Grr.

"I feel the same way." I dropped the stinky army bag and gently picked her up before I trudged up the wide steps. "I guess I can clip you to the porch."

Bark. Bark. Bark.

Wallace wasn't looking at me or at the Siamese. She yipped and struggled to get out of my arms. Her rib injury from Cheryl Morris' vicious kick wasn't bothering her at all. "Knock it off. They won't eat you. Much."

Wallace nipped my arm and I dropped her, barely keeping ahold of her leash. I struggled to hold her back as I rang the doorbell.

Mom should've come running with all the yowling and barking. The cats were practically frantic. If they weren't so evil, I would've thought they were happy to see me. But they were never happy to see me. They hated me. Frantic wasn't good. A zing went through me and I pounded on the door. "Mom!"

I dug through my purse and got my key. I inserted it and punched my code in the keypad. It made a beep that meant the alarm wasn't armed. My stomach twisted and I turned the key.

"Mom!" I yelled into the receiving room.

No answer.

Wallace yanked me sideways and I scooped her up a second before the cats got to me. I dashed in the door with them charging at my exposed ankles. "Mom! Your cats are nuts."

A creepy crawly feeling came over me, the hairs going stiff all over my body, but I didn't have time to worry about it. Swish and Swat slashed at my ankles, caterwauling like I'd never heard before. I got Wallace in a football hold and swung my purse at them, but my ankles were already bleeding. I ran through the entire first floor, chased by yowling cats and yelling for my mother. She wasn't there and I ran up the stairs, just ahead of the cats to the second floor. Empty as well. Then up to the third floor, where my room and Aunt Tenne's boyfriend's studio was. Both were empty. The smell of paint pervaded the floor, but it wasn't as strong as usual. Bruno had a show somewhere. I couldn't remember where or when.

Swish and Swat rushed into the studio, hissing and stalking around me.

"No one's here," I told the cats.

Yowl.

Bark.

"Not you, too," I said. "We're going home."

The cats went insane. I leapt over them and dashed out the door and down the three flights. I managed to make it through the kitchen and into the butler's pantry, slamming the door in the nick of time before the Siamese got through.

Bark. Bark. Bark. Bark.

I leaned on the back door and clamped her jaws shut. "Oh my god!"

The cats rammed themselves against the door. They were going to hurt themselves. Mom would kill me. "I've got to call the vet. They've got brain damage or something." I kicked the door as it rattled. "She's not here, you freaks!"

Long, plaintive yowls came through the door like it was made of paper instead of thick walnut.

My phone rang in my purse.

Please be Mom.

I went out the back door to get away from the clamor before answering in a rush. "Hello! Hello! Mom?"

"No. It's me," said Spidermonkey.

My knees went weak. I was sure it would be her. Spidermonkey was my cyber snoop, a hacker with tremendous reach. Normally, I was happy to hear from him. "Sorry," I said. "Not now."

"What's wrong? Where's your mother?"

"I don't know. Her cats are acting nuts and she's not here."

"You're at your parents'?"

"Yeah, I gotta go."

"Call her and then call me back," said Spidermonkey.

His strong fatherly voice steadied me and I hung up to call Mom. No answer. That wasn't unusual, if she was getting her nails done or something. I left a voice mail, but the creepy crawly feeling didn't go away. I could still hear the cats yowling as if they were in pain. Something was wrong. They didn't act like that. Not ever. I called Dad. No answer. I left him a voice mail. He was doing something for the FBI. Nobody had been able to get ahold of him all week.

My phone rang again. Spidermonkey. "You didn't call me back."

"She didn't answer."

"Do you have a feeling?" he asked.

I didn't want to answer. I did have a feeling, a feeling that something wasn't right. It was a Watts thing and we were rarely wrong, even me. But my intuition was nothing compared to my dad's.

"Mercy."

"Yeah?"

"You looked through the entire house?" Spidermonkey asked.

"Uh huh." I thought I would throw up the feeling was so strong.

His voice got tight. "I want you to go to the garage and see if her car is there. Okay?"

Why didn't I think of that?

"On my way," I said, jogging down the porch steps to the brick walk overgrown with a riot of flowers, dragging a yapping Wallace behind me. The smell was cloying and made my nausea worse as I got to the garage. I keyed in my code and flung open the door. "Oh, crap!"

"What? What?" Spidermonkey's voice burst out of my phone.

"Her car is here."

"Maybe someone picked her up. Your Aunt Miriam, for instance."

I said maybe, but in my heart, I knew it wasn't true. I just knew.

"Call the police," said Spidermonkey. "Or I'll call them."

I stepped out of the garage and turned back to the house. On the back porch, looking at me with unblinking green eyes, was a black cat.

CHAPTER TWO

"**O**h my God!" I exclaimed.

"What Mercy?" yelled Spidermonkey.

"The cat."

"Cat? What cat? Do your parents have cats?"

"Yes. I mean, no. It's the other one," I said, watching as the cat, known to my family as Blackie, went into a stiff, impossibly high arch and then slinked down the porch stairs.

"I don't understand," said Spidermonkey in a tight voice I'd never heard him use before.

"It's the cat that shows up when something's happened or is about to happen. He belongs to us. He's been with us forever."

"Mercy, what are you saying?"

"Call the police. Something's happened to my mother," I said."

"Mer—"

I hung up. Wallace had stopped yapping. Her leash was taut and she walked mechanically toward the house. I followed, letting her and Blackie lead me.

Instead of going up the stairs to the house, we veered to the left toward Mom's side garden. It was separated from the backyard by an eight-foot-tall wrought-iron fence. Through the bars, I could see the ornamental ivy and a couple of sculptures done by our neighbor, Sandy. I unlocked the gate and Wallace pulled me past a cubist-style sculpture that Mom said was a chicken and, in the same moment, I realized Blackie had disappeared and someone was lying on the ground behind a pair of trash cans by the side door that led to the servant stair.

Wallace exploded into barks and we ran through the garden. Mom. She lay face up on the hard bricks.

"Mom!" I dropped to my knees, shoved Wallace back, and put my fingers to her pale, exposed neck. Strong heartbeat. Thank God! "Mom, can you hear me?"

"Help," she whispered. I never heard anything so sweet.

I quickly ran my hands over her, finding no blood or obvious signs of trauma.

"Tell me what hurts," I said.

She didn't answer.

"Mom, can you hear me?"

"Yes." Her voice was odd, sort of high-pitched and nasally. I found out why the second I tilted her face toward me. The left side of her face drooped and it was clear from the way her left arm and leg lay limp that she was completely paralyzed on that side.

I brushed her hair out of her face and pulled out my phone. "Mom, it's going to be fine. I'm calling an ambulance."

"Ambulance? What for?" she slurred. "Help me up. I have to get up."

"You can't get up right now."

"Help me up."

"It's alright, Mom. It's okay. I'm here."

"Why won't you help me?"

I dialed 911 and the dispatcher said, "911 What is your emergency?"

"My mother is having a massive stroke. I need an ambulance right now." I gave her our address and she calmly asked for Mom's symptoms. I named them and she said a patrol car had already been dispatched to our location and she was sending firefighters and an ambulance.

"I have to go."

"Ma'am, you need to stay on the line with me," she said smoothly.

"I can't. It's a gated street. I have to call the guard."

"Well—"

I hung up and called Mr. Knox.

"Miss Mercy, what can I—"

"Open the gate," I said. "Right now. Open the gate."

"What?"

"Open the gate!" I screamed. "My mom's having a stroke. You have to let the police and ambulance in."

"Oh my god! I'm opening it. Hold on. I'm coming!"

I hung up and picked up Mom's limp hand. I rubbed it hard. "Can you feel that, Mom? Do you feel me holding your hand?"

"Where are you?" Her eyes were locked to the right and she couldn't see me. I dropped her hand, crouching down to get into her eye line.

"There you are," she said.

"It's okay."

"Help me up."

"You can't get up, Mom," I said.

She flailed out her working arm and grabbed at my tee. "If I can just get my feet under me."

"The ambulance is coming."

"What for?"

I had to work to control my panic. *When had she last called me? When was that?* "There's the siren. They're coming."

"Who's coming?" Mom was getting less intelligible by the second.

"The ambulance."

She said something I couldn't understand and Wallace crept around the side of her head to where she could see and licked her cheek. It was so sweet and gentle that I started crying.

"What's wrong?" The half of Mom's face that could move looked puzzled. She had absolutely no clue and didn't appear to be afraid at all. I didn't know what to make of that. You'd think she'd be terrified.

The sirens got closer and I heard a pounding of feet. Mr. Knox ran up, red-faced and missing his hat. "What happened? Carolina can't have a stroke."

"Did you leave the gate open?" I asked, wiping the tears off my cheeks.

"I did. They're coming. I can hear them."

"Go out front and wave," I said.

He ran back to the front of the house and I heard him yell, "Over here!"

I leaned down low, putting my face beside Wallace, who continued to lick Mom's cheek. "Do you remember what happened, Mom?"

"I can't get up."

I smoothed her hair back from her widow's peak. "I know. Do you remember what happened?"

"What happened?" she asked.

I guess not.

"Down here!" yelled Mr. Knox.

A couple of cops followed by four firefighters ran into the garden, trampling the shade plants.

"Be careful of the plants!"

What the hell am I saying?

Happily, they ignored me. I moved out of the way, holding Wallace to my chest, as they got to work. They confirmed and called for a stroke protocol. They put in an IV line and I pictured the ER springing into action, clearing a CT and calling neuro. The thought was comforting. It would be fine. It would.

One of the firefighters taped her line and then asked me, "When did you find her?"

"Like five minutes ago."

"Do you know when it happened?"

"No."

His grizzled face clouded.

"Maybe," I said.

"We have to know in order to treat her."

"I know. I'm a nurse."

"Do you have any idea?" he asked as the EMTs arrived hauling a gurney and winced as the rose thorns snagged their uniforms.

I picked up my phone from the bricks. "She called me. Let me look at my log."

"Good. Get the time. We need the exact time you talked to her."

I pulled up the log and calculated quickly. "One hour and fifty minutes ago. We're within the window."

"You're sure?" asked the lead EMT.

I held out my phone. "It kept breaking up, but I heard her voice."

They nodded and began talking to Mom, telling her what was happening. I could tell she didn't understand, but she complied with what they asked her to do. She answered questions, but she was thoroughly confused and kept asking why they were there.

When she was taped and ready, they lifted her onto the gurney and ratcheted it up to waist height.

At some point, Mr. Knox had put his arm around me, but I hadn't even realized he was next to me until he asked, "Where are you taking her?"

"SLU is Level I," I said.

"That's where she's going," said the EMT. "Can you follow?"

I nodded and they rushed Mom away. I heard her call my name and I ran after. My purse was gone. Where was my purse? Where was my truck?

They slid Mom into the ambulance.

"Mercy?" her voice was so soft; I could barely hear her.

"I'm coming, Mom."

"Mercy?"

"I'm coming." I looked at Mr. Knox. "I don't have a car."

He hugged me, careful not to squash Wallace between us. "I'll drive you. Wait here. I'll get my car."

"I can't wait."

We took off running down the formerly peaceful Hawthorne Avenue behind Mom's shrieking ambulance. It seemed to take forever to make it to Mr. Knox's pagoda, out through the gate, and to the designated parking spot where his Camry sat under an ancient oak tree.

The car roared to life and Mr. Knox peeled out, ignoring the looks from curious walkers. He was an amazing driver. My dad must've given him aggressive driver lessons. We went up on sidewalks, changed lanes on a dime, and scared the crap out of everyone we encountered.

I caught glimpses of the ambulance up ahead, but then I'd lose sight. Mom would be wondering where I was. Was she asking for me? Was she scared now? Had it dawned on her what had happened?

I squeezed Wallace so tight she yelped. "Sorry." I kissed her on her wrinkly head and kept looking for the ambulance. We turned onto Grand and I saw them again. "There it is!"

"Almost there," said Mr. Knox.

The ambulance turned and we followed, only a couple minutes behind, thanks to Mr. Knox's take-no-prisoners driving.

He screeched to a halt behind the ambulance as they yanked open the back doors. I jumped out of the car and ran to Mom's side as they pulled her out. "I'm here."

"Where'd you go?"

They pushed her through the trauma doors and things went fast. I never realized how fast until I was on the patient side. It was a blur. Running through the halls, signing things, finding CT, and watching Mom go in. I couldn't go. I wanted to go so bad. The ER doc came up and took one look at me. "Mercy Watts?" He looked at his chart. It was Dr. Calloway. I worked with him before. He was good. Thank God.

"The patient is your mother?" he asked like he didn't think I had one.

I nodded.

"I'm sure you already know the situation. She's had an acute stroke." Dr. Calloway glanced through the chart. "She looks good." He blushed furiously. "I mean, her vitals." A smile flitted over Mr. Knox's face. Unlike Dad, Mom wasn't a publicity hound. Lots of journalists wanted to interview her, mostly just to get her famous face on camera, but Mom had never been interviewed. She kept a low profile, but people knew her, and she didn't like that one bit.

"I don't know how she could possibly have a stroke," I said. "She has no risk factors. None."

Dr. Calloway kept looking through Mom's slim chart as if an answer would appear. "No family history?"

"No. What are you thinking?"

"AFib can go undetected until there's an event."

I nodded, but that didn't feel right. Mom was so damn healthy. She ate salads on purpose and jogged for fun. I couldn't wrap my head around it. I knew it had happened, but still...

"What are they doing to Carolina?" asked Mr. Knox and Dr. Calloway noticed him standing beside me for the first time.

"I'm sorry," I said. "This is Mr. Knox, a friend of the family."

Dr. Calloway tilted his head, noting the uniform.

"And the Hawthorne Avenue gate guard. He helped me get here."

"Ah, yes. The uniform was confusing. I couldn't place it."

Mr. Knox chuckled. "It was designed in 1948, so I get that a lot."

"I bet," said Dr. Calloway. "As for Carolina, she'll have her CT. It will show us if her stroke is hemorrhagic or ischemic."

I said nothing, the implications racing through my head.

"Okay," said Mr. Knox. "What's the difference?"

Dr. Calloway looked at me. Maybe he wanted me to say something, but I didn't. I was too busy praying for ischemic.

"A hemorrhagic stroke is caused by ruptured blood vessels in the brain," said the doctor.

Mr. Knox stiffened. "That sounds bad."

"It's not great. An ischemic stroke is caused by a clot that has blocked the blood supply to parts of the brain."

Mr. Knox just squeezed my shoulders. I think it was dawning on him that my mother might be screwed. "You can fix it?"

"Let's see what the CT tells us," said Dr. Calloway.

I stared at the door to the CT room and scratched Wallace's head. She gave me a gentle lick.

A single door down the hall flew open and a doctor jogged down to us, her long black hair flowing out behind her like a silky scarf. She shook my hand and said, "I'm Dr. Siddiqui, your mother's neurosurgeon. We've confirmed that she's suffered an acute ischemic stroke. We need to perform a contrast CT to visualize the vessels affected."

"Where do I sign?" I asked.

"Any questions?"

"How fast can you do it?"

"We're ready the moment you sign."

I signed and Dr. Siddiqui ran back through the double door.

"You'll be able to see her in a minute," said Dr. Calloway. "Do you know Siddiqui?"

"Not really. Neuro isn't really my thing."

"She's very good. If I had a stroke, she's the one I'd want," he said.

High praise and it matched what I'd heard in passing about Siddiqui: brilliant, intense, and at the very top of new treatments.

"So...is this good?" asked Mr. Knox.

"It's better than hemorrhagic," I said.

"What will they do now?"

"Hopefully, she'll get tPA."

"That sounds familiar," said Mr. Knox.

A nurse waved at Dr. Calloway. "Mrs. Fellows is ready for the cath lab."

He patted me and said, "I'll be right back."

I nodded and stared at the doors. I didn't notice someone else had come up. "Mercy?"

I blinked and, for a second, I had a hard time peeling my mind off my mother. "Yeah?"

She hugged me and it took a second to click. "Rita. I'm sorry. I..."

"I know. I heard you were here and I wanted to come down. I just love your mom."

Tears filled my eyes. Rita and I were in nursing school together. She was a senior when I was a freshman and had gone into the master's program for nurse anesthetist like Mom wanted me to. It sounded like a whole lot of work to me, especially with Dad's demands.

"Where is she?" asked Rita.

"Contrast CT."

She nodded and said, "I brought you something." She handed me a piece of red cloth.

I stared at it in my hand.

"It's a vest for Wallace."

It was so hard for me to concentrate. What was she saying? Wallace? Vest? "She's not cold."

Rita took the vest back and held it up, showing the International Therapy Dog emblem. "I'm amazed that they let the Wonder Pug in without it."

"She isn't a therapy dog," I said.

Rita took Wallace out of my arms and slipped the vest on. "Yes, she is."

"What?"

She gave me a wink. "It was in the paper and online. People will believe anything if it's online."

"What was online?" I asked, taking Wallace back from Rita.

"That Wallace the Wonder Dog is your therapy dog."

Mr. Knox chuckled. "I saw that." He nudged me. "You've got anxiety."

"I do right now."

"You told people in Sturgis that Wallace the Wonder Dog was your therapy dog," said Rita. "You just forgot to bring her vest."

"I just said that to get her in a restaurant."

"And now it's a fact. I got the vest from Cabot. He heads the program for our region."

"Cabot gave you this vest? He thinks I'm a slutty dingbat," I said with a sneer.

"And as such, he's deeply in love with you."

"Ew."

"I know, but you need this dog. Personally, I think we ought to have therapy dogs free-ranging in the ER. We'd get a lot less freaking out."

I tugged on Wallace's curly tail. "She's working for me."

"I doubt you'd be screaming," said Mr. Knox.

"I'm screaming on the inside."

Rita gave me another hug. "I'll be checking in." She crossed paths with Dr. Siddiqui, who had a new sheath of paperwork. "She's clear for tPA. We need to discuss the risks."

"I know them," I said. "Give it to her."

"I have to talk to you."

"Time is brain. Please just do it."

"You understand there is a possibility of death?"

"I understand that without it, my mother's screwed."

Dr. Siddiqui held out the release form. "Sign here."

I signed and Dr. Calloway returned. "So it's a go for the tPA?"

"Yes," said Dr. Siddiqui and she went through the double doors. I caught a glimpse of a pair of feet covered in a thin blanket.

"Would you like to go in and see her for a minute?" asked Dr. Calloway.

"Absolutely." I pushed Wallace into Mr. Knox's arms. She struggled to get back to me and more tears sprang up in my eyes. "You stay here. I'll be back in a minute."

"Mercy?" asked Mr. Knox.

"Yeah?" I turned around.

"Can I call someone for you? You're all alone."

I swallowed hard. "I have you. Nobody can get ahold of my dad." I tried to think of someone else. Mom wanted Dad. She needed Dad.

"I'll call Miriam. She'll know what to do."

Dr. Calloway's face froze with a look of utter dismay.

"I take it you know Sister Miriam?" I asked.

"She visits patients sometimes. Sister Miriam makes the hospice nurses seem disinterested."

"Sorry."

He shrugged and put his hand on the door. "We can't very well turn her away."

"Many have tried."

He gave me a wan smile before going in and I resisted the urge to bite my nails. It was definitely a time for biting nails if there ever was one, but Aunt Miriam hated that "nasty habit" as she called it and she wouldn't mind telling me wherever we were, loudly and repeatedly.

My Great Aunt Miriam was Grandad's older sister and ninety-three pounds of terrifying. The elderly nun had no fear and an opinion on absolutely everything, and she felt strongly that it was God's will that she share it. I was surprised that Mr. Knox both had her number and was willing to call her. She'd once cracked him with her cane at Mom's Easter brunch over a disagreement on a passage in Corinthians. She was right, by God, and she smacked that fact into Mr. Knox's shin.

I glanced back at him and he said, "She's not answering."

"Keep trying. It takes her a few times to find the button," I said.

"She'll probably yell at me for not calling right."

"That's a distinct possibility."

The door opened and Dr. Calloway waved me in. "Just for a minute. We don't want any pressure changes."

I did tend to change Mom's blood pressure and not in a good way. I tried to think of something soothing to say as Dr. Calloway walked me around the gurney. They'd already started the infusion. A nurse I didn't recognize checked Mom's nose and mouth for bleeding and then backed away. I bent over and said, "Hey, Mom." I sounded all squeaky and terrified, which I was.

The left side of Mom's face was still completely paralyzed, but the working side sort of screwed up and she said, "I have to go to the bathroom."

"Er...okay. You can go in a bit. You're getting some meds right now."

"What for?"

I glanced up at the doctors. Both faces were impassive.

"Well, Mom, you had a stroke. They're giving you tPA to break up the clot so you can move."

Mom just looked at me and then said, "I'll never remember."

"Remember what?"

"All the names."

"Oh, that's okay. Nobody cares," I said.

She scowled at me, which was really weird when half her face didn't do anything. "It's not polite."

"Of course. I'll get the names."

She smiled and closed her eyes. Dr. Calloway steered me out. They were starting more checks on her leg and arm. They didn't want family to freak if it didn't work. But it would work. It had to. I left the room and stood out of the way while a man in a wheelchair loved up Wallace. When his tech wheeled him away, I heard him say, "I feel so much better now. What kind of dog was that?"

"A pug." The tech winked at me over her shoulder. "She's a special therapy dog."

"She's good."

I kissed Wallace's wrinkly head. "Hear that? You're good."

Yip.

"Mercy, I got Sister Miriam to answer." Mr. Knox looked shell-shocked as many did after talking with my great aunt. "She's coming."

"Was she mad?" I asked.

"Not mad."

"Furious?"

His lip twitched.

"You should go. She'll have her cane."

"I can't leave you," he said.

"You can. Now that Aunt Miriam knows, everyone will be coming."

He smiled and said, "I'm more than willing to stay."

"She's my aunt. I'll take the cane. You've been great." I teared up again. "I don't know what I would've done without you."

He put his arm around my shoulders and gave me a squeeze. "I hear the stories. You'd have thought of something. You should go to the waiting room instead of standing out here."

Mr. Knox, a little teary himself, led me to the waiting room, sat me down, and got me a cup of coffee. He fiddled around, antsy with the occasional twitch.

"You can go. Seriously. I'm fine and there's nothing more to do for Mom."

"Do you feel that?" Mr. Knox looked around.

Everyone in the waiting room froze. There were moms with babies, an elderly couple trying to figure out their new cellphones, and a group of teenagers that had been skateboarding with predictable results. They all stopped talking and listened.

There was something. More a feeling than a sound. Sort of like the barometric pressure dropping before a hurricane.

"It's her," I said.

"How do you know?" Mr. Knox asked.

"How do you know? I can feel it. Go. Save yourself." I shooed him to the door.

"But she might hit you with that damn cane."

"I guarantee she's going to hit me with the cane. It's okay. I'll take one for the team. It'll take my mind off Mom."

A red-headed woman carrying a coffee the size of a Big Gulp

walked by and said to her friend, "There is a nun out at security yelling about mismanagement."

Mr. Knox said, "Good luck." He dashed out the door not a minute too soon.

One of the teens said to me, "She doesn't get to hit you."

"You're too hot to hit," said another.

I rolled my eyes. "Watch and learn."

"Carolina Watts!" yelled my tiny aunt. "Carolina Watts!"

I guess my day just wasn't bad enough.

"She can't hit you," said the boy again. "I'll call the cops."

Aunt Miriam charged through the door, scary as I've ever seen her and I'd watched her chase pimps and drug dealers off street corners. They called her 'The Angel of Asskicking'.

"Carolina Watts!" she yelled. "There you are. Skulking in here when you ought to be with your mother. What kind of daughter are you?"

"They kicked me out and stop yelling," I said. "Everyone in here is having a very bad day." I looked around for confirmation, but nobody moved, like rabbits in front of an approaching dog.

"You should've called me!"

"I did."

"Immediately."

"Kinda busy. Please sit down." *And shut up.*

"I will not shut up," she spat at me.

Did I say that out loud? No. Pretty sure I didn't.

"I heard that," said Aunt Miriam.

"I didn't say anything."

"You thought it."

"Please stop yelling."

"I should've been informed immediately."

I backed away slowly and set down my coffee. "Basically, you were. We haven't been here that long."

"Long enough to make decisions you have no business making," said Aunt Miriam, her voice now a venomous whisper.

"What?" I asked, my mouth falling open.

"As her closest living relative, I should make all relevant decisions."

"I'm her daughter."

Aunt Miriam cracked me on the hip with her cane so fast, I didn't have time to flinch. "I'm an adult."

"Ouch! That hurt. And I am an adult and a nurse, for crying out loud." I circled the room, looking for an escape opportunity. I'd seen Aunt Miriam mad before, but never like this. Like Mom's stroke was my fault. What the hell?

"You're practically a child."

"I'm twenty-six."

"Exactly."

Dr. Siddiqui walked in. "Miss Watts, I need to speak to you."

I scratched Wallace's head and she gave me a little lick. "What?"

"Please step outside for a moment."

Please say it worked.

"Miss Watts?"

I glanced at Aunt Miriam, but she didn't move. All the anger had drained out of her and she stood there, pale and shaking. I went over and took her hand. "Come on."

The doctor took us out into the hall and to my surprise, Aunt Miriam remained silent. That was almost as frightening as what Dr. Siddiqui had to tell me. The CT showed that Mom had two clots, a very large one and a smaller one behind it in the main artery to the brain. The tPA wasn't able to dissolve the whole thing. Forty percent of her brain was affected. It was a devastating stroke. They would have to go in and get the main clot.

"Do you understand what I'm saying?" asked Dr. Siddiqui.

"Are you going to break it up?"

"No, I will use a stent removal device threaded up through her groin into her brain. I'll retrieve the clot and pull it out."

"What about the second clot?" I asked.

"I believe the tPA will dissolve it once blood flow reaches it."

I thought I should ask what would happen if it didn't, but I couldn't make the words come out.

"We need a release signed so that I may perform neurosurgery on your mother."

Where the hell is Dad?

"There are inherent risks to all surgical procedures. We may cause a secondary stroke or damage the artery, causing a brain bleed."

Dad!

"There is a possibility of death," said Dr. Siddiqui, calmly as if she'd said Mom might get the common cold.

I looked at Aunt Miriam. Nothing. I don't think she was even blinking.

"There's really no other choice," I said.

"No, there isn't."

"How many times have you done this?"

"The procedure has been approved for a year. I've done it fifty-seven times."

"What are the outcomes like?"

She smiled for the first time, showing a row of small, very white teeth. "Excellent. Your mother is young and healthy. I see no reason that she shouldn't withstand the procedure well."

Withstand?

"Do you do it here?" I asked.

"Yes, we're ready to take her up now."

She handed me the release and I signed it. My hands were shaking.

"We'll take her up now and get her prepped." Dr. Siddiqui went into the hall and called for Carrie.

Carrie came and said she'd take us up to the neurosurgery waiting room. I nodded and turned to Aunt Miriam. She stood in the corner, clutching her cane and pale as paper. That's saying something since she was a red-head like my dad and Grandad. The only color they had was in their freckles. "Aunt Miriam, are you ready?"

"How could this happen to her?" she whispered.

"I don't know." I took her arm and steadied her as we walked down to the elevator.

"You should've called me."

"You're here now." I'd seen a lot of people freak out in my short nursing career. Usually, they yelled about the wait in the ER and pain meds being too slow. I think Aunt Miriam was straight up terrified. But nothing scared her and that was terrifying me.

We went up to the surgical floor. I put Aunt Miriam in the waiting room with Wallace and went in to see Mom. Rita was doing her anesthesia and that calmed me considerably. Rita knew Mom. It would be fine.

I leaned over into Mom's frame of vision. "They're prepping you now. It'll be over soon."

Her eyes dropped and I kissed her forehead.

"Out now," said Dr. Siddiqui.

I hurried out and returned to the waiting room, but I couldn't go in. I called Dad again, ready to scream like Aunt Miriam, but he didn't answer. Now I needed to scream. Why was he always gone? Why were dead people more important than us?

I dropped my phone and almost stomped on it. What good was it if he didn't answer? What was I going to tell Mom? The husband you adore couldn't be bothered to answer the damn phone?

A hand reached down and picked up my phone. Aaron stood there, looking off to the left and smelling of sausage grease and hot dogs. I flung myself at him. "Aaron, Mom had a stroke."

He patted my back and said, "You hungry?"

"Um...what?"

"You hungry?"

"I couldn't be less hungry."

Aaron picked up a cooler and a large picnic basket. "You're hungry."

"Okay, I guess."

He went in the waiting room, presumably to feed me a seven-course meal. There was an excellent chance that I would throw it all up, but that wouldn't stop my partner. The elevator door dinged and Uncle Morty and Grandad ran out, spinning in a circle before they saw me.

"Mercy, sweetheart." Grandad ran up and wrapped his bony arms around me. "She's in surgery?"

"Yes. It won't take long, like fifteen minutes," I said.

"It will be fine. Carolina is something else."

I wasn't sure what that meant, but I agreed. Mom was something else.

Uncle Morty peeled Grandad off me and gave me a fierce bear hug. "I can't get Tommy. I'm using every damn thing I got."

I burst into tears. "Where is he? I thought he was teaching some class."

"He is. All I can find out is that they went into the field. There ain't no freaking cell service."

"Won't they take a message out to him?" I asked. "This is an emergency."

"I'm working on it." Uncle Morty's lip trembled. "Is she scared?"

"Not that I can tell. She's mostly worried about remembering everyone's names."

"Who gives a flying fuck? She's paralyzed, ain't she?"

"Mom cares and I'm not altogether sure she understands what's happened," I said.

Grandad put his arm around me. "Did you tell her?"

"I did, but she just looked kinda blank about it."

He nodded and said, "Maybe that's for the best."

Morty looked around. "We lost Aaron. I don't know where he got to."

"He's in the waiting room. He wants to feed me. I don't think I can."

Grandad steered me in the waiting room. "You can."

He was right. I could. At least a little. Aaron opened a thermos and poured a thick hot chocolate that smelled seriously alcoholic.

"I don't think I should have any alcohol," I said.

He held out a cup and stared at me, unblinking.

I guess that doesn't matter so much.

I took an experimental sip and it was powerful, but I wasn't doing neurosurgery, so what the hell. I drank it and insisted Aunt Miriam have a cup, too. She sat with her brother, looking frail and shocked. I thought that I should do something for her, but what? Thankfully, she had Wallace on her lap and received little licks about every thirty seconds.

The hot chocolate made my head light, which was a huge improvement over the way it felt before.

"What kind is this?" I asked.

"Black Russian hot chocolate," said Aaron.

"Good for tragedy," said Uncle Morty, looking up from his laptop. "I'm going to get Tommy, if I have to drag him out my damn self."

I looked up at the clock. Procedure should be almost done. Mom's life. What would it be after this? I took another sip. "Black Russian hot chocolate. Appropriate."

CHAPTER THREE

Dr. Siddiqui walked into the waiting room with another doctor in tow. "Miss Watts, the retrieval was successful. Your mother is going into recovery now. The blood flow is restored. Due to her excellent health, it returned quickly. I believe her damage will be minimal, considering the nature of the stroke."

I fell back onto my seat and the Black Russian sloshed over my fingers. The other doctor knelt in front of me and took the cup from my hands. He pulled down his surgical mask. Pete.

"What are you doing here?" I asked in a fog.

"I assisted Dr. Siddiqui." He glanced back.

The surgeon nodded. "Cover the rest, Dr. Lindstrom. I have another acute coming in." With that, Dr. Siddiqui left and I never saw her again.

"I didn't thank her," I said vaguely.

"No need. It would just embarrass her," said Pete.

"Is Mom really alright?"

He brought me to my feet and tossed the cup. Uncle Morty was there in an instant, clapping Pete on the back and offering to buy him a bottle of whatever he drank. Grandad hugged him and couldn't speak. Aunt Miriam just stroked Wallace and shivered.

"I think she needs a blanket from the warmer," I said, heading for the door.

Pete took my arm and said loudly, "Fine. I'll show you where they are."

"I know—"

He squeezed my arm hard and practically dragged me from the room.

In the hall, I stopped short. "You said it went well."

"It did. It went great. Your mom has damage. That's unavoidable, but the blood just flooded her brain. We won't know how extensive her damage is until we get an MRI. Probably tomorrow. She'll go up to the ICU and we'll monitor her closely."

"Then what is going on?" I asked.

Pete's face was so intense. I'd never seen him look like that.

"You're scaring me."

"Your mom has no risk factors."

"Yeah, I know."

"How closely did you look at her?" he asked.

"Um...I don't know. Not at all. I was calling 911." My stomach started to tighten. "Why?"

"She has scrapes and bruises. Wrists, elbows, and a large hematoma on her hip. We didn't see it until we prepped her for surgery. Do you know anything about that?"

I shook my head. "No. Are they fresh?"

"Very fresh. Still developing."

"Her wrists?"

Pete nodded and he yanked his cap off, revealing his tousled dark blond hair. He grabbed my wrists. "Like someone had her."

"They were there when it happened," I said.

"I think so."

"Can you bring on a stroke?" I didn't remember strokes working like that.

"Maybe if it was Afib."

I bent over and put my hands on my knees. It had to be the stalker from Sturgis. He'd beat us back and had gone after Mom. Pete pulled me upright and folded me into his arms. I cried into his chest, breathing in the smell of antiseptic and sterile bandages that always clung to him.

"She's going to be alright," he said, bending over me and stroking my hair.

"You don't know," I whispered.

"I do know. I saw her brain come back to life."

"But she won't be the same."

"No," he said. "She won't be the same, but she won't be that different either."

I appreciated the honesty and that he didn't say she was lucky. Having a massive stroke didn't seem that lucky to me. I hated when people said, "They were so lucky." As if what happened didn't matter because the patient didn't die.

"Thanks."

"For what?"

"Everything. You've always been great," I said.

"Not that great," he said softly.

I pulled back and looked up into his kind face. "You were perfect. It's me that's not."

"It doesn't matter anymore," he said. "I've got to get back. She'll go up to the ICU in ten to fifteen minutes. Cardiology and Internal medicine will be coming in to discuss our next steps."

"So you're thinking heart?"

"She's young and healthy. If she was assaulted over a prolonged period, I think Afib makes sense."

"How long?"

"I don't know. Stress and exercise can trigger it."

"She'd have to form the clot and then throw it."

"Two clots, remember?"

I rubbed my eyes. "Right. Two."

"You'll be careful?" asked Pete with concern. "I heard about Sturgis. Your Grandad was the target?"

"Yes." I didn't expand on that. He didn't need to know about the stalking. He'd just worry more. Pete had always been uncomfortable with the crime side of my life, just one of the reasons we didn't work out. I'd have been happy to give up investigating, but crime came to me, not the other way around.

He hugged me again. "We'll let you know when she's going up."

"Thanks."

Pete took off down the hall. I watched him turn the corner, my mind spinning. An assault. A stroke. I couldn't find Dad. And that guy was still out there. Waiting.

I turned around and standing by the elevator was Chuck. He had a look on his face that I couldn't quite define. Rage. Sorrow. Nausea. Or some kind of wicked combo of the three. I, myself, felt instantly guilty, but I don't know why. Pete was on Mom's team. I had to talk to him, didn't I? Did Chuck see the hugging? That wouldn't be good what with the ex-boyfriend thing.

I took a breath and started for Chuck. He punched the elevator button and the doors opened.

Say the right thing. Say the right thing.

"My mom had a stroke."

Chuck's face instantly switched to concern and he came down the hall with his long strides and swept me up in his arms. "I know."

"Thank God you're here."

"Really?"

"Of course. I couldn't think. Mr. Knox called Aunt Miriam." I started blubbering like a five-year-old. "She hit me with her cane."

"Why does she have that cane? She walks okay."

"To whack people," I said.

He put me back on my feet and produced a packet of tissues. "Julia said you'd need these."

I blew my nose. It was juicier than I expected and I regretted it. "Who's Julia?"

"New to the squad," he said, eyeing me. "So you remembered to call Pete?"

"No, I didn't. He assisted on Mom's neurosurgery. They had to pull the clot out."

"Holy shit. Did it go okay?"

"He says she's doing really well. We won't know exactly how much damage until we get an MRI."

His broad shoulders relaxed. "So that's why you were hugging. Okay."

"That's not why."

He stiffened and got all hawk-eyed. Jealous, I guess.

"I mean, that's part of it. Mom was assaulted. Pete just told me," I said quickly.

It took a second to sink in.

"Assaulted? What do you mean, assaulted? I thought she had a stroke."

I explained the bruising and Pete's preliminary theory. Chuck took me by the shoulders. "How thoroughly did they go over her?"

A zing of fear went through me. "He just saw the bruising when they prepped her. The stroke was the major concern."

"Has anyone talked to her?"

"I did, but I didn't see the bruising. She had a long-sleeve tissue tee on."

"What did she say?"

"Nothing about any attack," I said. "She wanted to go to the bathroom."

"What?"

I hugged him again, just to feel his heat and strength. "I don't think she understood what was going on."

Chuck kissed the top of my head and pushed me back before pulling out his phone. "Okay. Who are her doctors, besides Pete?"

"Dr. Siddiqui and Dr. Calloway in the ER. She might've said something to him or the nurses, but I doubt it. I'm telling you she was in a fog. Forty percent of her brain was shut off."

Chuck stopped typing. "Forty percent?"

"It was a massive stroke."

"I don't know what to say."

"Pete said it's okay."

He nodded and went back to his phone. "Give me everything you know."

There wasn't much to say and Chuck wasn't happy.

"When will I be able to interview her?" he asked.

"Not today. She's going up to the ICU."

"But you can talk to her?"

I took his hand and tugged him toward the waiting room. "I can, but you shouldn't expect much. This was a big trauma."

Chuck pulled his hand out of mine. "I have to call this in and get to the house."

"Uncle Morty, Grandad, and Aunt Miriam are in the waiting room. They might've talked to Mom today."

"Right." He took two strides toward the door before spinning around. "Where the hell is Tommy?"

"We can't find him."

"Still?"

I shrugged and he darted into the waiting room. I walked in more slowly, trying to think if I'd seen anything unusual at the house other than the insane Siamese. I hadn't, but I wasn't really looking for anything other than Mom.

When I went in, Uncle Morty was cursing like he'd stepped on a rusty nail, Aunt Miriam hadn't moved, and Grandad was talking to Chuck, going over the Sturgis stuff. He got a week's worth of evidence out in concise bullet points like the police detective he once was.

"There's nothing you're leaving out?" asked Chuck.

We all shook our heads.

Chuck looked hard at me.

"Well, there was Hunt," I said.

"You went to see Blankenship? Why the hell—" He looked at Aunt Miriam and her cane, but she didn't move.

I told him about Blankenship's visitor, but it didn't seem that important.

"Alright," said Chuck. "Are you okay here? I have to go."

"I'm fine." I didn't feel fine. I felt needy and overwhelmingly sad.

"Good." He kissed me. "Do not leave the hospital."

"I'm not going anywhere."

Chuck left and I sat down for a whole thirty seconds, listening to Uncle Morty scream into his phone, trying without results to find my father.

Rita walked in and announced, "Your mom's going to the ICU."

Everyone stood up and she quickly said, "One visitor at a time, but there's a very nice waiting room." Her normally smooth forehead creased. "What is that smell?"

"Aaron," I said.

"Huh?"

"My partner. He comes with food."

"I thought you were with that gorgeous cop?" asked Rita.

"I am. Aaron's not that kind of partner."

Aaron, true to his nature, announced that Rita was hungry. He decided she needed a Monte Cristo sandwich. I know those sound gross, but when Aaron made them, they were amazing. Rita took a bite as ordered and exclaimed, "Oh, my God. It's fluffy and salty and sweet. How did you make this?"

Aaron shrugged and made it seem like he didn't know. He had to know. He'd made it, for heaven's sake. Instead of revealing his secrets under Rita's barrage of questions, he gave her fresh peach hand pies and some kind of smoothie with mango. It was green. I don't know why.

Rita was so full she could barely talk, a common problem with Aaron around. She did manage to give us directions to the ICU before she headed off to tell the other nurses of her good fortune.

We went upstairs and I put Aaron, Aunt Miriam, and Uncle Morty in the waiting room against their objections.

Aunt Miriam, in particular, was incensed. "I need to go in there. I can give her spiritual counsel."

"They only allow one visitor at a time in the ICU," I said, gritting my teeth.

"Then it should be me," she said, banging her cane on the floor with each word. "I am—"

"I know who you are!" I yelled. "And I don't care. Sit down. *I'm* going in to see *my* mother."

They sat down and Aunt Miriam's lower lip poked out and trembled. I doubt anyone had spoken to her like that in fifty years, if ever.

"Aaron, do you have any non-alcoholic hot chocolate?" I asked.

He pulled a second thermos out of the basket. I handed over Wallace and took the thermos. "Thank you." I think it came out as aggressive, not grateful, but I didn't care. I stalked off to get buzzed into the ICU. An older nurse named Patsy gave me a badge and took me down to Mom's room. A pretty young nurse with cornrows and luminous brown eyes looked up and recognized me We'd never met, but my reputation preceded me. Usually, that was a bad thing.

"Mercy, I'm Takira. I'll be your mother's nurse today. We just transferred her to the bed without any problems and she's asking for you."

I glanced through the window above Takira's desk, fearfully, if I'm being honest. Pete said it was good, but good to a doctor was sometimes very different to patients. Mom was lying flat on her back and surrounded by equipment, most of which wasn't being used. She wasn't on a vent or anything. Thank goodness.

Takira touched my arm and I jumped.

"Sorry," she said. "I was just about to go in and talk to her about what to expect for the next few hours."

"But..." There was definitely a *but* at the end of that sentence.

She took a breath and I could see her choosing her words. "But... your mother has suffered trauma other than the stroke."

"I know," I said. "Dr. Lindstrom told me."

Takira blew out a breath. "I was dreading telling you that after what you've been through recently. What did Dr. Lindstrom tell you?"

"That she has bruising consistent with an attack."

"Yes. There are also scrapes and what looks like a minor blow to the head. We didn't notice it until we transferred her."

"Where?"

"Below her right ear. Her hair was covering it."

Takira watched me for something. I couldn't tell what.

"I take it that's not all." My chest was so tight I thought I might have a coronary if she didn't just come out with it.

"I think we need to do a rape kit."

The room went swimmy. Patsy and Takira had me in her chair and breathing into a paper bag before I could put two thoughts together. I was such a wuss. Mom was lying in there and I was having a panic attack.

Patsy squatted in front of me with her hands on my knees. It was oddly soothing. "We don't know that she's been raped. She does have bruising that fits."

I lowered the bag. "Underwear?"

"On but torn," said Takira. "I have to say there was an attempt."

"I should've stayed with her. My Aunt Miriam said that someone was trying to break into the house before I went to Sturgis. She wanted me to stay with her, but I didn't. I went to Sturgis with Grandad."

"There's no use thinking of that now," said Patsy. "Let's order the kit and inform the police."

I told her about Chuck, but they called anyway, saying it was procedure. There'd be a rape counselor called in. The works.

"Do you think you can go in?" asked Takira.

I gave her the bag and got to my feet, shaky as hell. "Yes."

Takira took the lead. Like all ICU nurses, she was efficient, attentive, and kind. "Mrs. Watts, your daughter is here. Are you having any pain?" She checked Mom's IV line and the incision in her groin. There was bruising from something other than the surgery and minor swelling on the hip.

"Mercy?" Mom said, her voice high and breathy.

I came to her side and felt a load fall off my back. Mom's eyes weren't locked anymore. They moved to me and she tried to sit up.

"I'm here. Don't move," I said.

"Mrs. Watts—"

"Carolina," said Mom.

"Carolina, you have to stay flat on your back for three hours," said Takira.

Mom frowned and even though her left side still sagged, it did move a bit. "Why?"

"You've been given a medication called tPA. It's usually referred to as a clot-buster. We need to keep you still while it's working."

"I have to go to the bathroom."

"You can't get up. I can give you a bedpan if you can't wait."

Mom made a face and said, "I heard someone say I was going to the ICU."

"You are in the ICU, Mom," I said.

"Why? I feel fine."

Takira and I glanced at each other. Takira said, "This is not unusual."

"What?" asked Mom.

I told her again what happened, at least the part I knew. She didn't seem to get it.

"Why would I have a stroke?" she asked.

"We're going to figure that out, Carolina," said Takira. "Are you having any pain?"

Mom thought about it and said, "I'm all achy and my head hurts."

"I'll see what the doctor will give you for that." She patted Mom's leg and left to call Pete or whoever.

"I had a stroke," said Mom with wonder in her voice. "Are you sure?"

"Very sure," I said, picking up her hand and looking at the ring of bruising around her slender wrist. The other one matched. Pete was right. They looked like someone had grabbed her by the wrists and held on. I lifted the hair off her ear and saw the bruise that Takira described. Large enough to be a fist, but a glancing blow. Dad would know for sure if he ever bothered to call me back.

"What are you looking at?" asked Mom.

"Do you remember what happened?"

"You said I had a stroke."

"You did. Do you remember it?"

Mom looked down at her bruised wrists and a line of drool slipped down her chin. I grabbed a tissue and dabbed it away. "What are you doing?" she asked.

"Nothing," I said. "You just had something. It's gone."

She reached up to brush the hair out of her eyes and ended up jabbing herself in the eye. Mom began to cry and wiped away the tears. Takira watched me with a sorrowful expression. I had to start asking questions, but I didn't know where to begin. Dad would say you begin at the beginning. But I didn't know where this all began. Someone hated us and not just garden variety hate. Hard-core hate.

But that wasn't Mom's story. That was his.

"Do you remember this morning, Mom?"

She did remember. She got up. Aunt Tenne came over with Bruno and they packed the rest of his stuff for the show he was doing. Bruno was an exceptional painter and his work was in high demand, thanks to Aunt Tenne's crafty publicity.

They left for the airport after the packing, but Mom didn't remember exactly. Things were fuzzy. She remembered making tea and Wilson Cleves calling from Hunt. She definitely remembered calling me and being mad. She was still mad, but she wasn't sure why. I was her daughter. That seemed to be enough for now.

"I couldn't get up," she said.

"Wait. The next thing you remember is being on the ground?" I asked.

"Yes. And you came. And a dog. There was a dog, wasn't there?"

"Wallace. Pete's mother's dog."

"Didn't you break his heart?"

Let's not go over that again.

"Was there anyone else there?"

"Where?"

I had to be patient, not my forte. "When you went outside? Was there someone there?"

Mom pursed her lips and I dabbed her cheek again. "I think so. Who was it?"

"I'm hoping you'll tell me. Did someone hurt you?"

She looked at her wrists. "I think...I can't quite. There was someone there." She put her hand to her ear where the bruise was. "He hit me."

My voice caught in my throat. "Who hit you, Mom? Who was it?"

"It all seems so strange, like a dream but not. Did it really happen?"

"I think so," I said.

Mom turned her head. "Where is that nurse?"

"Why?"

"I have got to go to the bathroom."

"Please, think. Do you remember a face?"

She shook her head. "No. Just pain. And...it was a man. I'm certain of that. He smelled like mothballs and cigarettes."

"Mothballs?"

"You know, we use them to keep out the moths," she said like she was highly disappointed in my lack of housekeeping knowhow.

"I know what mothballs are," I said. "It's just weird."

"Why would anyone be wearing wool in the summer?" she asked, looking me straight in the eye for the first time.

"Good question. I will find out. I promise."

"Can you find me a bathroom first?"

I chuckled and she even smiled, sort of. I didn't find her a bathroom. I found her a bedpan and it was a no-go. Takira and I managed to get her on it. No mean feat, considering she wasn't supposed sit up or roll. Once we got her on it, she couldn't go. It happened all the time. Peeing while lying down is practically impossible. We were considering a catheter even though Mom said she'd rather die. Takira finally badgered Dr. Siddiqui into letting her get up. Apparently, Mom had moved herself from the gurney to the bed with little assistance. Takira thought she'd be fine as long as we were careful.

She peeked around the door. "She can get up to go, but we have to be super careful."

"Where's the bathroom?" asked Mom as I put the head of her bed up.

"Behind you. There's a curtain," I said hesitantly.

"I'll take it. This hurts so much."

Before I could get around the bed, Mom had swung her legs over the side, stood up, and taken two shaking steps.

"Holy crap, Mom!" I steadied her and I think Takira had a minor heart attack.

"I have to go."

"You can't get up like that."

"I just did."

"Good point," I said. "Let me help you. We have to be very careful with the meds still in your system."

Takira and I helped her and pulled the curtain. We backed away and Takira mouthed to me, "You saw the underwear and bruising?"

"Yes, but there's no fluids and the bruising looks more about trying to get her panties down."

"I think she's okay," said Takira. "But the counselor will come anyway."

"What are you two talking about?" asked Mom from behind her curtain.

"Nothing," we said simultaneously.

Mom pushed back the curtain and lurched toward the bed.

"You were supposed to wait," I said, diving for her.

She rolled her eyes. "I can't imagine why."

"You had a stroke."

"That doesn't seem right."

"I totally agree."

We got her back in bed and tucked in. She looked at her left hand, the one that jabbed her in the eye. She opened it and closed it. It worked but not right, not even close. "Where's your father?"

"We're trying to find him."

"That's right, you said that." She gave me the stink eye that I knew so well. "What were you two talking about?"

I decided to go ahead and tell the truth. I'd rather it came from me than some counselor she didn't know. "We were talking about who attacked you. There was some suggestion that you might have been sexually assaulted."

She looked at Takira. "Who suggested?"

"Me," answered the nurse, "the ER staff, and your neurosurgeons."

"I don't think so."

I took her hand and kissed it. "Would you remember?"

She began to cry again. "I don't know. I don't think so. There's no pain down there."

"That's a good sign," said Takira. She explained that a counselor would be coming to talk later. Mom didn't want a rape kit and I didn't blame her. I'd done a few and they were miserable from start to finish.

Mom asked me for Dad again and I checked my phone. Nothing from my father, but there were messages from just about everyone else, including Spidermonkey. He said he'd like to come to the hospital but didn't want to expose our connection. Mom's best friend, Dixie, was driving back from Pennsylvania where she'd been visiting her sister and Mom's parents were freaking out that I wasn't answering the phone. I had it on vibrate and never felt it buzz.

"Tommy?" Mom asked hopefully.

"No, but Nana and Pop Pop are coming."

She nodded and looked away. Damn my father. I would kill him for doing this to her.

"Mercy?" Takira called into the room.

I went out and she told me that the internist and cardiologist would come in the next day, but they'd put in orders already. I should've cared, but at that moment I really didn't. Mom was alive and likely to remain so. But Takira wanted to tell me the treatment plan so I listened. It included tests for Afib and an MRI. No surprises.

I went back in and told Mom, but she just wanted Dad. She was starting to get pretty upset about it. Takira didn't like how her heart rate was increasing, along with her pressure.

"Mom, I was thinking of going home and getting your stuff," I said quickly. Two birds, one stone. I had to see the crime scene.

"My stuff?" she asked.

"Your cozy pjs, your perfume, and that quilt Nana made you for your birthday."

She brightened up. "That would be nice."

"Aunt Miriam can come—"

"No!" she yelled.

"Mom?"

"No one is coming in here. Promise me." Her blood pressure alarm went off and Takira ran in. "Mrs. Watts, you have to stay calm. Please don't jerk around like that."

"No one," Mom cried. "No one but you. I don't want anyone to see me like this."

"You look good."

She held up a wet hand. "I'm drooling."

Takira tried to gently press her back into the bed. "We have to calm her down. The tPA is still in her system."

Calm her down. She needed Dad or her mother. Somebody. Something.

"I have an idea. I'll be right back."

I raced out of the room with the wail of my name chasing me.

CHAPTER FOUR

"I could get in big trouble for this," said Takira.

"You won't," I said. "I know people and she has the vest."

Takira looked doubtfully at Wallace, who was snuggled up to Mom's side and licking her tearstained cheek. The pug whined a tiny bit every time she moved. The ribs had caught up with her.

"Doesn't she pee on your feet?" asked Takira. "How is she a therapy dog?"

"I have anxiety," I said, trying to look nervous or something.

"Well, I'd have anxiety if I had your life. I'll give you that."

"So we're good?"

"For now. I'm only on until seven," said Takira.

I glanced at my phone. Holy crap. It was almost seven. Chuck was going to haul off the evidence and I'd get nothing. Dad would kill me. Right after I killed him for leaving Mom high and dry.

"Mom, I'm going to go get your stuff from the house. Is there anything else you want? Aaron will make you any kind of food known to mankind and even some that isn't."

"I'm not hungry."

I smoothed her tangled hair and said, "You'll be alright? Are you sure about being alone?"

"She's not alone," said Takira. "I'm with her and after me, Mark will be here. Ex-marine. He tells the worst jokes."

"How is he with pugs?" I asked.

She shrugged. "We'll see."

"Go ahead," said Mom.

I managed to stuff a painkiller down Wallace's throat with the help of a peanut butter pack that Takira gave me and I left Mom with plenty of anxiety. I could've used Wallace, for real. And even more than that I could've used an escape route.

"Mercy!" yelled Uncle Morty.

He snagged me and demanded to know what was going on. I told him everything I knew. He got sweaty when he heard about her lack of memory and went straight to his computer, typing furiously. His hacking skills were legendary. He was as good as Spidermonkey, maybe better. It was hard to tell.

"Can I go in now?" asked Aunt Miriam. She seemed old and small. I hated to say no. She had the cane at the ready, but I had to.

"I don't understand. I'm family," she said, tearfully.

"She doesn't want anyone. Just Dad and Nana."

Aunt Miriam scowled. "Tommy. I'm going to beat that boy bloody."

"Stand in line," said Grandad. "I'm getting the runaround from the feds. I think they're up to something. Bennett called from Sturgis. They've taken over their investigation of Cheryl Morris."

"On what grounds?" I asked.

"Crossing state lines. US mail violations. You name it. They're using it."

"That sucks. Bennett and Trevino deserve the kudos."

"I agree, but there's nothing we can do. Maybe Tommy would have some pull, but he's out."

I bit my lip and picked a Wallace hair off my chest. "You think they're keeping Dad away on purpose?"

"The bastards will do anything," said Uncle Morty.

Grandad nodded. "It doesn't look good for getting to Tommy any time soon."

"Fan-freaking-tastic. What about Nana? Where are they?"

"Can't get a flight. Everything's booked solid. They're looking at booking a private plane."

"No!" I yelled.

Aunt Miriam almost toppled over, but Aaron stuck a hand out to steady her. He was the only one who didn't look startled.

"Mercy? What on earth?" asked Grandad.

"No private planes," I said. "They'll have to drive."

He and Uncle Morty glanced at each other. Uncle Morty watched me like a video game, intense and calculating. It would've unnerved me if I wasn't so stressed already.

"They can't drive," said Grandad.

"Why not? They have a car. It's like eleven hours."

"They can't drive at night anymore. It's not safe."

My hands went into fists and I felt my face flush. That just made me angry. "No private planes. Absolutely not."

Grandad stayed very still and said slowly, "What are you afraid of?"

If it hadn't been such a disastrous day, I might've thought of something else. But I told the truth. It just popped out like a piece of PEZ. "Because I don't want them to die."

"Why do you think they'll die?" He said it like he knew the answer.

"It happened to Daniel and Agatha. Our family is full up on murders, don't you think?"

"Murders?"

"They were murdered, Grandad," I said, barely aware that I was yelling at my grandfather. A man who'd never yelled at me in his life.

"Who told you that?" asked Uncle Morty, his beady eyes boring into me.

"Aunt Tenne. She thought I knew."

Aunt Miriam shook off Aaron's hand and stomped over to me. "Why would she tell you that?"

"You don't think I had a right to know my own great-grandparents were murdered?" I asked.

Nobody said anything. I took that as a no and crossed my arms, determined to wait them out. I wanted them to say something. To be honest. I should've known better.

Agatha and Daniel's murders were related to The Klinefeld

Group, a so-called nonprofit. They were after something they thought my godmothers, Millicent and Myrtle Bled, had or knew the whereabouts of. They were more than willing to kill to get it. Chuck, Spidermonkey, and I had been working on it for months. So far, we'd figured out that it had something to do with Millicent and Myrtle's cousin, Stella Bled Lawrence. She'd met my ancestors, Amelie and Paul, in Paris in November of 1938 and given them something to conceal.

That was the beginning of my family's connection to the powerful Bled family, a connection that everyone pretended started with Millicent and Myrtle meeting my mother. It went way deeper than that. The Bleds knew my dad's family, too. They took care of us. There were scholarships, jobs, and, of course, me. I'd practically been raised in the Bled mansion, despite being the daughter of a cop and a paralegal. I never questioned it until The Klinefeld Group tried to get ahold of the Bled art collection. After that, weird things started happening: break-ins, the Bleds' chauffeur was murdered, and a mysterious man named Jens Waldemar Hoff started sniffing around.

Agatha and Daniel had been up to something when they unexpectedly flew up to St. Louis from New Orleans. They'd had break-ins and men had followed them. I was sure The Klinefeld Group had murdered them. I just didn't know why.

"Well?" I asked when I couldn't take it anymore.

"Why did she tell you?" asked Aunt Miriam.

I wanted to scream and I very nearly shouted out that I'd been investigating the family just to see what they'd do. It would've been a disaster. My family was nothing if not good at keeping secrets. Luckily, another family secret burst from my lips. "I saw the cat."

"What cat?" said Grandad and Aunt Miriam.

"Oh, please. Blackie. The cat that came with Nana and Pop Pop's house when the family bought it in 1830."

"I don't know what you're talking about," said Aunt Miriam primly. "You should get back to your mother."

She so knew about that cat. She'd seen him in New Orleans, even though she acted like she didn't. "You know, the cat that shows up when something terrible happens to the family."

"Mercy, you're overwrought." Grandad tried to extend a bony arm around my shoulders, but I shoved him off.

"He showed up when Agatha and Daniel died, when Aunt Tenne had her accident, and before Richard Costilla tried to stab me in New Orleans. Blackie saved me."

Shock was written all over their faces. Not Aaron's face. He never had any expression so he didn't count. I watched Grandad and Aunt Miriam for a second as they tried to look normal and failed. For once, I knew something they didn't. Mom didn't tell the family what had really happened in New Orleans. Weird.

"How do you know—" started Grandad.

"I saw him in Paris before the bridge. *And* I saw him today. He led me to Mom."

Aunt Miriam rammed her cane into the floor. "That's just a family legend."

"I. Saw. Him."

"Well...even if you did, it doesn't mean anything," said Grandad. He even looked like he believed it.

"Doesn't mean anything?" I yelled. "That cat is the harbinger of death and destruction."

Aunt Miriam gave me a swift whack with her cane, cracking me on the leg and nearly buckling my knee. "Don't exaggerate."

"Someone tried to murder my mother. Is that exaggerating? Are we going to pretend that didn't happen?"

"Don't be ridiculous," she said, lifting the cane for another go.

"You want ridiculous? How about this?" I snatched the cane right out of her hand and snapped it over my knee, throwing the pieces in the corner. "That's ridiculous. You'll just buy another cane and hit me with that. Now I'm going to my mother's house and attempted murder scene to get her pajamas and perfume. You got a problem with that?"

They shook their heads.

"Aaron, can you make Mom some dinner? She's having a hard time swallowing. It needs to be easy to chew and swallow."

"And Wallace."

"Huh?"

"Dog food," said Aaron, blank as ever.

"Yes and food for the dog." I gave him a smacking kiss on his pudgy cheek, leaving a smear of lip balm. "Is my truck here?"

He handed over my keys and gave me the location in the garage.

I pocketed the keys and pointed at the rest of them. "Nana and Pop Pop are not taking a private plane, now or ever. Mom wants her parents alive. Got it?"

They nodded silently and I marched out triumphant.

It didn't last long. Triumph never does.

I turned left and saw Spidermonkey standing at the elevator, holding an enormous bouquet of yellow roses with a card that said, "Happy Anniversary!"

He pushed the button on the elevator and I glanced back at the waiting room. No one had followed me, to my surprise so I darted over and tried to shove him in the elevator as the doors opened.

Spidermonkey looked past me. "Hold on." He plucked the card off. "Give these to your mother. I'll hold the elevator."

"Morty is in the waiting room. He can't see you."

"He won't. Go."

I screeched a little, ran the flowers to the ICU, and gave them to Patsy. "Be back soon," I said, closing the door in her face. I ran back to the elevator, passing Uncle Morty as he was coming to the waiting room door. He saw me, his face deeply etched with a frown. I darted into the elevator with Spidermonkey and punched the *Close Door* button like a crazed woodpecker.

"Are you crazy?" I asked.

"I was bringing my wife flowers for our anniversary," he said in his honeyed South Carolina voice.

The doors closed and we started down. I spun around. "It's not your anniversary."

"It could be."

"But it's not."

Spidermonkey crossed his arms and leaned on the wall, a warm smile wreathing his face. "Morty has never seen me. He has every reason to believe that I'm a twenty-five-year-old snowboarder who's obsessed with eighties punk bands instead of a seventy-year-old married father of four who prefers Muddy Waters."

"You're going to give me a heart attack and I've already had about three today," I said.

"I want to hug you, but Loretta says that might be creepy."

My eyes filled. "It's not creepy, but I'm hugged out. Why are you here?"

"You didn't answer my texts and I heard that Carolina was attacked. I was worried that you'd run off and start investigating on your own. Aaron doesn't need to make food. He needs to stick to you."

"You heard all that."

"I did and it was fascinating."

"Don't break out the strait jacket," I said, more fearful than I wanted to admit.

"The most beautiful thing we can experience is the mysterious," said Spidermonkey.

My brain cramped for a second. "Einstein?"

"Check. I know I usually leave the intuition to you, but I have a feeling about that cat."

The door dinged and I braced myself, but it was just some volunteers crabbing about being transporters. They got off on the next floor down and I asked, "What about the cat?"

"I don't know yet. I have to talk it over with Loretta. She focuses me."

"I don't think it has to do with The Klinefeld Group," I said.

He looked down at his spotless loafers. "But there's something..."

The door dinged and opened to the lobby. "Well, let me know." I left to head for the garage.

Spidermonkey followed me. "Where are we going?"

"*I'm* going to my parents' house. Where are you going?"

"With you."

"Because...?"

"You can't be alone. Somebody is targeting your family."

"I'll be fine."

He continued to follow me as I walked into the garage. "To be blunt, I'm sure that's what your mother thought."

I sucked in a breath. "I know."

"Don't ditch me. I'm too old to chase you."

"I won't. I might be crazy, but I'm not a fool." We walked through the rows looking for my truck. "You said you wanted to talk to me and Chuck about something?"

"I don't think now is the time," said Spidermonkey.

"It's the perfect time. I need something else to think about."

He took my arm. "I see the roof. Your Chevy is unmistakable."

"I hate being short."

"You're not short. You're travel-size, like Wallace."

"Please do not compare me to that incontinent pug."

He grinned. "She's a good pug."

"She's okay. What do you have?"

"The police report on Agatha and Daniel's accident, for starters," he said.

We turned onto the right row and I asked with a sick feeling, "Is it interesting?"

"Only because it's practically useless. The investigation was done by Jeff City and it appears they didn't have the resources to investigate properly or much interest."

"I thought the NTSB investigated crashes."

The NTSB did do a cursory investigation. Apparently, the crash wasn't quite as cut and dry as Aunt Tenne had said. Something to do with the wing flaps. The wiring had broken in flight. The Jeff City detective had flight experience and he thought it was tampered with, but it could've been worn out and snapped. The NTSB report said the wiring was fairly new and shouldn't have snapped, but it wasn't beyond the realm of possibility. There were several crashes during that time with higher profiles and larger body counts. The NTSB had their hands full and the case got filed as Cause Undetermined.

I stopped walking. "Do you think it was an accident?"

"No. Not for a minute. I had a friend of mine take a look, confidentially, and he says that the NTSB dropped the ball."

"He'd be in a position to know?" I asked.

"He would and, of course, there were the men seen in the hanger before Agatha and Daniel took off. No one followed up on them. There wasn't a whole lot of state-to-state cooperation back then. Louisiana thought it was Missouri's problem since they had the crash site. Missouri thought it was Louisiana's as the point of origin."

"What about Nana and Pop Pop? Didn't they want answers?"

"Everyone was interviewed. No one imagined that anyone wanted Agatha and Daniel dead. The only ones who had anything to gain were your grandparents and the cops saw them as devastated with no real financial motive. They were clean. And remember, this is before Ace met Millicent and Myrtle. Before they knew your parents personally, either of them."

"You mean, maybe they didn't know about The Klinefeld Group at the time," I said.

"The break-ins at the Bled mansion happened after the crash. I think The Klinefeld Group was following the trail that started with Dr. Bloom."

Dr. Bloom was an Oxford professor who'd inadvertently revealed the meeting of Stella Bled Lawrence and my ancestors, Amelie and Paul, to The Klinefeld Group. Once they discovered that Amelie and Paul shipped something home to New Orleans after their meeting in Paris, they went after Agatha and Daniel, thinking that they must've inherited it. Since The Klinefeld Group was still looking, I guess they didn't.

"There was a big break between all that and now. I wonder what got them started again," I said.

A strange look came over Spidermonkey's face and he ran his fingers through his silver hair. "It is curious."

"But you have a theory."

"Let's go to the truck. Your mother needs you back."

"Just tell me. This day can't get any worse."

I really thought that. I am so stupid.

Spidermonkey sighed. "I think it was you."

"Why me?"

"Because you triggered Dr. Bloom. When you started making the news, your connection with the Bleds was mentioned. The Klinefeld

Group is nefarious, but they're not stupid. Maybe they thought they'd gotten it wrong back then. That Stella never sent it back to the States at all. There's no record of your grandparents' house here in St. Louis being broken into. The Klinefeld Group dropped it after they didn't find anything on the Bled properties. I assume they went looking elsewhere."

"And if they stopped looking at St. Louis..."

"They never saw your parents marry, your father's involvement in Josiah's disappearance, or your mother getting Josiah's house. It's a huge connection."

"Then I get into the news and they get interested again," I said, feeling so tired I wanted to lie down on the garage floor, sticky spots and all.

"I would," said Spidermonkey. "I'd think I'd missed the obvious. That Agatha and Daniel didn't have it. Your grandparents did. Agatha and Daniel were flying to St. Louis to tell them what was in their possession. Your being raised in the mansion would make me think that everyone now knew and whatever it was had been put back into The Bled Collection."

"Except it wasn't."

Spidermonkey was so excited he was bobbing up and down like Aaron. "Exactly. I think your parents have it."

"My parents don't have it," I said.

"There have been attempts to break through your father's security. They weren't successful. The Bled Mansion break-in was a fluke."

"Yeah," I said, reaching for my purse and then remembering I'd dropped it at the house. I needed a tissue in the worst way.

"What are you thinking?"

"Just that I left Mom to go to Sturgis. I knew about those attempts. Aunt Miriam told me, but I went anyway. It's my fault and, apparently, it's my fault that Lester got killed."

Spidermonkey drew back in horror. "That's not what I meant at all."

"It doesn't matter what you meant. It's what happened." I started off for the truck.

"I apologize for telling you that. You couldn't have known what would happen any more than Dr. Bloom knew that his interview would cost people's lives."

I said nothing.

"Mercy, please forgive me."

"Quiet," I hissed, going rigid.

Spidermonkey tried to put me behind him, but nobody puts me anywhere. "I don't see anything."

"There's someone sitting in my truck."

CHAPTER FIVE

The person saw us, got out of my truck, and closed the door before leaning on the cab.

Spidermonkey pulled me back. "We have to call security."

"Go ahead," I said.

The figure was too big to be the guy from Sturgis. This person was taller, not to mention broader. Football player came to mind.

"Mercy," said Spidermonkey. "Come with me."

Curiosity overwhelmed my good sense. It wasn't the stalker. Something about the way they got out so leisurely intrigued me to no end.

"Are you coming or what?" rang out a voice that was both deep and lyrical. Male or female. Could go either way.

"Who are you?" I yelled.

"Calpurnia sent me."

Crap on a cracker.

"That could be good," said Spidermonkey.

"Oh, yeah. I need the Fibonaccis showing up like I need another stroke in the family."

"You're boring me," the person called out.

"Leave!"

"It's my job to stay."

I rubbed my forehead. Calpurnia. Could you pick a worse time? I don't think so.

"I'm just going to call an Uber if you don't beat it."

"Miss Watts, there's nowhere you can go that I can't follow."

I slumped and took the long way around the row to come in facing Calpurnia Fibonacci's minion. As it turned out, minion wasn't a good description at all. This person wasn't small, yellow, or of indeterminate sex. She was a woman and holy crap she was big with a nice, rosy tan and a great makeup job. If John Cena had a sister, she would be this chick.

"Hi," I said, sounding like a twelve-year-old.

"Hello," she said. "Ready to go?"

I straightened up to my full five-foot-two. Impressive, I know. "I can't go see Calpurnia today." *Or ever.*

She got off the truck and cracked her knuckles so loud it echoed off the concrete. "She doesn't need to see you."

I couldn't decide if that was a good thing or a bad thing. Calpurnia Fibonacci was the head of a mafia family that went back generations in St. Louis. Her nephew called on me to do him a favor and I'd accidentally done it by saving his sister's life. Once you get onto the Fibonacci radar, it was damn near impossible to get off.

"Why are you here, exactly?" I looked for a weapon and none were obvious, but I wasn't sure I needed one. She was wearing yoga pants and a form-fitted top from Lululemon. I didn't know they made sizes that big. Her shoulders put Chuck to shame and I swear her thighs had to be bigger than my waist and I'm no twig.

"I'm here to collect you," she said in a voice that spoke of whiskey and good humor.

"Okay then."

Why didn't I call security? Seriously, why?

"You ready?" she asked.

To die?

Spidermonkey had my arm in a vise-like grip. "We'll just be going now. Have a pleasant day," he said, tugging on me.

"Wherever you're going," she said, "I'm going too, Grandpa."

"Why?" I asked.

"You need watching and I'm going to watch you."

"Watch me do what?"

"Do whatever you do," she said with a sigh as if I was seriously slow. Maybe I was. It'd been a long day already. "Get in the truck."

"I'm good."

"Are you going to cooperate?" she asked.

I shook off Spidermonkey's grasp and crossed my arms. "I don't really do that. Who are you?"

"Fats Licata. Calpurnia sent me to watch you," she said.

That name was familiar. Calpurnia had threatened to give me a bodyguard when she sent me to Paris to find Angela Riley. I'd narrowly avoided it by getting stuck with Aaron and Chuck on the trip.

"You're Fats Licata?" I asked with a mountain of doubt.

"You thought I'd be fat, huh?"

"I thought you'd be a dude."

She maneuvered her tongue. A toothpick popped out between her teeth and she chewed on it like a ginormous beaver. "A little sexist, aren't we?"

"I guess so. Calpurnia just said she wanted to send you to Paris to protect me."

The toothpick snapped in two and she ate it. I swear to God. The woman ate the toothpick. "Yeah. Thanks for that."

"What do you mean?"

"I could've used a trip to Paris. Instead, I got to watch over Calpurnia's meatball nephew in Atlantic City. Atlantic City is no Paris, let me tell you."

"Who?"

"Lorenzo. Worst instincts I've ever seen. The guy's a moron, but this time, I'm with you."

"What in the world for? I'm not going to Paris."

"I don't care where you're going. I'm along for the ride."

"Why did Calpurnia send you? Am I supposed to do something for her?"

"You're supposed to stay alive in case she wants you to do something."

"Huh?"

"Calpurnia heard about the Sturgis situation and your mother. She likes you. She'd rather you didn't get murdered."

"That's nice, but—"

"But nothing. I'm on you."

"You can't come."

"Wanna bet?"

Not really.

"Look, I'm just going to my parents' house to get some things for my mom. It's not a huge operation."

"Fine. I'll make sure you arrive alive. It's what I do." Fats opened the truck and said, "Keys? I can rip open your steering column, but it's expensive to repair."

"I'm calling Oz for confirmation on your identity."

She nodded. "Prudent."

I called Oz, who told me he was sorry about Mom. I asked him about Fats and he laughed. He'd figured that Calpurnia would send someone to protect me. He just didn't think it would happen so fast. Fats Licata was one of a kind and I had her for the duration.

"Is there anything I should know about her?" I asked him.

"She's unbelievable in bed."

"Ew. Too much information."

He laughed. "You asked."

"I really didn't."

We hung up and Fats grinned lasciviously. "Oz remember me fondly?"

"I'd have to say yes," I said.

She held out a beefy hand. "Keys."

I tossed them to her and Spidermonkey said, "I guess you don't need me."

"Who are you, anyway? I don't remember you from the file," said Fats.

"I have a file?" I asked.

"Everyone has a file." She eyed Spidermonkey. "Who are you?"

I turned Spidermonkey and pushed him toward the exit. "Never mind him. He's leaving."

"You're sure?" he asked.

"Absolutely," I said. "Go before you get caught in the Fibonacci web."

He leaned over and whispered in my ear. "We still have things to discuss."

I nodded and he headed off, happy to leave me in the care of a woman who should've only existed in comic books. I was less thrilled, but sometimes you just have to go with it.

I got in the passenger side and Fats started the truck. "You smell like hotdogs and...chocolate."

"You smell like Shalimar," I said.

"Good nose. I think you and I are going to work well together."

"That's good, since neither of us has a choice. I'm afraid to ask, but does this mean that I owe Calpurnia again?"

"Now you're catching on," she said with a grin and pulled out of the garage and into the twilight.

"My life sucks."

"Looks excellent to me," said Fats. "I hear your godmothers have a leaf from the Gutenberg bible. Any chance of getting me in to see it?"

That was the last thing I expected her to say. If she'd said, 'I'm going to slit you open and eat your ovaries,' I'd have been less surprised. She looked a lot more like an ovary eater than an art lover.

"Um...they have three, actually, but they're on loan to the Smithsonian for conservation right now."

"Damn the luck. Any first editions?" She gripped the wheel, her eyes glittering.

"A few."

"*The Wonderful Wizard of OZ?*"

"Yes."

"*The Adventures of Tom Sawyer?*"

"They have it."

Fats beamed at me. "How lucky are you to grow up in the Bled Mansion, surrounded by those books and the art? I've heard they have a Giacometti."

"They do. It's really ugly. If I didn't know what it was, I'd be tempted to toss it in the recycling bin," I said.

"You can't be serious. Giacometti was a visionary."

"He had a vision to make ugly sculptures."

She snorted. "You are a philistine."

"I'm honest. The thing is ugly."

We bickered all the way to Hawthorne Avenue and that's how I got a new partner, a woman who could crack walnuts with her bare hands and had the soul of an artist.

"Stop the truck," I said.

Fats raised an eyebrow and stopped pelting me with questions about my travels with Millicent and Myrtle. She'd never been out of the country and was hot to go just about anywhere. "We're not there."

"You can't go. The entire avenue is swarming with cops."

She put her hand on her chest and said, "Are you ashamed of our relationship?"

"And the winner is Fats Licata in the role of I'm not supposed to know you," I said. "You want to be interviewed for half the night? I don't. My boyfriend will take one look at you and he will never let it go until he knows everything."

Fats licked her full lips. "I'd like to know *everything* about Chuck Watts. He has a file, too."

"Don't say everything like that."

"Everything," she drew it out to a full five seconds.

"You're grossing me out."

"Nothing in your file said you were a prude, leather bikini girl."

Damn that Mickey. In a fit of insanity, I'd agreed to pose for a bikini poster for the band, Double Black Diamond, and had been regretting it ever since.

"I hate that stupid poster," I said. "Pull over."

She pulled over three blocks from Hawthorne Avenue and said, "My grandpa has you up in his rumpus room."

"I hate you."

"Grandma has a theory about what he gets *up* to in there."

"If I had a gun, I would shoot you," I said, shoving her shoulder. It was similar to the punching bag at Chuck's gym that he made me hit. It didn't move either. "Get out."

"I've been shot before. Didn't make much of an impression."

"Really? How many times?"

"Three times. Flesh wounds."

"I bet. You're like all flesh."

"But no fat. Ten percent," she said with considerable pride.

I spun in the seat and started pushing with my legs. "That's not healthy for a woman. Get out."

She was unmoved. Literally. "Says who?"

"Everybody. Please get out. I've got to get Mom's stuff and go back to the hospital."

She grinned and opened the door. "Ah, the magic word. Finally."

I slid into the driver's seat. "Hopefully, this won't take long."

"I'll be watching," said Fats.

"Don't. You'll be seen."

"No, I won't."

"You're the most visible woman in the world," I said. "Chuck is going to make you."

"I've got skills." She slammed the door and gave me a finger wave. *Swell.*

I drove off and watched in the rearview as Fats darted between a hipster coffee bar, that for some reason also sold pool tables and fedoras, and an antique silver shop that specialized in tea urns. They'd been in business my whole life. And in my whole life, I'd never seen anyone actually go in. They had to be a front for something, but I'd never mentioned it to Chuck. He'd shut them down and the neighborhood would be pissed. The rich aren't crazy about change. Or crime, for that matter. It was okay as long as it wasn't near them or if they didn't have to notice it.

Knowing that, I should've seen what was coming, but I had murder on my mind. I turned the corner to see a crowd around Mr. Knox's pagoda. You'd think it would be news crews and there were three, but the rest were our neighbors and some servants. Mr. Knox had his hands up as if he was about to be shot.

I sighed and edged around a news van to go to the service alley, but the crowd extended into the street. Mr. Knox spotted me and waved. The entire group turned and converged on my truck. What did I say about how it couldn't get any worse?

I rolled down my window and listened to a barrage of complaints from the street being blocked to the unseemliness of crime scene tape on their beloved avenue.

Mrs. Haas, The Girls' neighbor and a woman I usually considered to be normal, said, "I knew this would happen. It was inevitable."

"My mom getting attacked was inevitable?" I asked.

Mr. McCallister's butler said with his nose in the air, "I said it then and I'll say it now. That element should not have been allowed to move in."

"Please, Palfry," said Mrs. Haas. "That is not what I meant."

It's exactly what she meant. Heaven forbid a cop without an ounce of blue blood move in. Crime must certainly follow.

"We've lived here for twenty-six years," I said.

"And we've had Lester's murder and now this thing," said Nina, the Coventrys' maid. "We have to do something."

"Are you at all worried about my mom, a woman who bakes you cakes and the wife of a man who did your security systems for free?"

They looked guilty. A look that immediately turned to defiance. "You have to get them off the street," said Mrs. Haas.

"Them?" I asked.

She leaned in my window, filling the cab with the scent of gardenias from her incredibly thick grey hair. "The police and those crime scene people. They have vehicles parked in front of your house."

I looked at the ceiling and practiced some deep breathing techniques meant to control rage. "So what?"

"So what?" asked Palfry. "People will think there was a terrible crime on our street."

"There was."

He pulled up to his full five-eight and said, "A person like you couldn't possibly understand. You, with your rock band and unseemly habit of being on the news."

My hand shot out my window, grabbed him by the silk tie, and yanked him into my door. Hard. "You know what, Palfry? An unseemly person like me might just get out of this truck and grant an interview to every single reporter that asks."

"What would you say?" His beady eyes darted around, looking for a way out.

"I might say that the residents of Hawthorne Avenue couldn't care less about the wife of a celebrated detective who's lying in the ICU with a traumatic brain injury. They only care about traffic and how it looks."

Mrs. Haas gasped, "Brain injury?"

"What did you think happened? They gave her a cuddle?"

Mrs. Haas and Nina burst into tears, apologizing. That's how it was with the wealthy of Hawthorne Avenue. Appearances first. Reality later.

I shoved Palfry back. He did not apologize. I didn't expect he would. Dad had arrested his brother for solicitation of an underage boy in connection with a murder-suicide a couple of years before he retired. Palfry hated us like herpes, said we were trash, the works. He had no problem with his brother, oddly enough.

"Well, don't expect me to help with this mess," he said, straightening his tie.

"Do you know something?" asked Mrs. Haas. "You have to tell the detectives."

Palfry's eyes darted around again and he said quickly, "I don't know anything."

He glanced at me with loathing. He knew something alright.

"You'll help if I say you'll help." I put my truck in gear.

"I already gave my statement."

"You can always give another one."

He stepped back. "No. I can't. Good day." He turned on his gleaming heels and disappeared into the crowd.

I didn't bother to go after him. Like Fats said, there was nowhere he could go that I couldn't follow.

The crowd dispersed, wiping their eyes, shoulders hunched with guilt. I drove onto the avenue to see why Mrs. Haas was so unnerved. There were two crime scene vans, a command center, for some reason, and no fewer than six squad cars, not to mention all the unmarked cars. Half of them were parked on the sidewalks and there were uniforms meandering everywhere, drinking coffee and chatting. The avenue liked dignity and decorum. Cops have neither and I say that as the daughter of one.

I parked four houses away and cringed at the crime scene tape ringing the manicured lawns and trampled flower beds. I jogged down the street, waving at the greetings from the cops that knew me. Actually, they all knew me, if not then through Dad through Kronos, Aaron's restaurant. It had a Star Trek/cop/firefighter theme that kept it packed with uniforms of all types.

I ducked under the tape across our front walk and ran across the lawn to the side yard, where most of the action was. When I turned the corner on our house, I stopped short in astonishment. It was lit up with portable lights and swarming with cops and techs. I spotted Dr. Grace, the M.E. I didn't think he came out unless there was a body.

Oh shit!

"Chuck!" I went up on my tiptoes, not a huge help...or any help, to be honest.

Everyone turned to me, but Chuck wasn't among the faces.

"Miss Watts, you can't be in here," said a uniform.

"Do you have a body?"

His brow furrowed under the brim of his hat. "Why do you think that?"

"Dr. Grace is here," I said.

"Oh, yeah. Everybody wants to help."

My lip trembled.

"Are you okay?" he asked kindly.

I barely stopped myself from the ugly cry. Why does kindness make crying happen?

"Chuck," I managed to squeak out.

"I think he's in the house. I'll get him."

The uniform took off and I watched the flurry of activity. There was a lot going on, but not in the area in front of the side door where I'd found Mom. Dr. Grace was squatting in a bed of hosta. The shade plants were flattened and Dr. Grace was measuring something. I couldn't tell what. Crime scene techs were taking pictures of every inch of the garden, the house, and the door to Sandy's garden next door.

A couple of techs and a cop were looking at Mom's chicken sculpture and measuring it. They had some plastic sheeting and seemed befuddled about what to do with it.

Dr. Grace stood up, saw me, and walked over in his sterile booties as he pushed his horn-rimmed glasses up with a gloved knuckle. His unruly iron-grey hair was completely contained underneath a surgical cap. If it weren't for the glasses, I wouldn't have been sure it was him.

"Mercy," he said, snapping off both pairs of gloves. "How's Carolina?"

"Pretty good, considering."

"No interview yet?"

"Just me."

He nodded. "What does she remember?"

"Very little. She thinks she might remember a man," I said.

"Might?"

"It's very hazy. The stroke was major and she took a blow under her right ear. The memory might improve."

The doctor looked at his booties. "Or it might not."

I let him think for a moment, knowing, for once, when to stay silent.

He looked up after a minute and asked, "Tell me the condition of her body. I talked briefly to Calloway, but I'd like your view."

My view echoed Calloway's.

"So no other trauma?"

"What are you looking for?" I asked.

"Cuts, specifically."

"She has abrasions, but nothing that would bleed much."

He rocked back and forth. "I thought not."

I raised an eyebrow. "You've got blood."

"A hell of a lot of blood. At least four liters," said Dr. Grace.

I looked at the flower bed. "But no body."

"No body."

"A person doesn't just walk away after losing that much blood."

He turned and looked back at the hosta bed. "And yet..."

"Mom didn't have blood on her. Not really. Just a little from the scrapes. You know about the bruising?"

"Yes, but I need pictures."

"I'll take some tonight," I said. "I couldn't bring myself to ask right after she came out of surgery."

"I understand." Dr. Grace hesitated and then said, "What's the verdict on the rape?"

I suppressed a shudder. "Doesn't look like it. An attempt, at most, but a counselor will talk to her."

"Thank God for that."

We stared at the hosta bed until I said, "So we're thinking what? At least two other people were here."

"I would think so. The bleeder didn't walk away without help," he said.

"Could be two bleeders. Two liters each."

Dr. Grace tapped his chin. "A possibility. But my preliminary results say two blood types. This is just between us, you understand."

"Of course. What types?"

"B positive and O negative."

"Mom's B positive. So am I."

He turned toward the side door. "That fits. There are traces of B positive by the door. The large amount is O neg."

I looked around the scene, waiting for something to jump out at me, but nothing did. Still, there was an itchy feeling like I was missing something.

"Mercy." Chuck had come up behind me and even in his crime scene getup, I would've recognized him anywhere. Nobody had a body like Chuck. "I thought you were staying at the hospital."

"Mom wanted stuff," I said.

He thought it over and surprised me by not getting pissed. "How are you doing?" he asked.

"Okay, I guess," I said. "Can I get Mom's PJs and whatnot?"

He gave me a faint smile. "I'm surprised you didn't just barge in the house and get what you wanted."

I crossed my arms and glared. "I understand about crime scenes. I'm not an idiot."

The smile fell off his face. "I didn't mean that. I meant, you don't ask permission."

Dr. Grace laughed. "That is your reputation."

"It serves me well."

"I can't disagree."

A tech from beyond the end of the house waved frantically. "Dr. Grace! I found more blood."

"Jesus," said the doctor under his breath before he gloved up again and headed off to the weird topiary Mom loved and Dad said looked like a penis. It kinda did, but I sided with Mom. She said it was an obelisk. Whatever, Mom.

"So can I get Mom's stuff?" I asked.

"Are you speaking to me?" Chuck asked in a contrite voice.

"You called to find out if Pete was really on Mom's team, didn't you?"

The muscles tensed under his lean cheeks. "Why are you asking that?"

"Because you look guilty and it's what Dad would've done," I said.

Chuck was my father's protégé. They were very alike in ways I wasn't crazy about. But that's what happens when you get adopted by my uncle and trained by Tommy Watts. Chuck was the only cop who could hold a candle to my dad and that made him the favorite. I was just the daughter who took forever (half an hour) to learn to pick a lock and insisted on having regular showers during stakeouts. 'Cause that's just ridiculous.

"Trust but verify," said Chuck after mulling over his options.

"Sounds like all verify and no trust to me, but whatever. Can I go in?"

"Sure. I need you to see if anything's missing."

"You didn't look?" I asked.

"I did, but you grew up here. I didn't."

I rolled my eyes. "You were always here. Annoying me. Being sleazy."

"You liked it."

"I really didn't." I went around to the front and trotted up the stairs, only to stop halfway up. "Where are the cats?"

Chuck's guilty expression went from mild to major.

This is going to be so bad.

"What did you do?" I asked.

Chuck backed away, holding up his hands still sheathed in nitrile gloves. "It was necessary."

"Oh my god."

"You hate those cats."

"Mom loves those cats. Did you kill them?" I asked.

He scoffed. "Of course I didn't kill your mother's precious Siamese. I shot them with—"

I think I blacked out for a second. When I opened my eyes, Chuck had me by the shoulders. "Are you okay?"

"You shot Swish and Swat. Mom will have another stroke. What the hell is wrong with you?"

"Wait a second. With a tranquilizer dart. They're asleep."

"You tranquilized them like tigers? Who does that? They weigh ten pounds each."

"Have you met the Siamese?" He pulled up his sleeves and his poor arms were etched with bloody scratches. "You should see Nazir. He was bleeding so much he had to leave. Grace thought he might contaminate the scene. You should've named those cats Beelzebub and Lucifer."

"They're upset. They knew something was wrong."

"Why did they attack us?" asked Chuck.

"Why did they lick off all the fur on my cat's butt the last time he was here? I don't know. They're evil. Where are they?"

Chuck clenched his jaw and said, "It's procedure."

"Where?"

"The ASPCA."

I grabbed a pair of booties out of the box by the front door and slipped them on. Chuck handed me a pair of gloves and I snapped them on before saying, "Mom is never going to know that."

"No problem."

"The cats went to the cat spa, willingly. They were angels."

"I guess I'll be wearing long sleeves for a while."

"Yes, you will." I walked through the front door and started going through the house, one room at a time. Nothing was missing that I could see, but my parents had a lot of stuff. The things thieves would normally target weren't anything special. Mom and Dad didn't care about electronics. The two TVs they had were over ten years old. There were a couple of stereos, but they were older than me. There were laptops. Mom's was in the kitchen, open to Allrecipes. She had some high-end kitchen appliances like an Italian gelato maker, but it was still there.

Chuck raised an eyebrow at me and I shrugged. "Nothing's gone. Do you think they were in the house at all?"

"Doesn't look like it. The side door automatically locks and it was closed," said Chuck.

I sniffed.

"What?"

Sidney Wick walked in through the butler's pantry door, reeking of cigars despite wearing the complete crime scene ensemble. I knew him but not well. Dad had a good opinion, which wasn't easy to get. "Well?" he demanded.

"Nothing," said Chuck.

"Figures. We got bupkis outside, except for the blood. We've got too much of that," said Sidney. "I suppose you didn't see anything."

"Sorry. The cats were going berserk and I was searching for Mom." I only paused for a second, but Chuck saw it.

"Chuck says there were attempted break-ins. What do you know about that?" asked Sidney.

"Nothing really. They were amateurish. Didn't come close to overcoming Dad's system."

"Was your mother frightened?"

"Not at all." I leaned against Mom's beast of a stove. "It wasn't unusual. Dad makes enemies."

Sidney snorted. "Tommy does that, for sure. Does your mother carry when he's gone?"

"No," I said, surprised. "Mom's not a huge fan."

"But she can shoot?"

"Sure. Dad made us both learn. She's a good shot."

"What weapon does she use?" asked Chuck.

"A .22 Remington. Pretty generic, but it's light and doesn't make a lot of noise. Haven't you found it?" I asked.

"Gun safe's biometric and I don't have access."

I yawned, a tremendous tiredness coming over me. "I can open it."

We went up the servant stair to the second floor. Dad's office was undisturbed and I opened the enormous safe. Chuck and Sidney went through the inventory and two weapons were missing, Dad's favorites, a Glock and a Colt revolver. Sidney got excited until I reminded him that Dad would've taken them with him. Dad was never unarmed.

Sidney groaned and waved me away. "Go check and give me the bad news."

It was bad news in a good way. My parents did have some expensive things, but a thief would have to know what he was looking for. Everything was there, including some pricey porcelain, Mom's Lalique perfume bottles, and Dad's fancy watches that he forgot to wear. If the guy had gotten in, it wasn't to steal.

After I checked the second floor and the third with the same results, I returned to Mom's bedroom. Her fabulous bed, nicknamed the Oasis, was made, all the expensive linens in place. The glossy wood floor was dotted with oriental rugs that were probably expensive. I'd never thought about it. And in the corner was Mom's favorite piece in the whole house, an enormous wardrobe that I'd once believed was the wardrobe from *The Lion, the Witch, and the Wardrobe*. I'd have given anything in that moment for it to be real. To escape into Narnia, even for just a little while, would've been an incredible gift.

But it wasn't real and there was no escape from what was happening at my parents' house. I turned the big key and the door swung open with a squeak.

"Well, that's creepy," said Sidney, coming up beside me. "What are you looking for?"

I rummaged around and came up with a small carry-on bag. I handed it to Sidney and when he looked away, I leaned in to touch the wood at the back of the wardrobe, just in case.

Sidney asked me some more questions while I gathered Mom's PJs and some stretchy yoga wear. Mom never wore workout clothes when she wasn't working out, but I hoped the hospital was an exception. She needed to be comfortable, not proper. I wasn't packing skirts or dresses. No silk. It wasn't happening. Just the quilt and comfort.

"Got everything?" asked Sidney.

"Almost." I went to the dressing table and breathed deep the multitude of expensive scents in their beautiful bottles. Which one would she want?

A hand snaked around my waist and I jumped.

"Sorry," said Chuck. "I thought you heard me."

I pressed myself back into him and kissed his hand. "I don't know which one to pick."

"What does she normally wear?"

I touched one of the plainer bottles, a tall, clear one with a pink tinge. It had pensive Roman ladies etched into the glass and a small amount of French perfume, a less-expensive scent for everyday.

"Not that one," said Chuck.

"No?"

"What's the one that she saves for special occasions?"

I pointed at the most impressive bottle. Millicent and Myrtle had given it to Mom for her fortieth birthday. It had a blue and clear-striped bottle, but the stopper was the fabulous part with a large spray of fat berries in blue that drooped down either side. It was nearly full.

"That's the one," said Chuck. "Surviving is a special occasion.

"You're right, but I can't pack up that bottle. It'll break."

"The perfume didn't come in that, did it?"

"Not hardly. It was made in 1920."

We went through the drawers until we found the perfume itself in a nice bottle from Italy. I packed that.

Chuck looked over Mom's small collection while I got underwear and shampoo packed. "How much do you think this stuff is worth?"

"I never asked. The Girls don't do cheap. I'd guess several thousand apiece."

He whistled. "If he got in, he doesn't know the good stuff."

I glanced at the door. Sidney had left at some point and his smell went with him, thankfully. "Not The Klinefeld Group, you mean."

"Yeah."

"I'm sure they would know what this stuff is worth, but what they want is a big-ticket item. Has to be."

Chuck gazed at the table. "I don't think he got in."

"Maybe not, but those bottles aren't the most expensive things in here," I said, zipping up the bag.

"No?"

I pointed at the pair of framed cameos above the table.

"Those? They're so tiny." He leaned in to get a better look. "Why?"

"Painted by the Le Bruns and they didn't do miniatures. One-of-a-kind doesn't begin to describe them."

"How'd your mom get them? The Girls?"

"Actually, they're mine. They gave them to me for a couple of birthdays."

Chuck looked at me like he'd never seen me before. "Are you serious?"

I shrugged. "So?"

"Dr. Bloom is right. You're a Bled. You have to be."

"Not necessarily. You know Millicent and Myrtle like to give presents," I said.

"Do they like to give art?" He pointed at the left miniature, the one by Louise Élisabeth Vigée Le Brun. "Who is it?"

"I don't know. The Girls didn't say."

"How much is it worth?"

I avoided his intense gaze. I was embarrassed and I didn't want to say. Those pieces shouldn't have been on our wall. They belonged in a museum or at least with the rest of the Bled Collection. I should've seen that, but I never thought about it.

"Mercy, I'm not going to steal it." Chuck was grinning at me.

"It's insured for two million. So is the other one."

"Holy crap! Why didn't you tell me? We need to lock this place down. The house has been open to every dipshit with a badge for hours."

"They wouldn't steal from my parents. That would practically be suicide."

"You know we have special procedures for situations like this."

"Not really."

He ignored that and started calling people. I looked back at the miniatures and wondered what Dr. Bloom could do with this information. He seemed like the kind of guy who could find out why these unusual portraits were done. And more importantly, who the girls in them were.

Chuck poked me. "Why are they so expensive?"

"The Le Bruns painted them."

His face was blank.

"Court painters to Louis the Fourteenth and Marie Antoinette."

Chuck explained the significance to whoever was on the phone and I kissed him on the cheek before I left, trotting down the stairs to go out the front. I was halfway down the walk before something made me stop and turn around.

I went to the side and was greeted by Dr. Grace. "Forget something?" he asked.

"Something. I don't know." I tapped my foot, still in its booty.

"You can go in. It might help."

I left the carry-on and walked through the side garden to the door with Dr. Grace trailing me. There were number markers on the bricks where Mom had been. I could still see her lying there helpless.

"Where's my purse?" I said.

Dr. Grace looked up, startled. "Your purse?"

"I dropped it here somewhere. Did you bag it?" I asked.

He spoke into the radio clipped to his waist and the response was no. He called the EMTs and the firefighters. The answer was no.

The doctor and I looked at each other. His face got more drawn by the second.

"He came back," I said.

CHAPTER SIX

The crime scene techs discovered why Mom's assailant came back after they reexamined the entire scene. I have to hand it to them. I never would've found it. Neither would Chuck, although he'd be the last to admit it.

Tucked up in the corner of the side door's frame was a bullet hole. No. Slash that. Not a bullet hole. A repaired section of frame that had been puttied and stained to match the original wood. It was a pretty good job. Not perfect, but perfect enough that no one looked twice, except one rookie tech named Cindy Amendola. She spent a half hour on her hands and knees with a pair of magnifying goggles strapped to her head.

Cindy found a splinter. One splinter. About an inch that was clearly from aged, stained wood, not anything in the garden. She went over the door frame inch by inch and finally found the putty. Mom's attacker came back and dug a bullet out of the frame and covered it up.

Chuck and Sidney thought that he'd disposed of the unknown victim's body and returned, recovering the bullet and snagging my purse as a trophy. They sent out a fresh wave of uniforms to canvass the neighbors about the period of time *after* Mom went to the hospital.

That was the only period of time Mom's assailant had to get in and muck with the scene. The first canvass, asking about the time before I found Mom, had turned up nothing.

Sidney and Chuck stared at that bullet hole, silent and fuming. The nerve of that guy coming back to cover up. It really galled them. They knew very well that Cindy's finding that splinter was akin to catching the Freeway Killer due to a traffic stop. She could've missed it. Two other techs did.

Chuck was about out of his head. He felt the guy was taunting them, what with him being on camera stalking me in Sturgis. Everyone was convinced that it was the same guy, without any evidence, I might add, but it was a hell of a coincidence if it was someone else entirely.

Sidney kept asking me questions about Sturgis, like if he asked the question a different way, my memory might change. It didn't. What did change was my feeling about the crime scene. The more I stood there, being pelleted with questions, the more I felt something else was wrong about the scene.

"Describe the man you encountered at the Bear Butte visitor center," said Sidney, poised to write down something incriminating. I barely remembered the guy. Not gonna happen.

"I think something else is supposed to be here," I said, staring at the ground where I'd found Mom.

Sidney ignored me. "Height? Weight? What was the ranger's name?"

"For crying out loud, be quiet."

Not only was Sidney quiet, but everyone else went silent as well. Chuck came to my elbow and followed my eye line.

"I almost have it," I said.

"Describe finding your mother," said Chuck so softly I could barely hear him.

I closed my eyes and described being dragged to the gate by Wallace. I left out the cat. My credibility didn't need to take that hit. I told them about seeing Mom on the bricks and opening the gate. I went on to my assessment and calling 911.

"Stop," said Chuck. "Rewind. Describe Carolina lying on the bricks."

I didn't want to think about exactly how she looked lying there so helpless. If I could never think about that again, it would be okay.

"Was her face turned toward you or away?" asked Sidney.

"Away."

"Her clothes?"

I could see it in a flash. Mom on her back, wearing a black tissue tee and a full silk flowered skirt. The skirt was hitched up, exposing her pale thighs. The heel of her working right foot was digging into the bricks, trying to push herself over so she could get up.

My eyes flew open. "She was barefoot. That's it!"

The detectives looked at me. Their faces had *so what* written all over them.

"You think he took her shoes?" asked Chuck.

"No. There weren't any shoes," I said. "She was barefoot."

Sidney shrugged. "So..."

"*So,* my mother doesn't go out into the garden barefoot." I pinched Chuck's coveralls. "Look at all these snags. Mom likes heritage plants, the ones that haven't had the thorns bred out of them. If you walk around here without shoes, you're liable to get a thorn. I don't listen, so I've had about ten thorns in my feet. It drives Mom crazy."

The wheels were turning behind the eyes of the detectives, but they weren't quite there yet. I guess neither of them had mothers that were as predictable as mine.

Beyond them, Cindy slowly raised her hand like she was in some horrible math class and thought this was the one time she might've gotten the problem right. "If your mom doesn't go outside barefoot, something had to happen to make her change her pattern."

"We have a winner," I said with triumph.

Sidney wrote furiously in his notebook. "Are you absolutely sure about the shoes? No exceptions?"

"Carolina Watts doesn't make exceptions," said Chuck. "Mercy's right. Something made her come out here."

"The second victim being attacked," said Sidney.

"Possibly."

I bit my lip and then said, "I don't know. That's weird. Who is this person? Is anyone missing in the neighborhood?"

"Not that we've discovered," said Chuck. "Homeowners and staff are all accounted for."

The picture of Palfry's smug face popped into my head and I told them about our brief conversation. "I have a feeling he's holding something back."

Sidney smacked his lips and hunched his rounded shoulders, flipping a notebook page to write down my info. "You Watts' and your feelings. Pisses me off."

"Why?" I asked, genuinely curious.

"I get sick of your father being right. It's fucking irritating."

"I know exactly how you feel."

Sidney eyed me. "I bet you do. Alright. I'm going to go pick up this Palfry and see what he has to say."

He took off and Chuck said, "Call your Grandad and get the whereabouts of the rest of the family and friends. We have to find out who was here."

I called Grandad and was surprised to find out that Mom had relented after talking to the rape counselor and had let Aunt Miriam in. Aunt Miriam was so happy she cried. Since before that day, I'd seen Aunt Miriam cry exactly never, I wasn't sure what to do with that.

Between Grandad and Uncle Morty, we were able to account for everyone who was likely to be there on a weekend. Mom's best friend, Dixie, had been with her sister in Pennsylvania, touring Amish country. Grandma J was out with Dr. Watts at Cairngorms Castle. Grandad insisted that they move in there so the owners, John and Leslie, could look after them. That was a huge relief. The two former spooks wouldn't let anything happen to Grandad's wife and ex-wife. If we were lucky, our guy might try and be neatly disposed of with no trouble to us. John and Leslie were more than capable of doing that.

Aunt Tenne and Bruno were flying back from Miami as soon as they could get a flight and nobody else was missing. Flowers were pouring into Mom's hospital room once word got out and Grandad had been on the phone almost constantly with people who knew and loved Mom, everyone from her manicurist to the committee members of her various charities. All of Dad's detectives had checked in, except for Denny, but he was undercover on a ranch in Montana, roping steer and trying to figure out how the owners were connected to some drug outfit.

"I've got to go, sweetheart," said Grandad. "Miriam's coming out and she wants something, probably a new cane."

"Wait," I said with a sinking feeling that plunged to my feet and bungeed up into my throat. "What about Claire?"

I heard Grandad ask Uncle Morty and he started a cursing streak that impressed me with its sheer volume and incredible foulness. Technically, a lot of the words he used weren't actually cuss words, but he had a way of making them seem like they were.

"We don't know where Claire is," said Grandad, his voice tight and throaty.

Chuck nodded at me and called in Claire Carter's name and sent a squad car over to her apartment. I looked at where the blood was in the hosta bed and barely managed to hold down a heave. Claire was my dad's transcriptionist and secretary. He referred to her as his Girl Friday, whatever that meant. Claire ended up working for Dad because of me. A while ago, I'd traded my investigating skills for her transcription skills. The exchange was for tracking down her bigamous husband. Claire turned out to be just what Dad and I needed. He needed someone with her passion for organization and I needed to never file for my father again. It was a win-win until now.

"We don't know it's her," said Chuck gently. "She doesn't come here on Sunday, does she?"

I perked up. "That's true. I don't know why she'd be here. Dad's out of town. Claire usually works at home, doing the calendar and transcription there, if he's not around." I leaned on Chuck's shoulder. "Thank God."

"We still have to find her. I assume Morty's tracking her down."

"Yeah." My stomach went queasy again. "But it's weird that she hasn't called." I checked my phone to make sure. "Grandad says it was all over the news"

"We'll find her," said Chuck. "It's not Claire. It doesn't make sense."

Things didn't always have to make sense. Chuck knew that as well as I did. Somebody was at my parents' house at the wrong time and they paid for it with their life. It could be Claire and the thought made me feel sick all over. Claire was my old high school rival. I scared boys and she attracted them like gnats around a brown banana. Since I tracked down her so-called husband, we'd become friends. She understood what dealing with my father was like and was one of the few that sympathized with me. If I got her a job, that ended up killing her...

Chuck rubbed my back. "Go back to the hospital. There's nothing you can do here."

"I can't. I have to go talk to Millicent and Myrtle," I said.

"Didn't Ace call them?"

"He did about an hour ago, but I should've done it. They're really upset."

He kissed me lightly. "Of course, they are, but your being the one to tell them wouldn't change that."

"Still, I'm going over and then I'll go back to the hospital."

"I'm sending a uniform with you," said Chuck.

No. No. No.

"I'm okay. I don't need a watchdog," I said quickly. Too quickly, as it turned out.

Chuck gave me the stink eye. "Why? What are you up to?"

I'm ashamed to say that I batted my eyelashes and got teary-eyed, but I did and it worked. What a sucker my boyfriend was. "I'm going to Millicent and Myrtle to calm them down and then to spend the night in the ICU on a foldout something."

He hugged the breath out of me. "Did I say I was sorry this happened?"

I snuffled into his shoulder, pretty convincingly if I say so myself. "I don't know."

"Well, I am and I'm sorry about the Pete thing."

"It's okay," I said. "I'll call you from the hospital."

"He shook his head. "You can't run around alone."

I tried to work up some more tears to distract and then it hit me. I didn't have to. "Tiny," I said.

"Tiny?"

"How about I take him with me? Dad sent him to bodyguard me at Cairngorms."

Chuck's shoulders relaxed. "That works. Millicent and Myrtle won't mind losing their temp chauffeur?"

"I doubt it."

We agreed and I jogged away down Hawthorne Avenue before Chuck could think of a reason Tiny wasn't a good idea. I didn't know where Fats was, but I had no doubt she was lurking somewhere. If a uniform got a load of her, Chuck would be all over me. It would probably take all of three minutes to find out who she worked for and I'd be screwed.

I'd have to figure out what to do with Tiny. He worked for Dad and right then, he was chauffeuring The Girls, since Chuck had discovered their new chauffeur was a pedophile and arrested him. Would Tiny's loyalty be to me, his beloved cousin, or to my dad, signer of the paycheck?

I dropped the iron crow knocker and heard the heavy plinking noise that echoed off the high walls of the Bled mansion for a second time.

No answer. My stomach started to twist and I let myself in through the over-sized front doors and called out, "Hello? Millicent? Myrtle?"

I turned back to the security panel. It had been armed and no doors had been open for the last hour.

"Tiny?" I yelled, my voice going high-pitched with fear.

I headed for the kitchen with my heart in my throat, but before I got five steps, a voice called down from the second floor, "Miss Mercy!"

Leaning over the second floor landing was The Girls' housekeeper, Joy. Her long brown hair tinged with grey was falling out of the neat French twist that she perpetually wore. "Thank goodness you're here."

"Why?"

"The Girls are in an absolute panic. I've never seen them like this. Not even poor Lester's murder got them this upset."

"Are they upstairs?" I asked.

"No. I'm packing bags for them," said Joy.

"Where are they going?"

"The hospital."

"With bags?"

Joy grimaced. "I think they plan on staying for the duration."

"They can't stay at the hospital," I said. "It's not a hotel."

"It's whatever they want it to be. The family are big donors."

I groaned. Mom let in Aunt Miriam, but that was no guarantee that she'd let in The Girls. It would break their hearts if Mom said no. It broke Aunt Miriam's heart to be refused at first and I was pretty sure her heart was made of titanium or whatever they used for the space shuttles reentering the atmosphere. The Girls weren't nearly so tough.

"I'll take care of it," I called up to her.

"Please do. It's not good for them to be so upset."

"Where are they?"

Tiny came around the corner at the end of the long hall and said, "The left conservatory."

"I'll keep packing, just in case," said Joy and she disappeared, probably making lists of hats and shoes in her head. The Girls didn't go anywhere with fewer than five suitcases each. All weather and social situations must be planned for and tragedy might occur. I had a full wardrobe upstairs in my room for traveling with them. It included designers like Valentino and John Galliano. Those clothes were way too fancy for real life and they remained safely tucked away in their wardrobe.

Tiny trotted down the hall. "Joy told you?"

"Yeah. Kinda losing it?"

"They're in there cutting flowers like they're for the Rose Parade."

"So a lot then?"

"Girl, this is crazy." My cousin wiped the beaded up sweat on his dark brow. "They had me bring all the vases in the house. Did you know that they have fifty-two vases?"

We walked through the house to the large arched doors that opened into the conservatory. "I never counted. They seriously filled fifty-two vases?"

"They working on it. There ain't a flower left in the garden and now they at the orchids."

"Not the orchids. You can't cut orchids."

"I know, but they aren't listening to me," said Tiny.

I grabbed the wrought iron door handle and asked, "Are they crying?"

"That's the one thing they aren't doing. Not a tear. Just flower cutting and ordering baking supplies. They ordered ten pounds of that special Brittany butter they love. What the hell they gonna do with ten pounds of butter?"

"I don't know, but I'm guessing pounding will be involved." I opened the door and a rush of hot, humid air hit me. Butterflies flitted between banana trees and prehistoric looking ferns.

"I'm not going in. I gotta go rent a van," said Tiny. "You got to calm them down."

"A van?"

"For takin' fifty-two vases to the hospital. What do you think?"

"Hold off on that."

He stopped dialing his phone. "Yeah?"

"We'll have to do something with all those flowers, but I have to think. Mom's room isn't big enough for ten vases, much less fifty-two."

"I got ya," said Tiny. "Still not going in. I'm sweating already."

"Go get some water. I'll...do something."

I walked into the conservatory, instantly feeling my hair start to curl in the humidity. The soft patter of my godmothers' voices led me to the far corner of the conservatory. Darkness was rapidly descending and the enormous glassed-in room was fully lit, highlighting all the ironwork that held up the three-story glass walls.

"We must find out," said Millicent.

"Tommy will, but it can't be," said Myrtle.

"It's happened before under this very roof."

"Dear Lester."

I stopped walking. I didn't mean to eavesdrop. It wasn't a conscious decision. I just did it. I stood behind a potted palm and held my breath.

"They wouldn't go after our Carolina," said Myrtle.

Someone blew their nose and Millicent said, "They murdered Lester and for nothing. He couldn't tell them anything and neither can Carolina."

"They murdered Lester out of frustration. It wasn't planned. Carolina—"

"If only we hadn't interfered."

There was the scrape of a heavy pot being dragged. "It isn't our fault. We love them."

"But if our love led them to Carolina…and Mercy."

"Mercy is safe. No one knows."

"Dearest," said Millicent. "I don't think it matters anymore. We loved her too much. The world has noticed."

Another scrape. "I suppose you're right. But they must give up some time. All these years. All of these deaths to no avail. They won't find it," said Myrtle.

"They'll never give up," said Millicent. "We should've understood that when Agatha and Daniel died."

There was a metallic thump of something hitting a pot. "I would tell them," declared Myrtle. "Why don't they understand that?"

Say what it is. Say it. Please.

"As would I, my dear sister. I would tell them in a minute if I could."

A strange thought entered my mind. Was it possible that The Girls didn't know what it was that The Klinefeld Group was after? I'd always thought, deep down, that they must know. How could they not? It was to do with Stella, their favorite cousin and a great friend of their mother. But maybe they didn't. Maybe that secret died with Agatha and Daniel on that plane. Could they have been coming to St. Louis to tell the Bleds what they knew? They didn't have it, so knowledge had to be what they were carrying. Dad always said that the best way to keep a secret was to shut the hell up. You'd have to keep the secret between the people who brought it back and their descendants and a line in the Bled family. If our side died with my great-grandparents, what happened to the Bled side?

There was another nose blowing and something being set down. "I think we must stop and settle ourselves."

"Yes, we can't change it. The orchids are a mistake. Tiny was right. The flowers are enough."

"And yet they can't do anything but be beautiful."

"It's all we have."

"Yes."

They don't know. They really don't know.

I tiptoed back to the door, pushed the door open hard so it squeaked, and called out, "Millicent? Myrtle? Are you in here?"

"Mercy, dear, we're back by the potting table," said Millicent.

I jogged back to find my godmothers disheveled. That alone made me skid to a halt on the stylized Art Deco tile floor. "Are you okay?"

My darling godmothers' eyes widened in surprise. "We're fine," said Millicent, immediately coming to me and hugging me gently. Myrtle followed suit.

I breathed deep the scent of expensive perfume, baked goods, and good clean dirt. For a second, everything seemed like it would be alright. They loved me. They loved Mom. These little old ladies had plenty of secrets, but not the one that got my great-grandparents killed. I didn't know how much weight I was carrying until that particular one was lifted away.

Millicent stepped back and asked, "Why are you worried about us? Dearest Carolina—"

She got choked up and couldn't continue, so Myrtle took over. "How is your mother? Ace says that she came through the surgery well."

"She did. I think she'll have some issues. That's pretty much unavoidable, but everything happened just the way it should with a stroke. Nothing was missed. I was worried about you because...you're all...messy."

The Girls looked over themselves seemingly surprised to find the prim Chanel suits that they'd probably worn to the cathedral that morning were smudged with dirt and had leaves and sticks stuck in the fine fabric. Their silver hair, usually done in ringlets and elaborate waves, was hanging loose with pins dangling from the tips of their locks.

They brushed their skirts and patted their hair, as surprised as me to find themselves a mess.

"Your mother," said Millicent helplessly.

"We wanted to bring her favorite flowers," said Myrtle.

I hugged them both. "She's going to be fine. I'm sure there are lots of patients that would love your flowers, not just Mom."

They nodded.

"But you should change and rest." I could see a flash of stubbornness in their lined faces. "Mom will be sleeping for some time. They gave her a painkiller. She won't even know you're there. Come tomorrow after we get her out of the ICU."

"The ICU," whispered Myrtle in horror.

"It's not that bad. Trust me," I said with a smile. "She's getting great care and Aunt Miriam is with her."

"Miriam?" they said with silver eyebrows shooting up.

We had to have a discussion about Dad, but I got them upstairs, had Joy unpack, and talked them into dinner on trays in bed, which they considered the height of decadence. I reminded them that Mom was eating in bed and it became a solidarity thing.

Once I got them settled in Millicent's bed with cups of Tension Tamer and *The Crown* on the TV I carried in from the sitting room, they seemed to relax. Joy promised to stay with them overnight to make sure they'd get up and start trimming hedges or something instead of coming to the hospital. Then I ran downstairs to try and sneak out the back.

No such luck. Tiny snagged me at the back door. "I got Mrs. Haas to handle the flowers," he said. "Some florist is going to take them to the hospital."

"Not the vases, I hope."

"Not the vases."

"Good. She owes us."

"Who?"

"Mrs. Haas." I told him about the fuss at the gate and watched as my cousin's face went into a downright scowl. That wasn't Tiny at all. Despite all he'd been through with his military service, he managed to stay cheerful.

"They acted that way about your parents? These people are trash around here. I don't care how much money they've got. Can't buy class."

"I think Mrs. Haas lost her mind. She thought Mom wasn't hurt badly at all."

"No excuse. I might give her a piece of my mind iffin' I could spare it."

"You can spare plenty," I said. "I got to go. Mom's probably asleep, but I've been gone a lot longer than I expected.'

"I'm ready," Tiny said and the cheerful expression that usually decorated his face returned.

Please, no.

"For what?"

"Chuck called. I'm gonna watch you."

Dammit, Chuck. No trust.

"I'm good. See ya."

"The hell you are. I know all about that guy in Sturgis trying to kill Ace and following you."

I went out the back door into the denuded rose garden. It was a pretty sad sight with all the fat bushes stubby and not a whiff of the heady scent that usually filled the air. "I'm fine. I've had stalkers before."

"Not like this asshole. He attacked your mother and killed somebody feet away from her," said Tiny as he chased me through the garden. He was pretty quick, considering that he was a huge guy at six six and over 300 pounds.

"I'm really fine," I said, trying to wiggle out of his iron grasp. Not gonna happen.

"This got something to do with that chick you got with you?"

I froze and then got overly casual. "What chick? I don't know what you're talking about."

He snorted. "I seen her lurking down the avenue behind you."

Crap on a cracker.

"What makes you think she's got something to do with me?"

"You acted like she wasn't there and you got skills," he said.

Not that many skills, apparently. I suck.

"I don't know who you're talking about." I tried to drag him down the walk toward the stable/garage. It was like trying to drag a chatty dump truck. Tiny kept yakking about Fats, trying to convince me of how he knew we were connected. I didn't care. I just had to get away.

"You know you're not going to move me, right?" asked Tiny.

"I can do it." My feet were moving. My body wasn't. "I believe."

"Believe all you want. I ain't moving. Unless..."

I stopped struggling. "Unless what?"

"You tell me who she is."

I eyed my cousin and his brown eyes got all shifty. "What are you up to?"

"Nothin'." He wouldn't look at me.

"You want to meet her. For crying out loud, Tiny, I've got stuff to do," I said.

"She's behind the garage."

"Unbelievable. Her name is Fats. Do you really want to date a woman named Fats?"

Tiny chuckled, a deep and reassuring sound. "She's fat like I'm tiny."

My hands went to my hips. Maybe my cousin's inexplicable attraction to Fats could outweigh Dad's influence. "Do you have my back?"

Tiny dropped my arm. "You know I do."

"Over my father?"

"They aren't different."

"Well..."

Without a word, Tiny charged past me. He was so big he created a breeze. I chased him down the walk to the stable, grabbing his belt loop and trying to hold him back. I actually went airborne a couple of times and didn't slow him one bit.

Tiny reached the keypad and punched in his code. In one swift movement, he whipped open the door and dragged me inside. We flew down the aisle between the old stalls filled with fresh hay. The smell was intoxicating, reminding me of a childhood when I studied there, hiding from my nosy mother and eating the pastries The Girls and I had spent hours making. Why had I never realized how unique my position was? It seemed everyone else had.

In thirty seconds, we were out the door. Tiny made sure he'd secured it before calling out, "I saw you."

Fats stepped out from behind the corner of the garage and said, "Because I let you."

Tiny scoffed. "Yeah, right."

She advanced on him like a lioness on prey. "I decide."

"Why are you watching Mercy?" asked Tiny, letting her slink up to him without any reaction. I would've backed up or run. I'm tough that way. "That's my job."

"You chauffeur old ladies."

My cousin twitched. "That ain't permanent."

"Looks permanent."

"Who are you?" he asked.

Fats jerked a thumb toward me. "She didn't tell you?"

"She said you're called Fats, for no good reason."

"For the same reason you're called Tiny. It's incongruous." She smiled, revealing sharp, rather large canines and another toothpick, just hanging out in there.

"I been called Tiny since kindergarten."

"Same here." Fats looked him up and down in a blatantly sexual way.

Ew.

"Okay. You two get a room. I'm going to the hospital."

Fats made a purring noise.

"Oh my god! Stop that. You're grossing me out."

"Prude."

I rolled my eyes. "Whatever. I'm leaving."

"Not a chance. I follow orders, even if you don't."

My lip poked out. I don't know why. Following orders wasn't my jam.

"Yeah, she's not good with the orders," said Tiny.

"Hey! Stop bonding," I said. "She works for Calpurnia Fibonacci."

Oops.

I pushed on Fats, trying to turn her around. "Let's go. Stroke patient waiting."

"Calpurnia Fibonacci?" asked Tiny. "The mob boss?"

"Businesswoman," corrected Fats.

"Tommy Watts won't see it that way."

"Not my problem." Fats turned and walked down the alley. I noticed she had a lot more swing in her hips. Tiny followed her as he was meant to. Men.

"I take it we're going now?" I said, jogging along to keep up with their long strides. It was a workout just to get back to my truck. They ignored me for the most part while trading zingers and innuendos while scanning the area and avoiding being seen, sharp-eyed and, frankly, scary as hell.

When we got to the truck, I was breathless and stupid. I thought I could keep Tiny out of the truck. We're talking a 1958 Chevy, not exactly a crew cab. Fats unlocked the driver's side. I hopped in, sliding over and trying to make myself look big like you're supposed to when being charged by a bear.

Fats got in and reached over to pull up the door handle. I pushed it down. "Sorry. Won't fit."

Tiny knocked on the window. "Open up."

Fats pinned me against the seat—breathing was optional—and opened the door. Tiny pushed me to the middle of the seat and eased his bulk in, squashing me against Fats. I felt like a pea between two slices of Texas toast.

"Why is this my life?" I asked.

"Some people have all the luck," said Tiny, barely getting the seatbelt around his waist.

Fats pulled out and said, "Think of it this way—there's little chance of you getting shot right now."

"I can't breathe."

"You're fine," she said and turned her attention to Tiny. The two of them talked over my head. Literally.

"I don't like this," I said.

"Good thing you don't get a vote," said Fats.

They began discussing whether I should wear a bullet-proof vest. What the odds were of a sniper taking me out. Cheerful stuff like that.

"Can we talk about something else?" I said like I was included or something.

Tiny leaned toward Fats and I squeaked as my shoulders went up into my ears. "I gotta tell you, Fats, you smell as good as a woman can smell."

"I love your tattoo," she replied.

"Ew. Not that," I said.

"Ever have a couple's massage?" asked Tiny.

"No, but I will. Soon," said Fats.

I managed to free an arm and waved over my head. "Gross. Let's play the quiet game. Loser gets shot with Grandad's Mauser."

"You know what they do in couple's massages?" asked Tiny.

"I want to find out," purred Fats.

God help me.

CHAPTER SEVEN

The drive to the hospital was the longest ten minutes of my life. Fats and Tiny's conversation bounced between gun caliber and massage oil. They were sweaty by the time we got there and I was scarred for life.

Fats pulled into a secluded section of the hospital garage. Gee. I wonder why. Tiny physically pulled me out of the truck and said he'd escort me in. Fats ordered me not to leave the hospital or else. I didn't know what the "or else" meant, but since I had sweat stains on my shoulders, I didn't care.

Tiny practically ran me through the lobby to the elevators. He tapped his big foot and glared at the *Up* button that refused to light up. He held up Mom's carry-on. "You're spending the night, right?"

"Yes and no need to tell me what you're going to do."

He smiled and got all dreamy. "I'm gonna take her to dinner at Kronos. I don't think she's eaten there. She'll love it."

"Are you crazy? Kronos is cop central."

"Nobody'll say anything. They wouldn't dare."

"But they'll tell my father that you're dating one of Calpurnia Fibonacci's thugs," I said.

The elevator doors opened and he pushed me in. "She's not a thug. She's a lady. The hottest lady I ever laid eyes on."

"That's enough."

"No. She's not hot. She's scorching. You know what I'm gonna do?"

I held up my hand. "Too much information."

"I haven't told you anything yet."

"The less I know, the better."

"I think I'm in love," he said with all sincerity.

"I know. I can smell it on you and on me, come to think of it."

The doors opened on Mom's floor and, just my luck, Uncle Morty was standing there glowering. "What took you so long?" He reached in and snatched me out of the elevator.

Tiny put the carry-on in the hall and waved.

"Where you going?" asked Uncle Morty.

"I gotta date with the hottest lady you've ever seen."

"Date? You stay here."

Tiny shook his head. "She's with you and she ain't leaving."

"You got a hole in your head?" asked Uncle Morty. "This is Mercy."

"My lady. You should see her thighs."

Doors. Please close.

"I don't care about no thighs," said Uncle Morty.

"They ripple."

Uncle Morty looked at me. "What's wrong with him?"

"He's in love," I said.

"Since when?"

"About twenty minutes ago."

Uncle Morty growled and the doors closed, cutting off a comment about massage. Thank goodness. I sighed. "You know it's bad when it feels good to be on the ICU floor."

Uncle Morty yanked me down the hall. "Shut up and come on."

My stomach tightened up. "What? Grandad said Mom's fine."

"She is."

He didn't lead me to the ICU doors but instead tried to shove me into the waiting room. "Fix it."

"What happened?" I turned to the ICU and he spun me back around. "Carolina's sleeping. Miriam's with her. Get in there."

"But what—"

He pushed me in, straight into the quietest argument I'd ever witnessed. Aaron stood on one side and Uncle Morty's girlfriend, Nikki, on the other. They stared at each other. Aaron had a basket and Nikki had a cooler.

"Um...what's going on?" I asked.

Nikki didn't take her eyes off Aaron. "She'll want my food. I'm a woman and a mother. I know."

Aaron said nothing.

"Mercy will decide," said Uncle Morty.

"Decide what? Mom's asleep," I said.

"What food Carolina wants," said Grandad.

Oh, hell no!

"Er...maybe she got a tray?"

They looked at me like I'd sprouted candy corn horns.

"She won't eat that stuff," said Grandad. "Pick something out."

"Um...I'll go ask Mom." And I'll never come back.

Uncle Morty peeked in the door. "Don't be a coward."

"You should talk."

"Carolina needs to eat," said Grandad before going back to his phone.

I sucked it up and said, "Okay. What've you got?"

Aaron pulled out a thermos and slapped it on the table. Nikki scoffed, "Chai tea? Please. I've got a Belgian chocolate malt. Easily digestible and plenty of calories. Top this." She slapped down a covered dish and popped off the top, revealing a green stew that smelled of lemon and spinach. "Horta Vrasta, packed with vitamins."

Aaron laid down Mom's favorite Kale salad with pomegranate. He didn't say anything. His food spoke for itself. Unfortunately, this time it said delicious and hard to chew.

Nikki rolled her enormous dark eyes. "Foolish man. She can't eat that."

Aaron looked at me.

"Er...what else you got?" I asked.

Aaron slapped down eggplant parmesan. Nikki countered with moussaka. That was a draw. Next, Aaron produced chicken and

　　　　　　　　　　　　　　A.W. HARTOIN

dumplings and I started drooling. His dumplings were so fluffy and they came in a stew of wood-roasted chicken delicately flavored with a pricey sherry and some mystery spices in the golden sauce. Nikki brought out a chicken soup made with lemon and egg. Sounds weird, but it smelled fantastic.

It went on from there. Stuffed peppers vs stuffed tomatoes. Chocolate mousse cake vs bread pudding.

"I've only been gone three hours. How did you make all this?" I asked.

"Sheer talent. I don't have a staff," said Nikki haughtily. She was sure I'd pick her food. I couldn't. Aaron was my partner. He'd literally saved my life. On the other hand, Nikki's food, overall, was easier to eat and swallow, which was huge for Mom. Plus, Uncle Morty was standing there in a brand new Under Armour track suit with zero stains, his hair had been recently cut, and for the first time in my life, his nose hair wasn't an issue. Mom had said that he even smiled. I didn't really understand what was happening, but Nikki soothed the savage writer and he smelled good, too.

"Just pick, sweetheart," said Grandad, looking up from his call. "There's no wrong answer."

"Wanna bet?"

From the corner of the room, a soft voice said, "It all looks good to me."

I turned and realized that we weren't alone. The left side of the room had what looked like several different families having the worst day of their lives, too. It was just like a Watts to forget that anyone else existed. I'm such a jerk.

To make matters worse, we had two gourmet cooks and they had hospital coffee and vending machine food. Gag.

"You know what?" I said. "I'll pick out what will be easiest for Mom to eat. Let's face it, she won't eat more than a few bites of anything. The rest should be eaten in here." I gave Nikki a significant look. I didn't bother with Aaron. Nikki was pretty normal if you ignored the enormous Jersey hair and the fact that her track suit matched Uncle Morty's. Plus, she had expressions, which was more than I could say for my partner. "Everyone is waiting to see how things will turn out for their family."

I looked at the woman who spoke so softly. "Who are you here for?"

She got teary. "My husband. He had a heart attack. His fourth."

Another woman said, "My sister overdosed. But she's not a bad person," she said hastily.

"My son went skateboarding without a helmet," said a man with eyes so puffy they were mere slits. "He has brain damage. We don't know how bad. His mom's in with him now."

Nikki nodded at me, left, and came back with a stack of plates and plastic ware. She started serving without asking if anyone was hungry. Such a mom. I made my mother a plate, choosing some of Nikki's and some of Aaron's. He didn't seem mad, but honestly how would I know?

The families began talking and smiling, taking big bites and patting shoulders. Aaron's food had that effect on people. I guess Nikki's did, too. Grandad gave me a thumbs-up and said, "You want to talk to your cousins? I've got Weepy and Spoiled Rotten here."

"I'm good." I took a tray for Mom and high-tailed it out of there while I had the chance. Aaron followed me, trotting along behind me on his short little legs. I balanced the tray and pushed the intercom button for entrance. "What's up?" I asked him.

He put a pint-sized thermos on the tray.

"Hot chocolate?"

Aaron gave me the tiniest of nods before trotting back to the waiting room. I bit my lip and had a hard time answering the gruff male voice who asked who I was there for. I finally got Mom's name out and he buzzed me in. I crossed paths with Aunt Miriam, who was back to her hawk-eyed self. Not a tear or a trace of weakness to be seen.

"How is she?" I asked.

"You have to find out who did this." She gripped her square black leather purse like a weapon. Since she'd been known to carry bricks in it, it was entirely possible.

I eased around her and said, "I will. I promise."

"And punish them."

"Er..."

Aunt Miriam pointed a bony finger at me. "You know what I mean."

"I really don't," I said.

"An eye for an eye."

"So you want me to go all Old testament on them?"

"I trust that you will do what is right for the family." The elderly nun marched off, her back ramrod straight and unyielding. There'd be hell to pay if I didn't succeed and she was hell.

"She wants you to kill them," said Mom's new nurse, Mark, giving me the once-over to see if I might come through on that.

"I'm not killing anyone," I said.

"I think I might rather kill than explain to your aunt why I didn't."

"No kidding. How's my mom?" I asked.

Mom had weakness on her entire left side. He thought her peritoneum was partially paralyzed. Her breathing was somewhat labored and she couldn't manage a productive cough. The rape councilor thought she wasn't raped, but there was definitely an attempt. She thought Mom would eventually remember because she was getting clearer already. She had an MRI scheduled and a TEE to test for the Afib, so she wouldn't be able to eat in the morning.

"Swell," I said. "She's going to hate that."

"You'll get her through it."

I nodded and went in Mom's room. Through it. Right then, it was the best I could hope for.

Wallace woke at five. The pug rooted around on Mom's bed before setting her wrinkly snout on Mom's hip. It'd been a rough night. Mom slept on and off, often crying for Dad and asking why he hadn't come to her. I had no answers for her, but I promised I'd get them.

Mark waved to me through the window and I went out, closing the door behind me. "What's up?"

"Your Aunt Tenne's here," he said. "She wants to come in, but I don't know how Carolina feels about that."

"Me either."

He handed me a cup of coffee and I returned to Mom.

"Is something wrong?" Mom held a tissue to the corner of her mouth. She couldn't feel the drool when it happened and I feared the tissue would become a permanent fixture.

"No. Aunt Tenne's here and she wants to come in." I picked up a packet of creamer and mixed it in the coffee.

Mom looked away. "I don't want to see anyone."

"You saw Aunt Miriam and that was okay."

"She was upset."

I opened a straw and popped it into the coffee. "Everyone's pretty worried about you. Want some coffee?"

She nodded and I helped her take a sip. She gagged and began coughing these weird coughs like she couldn't get enough air.

Mark came in. "Let's get you upright." He helped her sit up, but the coughing got worse. I grabbed a pillow and told her to wrap her arms around it, squeezing it tight when a cough came. The pressure from the pillow helped her clear her throat.

"Nice one," said Mark. "I'll have to remember that."

I grinned at Mom. "See? I know stuff. I'm not just a dufus that forgets to turn in homework and do the dishes."

Mom took my hand. "You're still a dufus."

"Want to try some more coffee? You just have to think about swallowing and do it on the right side."

Mom looked doubtful, but she tried it and it worked.

Mark checked her pressure and oxygen levels. "Looks good. How's the pain?"

"Maybe something," said Mom. "I have another headache."

"Will do," said Mark. "Mercy, you might want to walk the pug. She's got the look."

Wallace did have the look. She was hopping around, wiggling.

"Okay and I'll go see Aunt Tenne."

Mom nodded, but I could see from the set of her jaw that Aunt Tenne had come a long way for nothing. I didn't say that, of course. The last thing Mom needed was guilt.

I picked up Wallace and clipped on her leash. "Can Aunt Miriam come in again?"

"Will she still be mad?" Mom asked, almost childlike.

She'd better not be.

"I'm sure she'll be calmer," I said. "You want me to get you a latte from the cart in the lobby? They're pretty good."

"Okay."

Mark came in with a syringe and I headed out, dreading telling Aunt Tenne that she wasn't wanted. I found her and Bruno in the waiting room. Bruno sat on a chair, sketching wildly on a big pad and didn't even look up. Aunt Tenne got to her feet slowly, the sleepless night in an airport showing on her pretty face so much like Mom's, only a little older and heavier.

"How is she this morning?" she asked.

"Pretty good," I said. "Aunt Tenne..."

My favorite aunt held up a hand. "I already know. Ace told me she won't see anyone."

Two steps and I was in her warm embrace. I should've known Aunt Tenne wouldn't kick up a fuss. She was the sweetest person in the family and now the happiest, since she'd met Bruno, a Honduran artist fifteen years her junior. They seemed like an odd pairing, but it worked.

"I'm going to paint your mother a work that will lift her spirits," said Bruno in his shy way.

"Good. She'll love it."

Bark.

Wallace danced around my feet, smiling her pug smile. If I didn't hurry, she'd pee on my feet. I had the feeling that only being in the hospital restrained her.

"I gotta walk this nut."

Grr.

"This fabulous therapy dog," I said quickly.

Bark.

I rolled my eyes and Aunt Tenne said, "We'll be right here. Make sure you stay by security."

I said I would and I did. Wallace missed my foot and peed on a petunia instead. I got Mom a latte and got back on the elevator with two men in dark suits that eyed me in a cold, penetrating way. Men looked at me a lot, mostly in ways I didn't like, but that was particularly uncomfortable. I scurried off the elevator and back into the ICU.

Mom drank her latte through a straw with shaking hands and Wallace got right in there, calming her almost instantly. "Anything wrong?" I asked.

"You were gone a long time."

It was fifteen minutes. "Sorry. Aunt Tenne totally understands that you want privacy. She'll stay out there. No problem."

Mom teared up. "She's a good sister."

Mark waved to me. He could've come in, but the expression on his face said something was up.

I went out. "What?"

"The FBI are here and they want to interview your mother," he said.

"Not just no, but hell no."

"That's what I said and I've got a call in to Dr. Lindstrom."

I called Chuck and said in a burst, "Why are the FBI here?"

"Dammit. They beat me."

"You knew."

"Yeah and don't think I'm happy about it. Coming up the elevator now."

I glanced in the room and Mom was eyeing me. Even with Wallace, the shaking had returned. I went in and she said in a whisper, "Is it about the rape?"

"No. Do you remember what happened, Mom?" I asked.

She didn't remember, not exactly, but some things were coming back. Mom remembered being in the kitchen and hearing something. She didn't know what. Then she was on the ground. There was pressure on her chest.

"Do you remember someone being there?"

"Yes, but I don't know. It's just an impression," she said with a yawn. "That medicine makes me so sleepy."

"How's the headache?"

"Better. Why did you have that face?" The slurring got worse as the painkiller kicked in. "Tell the truth."

Like a moron, I did. When will I learn? You never tell the truth, even when you don't think it can get you in trouble. "The FBI wants to interview you."

Mom's green eyes flew open. "I don't want to see them."

"You don't have to. You're safe in here."

"You won't let them in."

Mark came through the door. "I won't let them in. Count on it, Carolina."

Mom pulled Wallace into her lap. If it weren't for Wallace, I think Mom would've burst apart at the seams. "What do they want?"

"I'll handle it," I said. "And Mark will keep them away."

Mark took her latte from her and lowered the head of the bed. "Try to rest now. We're going to take you down for your MRI in a couple hours."

"Mercy?"

"It's no biggie. They'll sedate you if you're nervous."

She nodded and I went out to meet the FBI, ready to kick ass and take names as Dad would say.

Chuck and Sidney stood in the hall, talking with the two guys from the elevator. They were doing what I can only describe as quiet yelling. All their fists were balled up and Chuck had color on his high cheekbones, making his blue eyes glitter.

"What the hell do you mean we're off it?" he asked.

"Exactly that, Detective Watts," said the agent on the right, a bald man with a red-tipped hatchet nose.

"By what right?" asked Sidney.

"We don't have to explain ourselves to local cops."

"You son of a bitch," said Chuck.

I walked up as casually as possible. "Well, maybe you can explain it to me."

Hatchet nose introduced himself as Morley and his partner, a weasely guy wearing what had to be a toupee, as Harwood.

"Miss Watts, we'd like to ask you a few questions," said Hatchet nose.

"Not until you answer some of mine."

That stopped him for five whole seconds. He looked vaguely surprised that I could string together a full sentence. Men are like that with me sometimes. It makes me hate them, and they can never understand that. It didn't help that his partner was looking at my chest. Dirtbag.

"We'd like you to go through all the events in Sturgis through this morning."

"Oh, yeah?" I said. "Interesting. Where's my father?"

"We have no information on the whereabouts of Tommy Watts."

I crossed my arms. "Fine. Then I have no info on Sturgis or my mother or lipstick or how I'd like to kick your ass."

Chuck and Sidney started grinning.

"We can issue a material witness warrant," said toupee.

"Go ahead and try it. I've got a great lawyer, Steve Warnock. He teaches a course on constitutional law at Wash U. Give him a call."

"Miss Watts, your mother was viciously attacked," said Hatchet nose.

"You think I don't know that? You're taking the case away from the only cops that have a chance of solving it."

"Do you think *you* have a chance of solving it?" asked Toupee.

"Where's my father?"

"We have no information on the whereabouts of Tommy Watts."

I resisted the urge to kick him in the shin. "Why are these two off the case?"

"That's not your concern, Miss Watts," said Hatchet nose.

"The hell it isn't," said Chuck. "She's the victim's daughter."

"Department policy."

I turned on my heels and went back to the ICU door before I did something they could actually arrest me for. "I'm going back. Don't bother to stay."

Hatchet nose called after me. "I advise you to reconsider your position, Miss Watts."

"Right back at you!"

I rushed into the ICU and Mark jumped up. "Didn't go well?"

"Not hardly." I looked in Mom's room and she was trying to touch her thumb to her fingers on her left hand. It wasn't working out.

"Any word on your father?"

"They're not going to cough him up anytime soon," I said.

"What are you going to do?" he asked.

"When is the TEE scheduled?" I asked.

Mark checked the schedule. "Hard to say. Not before eleven. You really should be there for it."

Missing the TEE wasn't an option. Mom had to swallow a probe to test her heart from the back. It would be uncomfortable at best.

"I won't miss it."

"Sounds like you have a plan."

"I'm going to give the FBI an incentive to give up my dad."

Mark frowned at me. "How are you going to do that? They're the government. They don't care what you think. I'm a marine. I should know."

"They don't, but I can make them want what I have," I said.

"What do you have?"

"Nothing yet."

"Huh?"

"It's an idea in progress." I went in and gave Wallace a scratch. "Mom, I have to leave for a while."

She looked up, startled. "No. I need you here."

"You need Dad here."

"Where is he?" Her lower lip trembled.

I took her left hand and rubbed it between mine. "I don't know, but I have an idea on how to find out."

"I don't want you investigating."

Bark.

"Nobody asked the dog," I said.

Grr.

Mom smiled, sadly very lopsided. "I agree with the dog."

Bark.

"You need Dad. He probably doesn't even know. The FBI has no interest in telling us where he is."

"Why are they keeping him from me?"

"Dad's the best. I assume they have a reason for keeping him away from this investigation," I said.

"I don't like the sound of that."

"They took over the police investigation, too. Chuck's off it."

Mom started wringing her hands and Wallace crept onto her lap, nosing under her hands. "They're covering something up. Chuck's the only one to hold a candle to your father."

"Hey. I don't exactly suck," I said, hands going to hips.

"I didn't mean that."

"So you think I can do this without Dad or Chuck?" I gave her the puppy dog eyes.

"Well…"

"You don't think I can. I knew it."

"Mercy, someone tried to kill me and…rape me," Mom said and the trembling came back.

I hugged her. "I know, but I'm not going to sit here and do nothing."

Mom gave me a sly look. "What are you going to do?"

I thought about it for a second. A good general rule was to tell Mom nothing. I learned that when I wanted to go to my first rave. Like an idiot, I told her where I was going and got grounded for two weeks just for thinking about it. But Mom couldn't ground me anymore and she wanted Dad.

"I'm going out to Hunt."

"No. That's out of the question. Blankenship could be behind this."

"That's why I'm going."

"No."

"You want Dad. This is how to bring him back. I'll get something the FBI wants," I said with more confidence than I felt. Blankenship was slippery at best.

Mom said nothing and I knew I had her.

"I'll take a bodyguard, if that helps."

"Tiny?"

"Sure."

She took my hand. "You promise?"

"I promise and I'll be back for your test."

"What test?"

"Er...Mark will explain it. I've got to go if I'm going to get back in time."

Mom agreed. Her need for Dad was overwhelming. It blinded her to my lie about Tiny. Normally, she never would've believed me on that. Carolina Watts take my word for something? Nope. Not gonna happen. Or maybe it was the stroke.

Whatever it was, I snuck out through the service exit and dashed down the stairs. I got away clean. Or so I thought.

CHAPTER EIGHT

I jogged through the hospital, trying to figure out the best place for an Uber to pick me up. It would cost an arm and three legs to have them drive me all the way out to Hunt, but it'd be worth it not to have Tiny or Fats dogging my every move. The thought of the two of them crammed together again was too gross to be considered.

The hospital lobby was nearly empty at six in the morning and a quick scan told me that nobody I knew was there. I hid behind a fichus and ordered an Uber to pick me up. I got the car description and a mere five-minute wait time. All I had to do was hang out and stay out of sight until a 2011 silver Camry showed up.

After three minutes, I broke down and got a latte. It was a dangerous move, but I was feeling good about it. No sense that I was being watched. No Dad feeling about something not being right. I was all good.

That is until the Camry pulled up and I went outside. My hand reached for the car door and an enormous hand wrapped around my wrist so fast, I didn't have time to squeak.

"Going somewhere?" asked Fats.

"Dammit. Where did you come from?"

"I can't give away all my secrets."

"Let go. I ordered this car and I'm leaving."

Fats didn't let go. Nobody listens to me. "I'll take you wherever you need to go. Calpurnia's orders."

"I'm good." I tried to reach the door handle but didn't manage to move my hand an inch. Kinda depressing. I didn't know I was *that* much of a weakling.

The window rolled down and a guy with a pair of thick glasses, greasy hair, and a washed out polo called out, "You ordered an Uber?"

"Yes," I said.

"No," said Fats.

"Did you order this car or not?" he asked, getting irritated and I didn't blame him.

Fats leaned down and looked at him. He quickly retreated to his side of the car and gripped the steering wheel tightly.

"She ordered it, but she changed her mind," said Fats.

"No, I didn't," I said.

Fats pulled out a hundred bucks and tossed it on the passenger seat. "Have a nice day."

"Sweet," said the Uber driver and he drove away with a squeal.

"Thanks a lot," I said.

Fats steered me toward the closest parking lot. "You were going to go with that guy? He looks like every serial killer ever."

"No, he didn't."

"I have one word for you. BTK."

"That's technically not a word," I said. "It's initials and hello, let go."

She didn't let go. She installed me in a Yukon Denali with a well-placed threat before getting in on the driver's side. I thought about making a break for it. But who was I kidding? Fats would catch me and I'd end up where I started. I might as well save myself the trouble, so I sat back in the cushy seat as she pulled out.

"Where are we going?"

"Hunt Hospital for the Criminally Insane," I said.

"Nailed it." She held up her hand and another hand came from the backseat and high-fived her.

"What the..." I swiveled in my seat and there was Aaron, dwarfed by the expanse of leather—not that that was hard—and eating a puffy taco with molé sauce dripping onto his grubby jean shorts. "You kidnapped my partner?" I asked Fats.

"Not kidnapped. Picked up."

"Is there really any difference with you?"

"Not much." She paused. "No, no difference. I told him to get in the truck and he did. They always do."

"Why did you get Aaron?" I asked.

"He's your partner."

I looked back at my partner and watched him try to lick sauce off his chin. He gave up after a second and left it there. "Well, I don't know how you think he can help."

Aaron reached over and dropped a paper bag in my lap.

"There's that, for starters," said Fats.

I opened the bag and luscious smells wafted out: Aaron's homemade sausage, extra-creamy scrambled eggs made with heavy cream, no doubt, some kind of sheep's milk cheese, and paper-thin tortillas.

"That there is the best breakfast burrito you'll ever have," said Fats. "I can't believe I didn't know about Kronos until last night."

I groaned. "You went to Kronos."

"Don't worry. Everyone recognized me," Fats said with a grin. Somehow, the combo of Wayfarer sunglasses, pale pink lipstick, and the big sock bun on top of her head made her seem more threatening instead of less.

"That's swell."

"I thought so." She merged onto Highway 40 and flipped an after-market switch on the dash. There was a series of dings and then a green light flashed. Fats put on so much speed I was thrown back against the seat.

"What is that?" I asked a bit breathless.

"Newest generation of radar detector. Not available to the general public yet. Calpurnia knows a guy."

"I wonder if he wants to know her."

"Don't you worry. He's doing alright." She turned on the stereo. "You like Ludacris?"

"Uh..."

Fats didn't wait. Ludacris burst out of the speakers, making me feel like I was back in Sturgis surrounded by Harleys. I looked back at Aaron, who definitely did not seem like a Ludacris kind of guy and I was right about that. He had paper napkins sticking out of his ears and was writing furiously in his recipe notebook, apparently inspired by the driving beat.

He handed me two napkins without looking up and continued to write.

"Don't be a wuss," said Fats.

"Aaron's a wuss," I pointed out, desperately wanting to use my napkins. The music was rattling the windows.

"He's a weirdo."

"And I'm normal?" That didn't seem right.

"Closer to it," she said before singing, "I say move, you move."

I didn't stuff napkins in my ears. I'd probably regret it when I was seventy, but Fats gave me the stink eye and I caved, suffering the incredible clamor.

On the upside, we made it out to Hunt in record time. That happens when you're driving a hundred and twelve miles an hour. I feared for my life, but I wasn't about to complain. If we survived, I'd make it back to Mom in plenty of time for her TEE.

Fats pulled onto the long driveway and turned down Ludacris. "It's like we're going to a university. The psychos have it pretty nice." Her head swiveled as she looked at the wide, manicured lawns, mature trees, and the main building that would've fit right in in the antebellum South. The razor wire and guard towers kinda ruined the effect though.

"I don't think they let the psychos out to see it."

"Good thinking. I hear they've got some real whack-a-dos out here."

"Yeah, they do." My stomach threatened to bring up Aaron's excellent burrito with the thought of seeing Blankenship. Whack-a-do didn't come close to covering that guy.

Fats stopped at the first gate and we got out. They ran metal detectors over us and asked for Fats' ID. That was new. Of course, I usually came out alone and everyone with a TV knew who I was.

One guard took the ID and the other one told us to get back in. We drove through that gate and went through the process again with the addition of hand swabbing for explosive materials and a full check of the truck. They even checked the oil, which seemed over the top, but Fats didn't seem to think so.

The second set of gates opened and the guard handed back Fats' ID. We drove through and up to the main building.

"What was that about?" I asked Fats.

"Checking to see if I have any warrants out."

"Er…"

She snorted. "Please. I'm cleaner than you."

"I don't find that comforting," I said.

"As a cop's daughter, you shouldn't, but it's the way it is."

"What does your ID say?"

"Mary Elizabeth Licata."

I looked at the ceiling. "This is so going to get back to my dad."

"Maybe not. Nothing popped on me."

"I guess as long as they don't tell the director, I might get away with it."

"Do you really care?" she asked. "You've got to do this."

I thought about Mom, sitting in her hospital bed all alone. "No. Not one bit."

"Good. Glad to have you on board." She inclined her head to the right. "FBI."

I followed her gaze. Sure enough, there were two men loitering by the visitor's entrance, smoking cigarettes and gnawing on long strips of jerky.

"How do you know?"

"I know."

"Well, you can't come in. They might know you."

"It's the FBI. They know me alright. I don't exactly blend."

"I guess not. I wonder if they'll tell my father about you?"

"Depends," said Fats.

"On what?"

"On how they feel about him."

"Well, they're keeping him on the down-low instead of telling him about my mom."

She parked and gave them a finger wave. "Then you're probably good for now, but they'll blackmail you later."

"Swell."

"Feds. What are you going to do?"

"Back soon, I hope."

She nodded and pulled a battered copy of Cormac McCarthy's *Blood Meridian* out of the zebra-striped backpack at my feet.

"Do you understand that book?" I asked as I got out. I'd tried to read it once in college. It cramped my brain.

"Not yet, but I'll get it."

"Good luck," I said.

"You, too." Fats started reading and I walked straight to the FBI. They were both young, blond, and handsome in a bland sort of way. I wondered if the Feds decided that they might get some cooperation if a more pleasant package was asking. Obviously, they hadn't done their homework on me. I didn't cooperate that well with anyone, even Chuck, and he was super-hot.

They flashed me their badges and I asked, "Here to arrest me or molest me?"

"I'd be more worried about that guy molesting you than us," said the one on the right, Gordon.

"She's a girl, dirtbag."

The one on the left, Gansa, almost had an expression and then said, "I don't think so."

That's when I smelled hotdogs with an after smell of tacos and turned around. Aaron was standing right behind me, staring off to the left and holding two fat paper bags.

"Oh, for crying out loud," I said. "What are you doing?"

"Huh?'

"Go back to the truck and stay with...Mary Elizabeth."

"No."

"Why not?"

"You need me."

The FBI guys chuckled. "You need him like you need eczema," said Gansa.

Bastards.

"That's where you're wrong. I need him." I grabbed Aaron's arm. "Don't I?"

"Huh?" Aaron couldn't have looked more weird if he tried. He had on one of his beloved pink hairnets and an ancient Star Trek tee. Of course, there were the stained shorts and when I say stained, I mean it.

"Never mind," I said. "So what's the FBI doing at a looney bin like this?"

"Surprised to see us?"

"Thrilled beyond compare."

They just looked at me. If their bosses thought looks were everything, they were incredibly wrong.

I crossed my arms. "What do you want?"

"The same as you."

"I doubt that."

Gordon said, "Your family is under attack. We all want to know who is behind it?"

"Where is my father?"

"We are locating him," said Gansa. He whipped off his sunglasses in what I assumed was an attempt to show sincerity. Yeah, right.

"Are you?" I asked.

"Yes."

"It's been well over twelve hours. You're telling me that you can't find my father? He's working for you."

No answer.

"That's what I thought."

"What reason would we have for keeping your father out of the picture?" Gordon took off his sunglasses and smiled. I have to admit he was pretty good at it. Claire would fall for him hard, if we could find her.

"What are you looking at?" asked Gordon, his smile turning downward.

"Nothing." I pushed the question of Claire out of my mind. I had enough to worry about already. "I don't know why you're doing what you're doing and I doubt you two are high up enough in the chain to know either." I started to walk by them and Gordon grabbed my arm.

"Miss Watts, you will cooperate or we won't let you see Blankenship. Understand?" He screeched and danced away.

"What the…"

Aaron stood there with a lit lighter. No expression. Naturally.

"You burned him? Are you crazy?" I asked, but I was impressed. Aaron wasn't exactly a weirdo of action.

"I could arrest you!" yelled Gordon.

A car door slammed hard. Fats was out of the truck.

"Oh, shit," said Gansa under his breath.

"Oh, shit is right," said Fats.

"I have a gun."

"I don't care," she said, walking toward us in a way that made me pee a little and she wasn't even looking at me.

"Aaron, enough with the lighter," I said.

He extinguished the flame and pocketed the lighter before heading for the door.

"Where is he going?" asked Gansa.

"What's she going to do?" asked Gordon as Fats continued to advance.

I held up my hand. "We're fine…er…Mary Elizabeth."

She stopped walking and just stared at the agents through her dark glasses. Sweat beaded up on their smooth brows and I detected a nervousness that Hatchet nose and Toupee would never have had.

"You're rookies, aren't you?" I asked.

"No," said Gordon a little slowly.

"Well, everyone has to start somewhere. It's your bad luck that you had to start with me." I walked past them and through the door Aaron held open for me.

"Miss Watts!" Wilson Cleves said through the heavy bullet-proof glass partition next to the heavy metal door that led to the patient rooms or cells, depending on their condition. "I didn't think I'd see you here." He flicked a glance at the agents who were glowering beside me.

"Really? You usually come to work this early?" I asked.

"Um...well...I assume you're here to see Blankenship."

"And Greta."

He frowned. "You have time?"

"Mom says you always have time for kindness." Mom did say that. I only wished I'd thought to bring Greta something. She was technically a murderer that my dad had put away for killing her kids with cough syrup, but she had postpartum psychosis and Dad felt it wasn't her fault. He visited her and now I did, too.

A brief alarm sounded and the metal door opened. Shelley, the guard who usually handled me, waved me back. I walked through with Aaron trotting along behind me.

"Who are you?" Shelley asked him. "I thought you'd be alone, Mercy."

"Me, too," I said. "He's my partner."

She had Aaron sign paperwork saying he wouldn't sue if someone accidentally bit his eyeball and we went through the body scanner. The agents fell behind as their guard was in no hurry. He gave me a wink and fussed about their paperwork as we hoofed it down the corridor that looked like any office building on a budget until we got to the door that nobody in their right mind would want to go through. It was heavy barred metal, obviously designed to keep something terrible in. I felt a familiar panic as it made a clang and swung open.

It's fine. You're not really crazy. They'll let you out.

To distract myself, I asked, "So what's with that new alarm on the other door?"

"We had an escape attempt. Thwarted, but it was close," said Shelley.

I threw up in my mouth a little. "Not Blankenship?"

She smiled at me. "No. That little weasel is locked down so tight, he can't even scratch his balls."

Ew.

"Who was it then?"

"Harvey the head case. IQ in the mid-160s and always thinking."

"What did he do?"

"Attacked women and tried to eat their feet." She said it like eating feet was a common enough occurrence.

"What the hell? When did that happen?"

"In New Jersey before you were born. We got him after his third escape out there."

"Congratulations, I guess."

"Thanks," she said with all seriousness. "We are good. So, Greta?"

"Yes, please."

We got to Greta's door, a pretty normal one.

"You moved her?" I asked.

"She's been more cooperative since you started coming. Hasn't been hurting herself or screaming. Doctors decided to give her a more comfortable room. Your dad's been lobbying for it."

"Good."

Shelley opened the door and said, "Greta, Mercy's here and she's been having a crap couple of days. Try to be perky."

I went in and saw Greta sitting up at a metal desk bolted to the floor. She had a set of watercolors, like the ones they give kids, in front of her. I guess they didn't trust her with brushes yet because she was using her fingertips to paint.

Greta brushed a greying lock of blonde hair out of her eyes, leaving a smear of blue across her forehead. She looked the best I'd ever seen her, not so painfully thin and there weren't any new scabs on her arms.

"Mercy," she said softly. "I knew you'd come."

"Are you going in?" asked Shelley.

I turned and Aaron thrust one of the paper bags at me. I took it and looked at Shelley, who shrugged. She'd x-rayed Aaron's bags and didn't find anything objectionable in them.

"What is it?" I asked.

"For Greta," said Aaron and he stepped back for Shelley to close the door.

There was a heavy clang and a grind as she locked me in, an ominous sound if there ever was one.

"I don't know what it is, but if Aaron made it, you're in for a treat." I gave her the bag and she actually smiled as she pulled out wax paper-wrapped chocolate chip cookies and little Italian butter cookies that smelled of orange.

"Thank you," she said.

"How'd you know I'd come?" I asked.

"First, tell me what has happened to you."

So I told her about Sturgis and Mom. I managed not to cry and I was pretty proud of that. She stood up off her metal stool and hugged me, her painfully thin body trying to soothe my curvy one. I ended up wanting to soothe her. My mother was alive. Her children were dead.

"I know there is nothing I can do. I wish there was."

"You listened. That's enough."

"Not really," she said, going back to her stool. The effort of moving seemed to exhaust her. "You will go see Blankenship now to get information?"

"And it's useless to me. The FBI will hear it and take over. Dad would hate that."

Greta smiled wanly. "Yes, Tommy is all about control. But there's no reason they have to hear everything."

"We'll be in the fishbowl," I said.

She slid a blank piece of paper over to the side of the table and gave me her watercolors. "Warn Blankenship."

I grinned at her. "I knew there was a reason I liked you." I stuck my finger in the flimsy water cup on the table and wrote in red, "Whisper. FBI is listening."

"It will only take a few minutes to dry," said Greta.

I ripped the paper into a manageable size and waved it in the air. "Now it's your turn."

Greta turned solemn. "You know that I have bad days."

"Sure."

That's what I said, but I didn't know that Greta had a problem with catatonia. It happened infrequently, usually on her children's birthdays. It was her middle son's birthday last week and she'd been catatonic for three days.

"When it happens, the doctors like to put me in the sunroom," said Greta.

I had no idea where she was going with this, but she was pretty intense about it. "Yeah. Did something happen in the sunroom?"

Please don't say that someone assaulted you.

"Yes. When I'm like that, I'm completely immobile and mute."

"Uh huh."

"But I can hear perfectly."

I got all tingly. "What did you hear?"

Greta told me in great detail how an orderly came in, checked the room, and since it was only Greta, he answered a call. A call about Blankenship. This was after Blankenship's visitor, a man who got nothing out of him and that's what the orderly said. He was trying to get access to Blankenship to 'persuade him,' but only high-level personnel got near him. The person on the other end of the line talked for a long time and the orderly sounded nervous to Greta when he said that he didn't think he could do that. 'That' was never specified. But the orderly was worried about getting caught. That was the end of the conversation and the orderly left, but not before calling Greta a smelly vegetable.

"What was his name?" I asked.

"I've never heard his voice before, so he's not on my team, but when he answered, he said, 'Jones'."

"I can't believe catatonia came in handy," I said.

"Me either," said Greta. "I hope this helps you. I think that orderly was told to kill Blankenship."

"I agree." I wasn't against Blankenship dying, but if someone wanted him dead, we definitely needed him alive. I thanked Greta and rapped on the door.

Shelley unlocked the door and let me out. I waved to Greta before the door slammed again. She was smiling and it warmed my heart.

I turned to the guard and asked, "Do you have anyone working here by the name of Jones?"

"Jones? Why do you ask?"

"Just something Greta mentioned."

She shrugged. "I don't know any Jones. By the way, your partner is quite a storyteller," said Shelley while we walked down through a warren of corridors.

"Who?" I asked.

She jerked a thumb at Aaron. "Him, obviously."

"You told her a story?" I asked.

Aaron shrugged.

"How come you don't tell me anything? I asked you how to make Waldorf salad and you wouldn't say a word."

"Maybe because Waldorf salad is gross," said Shelley.

"My boyfriend likes it."

"Your boyfriend needs help. Here we are. The Fishbowl. Time for fun and games."

The agents ran up, tucking in their shirts and missing their jackets, weapons, and badges. Security did a number on them and Shelley couldn't stop smiling.

"What did you do?" asked Gordon.

"Visited a patient," I said. "You really need to keep up."

"Prisoner," said Gansa.

"Po-ta-to, Po-tah-to."

"This isn't a private hospital for neurotics," said Gordon.

"Everyone in this building understands that better than you," I said. "Shelley, I'm ready."

Gansa grabbed my arm. "We need to discuss strategy."

"I'm good," I said, shaking him off.

The agent clung to the material of my sleeve. "This has to go right."

"What's your problem, rookie? I've been here before."

"You have a reputation," said Gordon.

I struck a pose, very Bettie Page. "For being awesome?"

He stammered, "No."

"I'm so surprised."

They stared at me, making a concentrated effort not to look at my chest and not entirely succeeding.

"I don't like you," I said.

"Miss Watts, your opinion of us is irrelevant," said Gansa.

"We'll see."

I set Aaron's second paper bag on the metal table in the middle of the Fishbowl. The square, white room was the same as always, but the table situation wasn't. Where there had been two, one for Blankenship and one for me, there was now one. The table had been positioned so that my chair was at the head of the table and Blankenship sat heavily shackled at the foot. We were now ten feet apart instead of six with the two small tables.

"Oh, look," I said. "You made them redecorate."

Blankenship looked up, his mask of disinterest fully in place. "I had some tummy trouble."

"I heard."

Shelley went halfway out the door and said, "Ten minutes, as usual. Don't attempt to get closer."

"I need fifteen," I said.

She hesitated and then agreed. "I'm serious about the distance."

"No worries there." I sat down and put my elbows on the table. The paper was itchy in my bra and I longed to pull it out.

"What's in the bag?" asked Blankenship. I would've thought he was curious if I didn't know he was a sociopath with psychotic features, making him unable to feel normal emotions. Honestly, I don't think the diagnosis was complete since he refused to cooperate with any examination. It'd gotten to the point that he only communicated with me. I'd been told that the doctors and researchers were jealous and frustrated, but I'd gladly have traded places with them, just not on that particular day.

"Could be fish tacos," I said. "I have no idea."

"If it's fish tacos, you want something," said Blankenship.

"Always. We're not friends."

A look of sorrow passed onto his bland face. It was gross in its mimicry of emotion. "You wound me."

"You disgust me."

"Miss Watts." Gordon's voice came through the hidden speaker system. "Watch yourself."

I looked up at the camera over Blankenship's head. "How about you shut up? If I need help, I won't be asking you."

Silence. I pictured Shelley and the other guards telling him off.

"Let's get serious," I said to Blankenship.

"With pleasure."

I pulled the note out and held it under my tilted chin, pressed against my throat so it might be obscured from the camera.

Blankenship squinted and then gave me a twitch of a smile. I'd discovered that he could feel pleasure of a sort. He enjoyed hurting others and thwarting the FBI would do.

"Miss Watts, what do you think you're doing?" asked the agent.

I crumbled the note and ate it. "Having a snack."

"We will pull you out."

Blankenship got tense. "You do and I will give up nothing ever. She belongs to me."

Silence.

I mouthed, "I want to know about the guy that visited you."

"Open the bag," he said.

"Do you know him personally?" I mouthed.

"No. Open the bag."

I opened the bag and found a tubular object heavily wrapped in foil. I knew what it was and I couldn't believe Aaron understood men, or whatever you wanted to call Blankenship, that well.

"Is it..." Blankenship trailed off.

"A hotdog," I said with a smile. "It's no popsicle but I imagine you want me to eat it."

He shifted in his chair and his chains rattled. A shiver went through me, but I concealed it. This was for Mom and Dad. I could do it. I could do anything.

"Do you want to eat it?" asked Blankenship.

"Hell, no."

"Why not?" He looked a bit suspicious.

You're losing him.

I unwrapped the package and involuntarily horked. Damn that Aaron. Did I say I could do anything? "It's eight thirty in the morning and this thing is made"—I swallowed hard— "is made of bacon and crab."

Blankenship sniffed the air like a feral dog. "And you don't like crab."

"You know I hate it and it's...lumpy."

"Where'd you get it?"

"A friend of mine made it. Apparently, he hates me," I said.

The grotesque sorrow settled onto Blankenship's face. "Poor Mercy."

"You gonna talk to me or what?"

"Why are you here?" he asked. "It's not just because I had a visitor."

I told him about Sturgis and my mother, nothing the agents didn't know already.

"That's why you haven't showered in days."

"Do I smell?"

"Yes. I like it."

"You would."

He leaned forward, his chains going taut. "They think he's after you?"

Last time I checked, nobody knew what the deal was, but that wasn't the right answer. "That's the general consensus."

Something akin to anger replaced the sorrowful look. "You belong to me."

"Somebody doesn't agree," I said.

"He can't have you."

I shrugged. "Fine by me. You want to answer some questions?"

"Take a bite."

I took a bite and kept it down. Don't think it wasn't a struggle. It was lumpy crab and extra stank. But that's how I got more information than I ever imagined I'd receive.

Bite by bite, Blankenship mouthed the important details of his life that he'd kept so well-hidden. He was a part of an anonymous group called Unsub. It was short for a law enforcement term meaning unknown subject. It was a kind of support group for psychos. They shared techniques and triumphs.

"Triumphs?" I mouthed. "Is that how you knew about the bloody clothes in the safety deposit box?"

He nodded.

"Then your 'friends' are skilled."

No reaction and, more importantly, no agreement.

"Or maybe not."

His weird twitch of a smile passed over his thin lips.

Holy crap. He's jealous. They're out and he's in.

"Will you give me something?" I asked.

"No."

"Why not? They can't share their triumphs with you anymore."

There was a flicker of dismay in his eyes.

I took a big, disgusting bite. "You can be back in the news. Horrifying people on CNN. The focus of articles and speculation."

"Of you?" he asked.

"If you like, but I have to protect myself and my family first. What can you tell me about your visitor?"

"Someone sent him."

"Who?"

"I don't have his name."

"What do you have?"

His chains rattled again. "I want to touch you."

"You want to hurt me." It just popped out and he was surprised. It was a brief expression but I caught it.

"You're afraid," he said.

"I'm not a fool."

"I wouldn't hurt you."

"We'll see," I said.

"Will we?" The anticipation of hurting me was in his tone. He couldn't hide the pleasure.

I nodded. "What will you give me?"

Blankenship told me about his visitor, a Mr. Woods. His description matched the one Barney gave me in Sturgis, a middle-aged Hispanic male, except that Blankenship said he had a neck tattoo and a gravelly smoker voice. He didn't get a good enough look to say what it was. The visitor claimed that he was sent by a friend of Blankenship's, a guy in the Unsub group that was asking about me six months before Blankenship's final crime, the mass murder at Tulio's. The Unsubs were from all over the country and the world. This one focused on Blankenship because he figured out that he lived in St. Louis. This was how Blankenship first became aware of me. He stalked me and exchanged info, my routine and places I frequented, for this Unsub's victims. Victims were like catnip to those freaks.

If I can get a victim...

"But he wasn't real," said Blankenship.

My heart sank. No names. No lead.

"What do you mean?" I asked. "He was a cop?"

Blankenship didn't think the Unsub was law enforcement, mostly because he got a lot of info from the other members and nothing happened. No arrests. No bodies found. He spoke of murders but offered no proof as the others had, including Blankenship.

"But that's not why you didn't believe him," I said.

"You're learning," he said.

"What was it?"

"He described a crime I knew he didn't do."

"Really? What crime?"

"Cassidy Huff."

Huff was one of Dad's cases, one of the unsolved. Dad would obsess about those crimes and track the suspects. These were not good people. Most of the time, they got convicted of something else, but that wasn't enough for Dad. He wanted them punished for every crime, every time. Mom would say nobody's perfect. You can't get them all. Dad's reply was always that that was not acceptable. It ate at him.

"You recognize the name?" asked Blankenship.

I nodded and mouthed, "How do you know he didn't do it?"

"Because I helped and your father never knew."

I felt as though someone had turned me to stone.

"Blink," said Blankenship.

I blinked.

"You're shocked at your father's incompetence." It wasn't a question.

My body came back to life. "Will you confess to the murder?"

"No."

"Why the hell not? It can't affect you at this point."

"I didn't kill her," he mouthed to me.

I cocked my head to the side.

"I only put her in the wood chipper." Blankenship licked his lips at the memory.

This is never going to wash off.

I leaned forward and whispered, "How do I know you're telling the truth?"

"Does your father have a file on her?"

"I'm sure he does."

"Her green purse was missing and she had a secret heart tattoo on her left hip. That was never in the news. Check it."

"Count on it," I said. "Did the fake Unsub have those details?"

Blankenship looked me in the eyes. Something he rarely did. "He knew everything your father knew, except for the tattoo."

Cop? Prosecutor? Family? Friend?

"And what, exactly, did you do?"

"She was dead. I chipped her."

"Who killed her? Another Unsub?"

He nodded. "Brian Shill. He asked for help. I was happy to do it."

"Fine. You can confess to that."

"Would it make your father unhappy?" He was tense with anticipation.

"He'll be glad to have it solved," I mouthed.

"Not by him."

I threw up my hands and said out loud. "It's not great. Dad hates to be wrong."

"Then I'll confess." He looked up at the camera behind my head. "I, Kent Blankenship, of unsound—"

"No!"

"No?"

"I'll find out who's hunting my family and then you'll confess."

"Miss Watts, what are you doing?" asked an agent.

"Not your problem," I said to the camera.

"Miss Watts—"

"Pipe down, rookie."

"I'm not a rookie."

I pointed at the camera. "You're talking right now. That proves you are."

Silence. Thank goodness. So distracting.

"You're getting more and more interesting," said Blankenship. He didn't look remotely interested.

I put my elbows on the table. "I'm glad I amuse you."

"Are you?"

I thought about it for a second. "Yes. It's useful."

"How else can I be *useful?*"

"I need to give them something to keep them off my back and get my dad back," I mouthed.

"Then you can tell them he was wrong about Cassidy Huff."

"He'll be thrilled."

The pleasure of outsmarting Tommy Watts really got him going. He gave up the name of the man whose clothes were in the safe deposit box. Joseph Cranmer. He didn't know the name of the killer. He was one of the Unsubs and, even though the box was local, he had a feeling that the killer wasn't.

This was good stuff, but it wasn't enough to get everything I wanted. "What else?"

"You need something big." Also, not a question.

I looked up at the camera. "Yes, I need something big."

And Blankenship gave me something big. Huge. Career-changing. He gave me a location in Russell, Kansas, near the grain silo. An Unsub claimed it as his main burial ground. That's right. He said 'main' as in there were other sites.

I had to push down the horror and try to think of this information just as a bargaining chip. But it didn't feel like a chip. It felt like I was opening the proverbial Pandora's box and the horrors would keep coming out forever.

"Finish your hot dog," said Blankenship.

There were two bites left. I didn't think I could do it. "Why should I?" I asked to delay.

"Because you'll be back."

"Good point." I ate the rest of that hot dog and I didn't regret it. Mostly.

CHAPTER NINE

Gansa pushed me against the wall of the hall as the Fishbowl door clanged shut. "What did he give you?"

"Nothing," I said.

He shoved me hard, banging my head on the cinderblock wall.

"Hey!" yelled Shelley and she pounced on him. Shelley had him facedown on the floor with an arm cranked behind his back before he or the other agent could react. Don't mess with a woman who wrangles psychos for a living. It's not a good idea.

Gordon kept patting his waistband frantically.

"You don't have a gun, dipshit," said one of the other guards, a scrawny guy with a goatee and a ponytail. His name tag said 'Jack', but he looked more like a Phil to me.

"He's a rookie," I said.

"No kidding," said Jack. "My son could take him and he's in the Science Olympiad."

Gordon came at me, sticking a finger in my face and getting all red. "Don't push me."

I rolled my eyes. "Puhlease. You're not that frightening."

Shelley released her prisoner and stood up. "You should've researched Mercy."

"We don't need to research her. She's our informant."

The guards all laughed and the agents looked confused.

Shelley slapped Gordon on the shoulder. "Mercy doesn't work for you, pea brain. You work for her. Why do you think the bureau is keeping her father away? Tommy Watts is large and in charge, same as his daughter. Now get a clue and make an offer."

"An offer?" asked Gordon. "She works for us!"

Gansa held up a hand. "Wait. I get it. She wants something."

I leaned on the wall and said, "So you're the brains of the operation. What does that make him?"

Gordon stuck his finger in my face. "Girl—"

"Do I look prepubescent to you? No, I don't. I'm a woman. Got it, moron?"

He stepped back, took a breath, and asked, "What do you want?"

"I want Chuck Watts on the Unsub task force, for starters."

The agents exchanged glances. "There isn't any Unsub task force," said Gansa. "Unsub is just a term for an unknown suspect."

"Hello. I know that. But there's going to be an Unsub task force if you agree to my terms."

"What do you have?"

"You'll never know if you don't agree, and I want it in writing."

They stood there, their jaws set.

"Alrighty then. I'm out."

"Okay. Okay," said Gordon. "You said for starters. What else do you want?"

"My father."

They shuffled their feet.

"That's the deal and, believe me, you want this deal," I said.

"Oh, yeah?" asked Gansa.

"You want to be the guys who bring in the critical information on a serial killer with only months on the job."

"I've been an agent for a year," said Gordon.

"Two for me," said Gansa.

Shelley slapped her forehead. "Jeez, what did they have you on? Traffic?"

"Background checks."

Jack laughed. "And they sent you to deal with a mass murderer and a Watts. You're expendable."

"Huh?"

I started to feel a little sorry for the not-so-rookies. "It means that they didn't expect you to get anything. You're nobodies. It's okay if your careers take a hit."

"You've got something good?"

"Oh, it's a sick dream come true and there's more to come if you cooperate," I said. "I want it in writing. Call your superiors and feel free to exaggerate your role. I couldn't care less who gets the credit, but I want to talk to my father within three hours."

"Why three hours?" asked Gansa.

"Because that's how long I figure it will take your guys to find the first body. Seems fair."

They dashed down the hall to get their cellphones at security. It was the wrong hall and it took them a half hour to get there, but they got everything they needed in the end.

An hour later, we signed a contract that my parents' lawyer, Big Steve Warnock, wrote. His negotiating skills were stellar and he handled the whole thing. The contract was twenty-five pages long and got witnessed by Wilson Cleves, the director, and Shelley. The head of the FBI field office in St. Louis signed, as well as Gordon and Gansa.

It took a lot of pages to say that I'd give them information. In return, they'd retain Chuck and Sidney on the newly-formed Unsub task force. Big Steve was very specific about their roles. He said we had them by the short hairs and ought to take advantage. On his advice, the first piece of info was the safe deposit box identity. The field in Kansas came after I talked to my dad and he was on his way home.

After the signing, I managed to get a moment alone with Mr. Cleves and he confirmed that there wasn't anyone named Jones employed at Hunt. Bummer.

Gansa and Gordon burst into the office, interrupting Mr. Cleves and asking me why I wanted to know about a Jones. They were jittery with excitement and followed me out of Hunt, peppering me with questions. I had the fat contract in a folder under my arm and Aaron by my side. If he was interested in the proceedings, he showed no signs of it.

"You hungry?" he asked.

"I just ate a crab freaking hot dog, so no."

He started bouncing up and down on the balls of his feet.

"If you think I liked that abomination, you're dead wrong. Only my innate dislike of vomiting is keeping it down."

"You ate it," said Aaron.

"You know I had to to get Blankenship to talk. He's always trying to get me to eat crap I hate."

"It worked."

"Yeah. Thanks a bunch." I started toward the truck where Fats was still reading, but Gansa rushed around me.

"You got your contract," he said, slicking back his blond hair. "What do you have?"

"Joseph Cranmer," I said.

"Who? What?"

I reminded the agents about the safe deposit box.

"That's it?" asked Gordon, visibly disappointed. "That's not going to make my career."

"You get the bodies when I get my father." I held up my phone. "You have about an hour and a half left."

"How many bodies?" asked Gansa.

"Beats me."

Aaron and I walked around the disappointed agent and got in the truck. Fats put a beer label in her book as a mark and said, "Get what you wanted?"

"I got a contract," I said.

Fats fired up the truck and flipped on the radar detector. I expected blaring Ludacris next, but she started singing The Stones with a smile. "You can't always get what you want."

That was fine by me as long as my mother got what she needed.

CHAPTER TEN

Fats dropped me off at the front door of the hospital despite my objections. She thought it was only a matter of time before my family found out about her family, so she couldn't see the point in sneaking. I still had hope there'd be a miracle to save me from the ultimate yell-a-thon about ethics from Dad. We couldn't be involved with a mob family. Crap like that. Dad didn't see me as a separate entity and insisting that I was me and he was him would get me nowhere. I knew. I'd tried it.

Aaron stayed in the truck, silent as usual, and Fats said she was taking him back to Kronos for the lunch rush. She called Tiny and said it was his turn to take me over. She issued a vague threat about me not running off without a bodyguard before turning her attention to Tiny again. I slammed the door in time to cut off her saying, "I missed you so much. I want—"

I didn't want to know what Fats wanted unless it was another job that got her out of my hair. She waved and shooed me into the hospital under the watchful eyes of a security guard and didn't pull out until I was safely inside. I wanted to run off just to be a pain in the butt. I didn't because I wasn't fourteen and because Mom was probably back from her MRI.

When I arrived on the ICU floor, there were no agents and no cops. Not quite what I expected, but I guess I'd given them something to do.

"Mercy!" Uncle Morty waved from the waiting room and I took a detour.

"I need some coffee," I said. "And a shower. Blankenship said I smell. I care, but I don't know why."

Uncle Morty held up a beefy hand and used his other hand to push up his glasses.

"What are you doing?" I asked.

"Whaddaya think? High-five."

I stared at the pudgy hand with its mouse calluses. "Are you okay?"

"Ya gonna leave me hanging?" he asked gruffly.

"Er..." I high-fived Uncle Morty for the first and last time of my life. "The question remains. Are you okay?"

"You did a good job, you pain in my ass."

"Yeah? How do you know?"

"How do I know that you forgot to pay your electric bill again last month?" He pointed at a coffee table that now had three laptops on it. Who needs three laptops? Seriously.

"I did pay it," I said.

"No. I paid it so they wouldn't shut off your power, ya moron. You forgot in December, January, and March, too. Your late fees are flipping ridiculous."

"I was working on cases in those months."

"Ameren don't care if you were busy shooting a guy in the face. They want their money. I taught you better than that."

"You didn't teach me anything except how to make margaritas when I was eight," I said.

"And a good job I did of it. A strong margarita's a good margarita."

"Okay then. I'm going to go see my mother in the ICU. Don't so much care about mixing drinks and electric bills."

"That's freaking obvious, but we ain't done here," said Uncle Morty, pointing at the sofa.

I groaned. "Mom wants me back."

"Tenne's in there. That male nurse talked Carolina into it."

"You can just call him a nurse."

"Whatever."

I went over to the sofa and flopped down. I got a whiff of myself and it wasn't good. I was going to have to take a sponge bath in Mom's sink if I didn't get home soon.

"So how'd that go?" My mom and Aunt Tennessee had a lot of love and rivalry. Aunt Tenne usually came out on the losing end. I wasn't sure how this reversal of fortune was going to be handled by either of them.

"They cried. Women."

"Have you seen Mom?" I asked.

I saw her when they took her down for her MRI." He turned away, his mouth twisting into a grimace, and I touched his arm. "It could've been a lot worse."

"That don't help."

"You didn't see her when it happened."

He nodded, still not looking at me. "Keep your phone close. They ain't got much time left."

"Huh?"

"Tommy ain't called you yet, has he?" Uncle Morty asked.

"Not yet." I looked at his screens. They had Dungeons and Dragons screen-savers up, so I couldn't tell what he'd been up to. "The FBI stuff is online already."

"Hell, yeah. And Big Steve called me."

Of course, he did. Nothing I said or did was considered private in the family and although Big Steve and Morty weren't blood-related, they were still family.

Uncle Morty put a laptop on his lap and gave me a hard look. "Let's hear it."

"Apparently, you've already heard it." I tried to get up, but he pushed me back down, none too gently.

"Cut the crap. I know you're holding back."

"Alright, but you aren't going to like it," I said.

"Of course, I won't like it. Some fucker tried to kill Carolina and the damn FBI is holding back Tommy. What did you get from that waste of skin, Blankenship?"

I told him about the Unsubs. He already knew about Kansas from Big Steve, but the lawyer didn't know the big-ticket item. I drew it out just because I could.

"Mercy, dammit."

"There was a fake Unsub and he was after me," I said.

Uncle Morty went stock still and then began typing like crazy. I told him about the Cassidy Huff case and he growled, "Bullshit."

"Dad's not infallible."

"Shut your yap."

"It's true. I can feel it. Blankenship knew who I was from the first and his interest wasn't normal. The cops and the FBI sent other women in, other women to play Clarice to his Hannibal, and nobody got past hello. These were trained agents, experienced cops, but I got in. Me. Why?"

"'Cause you're hotter than the Fourth of July," mused Uncle Morty.

"Come on. They sent in hotties. They sent in nerds. They sent in everybody they could think of. Nothing. Blankenship is protective of me. He says I belong to him."

"I don't like it," he said.

"Neither do I, but it's working for me. He doesn't like the idea that I might get killed and not visit him anymore."

Uncle Morty lifted his lip in a snarl. "And that's the reason he gave it up?"

"He didn't give up everything. There's plenty more in that twisted mind of his."

"There has to be another reason."

"Well...I did eat a crab hotdog for him."

He grinned. "And there it is."

"It was disgusting. I'm never doing that again."

"You'll eat a live crab if that's what it takes," he said.

"Thanks. You're all heart," I said. "So...did you find anything on Joseph Cranmer?" I believed Blankenship, but I wouldn't be the first person he'd fooled. Part of me was very afraid that I'd been played. I bit my lip in anticipation of the wrong answer.

Uncle Morty put one of his laptops on my lap. "You got to explain this to me."

Please don't let this be about Fats.

"Explain what?"

Please don't let this be about Fats.

"How this guy fits in."

Guy. Fats could be mistaken for...

I stared at the screensaver, unwilling to touch the mousepad. "Just tell me."

He reached over and tapped a key. The screen lit up with an Illinois driver's license. Joseph Cranmer, a moderately handsome white guy in his mid-fifties.

"So he exists," I said with a whoosh. "That's a relief."

Uncle Morty tapped another key without looking. He had extrasensory perception when it came to keyboards. I'd seen him type on two keyboards at the same time and he didn't misspell a single word. I wanted to make a YouTube video of it, but he wouldn't let me.

The screen changed to a police report filed in the Chicago suburb of Evanston three years ago. The report was extremely detailed, but I doubted that Mr. Cranmer would've been thrilled with what it contained. Joseph Cranmer was an ass. By that, I mean that he was so disliked that no one reported him missing. He worked at an H&R Block as a tax preparer and supervisor. He was so hated that when he stopped showing up for work, no one called the police. They had a party with cake *and* ice cream. His family, including living parents and two sisters, were relieved that he didn't show up for Thanksgiving and Christmas. They didn't call the police either. The only reason the police got involved was that his landlord, who detested him as well and let him slide on his rent for three months so he wouldn't have to talk to him, finally needed the rent and went to the apartment. He couldn't get an answer for a month and started eviction proceedings. The landlord used the guise of a gas leak to go in and discovered rotted food in the fridge and no Mr. Cranmer. True to form, he didn't call the police. They only got involved when a curious pawn shop owner questioned why the landlord was pawning an entire apartment full of stuff.

The cops investigated as much as they could. There were no signs of violence in the apartment or his car, which was in the garage. His wallet and credit cards were gone, but no one had used them. He just up and vanished. They collected a hair sample from his hairbrush but never ran the DNA since they had nothing to compare it with and no concrete reason to believe he was dead. It was the logical conclusion, but people had disappeared before and turned up in Florida twenty years later. Mr. Cranmer was declared missing and that was it until today.

"Well?" asked Uncle Morty.

I shrugged. "I got nothing. I don't see how this is related to Sturgis or Mom."

"Me either, but I thought you might get a feeling."

"I feel sad that nobody cared, not even his parents. He's the perfect victim. Did you see how people described this guy?"

"Yeah," Uncle Morty growled.

"The most used words were crabby, mean, and nose picker. How much nose picking do you have to do to have" —I scrolled through the pages— "twelve people use it to describe you to the police?"

"I'm crabby."

I looked over at him, but he didn't look up. "Er...yeah."

"Mrs. Davis says I'm mean."

"That's because you won't buy her kid's Christmas wrapping paper. It's a school fundraiser. I had to buy caramel turtles from Mitchell Braidwood. They tasted like feet."

"The kid was selling Christmas paper in April," said Uncle Morty.

"Okay. I'll give you that one. Anyone else say you're mean?" I asked.

"You."

"Me?"

"Once a week and twice on Sundays," he said, finally looking at me through his new glasses. We were so close I truly appreciated the lack of nose hair.

"You charge me for your hacking when I'm doing stuff for Dad."

"I got a business to run," he said, but a lot less gruffly than I expected.

"You realize that I don't get paid a dime, right?" I asked.

"So I am mean."

"Not always. You bought all my fundraiser crap and came into my school as a volunteer. Sure, you did convince everyone that you were a vampire, but they still learned stuff, mostly because they were afraid not to, but it was good."

"I'm crabby."

I put my hands up. "Yeah, you're crabby, but not a nose picker. That's the salient point here. I've never seen you pick your nose and I would call the police if you were missing and so would everyone else, including Mrs. Davis. You fixed her microwave that one time."

"Yeah?" he asked.

"Yeah. You are no Joseph Cranmer. Trust me on this."

"Alright then. Now who's paying for this research?"

Oh my god!

"Tell me you're just messing with me," I said.

Uncle Morty chuckled. "I'll do it for a bottle of your dad's special peach schnapps. I know he has a secret stash somewhere."

"Done. So did you find anything on that place in Kansas?"

He tapped a few keys on my keyboard, once again without looking, and a wide shot of a grain elevator appeared. Even if I didn't know it was Kansas, I would know it was Kansas. Talk about flat.

"That doesn't seem like a good place to bury bodies. You'd be right out in the open. Anybody could see you digging. The highway is right there."

He tapped again and the screen switched to a grainy satellite photo. The grain elevator was enormous, but there wasn't a lot else going on. Small town. Plenty of highway traffic.

"You think Blankenship's full of it?"

Uncle Morty tapped the screen so hard it tipped backwards. "Use your damn eyes."

I grabbed the computer before it tumbled off my lap and I did use my eyes. There was a whole lot of nothing in my view.

"Just when I think you got something going on upstairs," he grumbled. "Zoom in, ya nitwit."

I take it back. You are super mean.

I zoomed in and it took me about thirty seconds to get it. A chill raced down my arms. "That looks like..."

He tilted his screen toward me. It showed an aerial view from CNN.

"A mass grave in Bosnia?" I asked.

"Looks familiar, don't it?" Uncle Morty asked.

"Yeah. I mean, a lot smaller, but yes, it's similar."

"Blankenship wasn't playing you," he said. "That crab dog worth it now?"

"I'm kinda nauseous, but yes. How many do you think are there?"

Uncle Morty's fingers drummed his laptop. "Assuming they're not stacked, average height of five eight with...say a foot between each grave, I'd guess in the neighborhood of forty to forty-five."

"Isn't that a lot for one dude? How could nobody notice?"

"Ridgeway confessed to seventy-one, but they think it was closer to ninety."

"I wish I didn't know that."

"Not knowing don't change it."

His logic worked, but it didn't help me any. I put the laptop back on the table. "Unless you've got something else horrifying to show me, I'm going to see Mom."

He waved me away. "Yeah, yeah. I got to get through the Huff info and see if there's any connection to Blankenship."

I kept expecting him to say something about Calpurnia Fibonacci, but he didn't.

"You won't find anything connecting him," I said.

"'Cause he's full of crap. Go on now."

Does he really not know about Fats?

"I'm telling you he's not," I said.

Maybe I can get away with it. Maybe they'll never know.

"There's no freaking chance that guy's on the level," yelled Uncle Morty.

I stepped outside the door, heading for the ICU.

"Mercy, a moment, please," said Grandad from behind me. He leaned on the wall next to the door of the waiting room. I'd never seen my grandad lurk before. It couldn't be a good thing.

I glanced back at Uncle Morty and Grandad waved me down the hall.

"What's up? Uncle Morty said Mom's okay."

"She's snoozing. They had to give her a sedative for the MRI."

"So..."

"How do you know Calpurnia?"

Dammit. So close.

"Er...what are you talking about?"

Grandad had gone outside that morning with a respiratory thera-pist, who was having a smoke, and he saw Fats Licata snag me.

So not that close.

My voice went all squeaky 'cause I'm so smooth. "Who's Calpurnia?"

Grandad gave me the stink eye that usually came from Aunt Miriam. "Don't kid a kidder. Calpurnia put that beefcake on you and I want to know why."

"She's a girl," I said.

"Fats is still a beefcake," he said. "How did this happen?"

"It's a long story."

Grandad crossed his skinny arms. "Carolina's asleep. We appear to have the time. Explain yourself."

Wait a minute!

I crossed my arms. "Explain yourself."

Grandad's blue eyes went wide. "Explain what?"

"How do *you* know Calpurnia?"

"I didn't say I knew her."

"You didn't have to. You called her Calpurnia. Everyone who doesn't know her calls her Calpurnia Fibonacci. Both names without fail."

Grandad's eyes went shifty. "I don't know about that."

"I do. Calpurnia scares people. It's a respect thing, but when you meet her, it's different. You're still scared, but she's human. She's Calpurnia. How come she's Calpurnia to you?"

"You're changing the subject."

"Damn straight."

He relaxed and smoothed back his faded red hair. "I arrested her mother several times."

"Are you kidding me?" I asked.

"Why would I kid about that? What a woman. A real firecracker."

"What did you arrest her for?"

He grinned at me. "Public disturbance mostly. She brandished a firearm in Tulio's once."

"Was she crazy?"

"She was beautiful. Legs for days and she could dance. We did the tango once. It was ethereal."

"I don't know what to say about that," I said, starting to get a little uncomfortable.

His smile got wider. "She smelled like orange blossoms and good merlot."

"I got it."

"And when she walked, there was this swing to her hips."

I put my hand up. "That's quite enough."

Grandad focused on the wall like he forgot I was there. "I never get to talk about her."

"Let's keep it that way. So how does this connect to Calpurnia?"

"Well, she was there when I arrested her mother before and after they went to Italy. Beautiful girl and smart. You could tell, even when she was young. I used to do puzzles with her while her mother was being arraigned. When she was older, she'd call me to ask about certain arrests."

"Holy crap. You were a Fibonacci mole?"

He laughed. "Of course not. She could've gotten that information from anyone. Now it's online. We had a nice relationship. Her business is her own. She never gave me cause to arrest her. Calpurnia is a Fibonacci, after all."

"Her mother was a Fibonacci and you arrested her," I pointed out.

"Marcella was a Meucci. They have a totally different kind of luck," he said. "Now, how do you know Calpurnia?"

"Does Grandma J know that you have a huge crush on Marcella?"

"Had. The woman's been dead for twenty years."

"And yet..." My turn to give the stink eye.

Grandad started to protest his innocence, which wasn't going to work out for him. I'd seen that look in his eye. Men looked at me like that all the time. Grandma wouldn't care if Marcella was dead. That look said it all.

I just let him go on until the ICU door opened and Mom's day nurse, Takira, came out. She saw me and said, "Thank goodness. I was just coming to ask where you were."

My chest got tight. "Everything okay with the MRI?"

"Fine. I need you to make a command decision." She waved me inside.

"Your father should be making the command decisions," said Grandad.

"Well, he's not here, is he?" I went through the door.

Grandad dashed over and stopped it from closing. "We still haven't heard anything from him."

I glanced at the wall clock. Five minutes left. "We will," I said, more confident than I felt. If the FBI didn't come through, I had a real problem. If Uncle Morty was right about Kansas, how could I keep that from them? Blankenship's buddy might be on the prowl right now.

Grandad's forehead creased into a dozen lines, making his freckles stand out against his pale skin. "What are you thinking?"

"Don't worry. I'll take care of it." I meant it, too. Even if I had to go back to Hunt and eat a live crab, as Uncle Morty suggested, Dad would be coming back.

"How?" Grandad asked.

"Let's just say the FBI won't be thrilled with me."

"I like the sound of that."

I kissed his weathered cheek and went inside. In five seconds, I was wishing I hadn't.

CHAPTER ELEVEN

I'd been hanging out in hospitals since I started nursing school when I was eighteen and I've seen a lot of stuff, plenty of it weird. I'd never seen yelling in the ICU. Especially not doctors. ICUs are quiet. I rarely heard patients call out. Mostly, they didn't have to, being so closely monitored, but they endured tremendous pain while waiting for the morphine to kick in. They didn't scream when being moved despite the agony it caused. You want to see the definition of fortitude? Go to an ICU.

What I mean to say is go in a *normal* ICU. Mom's wasn't normal, not on that day. Two docs in scrubs and lab coats were nose-to-nose in front of Mom's window, yelling about each other's stupidity.

At some point, I became aware that my mouth was open and I snapped it closed.

"Doctors, please. Miss Watts is here and she'll settle this," said Takira.

"Are you off your nut?" I asked her. "Call security or psych."

"I did, but you're here," she said. "Psych has a two-hour wait and security's responding to unauthorized people in the surgical suites. Your grandfather requested these two and now we have this."

"Are you serious?" I asked.

"Just another day in paradise."

A couple of nurses tried to pull the doctors apart to no avail. Neither of them was large, but anger was fueling them.

"Call security again," said Patsy, almost tumbling to the floor after losing her grip.

"I'm calling," called out another nurse behind her desk. All the doors to the patients' rooms were closed, thankfully, but I'm sure they could hear that something was going on. There was a family member at every window. Tenne was at Mom's, watching with calm fascination.

The male doc grabbed the female by the scrub top. "You are a hack."

"You're a sadist pig."

"Look at the printout."

"You look at the CT."

I pulled Takira aside. "What is their deal?"

"They hate each other."

"I got that. Why?"

"Dr. Nishi slept with Dr. Millikan's wife."

I grimaced. "That's bad."

"Then Dr. Millikan keyed Dr. Nishi's new S-Class."

"Also bad."

"Seven times and he put super glue in the locks."

"Why wasn't he arrested?"

"Can't prove it was him. Plus, Dr. Nishi jimmied the trunk of Dr. Millikan's Aston Martin and threw fish guts in there."

"Can't prove it?"

Takira nodded. "It's been like *General Hospital* around here for the last two weeks."

"Who agreed to put them on the same case? That's just crazy."

"Your grandfather was warned," said Takira. "And they are the best."

"And you want me to stop them?" I asked.

"Yes, talk to them about your mother's case and make a decision," said Takira.

It didn't take a genius to look at those nutballs and know talking wasn't an option. If only I had my taser.

The ICU door flew open and a plump security guard ran in, red-faced from the effort. "Who called in a disturbance?"

Three hands went up.

"What's the problem?" she asked.

Everyone pointed at the obvious problem.

"Oh, well, is that all?" The officer sauntered over and politely asked them to be quiet and stop smacking each other.

They didn't. Imagine that.

I checked my phone. One minute left before I had to decide what to do—hold out for my father to help my mother or give up a serial killer to help strangers. Maybe it shouldn't have been a painful choice, but it was. Damn the FBI and damn doctors.

I walked over and grabbed a small fire extinguisher off the wall. I pulled the pin.

"What are you doing?" yelled the officer. "You can't do that."

People are always telling me what to do. Flirt with mass murderers. Solve murders. Eat crab. Enough.

I sprayed her and the doctors. Not a lot, but it sure as hell got their attention.

"What the frack?" asked the guard. "I could arrest you for that."

"You can't arrest shit," I said, handing the extinguisher to Takira. Aunt Tenne was clapping and the nurses were doing their best to hold in their laughter. "Now I've been having a very bad" —I had to think about it— "eight days. Now who wants to talk to me about my mother, Carolina Watts, a woman who had a stroke and deserves some doctors that aren't psycho?"

Dr. Millikan wiped the foam off his forehead. "I'm not psycho."

"I say you are and I just spent the morning at Hunt. Don't make me go all Harvey the Head Case on you."

Dr. Nishi got herself together and said, "Who is this Harvey?"

"He attacks people and eats their feet. I ate a crab hotdog this morning so I can eat me some feet. Who wants to try me?"

Nobody moved.

"No takers? Good. Let's talk diagnosis." I walked around and plopped down in Takira's chair, glaring at the docs.

Patsy whispered behind me. "I think she's lost it. Call Dr. Lindstrom."

"Already did," said Takira.

I threw up my hands. "Well?"

The doctors made their cases and it was fairly simple. Nothing had changed since the day before. What had caused Mom's stroke, a dissection or Afib? Dr. Nishi, the internist, believed it was a dissection. Dr. Millikan, cardio, thought it was the heart. They both had merits. Mom's heart monitor showed unusual activity consistent with Afib and her CTs showed the right carotid with thirty percent occlusion.

"There is no need to put your mother through a TEE," said Dr. Nishi. "It's a dissection."

Dr. Millikan gritted his teeth. "We think she threw the clot during the attack or shortly after. That's the heart."

"The attack could've caused her to throw the clot from a previous dissection."

"That is patently ridiculous."

"No more than your theory."

"I have data," said Dr. Millikan.

"So do I."

I stood up and said, "Show me your data."

They did and I had no idea which side to fall on. Lucky for me, Pete walked in just as the doctors were starting to insult each other again.

Pete took over in his calm, confident way. Even though he was junior to both of them, they piped down and listened

"I think you should do the TEE," he said after examining the CT.

"What?" asked Dr. Nishi.

"If she were my mother, I'd have to rule out the heart, although I think a dissection is likely."

Dr. Nishi beamed. "That is exactly what radiology said."

I shooed them through the ICU. "You should go talk to radiology. Maybe they made a mistake."

"That is highly likely," said Dr. Millikan, bursting out the door.

"You have a screw loose," said Dr. Nishi, chasing after him.

I sighed and craned back my neck. "Ten bucks says they sleep together at some point."

"Please don't say that," said Patsy. "The repercussions, I can't imagine."

"Somebody call Radiology and warn them," said Pete. "Why is there foam on the floor?"

Takira rushed up with a mop. "I'll get that."

"What did you do?" Pete asked me.

"I solved a problem," I said.

"With an extinguisher?"

"Could be."

The guard tried to take me by the arm. "This isn't in the handbook, but I think I have to escort you out of the building."

Pete took her off me and steered her to the exit. "I'll take responsibility for Miss Watts."

"I have to report this to my supervisor."

"We understand, Joanna," he said and politely pushed her out the door. "Alright then. Who wants coffee?"

Pete took orders and called it in to the cart in the lobby. I asked for a mega latte. I didn't know how big it was, but I doubted it would be big enough.

Aunt Tenne came out of Mom's room, smiling. "She slept through the whole thing. She's going to be so disappointed that she missed you in action." She hugged me and another weight was lifted off my shoulders. Aunt Tenne could handle things and she wouldn't hit me with a cane. On the other hand, Dad hadn't called. I couldn't believe it. The bastards welched on me.

Pete came over and shook Aunt Tenne's hand. "They're going to bring the cart up."

"They can do that?" I asked.

"Sure. Have coffee, will travel. It's just easier to bring the cart." He touched my shoulder. "Are you okay?"

"Not really. I sprayed them," I said. "I can't believe I sprayed them."

Takira came up and said, "And you threatened to eat their feet."

Aunt Tenne and Pete stared at me.

"I was just out at Hunt. It does things to you," I said.

"Clearly," said Aunt Tenne. "I don't think you should go back there if you're thinking about eating feet."

"I'm not. I lost it." I went in Mom's room and picked up her good hand. Her eyes fluttered and she murmured, "Tommy?"

My eyes filled and I kissed her forehead. "No, Mom. It's me."

"Where is he?"

"I'm working on it."

"Are you?"

"Yes. I'll think of something," I said.

Aunt Tenne took me by the shoulders and pushed me out of the room.

"What?" I asked as she closed the door.

"You're about to go to pieces," said Aunt Tenne. "She doesn't need that."

"I'm okay."

"Your hands are shaking."

They were. I was. My whole body. Pete put a warmed blanket over my shoulders and sat me in Takira's seat. "Carolina's doing very well. We'll figure out where the clots came from."

"It's not that. I mean, it is, but I can't get Dad for her. I had something to offer in exchange. They signed a contract and everything. They still didn't give him up."

"He must be worried sick," said Aunt Tenne.

"He probably has no idea what's happened. He goes into the field and we fade away. It's like he thinks we get paused when he's not around."

"You'll think of something," said Pete. "You always do."

"I could go back out to Hunt. Maybe I can get Blankenship to tell me something else that they want."

"Don't do that." Aunt Tenne pushed the hair off my forehead. "You should go home and rest."

"I can't rest. You heard Mom. She needs him."

My phone rang in my pocket and I almost jumped out of my skin. "Dad?"

"Dammit," said a vaguely familiar voice. "He didn't call."

"Who is this?" I asked, my heart sinking so hard it felt like it hit the floor.

"Gansa," he said. "Shit. I thought they'd do it. You really have something big, don't you?"

I put my head in my hands. "It's huge and I want to tell you. I really do."

"Is there anything you can give me, a hint to whet their appetites?" asked Gansa.

Short of saying, "Drive halfway through Kansas and turn right," I had nothing.

"Did he give you any proof?"

"What, about the Cranmer lead?" I asked. "That's panning out, isn't it?"

It was panning out. They were running the DNA, but the blood types matched. Gansa's boss wouldn't tell him or Gordon what was going on though. They'd been locked out.

"I don't know if they don't believe you or if they don't care," said Gansa.

"I have to make them believe so much that they have to care."

"Sounds good or you could just whisper right now. That works for me." Gansa had a sense of humor. Who knew?

"Fat chance," I said.

"I had to try."

Proof. I needed proof. What proof did I have that didn't give it away? Then it hit me. The CNN article had a headline that said, "Proof of Atrocities."

"I have proof," I said.

"Let's hear it," said Gansa.

"Give me a minute."

"Wait—"

I cut him off and called Uncle Morty. I asked him to use the satellite imagery of that field in Kansas to give me proof. He had to crop it so you couldn't tell where it was. Just a field that looked like a burial site. It could be anywhere. Sure, they might be able to use some program to figure it out, but that took time. Time was something they didn't have the luxury of. I'd call some reporters Dad knew. I'd give them the image. I'd tell them what was happening. This wasn't the kind of publicity that the government enjoyed.

Uncle Morty texted me the image. Actually, five images, a large one of the whole site and four individual grave sites. He'd managed to clean up the graininess somewhat and they looked like graves. It might've been my exhausted imagination, but I think I saw a foot.

"Is that a foot?" asked Pete, peering over my shoulder.

"I don't know, but I hope the FBI asks the same question." I texted the images to Gansa and he came back with a "What the hell is that?"

"Guess." I texted back.

"Graves?"

"A lot of graves."

Gansa said he'd take the images and my threat to his boss personally. He told me to hold tight. I couldn't have gotten any tighter. Every muscle hurt. Breathing took effort to care about.

"Good," said Takira. "Carolina's awake."

I didn't think it was good. Awake meant she'd be missing Dad and thinking about her stroke. "Yeah, great," I said.

"Takira just means that we can start her anti-coagulants," said Peter like that was a good thing.

"Swell."

Pete frowned at me, his smooth face filled with concern. "You want her on anti-coagulants."

"I assume you're starting her on Lovenox or something?" I asked.

Takira looked at Mom's orders. "Lovenox and warfarin."

"She's gonna love that. Shots in the belly are always good fun."

"I can do it," said Pete.

Takira and I both laughed, causing Pete to cross his arms. "Hey. I'm training to be a neurosurgeon. I think I can give a shot."

"Of course, you can," said Takira with a sly smile that made a dimple appear in her left cheek.

"I know you're humoring me, but I've given shots before."

"Oh, yeah?" I asked. "How many?"

"I've given...it doesn't matter," he said.

"It will to Mom. I'll do it."

Takira shook her head. "I'll do it. It's too hard on a family member."

"I'll be doing it when she goes home," I said. "There's no way on Earth that my dad can handle it. He couldn't take out a splinter she had last year. I had to come over and do it."

Takira took off to get the meds and Aunt Tenne said, "I don't know. How are your hands?"

"You want to do it?" I asked.

"Never mind."

"That's what I thought and I'm fine. This is what I do, after all."

"Not to your mother," she said.

"I do now."

Takira came back with a syringe and a video on anti-coagulants for Mom to watch.

"I can't believe that Millikan and Nishi agreed on this," I said.

She laughed. "It's the only thing they agreed on. That and that each other should drop dead and rot."

I chuckled and went in Mom's room.

"Have you heard from your dad yet?" asked Mom, moving the head of her bed into the upright position.

"Not yet, but I've put a plan in motion," I said.

Mom didn't look convinced of my ability to get the job done, which was oddly encouraging. That was the Mom I knew and loved.

Aunt Tenne gave Mom a kiss on the forehead and said she was going to go since we weren't supposed to have two visitors there, but the real reason was the shot and I didn't blame her. Takira and Pete explained the anti-coagulant thing to Mom while I practiced the positive thinking that my therapist, Dr. Witges, gave me. It worked. I was totally positive that this was going to suck.

"I can teach you how to do it yourself," said Takira, applying an ice pack to Mom's belly.

Mom just looked at her in horror.

"Or Mercy can do it."

Mom glanced at me.

"I'll do it," I said as a security guard poked his head in Mom's door. "Excuse me, is this Carolina Watt's room?"

"Yes," said Takira. "Can I help you?"

"Actually, I'd like to talk to Miss Mercy Watts, if I may," he said, straightening up and looking incredibly formal.

Ah, crap!

"I'm Mercy." I raised my hand like a bad kindergartner.

"If it's about the incident with the fire extinguisher," said Pete, "I can explain."

"Fire extinguisher?" asked Mom. "Did you hit someone with a fire extinguisher?"

"No," I said.

"It sounds like something you'd do," she said.

I rolled my eyes. "'Cause I'm such a violent person. Come on, Mom."

"You punched that boy in your freshman year of high school. We had to go to a meeting."

"He grabbed my breast."

The guard smiled and look down.

"Well, you shot that boy in New Orleans."

"He was a gangbanger, trying to kill me."

The guard was no longer smiling but looking at me like he'd rather not talk to me after all.

"What about Paris? You could've hit a tourist when you shot at that terrorist," Mom said.

"No, I couldn't. I—"

The guard cut me off. "It's not about the fire extinguisher. Can I see you outside, please?"

I went out with Pete and he gave me a quick hug. "I have to go. I'll check back later."

Pete left and I turned to the guard. He introduced himself as Will

Snyder and closed Mom's door. "There's been an incident, Miss Watts," he said.

"As long as we're not talking about my incident, I'm totally okay with that," I said.

He gave me a look that was somewhere between gas pain and explosive diarrhea.

"Unless I'm not," I said.

"You're not."

That was an understatement. Shortly after I'd returned from Hunt, a man had entered the hospital, a Hispanic of medium height and build, wearing a summer fedora pulled low and an over-sized jacket. His voice was gravelly and strained. He flashed a badge at information and asked for my mom's location. The volunteer told him that she was in the ICU but would be transported to a regular room soon.

Then he asked if she'd seen me, complete with a description of what I was wearing. It was totally accurate and the creeps came over me hard core. The volunteer hadn't seen me and she asked around. Nobody had.

"It could've been a cop," I said weakly.

Snyder nodded. "That's what I would've thought. In fact, this would never have come to my attention at all, but we've been having a problem with Wash U journalism students."

"What's this got to do with journalism?"

"Nothing and everything. They're doing some sort of exposé of hospital security and we're a target. They've been tailgating. You're familiar?"

I was. Tailgating was when an unauthorized person gained access to restricted areas like operating rooms by following someone going in with a badge. People's innate politeness sometimes led them to hold open doors if the person looked official. It was a real problem. In this case, the students had gotten past outer security twice but never into an actual OR before getting caught.

Because of their repeated attempts, Mr. Snyder was continually reviewing security footage, trying to catch them in the act. Because of his increased vigilance, he happened to see a man in a summer fedora loitering in the hall outside the ICU doors. He tried to tailgate several times, including with Aunt Tenne, but he wasn't successful. When the guard came running over to the doctors' fight and went in the ICU, he left.

Mr. Snyder tracked him with the cameras through the building and out the front doors. He would've gotten a license plate, but the man walked off campus. Then Mr. Snyder went through the footage before the man arrived on the floor and saw him questioning the volunteer. Snyder talked to her and found out who the man was asking about.

"Did you call the police?" I asked.

"I did and they're on the way," said Mr. Snyder. "I wanted to tell you myself. I've known your father a long time. We were in uniform together."

"Thanks. I appreciate your telling me. My mom needs an around-the-clock guard."

"I agree, but if I know your father, he'll want one of his own people with her."

Mr. Snyder was right. Dad would want someone on his own team with Mom, but who?

"Have you told this to my grandad?" I asked.

"Ace is here?" he asked. "Oh, that's right. I saw him pass our guy when he was loitering in the hall. I wasn't thinking about him."

I poked my head back in Mom's room and said, "Hey, Mom. I'm going to check on Grandad."

"He's still here?"

"I think so. Do you think Wallace needs a walk?"

Mom scratched the pug's belly. She was lying on her back, snoring away. The vet in Sturgis had given her painkillers for the kick she got and Wallace had gotten even more lazy. "Let's let her sleep."

"Okay. I'll be right back."

"When can I eat? I'm getting a little hungry," said Mom.

"After the heart test," I said.

Mom lowered her right eyebrow to match her left. "What are they going to do to me?"

"Er…I'll explain it later." I closed the door and went with Mr. Snyder, passing the female guard who was going to hang out in the ICU.

Out in the hall, a second guard was posted at the entrance. He was more interested in the coffee cart that was pumping out lattes at an incredible rate. It turned out that Pete had given the guy a couple of hundred bucks to caffeine up all the patients and family that wanted it in order to soothe everyone over the whole doctors versus extinguisher incident. Pete really was the best.

We went into the waiting room to find Nikki hovering over Uncle Morty while he ate her baklava. "Mercy," she exclaimed, rushing over. "You must have some."

I wasn't really hungry after the whole crab dog incident, but my opinion wasn't required. I was promptly seated in a big armchair by the window, fed baklava, and given a mega latte to increase my stamina, according to Nikki. It was delicious, so I didn't care.

"The Feds are talking," said Uncle Morty.

"Is that a good thing?" I asked.

"It ain't bad. You got them in a fix. They think you'll go to the press."

"I will. Where's Grandad?"

Uncle Morty chomped on another piece of baklava and said through spewing bits of filo dough, "Went to the cafeteria to get ginger ale with Tenne. Her stomach's upset. Something about an injection." He shot Mr. Snyder a hawk-eyed look. "You got bad news, Will?"

"Could be better," said Mr. Snyder.

"Let me have it then."

Mr. Snyder explained the situation as I stuffed an entire piece of baklava in my gullet, not one of my prettier or better decisions. My phone chose that moment to ring. I gagged, swiped the green button, and couldn't say a word. I sounded like I was being strangled, which I kinda was, just with sugary goodness.

Nikki walked over and plucked the phone out of my hand while I pounded on my own chest.

"Hello, Tommy," she said. "This is Nikki."

She paused.

"Yes, she's right here, trying to swallow an obscene amount of baklava."

Another pause.

Nikki smiled. "It is the best, if I do say so myself."

I swallowed hard and gulped some coffee, holding up my hand.

"Here she is, Tommy," said Nikki.

"Dad," I burst out.

"What the hell are you thinking, Mercy?" Dad yelled, loud enough for the whole room to hear and we weren't the only baklava-eating family in there.

"I had to—"

"You *had* to bother me while I'm working? Think, Mercy. I'm working. For the FBI. Do you understand anything? A damn helicopter flew in with a satellite phone. This had better be good. We're tracking a cannibal. He ate a cop, for God's sake!"

For a moment, I couldn't speak. Dad was pissed. What the hell? Did it ever occur to him that I didn't send a helicopter for nothing? No. I was just his daughter, the family moron.

"Somebody tried to kill Mom and she had a massive stroke, but I wouldn't want to interrupt your cannibal hunt! Clearly, you have your priorities, you self-involved nut job!" I screamed at him and hung up.

The entire room stared at me and I sucked down the rest of my coffee. "Well, he knows. It was totally worth eating that crab."

"Mercy," said Nikki. "Your father is—"

"A complete ass? I know."

"I don't think..." she trailed off.

Uncle Morty put down his laptop and stood up. "Tommy's a real fucker when it comes to work. Always has been."

Nikki sputtered. Obviously, it wasn't Greek to call a father a fucker. "Don't you think—"

Uncle Morty came over slapped me on the back, so hard I almost fell out of my chair. "I think I've been to more of Mercy's crap than Tommy. Graduations. Talent shows. Those idiotic powderpuff football games."

"Really?" asked Nikki, glowing the way women do when they find a caretaker.

"Yeah," I said. "He was there. My dad found other things to do."

"Like catching murderers and rapists," said Uncle Morty. "There's a price to pay for brilliance."

"And Mom's paying it right now. I could kill him. I could beat him to death with a bat."

Grandad walked in with Aunt Tenne. "You sound just like Jeanette in Sturgis and she did beat Steve to death."

"Great. Now I sound like that psycho," I said.

"What happened?" he asked.

I told him and Grandad got a shade paler. "He didn't."

"Oh, he did."

"Give me that phone. That boy, as Bill Cosby said before he was a criminal, I brought him in this world and I can take him out." Grandad reached for my phone just as it rang again.

"I got it," I said. "You can take him out later."

Grandad gritted his teeth and nodded.

"Hello," I said, steely and cold.

"What did you say to me?" yelled Dad.

"I said you're a self-involved nut job and I stand by it."

"Not that. About your mother."

I told him once again what happened, thinking that perhaps, just maybe, he would get upset. You know, ask about Mom's condition, what hospital she was in, stuff like that. But, oh no, not Tommy Watts.

"Where the hell is Denny?" he screamed. Everyone in the waiting room froze and Uncle Morty picked up his cellphone, nodding at me.

"How should I know where Denny is?" I asked. "It's not my day to watch him."

Dad went quiet.

"Well?"

"You haven't seen Denny?" he asked

"No. He's on a case. I didn't call him. I've been busy and it's not like he can do anything." I looked over at Uncle Morty and Grandad now sequestered on the sofa, working on the laptops. They didn't look happy.

"Have you been back to the house?" Dad asked.

I described the cops and techs at the house, finding the bullet with a sense of increasing doom. Somehow, I couldn't tell him about the blood. It was crucial information, but saying it out loud to Dad made it more real. "Why are you asking about Denny if he's in Montana on assignment?"

Dad's voice was thick and throaty. I'd heard him like that when his partner, Cora, was murdered and it scared the crap out of me. "Because I canceled the job and told him to watch your mother. Aunt Miriam was worried. We'd had some half-assed break-in attempts. Call him. I'm going to kick his ass up into his throat."

I pictured the scene, the trampled hosta and that bullet hole so well-concealed. We thought all our people were accounted for except Claire.

"Dad, where's Claire?" I asked.

"Claire? Why the hell are you asking about her? Call Denny."

"Uncle Morty's on it. Where's Claire?"

I could hear him violently scratching his scalp before he said, "She said she was going on some cruise. She met a guy from Parks and Rec. I didn't have time to run a background on him. Tell Morty to run her credit cards."

"He did. There's nothing." I mouthed to Uncle Morty, "She went on a cruise." Uncle Morty nodded and went back to typing furiously. "Do you remember this new guy's name or the cruise line?" I asked Dad.

"No. I don't remember the name. She said something about the Bahamas though."

I turned to Uncle Morty. "Bahamas."

He nodded and typed furiously. "On it."

Dad and I went quiet. If Claire was on that cruise with her latest loser, that left only Denny unaccounted for. Denny would never leave Mom alone when he was under orders to keep an eye on her. Never. Not going to happen.

There was a beep.

"Dammit," said Dad. "This phone is low."

I looked over at Uncle Morty. He shook his head at me and I said, "Denny's dead."

Dad grumbled, "Don't jump to conclusions. I taught you better than that."

I told him about the blood and Dad said there could be another explanation. Dumped blood to throw us off the track. Could be a service person that was at the wrong place at the wrong time. A Ron Goldman-type situation.

There was another beep.

"This phone's going to die," Dad said.

"Shocking."

"What do you mean by that?

"The FBI helicopter brought you a phone that's about to die. You don't think that's weird?"

He scratched his head again. "You think it's intentional?"

"Hell, yeah."

Beep.

Dad got thoughtful. "Why didn't you contact me sooner?"

"We tried," I said. "I had to make a deal with the FBI to get this phone call."

Two beeps.

"Tell me what you did, Mercy."

"No time. Get home. Mom needs you."

"I'm on it. What did you do?"

"I need your file on Cassidy Huff."

"Why the hell?"

Three beeps.

"Dad! Cassidy Huff!"

"My office. Bottom drawer on the right. Why, Mercy?"

I turned away and whispered into the phone so my spectators wouldn't hear. "Blankenship put her in a wood chipper. Don't tell the Feds." I paused. "Dad?" I'd lost him and I didn't know when. I closed my eyes. *Please don't tell them.*

A gentle hand landed on my shoulder. I looked up at Grandad. "We can't get ahold of Denny. No one has seen or heard from him since he ordered a pizza to be delivered to your parents' house yesterday at five. He obviously didn't go to Montana, but his wife was under the impression that he did go. He hasn't called her, which isn't unusual when he's working."

"Why would he tell his wife he was going to Montana when he was watching Mom?" I asked.

"Think about it."

"Come on," I said. "Mom and Denny wouldn't do anything."

Grandad hugged me. "I know that, but remember you said Grandma would be jealous of a woman who's been dead twenty years. How do you think Denny's wife would feel? Your mother is...well, your mother."

"I guess. What about Claire?"

"Looks like Claire is on a cruise, so that makes sense. She wasn't around to make the changes on the roster."

"He is so dead," I said.

"Who's dead?" Chuck walked through the door. His expression was half angry and half curious.

"Denny. He was supposed to be looking after Mom and he's missing."

Chuck stopped walking and Sydney bumped into the back of him. "Do you know his blood type?"

"No, but it should be on his insurance stuff." My chest was so tight it hurt. "I'll be right back."

Aunt Tenne touched my arm as I passed. "You really think Denny's dead?"

"Yes."

"I can't believe it. He's so young," she said. "Forty-two."

I patted her hands as she was wringing them. "I'm going to talk to Mom. I want you to go in when I'm done."

She nodded and I returned to the ICU, flashing my access badge at security. Takira was charting at her desk and I asked her, "Any word on the TEE?"

She picked up the phone and started dialing. "They're backed up. I'll check."

"Thanks." I went in Mom's room to see that Wallace was awake and amusing Mom by doing tricks for bits of Aaron's special kibble. To call it kibble was kind of an insult. It's main ingredients appeared to be black truffles, because all pugs should eat truffles, and filet mignon. I should eat so well.

"Who's a good girl?" asked Mom.

"I'm a good girl," I said.

Grr.

"I was asking Wallace," said Mom.

"I'm still a good girl."

Grr.

"Quiet, hound," I said and Wallace ran to the edge of the bed and peered through the safety rail at my feet. Happily, even Wallace's aim wasn't that good.

"Mom, have you remembered anything else about yesterday?" I asked.

Bark.

"Not asking the dog."

Grr.

I gave Wallace a chunk of gourmet kibble and asked Mom again.

"Why?" asked Mom, dabbing the drool away from her chin.

"Well," I tried to sound upbeat. "I was wondering if maybe Denny was at the house."

"Denny." She dabbed again. I think the drooling was getting worse like everything else in our lives.

"Yes, Mom. Try to think. Do you remember him being there?"

"Yes. I think...everything is so fuzzy. I think your father told him to watch me. I don't know why. I can take care of myself." She gave some more kibble to Wallace in exchange for sitting up and begging.

Takira came in and we exchanged a look. That guy almost killed her, but it didn't seem to have sunk in. "Was he outside with you when it happened?"

Please say no.

She frowned but only on the right side. "Denny?"

Oh my god!

"Yeah, Mom. Denny. You were out in the side yard and somebody else was there."

"Someone attacked me," she said. "He was there."

I swallowed hard and said, "I know that. But I think there was another person."

Mom blinked slowly and her eyelids didn't match. The left side was significantly slower than the right. She needed a neuro-ophthalmologist on top of everything else.

"I don't remember," she said. "It's all so indistinct. Dr. Nishi said I might have a concussion, but there wasn't any bleeding in the brain so that's good."

I pushed a curl off her forehead, revealing the widow's peak that was identical to mine. "That is good."

"Will I get better?" she asked softly.

"Absolutely."

"Tell the truth."

"I am." My eyes overflowed. "It will take time."

"How long will I be here?" she asked and I realized that with everything that had been happening, we hadn't discussed it. I didn't much want to discuss it then either.

Takira took over in her reassuring way. "You'll go to the regular floor this afternoon after your TEE at four. They're thinking maybe a week here total."

Mom sighed and reached for her water mug. "Then I can go home."

My mind was swirling with thoughts of Denny and blood and the man stalking Mom right in the hospital, but I managed to focus for a second. "I want you to go to rehab."

Mom looked confused. "Rehab?"

"For speech and physical therapy."

"Can't I do that at home?"

"It will be more intense in-patient," said Takira. "Mercy's right. You'll have a better outcome."

"I want to go home," said Mom.

I kissed her forehead. "I know. Please don't fight me on this. You really have to go."

Mom wrapped one of my limp curls around a finger on her good hand. "They tried to make me go to rehab. I said, no, no, no."

I laughed and sang back, "Yes, I been black. But when I come back, you'll know, know, know, know."

Takira picked up the rest, singing my favorite line from Amy Winehouse about how Daddy thinks I'm fine. Maybe I liked it because my dad never thought I was fine. I almost told her that I talked to Dad, but something held me back, a little niggling feeling that I shouldn't get her hopes up quite yet.

Instead, I hugged her. "You don't know how much I needed that."

"I do know. I'm still your mother. Isn't it odd that I can remember that song and I can't remember what happened yesterday?"

It was odd, but it wasn't the oddest thing about those days, not by a long shot.

CHAPTER TWELVE

Because I'd just claimed to be a good girl, I called Fats on the way out of the ICU. She was in the hospital garage, ready to go. I said I'd meet her at the front as I pushed through the door to find Chuck leaning on the wall opposite. He usually looked incredibly hot when he leaned like that but not that day.

"You and I have some business," he said without smiling and Chuck was a big smiler, even when he hated the person he was talking to.

"How about later?" I asked. "I've got to go to the house for...slippers. Mom's going to be up and about soon."

"Now."

I didn't know what his issue was and I found I didn't much care. If it was about Pete again, I might scream. Hell, I might scream anyway. It was a hell of a bad day. "Seriously, I have to go."

"I don't need your help," he said, raising his voice.

So we're doing this.

"Who said you did?" I asked.

He stood up straight, stiff, and unfriendly as all get out. "The FBI."

"Oh."

"Oh? Is that all you have to say to me?"

"I don't know. What do you want me to say?" I asked.

He wanted me to explain why in the hell I made him part of my deal with the Feds. I thought it was obvious, but I guess not.

"I was trying to help. You can't go undercover because of me. You can do this."

Chuck pointed a long finger at me. "It's a pity tasking. Thanks, Mercy. Now I'm fucking pathetic."

"No, you're not. You were pissed when the FBI took over the case and booted you off. I got you back on. What's wrong with that?" I crossed my arms and tried to control my temper.

"I'll get my own damn assignments."

Suddenly, I was so tired I wanted to sink to the floor and put my head in my hands. But I couldn't. I had to go read a file on a girl who got put in a wood chipper. Because that was my life and my boyfriend was looking at me like I'd committed a capital offense by getting him a job that he wanted.

"I don't understand. This is good," I said. "You want this. It's a huge case."

"And my girlfriend gave it to me," he spat. "What did you have to do to get me on it? A little breast goes a long way."

Now I'm awake.

"Don't say anything else," I warned.

"You don't want me to say it. I bet you don't," he said, flaming red with indignation.

Before I could respond, Uncle Morty came out of the waiting room and punched Chuck in the chest, knocking him on his butt. "Remember who you're talkin' to!"

Chuck leapt to his feet and said, "I know exactly who I'm talking to. The one who talks to her ex before she talks to me."

"We covered this already," I said.

"Pete was just in there."

"So? He's a doctor."

"Whatever," said Chuck.

"No whatever. You're losing it and that's not my fault." I turned to go and he yelled after me, "I'm not taking the assignment."

Uncle Morty stuck his finger in Chuck's face. "The hell you aren't.

Mercy traded good info for that assignment and you're freaking gonna take it."

"I don't want it."

"I don't give a shit. The Feds are trying to keep Tommy off this for some damn reason and we need you in there."

Sydney came out of the waiting room and calmly said, "We'll take it. I don't care how we got it. Tommy's a media whore, but he shouldn't be kept away from his own wife. I'll do it for the bastard and, with any luck, I'll become a media whore myself."

Chuck clenched and unclenched his jaw. "She needs a bodyguard."

"*She*," I said, "has one." Before I could name Fats Licata, Grandad said, "I took care of it. Called in a favor."

Chuck forcibly unclenched his jaw and turned his icy gaze on me. "Alright then. Fill me in on Hunt."

I was too angry, too hurt to deal with him. "That's a hard no."

"Where are you going?" asked Chuck, his face not softening one bit.

"To bat my eyes and who knows what else." I flipped my hair back and thrust a hip out.

The red drained out of his face and he took a step forward. "I didn't mean it."

I took two steps back. "But you said it."

Uncle Morty stepped between us. "It don't matter. You both got jobs to do."

Nikki came out of the waiting room with two spots of red high on her cheeks and a plastic container in her hands. "It matters. It just doesn't matter right now." She gave me the container and said, "For your bodyguard. I'm sure you'll give him a workout."

"Who is this guy?" asked Chuck, his voice going deeper.

Nikki winked at me and then turned me around, giving me a gentle push toward the elevator. "Go do your thing. We've got it here."

"Mom's got a test at four. After that, she can eat," I said.

"Aaron and I will take care of it," she said.

I pushed the elevator button, it dinged, and the doors opened. "Together?"

"We decided to join forces."

Why does that make me nervous?

"What does that mean?" I went in the elevator and punched the *Lobby* button. "You're cooking together?"

"We're exchanging techniques," said Nikki, her cheeks glowing brighter with excitement.

The doors started to close.

"Like what?"

"Today we're spit-roasting a goat. You'll love it." She waved and the doors closed.

"Oh my god," I said. "Goat."

Behind me, there was some twittering from a couple of candy-stripers wearing huge grins.

"You have to eat goat," said a willowy blonde, wearing electric tangerine lipstick that practically glowed. "I'm going to order from Pappy's."

"No barbecue for you. I bet goat stinks like roadkill," said the other one, who was inexplicably wearing pigtails. She really shouldn't have talked. Somebody forgot her deodorant. Even I didn't smell that bad and I had a good excuse.

They reminded me of the uber rich girls at my high school, the ones that only volunteered because they were serving time on community service.

I smiled back. "So is Marianne Goldberg still the head of the youth program?"

The grins fell off their faces.

"Yeah," said the blonde with suspicion.

"I'll give her a call," I said. "I'm sure she won't mind you coming to my mother's floor for some goat. Marianne's all about diversity and trying new things. Heck, she'll probably come with you."

The elevator dinged and the doors slid open.

"You won't," said the pigtailed one.

I stepped out and held the door open. "Do you recognize me?"

Aunt Miriam stomped by me with a brand-new cane. "They know who you are." She punched a button with the spiky brass tip. "And I know who they are."

The girls shrank back into a corner in horror.

"Oh, yeah?" I asked.

"Tiffany and Heather. They locked a disabled girl in the bathroom overnight at St. Elias Prep and posted it on the internet," said Aunt Miriam, giving them the laser-focused stink eye.

"We didn't do it," said the blonde with the ultimate confidence of the eternally idiotic.

"You're here, wearing a smock, so I'm thinking you did," I said, letting go of the door. "By the way, Sister Miriam hits."

The doors closed on a couple of terrified squeals and I said, "I feel better."

"Why do you need to feel better? Besides the obvious."

I spun around and Fats stood there, wearing a new set of yoga clothes and a holstered gun. She didn't even bother to wear a jacket to cover it up. All the passers-by were giving her a wide berth, but to be honest, they probably would've done that without the sidearm.

"I don't think you're supposed to open carry in a hospital," I said.

"I'm a licensed bounty hunter," said Fats. "There's nothing to say that I can't apprehend in a hospital."

"That doesn't sound right."

"It isn't. Why do you think I got the license?" Fats started walking me to the exit and I saw two security guards with big eyes watching us from behind a post. The cops really had to get someone on Mom quick if the hospital guards were scared to ask Fats what in the world she was up to.

"Is there anything else I should know about you?" I asked.

"Plenty, but we've got things to do. Why do you have that look on your face?" she asked.

"Why do men have to be jerks?" I asked.

"They aren't jerks to me."

"No?"

She grinned. "I scare them."

"I don't think I have that option."

She gave me an appraising look. "You need a weapon."

"I really do."

Fats took me to my apartment and cleared it for entry. Nobody had been in my place for over a week and it was super musty.

I bent over to pick up a fat manila envelope that had been shoved under my door, but Fats' big hand beat me to it. "I'll be checking that."

"For what?" I asked. "Ricin?"

"You think that's out of the question?" Fats gingerly placed the envelope on my breakfast bar and opened her striped backpack. In with a small collection of literary novels was a hand-held bomb sniffing device, explosive materials wipes, a taser, extra clips, and a couple of gas masks.

"Are we prepared for the apocalypse?" I asked.

Fats handed me a mask. "Yes. You know how to put that on?"

I did and Fats' masks were the same as the ones Dad bought Mom and me. He also gave us a class on how to use them. That was one of the longest Saturdays of my life and that included the time Dad made me take wilderness survival training in the Ozarks. It included digging trenches and worm-eating. But at least I wasn't bored for a change. For the record, I didn't eat a worm and only lasted twenty-seven hours because I passed out from hunger.

"You got a good seal?" asked Fats, her voice weird and muffled.

"This is ridiculous."

"Seal?"

I groaned. "Yes."

Fats used her wipes to check for explosives. Clear. Double-checked with the sniffer and then carefully unsealed the envelope, sliding the stack of paper onto the counter and checking it for powder. There wasn't any.

She gave me a thumbs-up and popped off her mask. I tried to take mine off the way Dad taught me, but it went as well as you might expect. My hair got wrapped around the rubbery straps and buckles.

"Help," I said.

Fats bent over my head, trying to unwind my hair while I glanced at the cover letter on the top of the stack. It was from Dr. Bloom, the history professor from Oxford. He said he'd gotten some interesting information from Big Steve about his mother, Constanza. Also, a man named Spidermonkey had contacted him with information about

Stella Bled Lawrence and he had some information regarding that, too.

I didn't know Spidermonkey had contacted Dr. Bloom. I was going to do that once he confirmed Dr. Bloom was on the up and up.

"How did you do this?" asked Fats as I stuffed the stack back in the envelope.

"My hair hates masks. Scuba's bad, too."

"I don't think I can get it undone. This hair. It's like it's alive."

"It is alive and it kinda hates me," I said.

"I'm not kidding. It's literally rewinding as I'm unwinding, like a Sci-Fi movie and it's an alien."

I laughed and tucked the envelope under my arm. "You're not the first to come up with that theory."

"I'm going to have to cut it," said Fats.

I tried to take off, but she snapped me back by the mask.

"What's your plan? Going to run around with this thing hanging off the back of your head?"

"Okay."

"I'm cutting it off. You look like an idiot."

"That's fine. I'm used to it," I said, making another break for it and failing.

Fats put me on a stool and asked, "Where are your scissors?"

"My mom can get it off. You wouldn't believe the stuff she's gotten off my head. A catcher's mask from the time Dad thought I could be a prodigy. Numerous pairs of sunglasses and the tiara from my first communion. That took her three hours. She's a genius with hair."

"Scissors, Mercy?"

"Nope. You are not going to make me look like I have mange," I said, crossing my arms. "Mom will do it."

Fats looked up from my over-stuffed drawers, her naturally aggressive face slightly softened. "Can she do it with one hand?"

That stopped me. "Um…"

"We've got to cut it. It can't be worse than your hair in Roatan. That was insane, like a blonde Brillo pad."

"Salt water is not my friend," I said, thinking about Mom's hand.

"There's no salt water in Paris," she said. "What happened there?"

"Did you look up all my bad pictures?"

"Not all. There are a lot."

"Thanks. You suck."

"That's what Tiny said." She gave me a huge grin.

I clapped my hands over my ears. "Noooo!"

"Scissors or else I start talking. A lot!" she yelled, grinning like a nutter.

"Drawer next to the fridge."

A few snips and I was free. I felt my head and it wasn't great.

"It's not that bad." Fats set the mask on the counter with three tufts of hair sticking out of the buckles. "You'll have to go with the shorter Marilyn do."

"I'm not trying to look like her, you know."

Fats stepped back and gave me the once-over. "What would happen if you tried?"

"It's creepy."

"I bet."

I took off down the hall. "I'm going to take a shower."

"Good. You stink."

"This day just gets better and better." I went into the bathroom and closed the door on my bodyguard's laughter.

I tossed Dr. Bloom's envelope on the counter next to the sink and hesitantly took a look. From the front I looked okay, greasy and snarly but okay. The back was definitely mangy. Awesome.

Since I couldn't begin to fix it, I took a boiling hot shower in record time. Then I put on a sundress. I'm not usually a sundress kind of girl, but Mom would like it.

I topped it off with a floppy hat and grabbed my Mauser out from between my sweaters. Then I rooted around and got my taser and a spare pepper spray. Remembering that I didn't have any ID, I dug out my passport. With my arms full, I went out to see what Fats was doing. I expected to see her watching *Downton Abbey* since I'd heard the petulant voice of Lady Mary echoing down the hall, but she wasn't watching the TV, where Mary and Edith were snapping at each other. They were enough to make me glad I was an only child.

Fats was reading and quite engrossed with her feet up on the coffee table as she devoured Nikki's baklava.

"What's so interesting?" I asked, grabbing my spare purse and stuffing my self-protection and passport inside. I'd have to see about getting a new driver's license and canceling my credit cards. Why'd he have to steal my purse? The DMV was a serious pain.

"You," said Fats after a minute.

"Me?"

She held up Dr. Bloom's envelope.

"How did you get that?" I snatched the papers out of her hands. "I locked the door."

"Please. You think I can't pick a lock?" Fats stood up. "Ready?"

"How much did you read?"

"Enough to know that you've got something interesting going on."

I marched to the door and flung it open. "This is just what I needed. Let's go."

We trotted down the stairs. Fats stopped me before we went outside. She checked the area and then put me in the truck for the short drive over to Hawthorne Avenue. Mr. Knox wasn't happy, but I swore to him that Grandad hired Fats to protect me and he opened the gate.

My parents' house was easily visible down the block, looking forlorn with all the fluttering crime scene tape and the trampled lawn. Mom was going to freak.

"I have to get a gardener to come fix this before Mom comes home," I said.

"I know a guy," said Fats as she trotted me up the front walk.

"I bet you do."

She smiled a devilish smile and kept an eye out while I let us in. Pounding footsteps came from the back. Fats thrust me out of the way and pulled her weapon. A young uniform ran into the receiving room, fumbling with his sidearm and choking on the enormous sandwich stuffed in his gullet.

"Febreze!" he yelled through the sandwich.

Fats kept her weapon on him. "Did you say 'Febreze'?"

The sandwich split in half and flopped on Mom's hardwood with a splat. "No. Febreze!"

"I'm hearing Febreze," I said, waving at him. "Mercy Watts. This is my parents' house."

The officer lowered his weapon and chewed with the grossest noises ever. Fats holstered her weapon and eyed the sandwich on the floor. "I bet that's your mom's food."

"Yeah. I recognized the bread. Mom makes it. She has a thing for poppyseed."

The officer gagged and turned purple.

"He doesn't look so good," I said with a yawn.

"I'm thinking about saving him," said Fats.

I shrugged. "You could."

"What's in it for me?"

He waved at us frantically and pounded his chest.

"No body to clean up," I said.

"Sold." Fats went behind him and did the Heimlich Maneuver, succeeding with one thrust. He spewed the rest of the sandwich. Part of it hit the wall and an oil painting that Mom bought at a garage sale a couple of years ago. Mom considered it priceless. It was really worth ten bucks, but I'd have to get it cleaned. The river scene was looking pretty gnarly.

"You cracked my ribs," choked out the officer.

Fats popped all the joints on her hands. "Yeah, I do that."

"Hurts."

I skirted his spew. "I don't doubt it. Clean that up, but don't touch the painting."

"Who is she?" he asked between short, sharp breaths.

"Don't worry about me," said Fats. "Get to cleaning."

"Hospital?" he asked, clutching his sides.

I went for the stairs. "Call an ambulance, but I warn you, living this down won't be easy."

His young face went all sad. "You're supposed to be nice."

"Who told you that?"

"Ameche."

"Oh, yeah. I guess I am nice. Keep in mind" —I pointed at the floor— "Ameche didn't do that." I ran up to the second floor to my dad's office and collapsed into his big leather chair before opening the bottom drawer in his battered old cop desk. Actually, opening the drawer was a challenge. Dad had kicked the desk so much the side was heavily dented. I braced my feet against the leg and pulled. It creaked but didn't open.

Fats came around the desk. "Let me do it before you give yourself an aneurysm."

It popped open for Fats. No problem. I suspect it was out of fear.

I went through the files, all unsolved, and found Cassidy Huff's in the middle right under my boyfriend, David's, file. My hand paused on the fairly thin file for a moment. I knew Dad considered David's disappearance unsolved, but I'd never seen the file before.

I eased David out of the way and pulled out Cassidy. Her file wasn't much thicker. Not having a body cuts down on a lot of paperwork.

"Who's Cassidy Huff?" asked Fats.

"Murder victim."

"2002. That's a blast from the past." She pulled up a chair and loomed over me. I thought about fighting it but couldn't work up the energy.

"Blankenship referenced it." I gave her the rundown on what he told me.

"Is that how you got Chuck Watts on the task force?"

I told her about the safe deposit box victim and she said, "Nice."

"He doesn't think so."

"Yeah, well. Men have their pride," said Fats.

"I was trying to help."

She chuckled and opened the file. "Men don't need help. Get with the program."

"I thought I was."

Inside, we found Dad's personal notes. He was super organized and liked bullet statements, which was handy for me.

Cassidy Huff was a high school senior, eighteen years old, blonde, pretty, and athletic. She disappeared from her high school after a Friday soccer practice. Her parents reported her missing when she didn't come home and they found her car in the parking lot. There were no signs of a struggle. Most of her belongings were in the car including her soccer bag and backpack. Her green purse was gone. In her physical description, there was a heart tattoo, but that was added a month after the disappearance. Her parents didn't know she had it. Only her best friend knew. Dad marked the tattoo as "Close Hold", meaning that it wouldn't be released to the public and only denoted in his personal file and his partner's. Dad asked Cassidy's parents and her friend to never tell anyone about the tattoo. From what I could tell, they kept it to themselves. Blankenship did what he said he did and it made me feel as bad as I could possibly feel.

There wasn't much evidence for Dad to go on. No one saw or heard anything. The other members of the team remembered her being in a great mood and going to her car, but that was it. No leads. Not a one, but Dad had a theory and it was Brian Shill, the killer Blankenship named. Shill was a janitor at the high school and was generally described as creepy. He did a good job, but during the investigation, several girls reported him hitting on them and making them uncomfortable with staring and comments. It wasn't technically criminal, but Dad had one of his feelings and he followed up hard on Shill. During a canvass of Cassidy's neighborhood, he found three witnesses who saw Shill on her street, driving slowly. His crappy old Firebird was unusual for the neighborhood. Once Dad knew Shill had scouted the area, he found surveillance footage of Shill driving around nearly every day leading up to Cassidy's disappearance, but he never returned after she was gone.

But all this was circumstantial. Dad interviewed Shill multiple times and he held up well. He passed a polygraph and claimed he was only in the neighborhood to visit friends. He didn't produce any friends and had no alibi and he showed up for work on Monday like nothing happened. That being said, the guy was weird and not well-liked. Shill lived mostly online. I thought since he was an Unsub, he must have other victims, although Blankenship hadn't said so. I'd have to tell Uncle Morty and see what he could come up with. I suppose I should tell Chuck, but he could bite me. Don't want my help? Good luck to you.

"So this guy walked free," said Fats. "What a douche."

I flipped through some witness statements to find an arrest report. "Sort of."

Three years after Cassidy, Dad arrested him for the attempted rape of a fifteen-year-old girl. He served five years and got five years of probation after that. Dad had filed a complaint against the judge, who knew Shill's grandparents, claiming a conflict of interest. It came to nothing. Dad testified at Shill's probation hearing and said he was a serial predator who would reoffend. The board shrugged and released him. He was currently out on bond for employing a minor in an obscene act.

"He's out right now." Fats put a finger on his address. "My parents live a couple of miles from this dirtbag."

"Shill targets teenage girls," I said.

"My little sister is seventeen."

"I'd give them a call."

"On it." Fats called her parents and gave them Shill's address and description. He was a standard white guy, so I doubt that would help much.

I leaned back and put my feet up on the desk. Shill was obviously important. How did that guy in the Unsub group know about him and Cassidy's murder details? 2002 was a long time ago and he did know about her green purse. General law enforcement might know about the purse, but friends and family would definitely know it was gone. Rumors swirled in high schools. Friends told friends, who told co-workers, etc. He could've found out. But as far as I could tell, interest in the case waned pretty quick. No witnesses and no body left the media with nothing to report on, so it was a fairly obscure case. Maybe that's why he picked Cassidy. It was just his bad luck that Blankenship helped Shill.

Fats told her mom goodbye and asked, "Does your father have a file on Blankenship?"

"Maybe." I told her about Donatella Berry and how I met Blankenship. "Dad didn't do much with the case and he didn't investigate the Tulio murders."

"Mind if I take a look?" she asked.

"Knock yourself out."

Fats went through Dad's files and found one on Blankenship. It only contained my information and some light background, but she read it anyway. I typed notes on Shill into my phone and thought about how he could possibly be connected to the Hispanic guy. It's not like Shill was full up on friends and asking someone to go to Hunt and stalk my Mom was a big favor. Maybe another Unsub member, but Blankenship got pleasure out of disposing of Cassidy's body. There'd be no pleasure in interviewing Blankenship—I should know—and the hospital was high-risk. Why would anyone agree to that?

"What's this?" asked Fats.

I looked up from Shill's file. "What?"

She'd gone through Dad's inbox and held out a letter from Dad's insurance. "Your mom had an accident."

"When?" I took the letter and the creepiest, crawliest feeling came over me as I read it. "Holy crap."

"Why is the day important?" asked Fats.

"Because I wasn't here. It happened the day I flew to Paris. Mom mentioned that she'd had a fender bender, but she wasn't hurt so I didn't think much about it."

"It wasn't a fender bender. The car was totaled."

I scanned the insurance claim twice. The details were sketchy, but one thing stood out. "It was a hit and run."

Fats sat on the edge of Dad's desk, making it creak. "And your parents' insurance had to pay out—"

"Because they never found the other driver," I said.

"I'm thinking that might have been the first attempt on your mother's life."

"And it might've caused her stroke," I said.

"How do you figure that?" she asked. "It was two months ago."

"One of Mom's doctors thinks a dissection caused the stroke. Car accidents can cause a dissection in the carotid artery, a clot builds up at the site, and they have a stroke later."

"Months later?"

"It happens," I said. "Is there a police report in the box?"

Fats leafed through and shook her head. "I don't see one. Seems like your dad would have one. He tracks everything else."

"He should, but maybe Claire was supposed to get it or it could be at her apartment. She takes stuff home. Can you check and see if there's a file on my mom?"

Fats went through Dad's filing cabinets and I called Uncle Morty. He was thrilled as you might imagine. "Whaddaya want?"

"Mom totaled her car in a hit and run," I said in a rush.

He paused and the clicking keys in the background stopped. "Yeah. What about it?"

"I need the police report."

"Tommy should have it."

I looked at Fats and she shook her head.

"I can't find it," I said.

The clicking started up again. "I'll get it. What are you thinking?"

"I don't know. It depends on the circumstances. Mom's a great driver. What happened? She acted like it was nothing."

"It wasn't nothing, but Tommy taught her well. His defensive driving training paid off."

"Um…what would've happened if Mom didn't have skills?" I asked, wincing in anticipation of the response.

"Oh, she'd be dead as hell."

"Tell me." I held out the phone for Fats to hear.

On that day in June, Mom had been returning from interviewing a witness for Dad in Illinois. She was on 270 passing over I44 when a SUV came up at high speed behind her. Mom saw it and anticipated them ramming her into the semi in front of her. Instead of jerking her wheel to the right as one might do on instinct, Mom went left. Her car hit the back left corner of the semi and was pinned briefly between the semi and the SUV with the SUV crushing the rear driver's side door. Mom's airbag deployed and the SUV slammed on its brakes, freeing itself from Mom's car and speeding off.

Uncle Morty said that the responding officer called it a miracle that Mom survived. She was sore from the airbag, but that was it. She could've easily been launched off the bridge or been crushed when the car was rammed under the semi. No one got a look at the other driver. Mom said he was a middle-aged white male, but that was just her impression a second before he hit her.

"Nobody thought this was suspicious?" I asked.

"I do now, but then...hell, who would want to kill Carolina? Tommy, I can see, and you, of course, but Carolina, no. She's not the hell-raiser around these parts. We thought it was careless driving, an accident."

"Well, someone has a problem with her. With all of us, I guess."

"Looks like it. You do anything to piss people off?" growled Uncle Morty. "What am I saying—you did. You're a trouble magnet."

"This can't be about me. He was working on siccing Cheryl on Grandad for months. Look at him."

Uncle Morty snorted. "Ace has been a professional whittler for the last ten years. It ain't him."

"Well, it's not me. All the people who hate me that bad are in prison."

"Yeah, my money's on Tommy, but why not kill him?"

"It could be a random lunatic who picked your family because of the media coverage," said Fats.

Uncle Morty stopped typing. "Who the hell is that?"

"Er...my bodyguard. Grandad got her for me," I said quickly.

"Ace hired a freaking girl?" he growled.

Fats slammed her fist on the desk and added a new dent. "Look, you old dump truck. I'm not a girl. I'm a professional."

"A professional what?"

"Bodyguard, obviously," I said.

"What's your name, bodyguard?" Uncle Morty couldn't have been more sarcastic and that's saying something. He was a master.

"Mary Elizabeth," I said. "You and Grandad come up with a name? We have to put someone in with Mom."

He ignored that and said, "You're being protected by a Mary Elizabeth? That's freaking ridiculous."

"You are a chauvinist pig," said Fats.

"What of it? Mercy needs a 200-pound gorilla next to her not some chick with penis envy."

"Old man, I could crack you open like a nut."

"Come here and try it," he said.

What is happening?

"Did you hit your head?" I asked.

"Who you talking to?" asked Uncle Morty.

"You, of course. Since when do you think women can't do stuff?"

"Women can do all kinds of stuff, but I don't want no *Mary Elizabeth* protecting you. End of story. Tiny can watch you."

"I'm calling Nikki."

"Huh?"

I shoved Cassidy's file back in the drawer and slammed it shut. Wow, that felt good. "I'm going to call your girlfriend and tell her that you think a woman's name is cause to fire her, 'cause obviously, she's incompetent."

"That ain't what I meant." He was gruff, but I heard a hint of nervousness. "You need somebody who can take a bullet."

"Whatever. I'm keeping her and *I'm* calling Tiny. Dad would want him with Mom. She's still a target and he's family."

"He's already here," said Uncle Morty, noticeably more subdued. "I'll tell him."

"We need to get The Girls another chauffeur." My stomach got queasy. "Unless they could be a target, too."

"They ain't family. He's only hitting the family."

Fats and I exchanged a look. Whatever was in Dr. Bloom's file clued her in that the whole family question was in play.

"But they're closely associated with us like family."

"Yeah, the old bats have been hanging around forever, but I got nobody to put on them without Tommy's connections."

Fats held up a finger. "I have somebody."

This is so going to bite me in the butt.

I cringed. "Who?"

"My brother."

Uncle Morty groused, "Ace know him?"

"I don't know. Ask him," she said.

"Alright. In for a dime, in for a freaking dollar. What's the name?" he asked.

Please don't say Knuckles or Icepick.

"Rocco," said Fats. "Rocco Licata."

Not much better.

"So ask Grandad about" —*God help me*— "Rocco," I said. "I'm coming back. Mom's got a test in a half hour. Any word from Nana and Pop Pop?"

"They got here an hour ago. They're in with her now. Nurse made an exception."

"Thank goodness. And they're okay. Nothing happened."

"Hell yeah, they're fine, but freaking exhausted. Had to drive after your hissy fit."

Fats raised an eyebrow at me and I shrugged.

I hung up and stretched. "Does Rocco work for Calpurnia?"

"Occasionally, when she needs some extra muscle. He's mainly a golf pro with Oz."

"I'm glad you didn't mention that." I left the office and ran down the stairs to find the officer still scrubbing the floor.

"It's clean," I said. "You're going to strip off the poly."

He got to his feet and eyed me warily. "Are you going to..."

"Tell my parents? We'll let this one slide. Don't run with a sandwich in your mouth. It's not a good idea."

"Tell me about it. My throat's killing me."

"My mom's got a collection of lozenges in the drawer next to the sink. Help yourself."

The officer looked doubtful.

"If my mother were here, she'd give you a lozenge and probably bake you a cake. Fix your throat."

He nodded and we left, trotting down the front stairs in the increasingly hot August sun.

"I'm thinking you might want to keep me on after this is all over," said Fats.

"Oh, yeah, 'cause I'm dying for you to meet my dad. That would totally make my life better."

"Better that than dead." I got in the truck and turned to her as she got in. "What makes you think I might get dead? I mean, other than this whole mess we're dealing with?"

"I've heard of The Klinefeld Group before. They're not the kind of people you mess with and you're messing with them."

Great.

CHAPTER THIRTEEN

Fats did know about The Klinefeld Group and it was not good news. Of course, nothing with them was, so I don't know why I was surprised. A couple of years ago, they'd approached Calpurnia with an offer. They'd help her expand her operations into Eastern Europe, if she'd do them the teensiest favor—help them get control of the board of the art museum. Why they wanted control wasn't part of the deal and Calpurnia turned them down flat. She might be the head of mafia family, but she wasn't for sale and she didn't care for outsiders interfering in St. Louis's affairs. They went elsewhere and were rewarded with two seats on the board, according to Fats. The new board members were from St. Louis, but they answered to The Klinefeld Group. This was the board that cooperated with the lawsuit against Myrtle and Millicent in a blatant attempt to get control of The Bled Collection.

"I always wondered how they got the board to go along with that crap. The Girls are generous to the art community and what some of the board members said about them and later about Stella was vile."

"Getting the board to go along isn't really the right question," said Fats.

"No? What is?"

"What happened to the board members that their hired hands replaced?"

I looked sideways at her. "Retired?"

"Dead."

"When you say dead, do you mean murdered?"

She fired a finger gun at me. "Calpurnia was seriously offended. As if she's in the business of hiring out hitmen."

I decided not to broach that subject since I had no doubt that Calpurnia would have someone killed if it suited her purpose. "I don't remember any museum people getting murdered."

"Well, you wouldn't, would you? Not if the job were done right. One died of carbon monoxide poisoning and the other committed suicide."

I didn't know what to say to that, so I said nothing. It wasn't beyond the realm, considering Agatha and Daniel's plane crash and Lester's murder.

Fats dropped me at the front door of the hospital with Tiny. They kissed and made plans for later, a romantic dinner on the hospital roof if they could get Rocco on board to hang with me and Mom.

Tiny practically dragged me inside. My stumpy legs couldn't keep up with his tree trunks.

"So, what did she say?" he asked.

"A whole lot. I don't want to talk about it," I said.

Tiny's face fell. "Damn. I thought I was in there."

I blinked and craned my neck up to look at my cousin's face so far above my own. "In where?"

"With Fats. That woman. I thought we had something special. The way she kisses make a man forget his name. Last night—"

"She likes you. A lot. So much that you never have to talk about the two of you again. Ever."

The elevator doors dinged and opened. The candy-stripers from before were in there.

"Oh my god!" exclaimed the blonde, woodpeckering the buttons.

"I'll scream!" yelled the one with pigtails.

Tiny put a heavy hand on my shoulder. "You know them?"

"We've met," I said.

"You make an impression."

The doors started to close and Tiny put his hand out to stop it. The girls screeched and I pushed his hand down. "Let them go."

"Maybe it was me. I make an impression, too," said Tiny.

"You're a gentle giant." I pushed the *Up* button again. "It might have something to do with Aunt Miriam."

"Oh, lord."

"You have no idea."

"I know you've got new bruises."

I looked down. "Oh, yeah. She does know how to get my attention."

"And theirs, too."

We laughed as we rode up to Mom's floor. Chuck and Sidney weren't there anymore, thankfully, and The Girls were standing in the hall with Grandad.

"Mercy, my dear," said Myrtle, coming over to kiss my cheeks. "How are you?"

"I'm fine." I exchanged kisses with Millicent.

"Are Nana and Pop Pop still in there?" I asked.

"No, dear. They've gone down to the cafeteria," said Myrtle.

Nikki came out of the waiting room with her ginormous purse. "I will have dinner here in two hours, but I guess they're hungry now."

Millicent took Nikki's hand. "They will enjoy your lovely dinner later. They aren't hungry. They needed to get away."

"Of course. Seeing their daughter in the ICU must've been terrible." Nikki ordered me to go eat the array of antipasti Aaron had brought over and took off, presumably to get the goat. Gag. If it was anything like crab, my life was going down the tubes.

"How upset are they?" I asked. "Should I go find them?"

"Let them have some time. They've dealt with tragedy before. Your grandparents are strong people."

An opening. Yes.

"I probably made it worse," I said, doing the hound dog eyes.

Grandad shot me a look.

"Whatever do you mean?" asked Millicent.

"I made them drive." I told them about the private plane thing.

"I'm sure that has nothing to do with how they're feeling," said Myrtle.

"I couldn't bear it if something happened to them."

Grandad crossed his bony arms and said, "Mercy."

"Agatha and Daniel being murdered was bad enough," I said. "But it could happen again."

The openness vanished, quickly replaced by distant expressions similar to the ones they used to have when they grounded me.

"It won't happen again," said Myrtle.

"Why not?" I asked.

"Because we're not sure it happened in the first place," said Millicent.

I crossed my arms just like Grandad and said, "Aunt Tenne told me what happened."

"It wasn't proven, dear."

They knew it was murder. I could see it in their shifty eyes. "Sounds like murder to me and I'm getting good at this stuff."

"That's true," said Myrtle. "You're very talented, but why would anyone murder your great-grandparents? It doesn't make any sense."

"It doesn't have to make sense to us," I said. "And whatever the reason, it sounds like it died with them."

Millicent and Myrtle appraised me quietly. "How would you know that?"

Be careful.

"Aunt Tenne said no one was arrested and no motive found."

The Girls hooked their arms through mine, their faces now wreathed with relieved smiles. Grandad wasn't buying it. His blue eyes evaluated me from under half-lowered lids. I knew that look. He was thinking and that wasn't good for me.

The Girls started to lead me into the waiting room. "How much do you know about Agatha and Daniel?" asked Millicent.

"Almost nothing," I said. "I've seen their tombs in New Orleans, but nobody talks about them."

"You should visit their memorial," said Millicent. "It's a lovely spot."

"Carolina could never bear to go, but we've been several times with Caro and Henry," said Myrtle.

I stopped walking. "You went with Nana and Pop Pop? When did you go to New Orleans? Recently?"

"Not New Orleans, dear," said Myrtle. "The memorial is just outside St. Sebastian. You should really go."

"Why in the world is the memorial there?"

The Girls tilted their head in exactly the same way. Sometimes, people thought they were twins when they did that. "Because that's where it happened," said Millicent. "Didn't you know?"

St. Seb? What the what?

"I guess I thought it was...farther south."

"Come. You should have something to eat," said Myrtle.

The ICU door opened and Aunt Tenne came out. "Thank goodness you're back. I thought I was going to have to go to that test."

"No, no. I'll do it," I said.

Behind Aunt Tenne, Mom was wheeled out on a gurney and followed by a young cop who'd been assigned to her. Mom didn't look happy. "I could've just walked."

"You haven't been evaluated by physical therapy, so no walking."

"You're coming?"

"Of course," I said.

"Tenne said you talked to your father," said Mom hopefully.

"I did. He's on his way." *I hope.*

Wallace was running in circles at the foot of Mom's bed and I picked her up. "Wallace should stay here."

"No," said Mom. "I need her."

"She can't be in with you during the test."

Mom began to look shaky, so I got Aunt Tenne to carry Wallace. We left everyone and went down to the cardiac lab. Officer Gish checked the room for unauthorized personnel and Aunt Tenne stayed outside with the pug, who was not happy about it.

I heard Aunt Tenne exclaim through the closed doors. "Don't bite me, you overgrown weasel."

The procedure nurse looked at me. "What kind of therapy dog is that?"

"She's...special," I said.

"Wallace is a wonderful dog," said Mom. "So sweet. So patient."

"Dear Lord! She peed on me!" yelled Aunt Tenne.

I ran out with Officer Gish and found Aunt Tenne standing as far from Wallace as possible with the pug at the end of her rhinestone leash and looking adorable. Gish groaned and muttered, "Of course this would happen." I guess getting stuck with us wasn't high on his list of fun things to do.

"Something is wrong with this dog," said Aunt Tenne. "She peed on my feet. I think she did it on purpose."

"Oh, she did it on purpose alright. She's Wallace the Wonder Pug."

"What are you talking about?"

"Google it." I ran to the bathroom for some paper towels and returned, giving them to Aunt Tenne and Gish. "I have to go back in. Be careful. She'll do it again."

"Not possible. It had to be a whole cup. She's a tiny dog," said Aunt Tenne.

"Trust me. There's more where that came from. I have like two pairs of shoes left."

Bark. Bark. Bark.

"It wasn't a compliment, Wallace," I said. "If you pee on my aunt again, I'll change your online persona to Wallace the incontinent pug."

Grr.

"Mercy, you're talking to that dog like she understands English."

"She understands." I pointed at Wallace and she plopped down on her wrinkly butt. "I'm watching, dog."

Aunt Tenne touched my arm. "I'm concerned about you."

"Join the club. I have to go back."

I returned to Mom as they were setting up the equipment.

"Is this like an x-ray?" Mom asked.

I'd given her a short explanation on the way down, but I hadn't gotten into the details. In short, I wussed out.

"It's to look at your heart from the back so we can see if you have a hole that might've caused your stroke."

Mom gave me the stink eye. "How are you going to do that?"

"Don't worry, Carolina," said the nurse. Her name was Nellie and she was a little more jittery than I would've liked. "We do these all the time."

"That doesn't answer my question."

"You're going to swallow a probe," I said. "It's not that big."

Mom's eyes got huge and she started grabbing at the sheet.

Nellie patted her leg. "We're going to give you a sedative, but you'll stay awake and be able to follow commands."

"Why would I want to stay awake? Knock me out."

"We can't, Carolina. We need you to hold your breath and exhale on command."

"What does the probe look like?" Mom asked.

Nellie held it up and it didn't look so bad to me, but, then again, I didn't have to swallow it. "I'll spray your throat with an anesthetic to numb it. You'll hardly feel anything."

That was such a load of crap I almost snorted, but I turned it into a cough instead.

Mom turned the stink eye on me. "Was this your idea?"

"What? Me? No."

"You sound guilty."

"The cardiologist ordered the test, Mom, not me."

Nellie gave us a big smile. "We're all set up here. I'll go get your sedative and check on when Dr. Reddy will be here.' She left and Mom glared at me.

"Seriously, Mom, it only takes twenty minutes."

"Twenty minutes? Are you crazy?"

"It's not that long," I said.

Mom balled up her fists. "You do it."

"I can't. You had the stroke."

"That's what they all say."

I took her hand and squeezed it. "I don't know what to do with that, but I'll be right here."

"As if that helps," she said.

"It's supposed to."

Mom made a strangled noise that I supposed was a snort. This was going to be fun.

"Mercy!" yelled Aunt Tenne. "Come get this dog."

I ran out the door and found Aunt Tenne and Gish standing next to a fresh puddle.

"Come on, Wallace," I said. "They're going to kick you out. Therapy dogs don't pee in the hospital."

Grr.

"They don't. It's a fact." I ran and got more paper towels.

"You know what," said Aunt Tenne. "I'll do the test. You take the dog. You have experience."

"All bad."

Grr.

"Don't growl at me. You're a bad dog. I have to call housekeeping and schmooze them."

Bark.

"So we'll switch?" asked Aunt Tenne.

"Sure, but I warn you, Mom is not happy," I said.

Aunt Tenne brushed a lock of hair out of her eyes and said, "I'm her sister. I can handle it."

I was by no means sure she could, but I agreed. I called house-keeping on the wall phone and she went inside for a split second and then poked her head out. "Where is she?"

"In there."

"Where?"

"In the room you're in," I said, feeling exhausted from explaining the ridiculously simple.

"No, she's not."

Oh my God!

I looked through the door and Mom's gurney was empty.

"Oh, crap!" said Gish, running through the door while pulling his piece.

"Can she walk?" asked Aunt Tenne.

"Apparently. Here." I thrusted Wallace's leash at her and ran through the lab. There was a second exit into an office and that's where I found my mother, pushing her IV pole, barefoot with her gown tucked up into her panties.

"Mom! Where are you going?" I chased her through the office with Gish at my heels. I guess we didn't need physical therapy so much.

"I'm not doing it."

"You have to do it."

"No. Thank you. I'm going home," said Mom, banging her hip on a desk because she couldn't corner.

"You can't go home. You just had neurosurgery."

"I survived that just fine. I am not swallowing any probe for you or anyone else."

I pulled out the big guns. "How about Dad?"

"Your father won't care. He always wants me to be happy." Mom was tiring. She couldn't make it to the other door. I caught her around the waist and lowered her into a chair.

Mom sighed. "I'm so tired and I have another headache."

Gish was almost as tired. He nearly keeled over in relief.

A nurse came in and started when she saw us. "What are you doing in here?"

"Tell the Cardiac lab that we have a runner."

"Wheelchair?" she asked.

"No," said Mom.

"Yes, please," I said.

"Why are you so difficult?" asked Mom. "You've always been difficult."

"That's what you pay me for." I squatted in front of her. "Dad loves you. He'll want to know why this happened."

"What does it matter? They put me on those shots and pills," she said. "Pete said I'd be on the pills for life."

"If it's the heart, we might be able to repair it," I said.

"Repair it? Why didn't you say so? Where's that wheelchair?"

Mom swallowed her probe and by the end of it, *I* needed a sedative. It was that hard to watch her in distress. Another one for the list of things never to do again.

Mom didn't return to the ICU. We took her directly to a regular floor and my anxiety level went up twenty notches. Anybody could walk right onto the floor and it was freaking me out. Officer Gish stood outside while we transferred Mom to the bed, but it wasn't much of a comfort. If I could've put her in a vault, I would've.

But in a few hours, I wouldn't need a vault. Dad was on a flight to Chicago. He'd change planes there and land at one in the morning. As soon as Uncle Morty confirmed Dad was actually on the flight, Agent Hatchet Nose showed up without being told, blowing past Gish with a flip of the badge.

"Get out," I said, stepping between him and the bed.

"We had a deal," he said.

Mom leaned to the side, grabbing her side rail and peeking around me. "What deal?"

"The one I had to make to get Dad back," I said.

"We've fulfilled our part," said Hatchet Nose. "I want the location."

I pushed him out of the room with Mom calling after us that she wanted to know what I had. I gave Hatchet Nose the location of the burial ground in Kansas. He got on the phone, ordering a full out CSI assault on the area. By the sound of it, Uncle Morty's pics were pretty convincing.

He hung up and tried to dart by me into Mom's room, but I was ready for that and blocked him so fast that he ran into me. "Back off," I said with a gesture to Gish for help. The officer wasn't enthusiastic about standing up to the FBI. I had no such problem. "You're not going in."

"I need to interview your mother," said Hatchet nose.

"Nope."

"You don't want me to solve this?"

I blocked him again. "You won't be the one to solve it. That's all Tommy Watts."

"Your father isn't as gifted as you think he is."

"Then why did you bother to hold him back?"

"Not my call," he said, making another break for it. He shoved me into the door frame and Gish exclaimed, "Hey!" The officer wasn't fast enough to nab Hatchet Nose, but that wasn't a problem. Tiny stepped in front of the agent and he bounced off my cousin's broad chest and hit the wall.

Tiny held up a finger. "Didn't your mama teach you that no means no?"

"Where'd you come from?" I asked.

"Bathroom," said Tiny.

"I am going to interview her," said Hatchet Nose, gathering the shredded remnants of his dignity.

Mom called out from behind Tiny, "Even if you got in, I have nothing to say to you!"

The agent went stiff and did an about face. "Your father will have her talk to me."

"Don't count on it," I said. "But since I'm such a nice person, I'll let you in on something. She doesn't remember anything of value, so you may as well beat it."

Hatchet Nose didn't reply. He left, which was all I wanted.

"Is he gone?" asked Mom. I couldn't see her with Tiny being so huge.

"Yep," I said. "Tiny's the best barrier ever."

He spread out his arms and grinned. "Size has its advantages."

"I bet you've never used a step stool in your life."

"I was taller than you in the fifth grade." Tiny went and wedged himself in the armchair beside Mom's bed and handed her the water mug she was trying to reach.

"My throat hurts," said Mom.

"I'll get you some ice cream," I said.

"I'm not hungry anymore."

"I know, but you need to eat."

Mom's lower lip poked out, but I didn't budge. She was going to eat.

"Did someone mention eating?" Nikki walked in, carrying an enormous platter. She could've fit an entire goat on that thing.

"Mom claims she's not hungry," I said.

"I don't want to hear anything about not eating." Mom's best friend, Dixie, appeared behind Nikki and Mom burst into tears.

"Now, none of that." Dixie lowered Mom's side rail and got right into bed with her. After twelve hours of driving, that woman looked more together than I did on any given day. Her hair was in a perfect

French twist and her makeup flawless. Dixie had a forties movie star quality that I always envied. She looked like she'd stepped off the MGM lot at any given moment.

"I'm so glad you're here," snuffled Mom.

Uncle Morty stomped in. "I guess the rest of us are chopped liver."

Mom blew her nose. "Hardly."

"Good. Let's eat."

Aaron trotted in with another platter and put it on the foot of Mom's bed. She was so short it fit with room to spare. Nana and Pop Pop were behind him and they looked like they'd driven for twelve hours. Nana's blonde hair looked like she'd been in a hurricane and Pop Pop had bags under his brown eyes that reminded me of swag curtains. They hugged me until they ran out of energy. Then we ate. Mom got a malt and we got goat. And not just goat. Goat five ways. Nikki had roasted a full-sized goat in her father's special goat-roasting pit. Who knew people had pits for that?

Nikki loaded up a plate for me and the big winners were her goat gyros with some kind of fabulous garlicky sauce and Aaron's Moroccan goat burger. Goat wasn't like crab. I could eat that burger every day and I just might. Aaron was going to put it on the Kronos menu after I gave it a great review. The little weirdo was so happy he was vibrating. Everyone loved the goat, including Myrtle and Millicent. Mom's room was so packed we could hardly move, but nobody minded.

After the main courses, Uncle Morty produced a bottle of champagne and announced that my dad was on his way back. We toasted and Mom wept in joy. I was so happy and full of goat that I couldn't bother to be nervous about it.

While we were eating Nikki's dessert, a sticky semolina cake that didn't look good but tasted great, Fats and her brother, Rocco, showed up. They didn't make it all the way in. That wasn't possible, even though Rocco didn't fill up a room the way his sister did. He was only about five-ten, extremely fit but not hulking. Uncle Morty gave him the thumbs-up and Rocco drove The Girls home.

Uncle Morty whispered to me. "Interesting how Ace knows the Licata family. I have to check that out."

I just nodded, afraid I'd give myself away.

He leaned closer. "Feds found the burial site with no problem. It wasn't hidden."

"I'm kinda afraid to ask but was that a foot in the picture?"

"Oh, yeah," he said. "From what they're saying, it was a fresh one."

My heart sank. "How fresh?"

Uncle Morty clapped me on the back, almost making me spew goat. "Look at you getting all guilty. That body was three days old at least."

"Thank God."

"You done good. You gonna eat the rest of that burger?"

Uncle Morty cleaned my plate and left with everyone else at nine. Everyone except Aaron. He stood beside Mom's bed, watching her sleep. It would've been a bit creepy if I hadn't been sure he was only trying to figure how to feed her more.

Tiny had come back from his romantic dinner with Fats on the roof. If I went by the sweat on his brow, more than eating went on, which didn't bear thinking about. Tiny rhapsodized about Fats for a good ten minutes before he situated himself between Mom and the door and started snoring. You'd think a bodyguard should stay awake, but, with Tiny, it wasn't necessary. You'd have a hard time getting the door open with him there and you'd have to climb over his body to reach Mom. I felt the stress start to drain off me as I settled into the fold-out chair/bed.

"You're going to have to pole vault over Tiny," I said to Aaron. "Good luck with that."

"No," he said, looking to the left of my face.

"No what?"

He didn't answer, as usual, but pulled out a crusty backpack from under Mom's bed. He handed me a thermos and a chipped mug the size of a large measuring cup. The thermos contained my favorite style of hot chocolate, French with no flavoring except incredible chocolate from Belgium.

"You always know what I need," I said after a sip.

"Yeah."

"You're staying, I take it?"

"Yeah." With that, Aaron curled up in a ball at the foot of Mom's bed with Wallace and immediately began snoring in rhythm with Tiny.

I covered him with a blanket and settled down in my chair with thoughts of Dad comforting me. My father would be arriving in a few hours and he'd take over, the way he always did, bossy with a load of ultimate confidence. It would be fine. Mom's attacker was as good as caught.

But as Grandma Fontaine said in *Gone with the Wind*, "Don't think you can lay down the load, ever. Because you can't."

CHAPTER FOURTEEN

I knew something was wrong before I opened my eyes and it wasn't just the cloud of stank pug breath I was enveloped in. I felt good, all warm and relaxed, and that wasn't right. I was in a hospital. They were a lot of things, but relaxing isn't one of them.

Bark.

"No." I didn't want to wake up and face it.

Bark.

"Nope."

Wallace nudged my chin with her slimy nose and I snuck a peek. The pug was right in my face, breathing like she'd run a mile with her slobbery tongue hanging out. I groaned, "What's your problem?"

But even as I said it, I knew. Mom's room had the glowing warm morning light flowing though the drawn curtains, not to mention the chorus of snores from Aaron and Tiny. I turned over and Mom was looking at me, her green eyes sad. "He didn't come."

He didn't. There was no possible way that Dad arrived in St. Louis and didn't come to Mom's bedside. Something happened. Part of me wanted to cry, but a bigger part wanted to hit someone, specifically Hatchet Nose. This was the FBI's doing. I had no doubt about that.

I tucked Wallace under my arm and whispered, "I'm going to walk Wallace and figure out where Dad is."

Mom bit her lip.

"I will. I swear. They're not going to keep him from you."

She nodded. "Take your bodyguard."

"No problem."

Tiny was a problem. I didn't want to wake him, but I couldn't see a way around it. I tiptoed around Mom's bed and squatted. Maybe I could crawl under his chair. Nope. Not enough room. I stood up and found Tiny watching me. "Tommy didn't come."

"I know."

"I called Morty at two. He's on it." Tiny got to his feet and opened the door for me.

"Thanks," I said. "I'm going to walk Wallace and check in with Morty."

He checked his phone. "Fats is on her way. Should be here at six on the dot. Don't be going out without her or Chuck." He gave me a sly look.

"Chuck is not part of the equation right now." I clipped on Wallace's leash and headed out the door while calling Uncle Morty.

"Yeah." Uncle Morty's voice was oddly gentle. "Whaddya want?"

"Where's Dad?" I asked.

"Chicago."

"What the hell? There's no weather. I checked last night."

"It ain't weather."

And it wasn't the FBI, not technically, anyway. Dad's plane had arrived in Chicago right on time. He got on his flight to St. Louis as expected and then proceeded to sit on the runway for over three hours. At first, it was fuel. Then water. Then mechanical failure. They wouldn't let anyone off and the passengers were getting restless. Dad, at his charming best, had made friends with everyone on the flight. They all knew where he was going and why. Several passengers had seen Mom's attack on the news and they were sympathetic. One of them had overheard the flight attendants talking. They were just as exhausted and pissed. Their conversation confirmed that nothing was wrong. The flight was being held for reasons they didn't know.

The passenger told Dad and he lost it, demanding to be let off the flight and citing some rule about letting people off after three hours on the tarmac. The other passengers joined in. Nobody got violent and they finally went back to the gate after four hours. The passengers were let off and Dad was arrested by Homeland Security for causing a disturbance on a flight. They still had him in custody.

"They did that on purpose," I said, tears of rage filling my eyes.

"Yep."

"What do we do?"

"Big Steve's flying up. He'll get him out." That's what Uncle Morty said, but I heard the doubt in his voice.

"They're the government. They can hold him for all kinds of stuff."

He was quiet.

"Why are they doing this? It can't be just keeping Dad from solving Mom's attack. What do they care? Dad gets all kinds of glory. Why this case? Why now?"

"I'm working on it," he said.

"Any leads?"

"They got this wrapped up tight."

That was the last thing I wanted to hear. If it was on a computer, Uncle Morty could get access. If it wasn't, Dad was screwed.

"I'm going to interview Shill," I said, mostly because I couldn't think of anything else to do.

"Hell, no, you ain't. He murdered that girl and she's probably not the only one."

"People have tried to murder me before. It hasn't worked out for them."

Uncle Morty chuckled deeply. "You sound like Tommy, but you're all hat and no cattle."

I pushed the button for the elevator and said, "Hey. I've got all kinds of cattle. I killed Richard Costilla. Shot him right in the face."

A woman who'd joined me at the elevator, lured over by the so-called pug adorableness, backed away slowly like I was waving a handgun. I covered the phone and said, "It's okay. He was trying to stab me. Self-defense."

It didn't help. She literally turned around and ran away. Some people. I get to shoot people in the face when they're trying to stab me to death. Look it up, woman.

"What was that?" asked Uncle Morty.

"Nothing. I just scared the crap out of some woman."

"Fats? That woman's a beast."

"No," I said. "It wasn't Fats. I can scare people, ya know."

"Whatever. I don't want you interviewing that Shill."

"I'll take Fats. Her mere presence might terrify the name of our unknown Unsub out of him."

Uncle Morty thought it over and said, "That's a decent idea."

"Don't sound so surprised," I said.

"Your ideas run the gamut. You jumped off that damn bridge like a freaking idiot."

"Why does everyone act like that was stupid? I was saving Angela Riley."

"Still stupid."

"Not."

"Was."

The elevator dinged and the doors opened, revealing Chuck and Sidney, looking exhausted and dirty. I'd never seen Chuck dirty like that before, like with actual dirt all over him. This couldn't be a good sign.

"Got to go." I hung up amid protests.

"Where are you going?" asked Chuck abruptly.

Sidney punched him in the shoulder. "We talked about this."

They walked off the elevator and I went to get on, but Sidney snagged me. "We need to talk to you. It's important."

I glared at Chuck. "Will insults be included?"

Spots of pink appeared on Chuck's chiseled cheeks and he had the good sense to appear embarrassed, even if he wasn't. "I'm sorry. I shouldn't have said that. I know you weren't doing anything wrong."

My hands went to my hips. "Oh, yeah?"

"Yeah."

Sidney pulled me away from the elevators, where people were gathering and keenly interested in us. "He's sorry, I swear. We've got to talk to you. Is there a room somewhere?"

"A room? Is it Dad? Why can't you tell me here?" My stomach lurched. For a second, I thought I might hurl right there.

"Tommy's fine," said Chuck. "Wait a minute. Isn't he here with Carolina?"

I told them about Chicago and they kept a lid on the cursing.

"We need a place to talk," said Sidney.

"Fine." I called down the hall to a nurse. "Do you have an empty room we can use for a minute?"

She said Room 23 was empty for the moment and the detectives hustled me down there and closed the door.

I leaned on the foot of the bed. "Well?"

"We found Denny," said Chuck softly.

"Dead, I assume."

"Shot multiple times. We believe he was killed at your parents' house."

I went to the window and looked out on the busy street, coming alive on a sunny Monday morning. Denny was dead. The heavy weight of grief nearly buckled my knees and I grabbed the sill for support.

"How well did you know him?" asked Sydney, poised to write down whatever I said on an old school pad.

Denny was Dad's first hire when he retired and set up his own shop, but I'd met him before that. David's dad hired him to look into his son's case. He was at the trial of the homeless man they pinned it on. Denny was very kind to me when the defense called me and I had to say things I didn't want to say. He never believed the conviction was right any more than my father did. Dad liked Denny instantly and his attention to detail, his absolute commitment to each and every client. He had a wife and three kids. He liked to waterski and brew beer. He hated salmon, but he loved trout. His birthday was in four days and they were supposed to go to Myrtle Beach in a couple weeks.

My mind wouldn't stop swirling on the details of Denny, how he was dead, and Mom wasn't. I couldn't understand it. Like David's disappearance, maybe I never would.

"Not that well," I said.

"Mercy," said Chuck. "Your mother was left alive. He could've killed her easily, but he didn't. He killed Denny and..."

"And?" I asked without looking back at him.

"And there's evidence that some of the shots were fired after Denny was already dead."

"There's a lot of rage in that act," said Sydney. "Denny may have been the target after all."

"No," I said.

Sydney came closer. "Why do you say that?"

"Because it's not Denny. I don't know what happened. Maybe he went outside to take out the trash, surprised the guy, and he shot him. Mom heard and ran outside in her bare feet. If you want to murder Denny, you don't come to Tommy Watts' house. That's just asking for problems. But Mom, she's fairly quiet. She's a homebody if she's not doing something for Dad or charity."

"Okay," said Chuck. "Then why not kill her or kidnap her? It was the perfect opportunity."

I turned around to face him, wrapping my arms around myself against the chill that may or may not have been in the room. "He was probably going to kill her, but the stroke stopped him."

Sydney rubbed his bald head like he was trying to make sparks. "So she had a stroke. So what?"

"Time is brain," I said, my mind working furiously. I could see Mom on the ground, her eyes locked, nearly half her brain gone.

Chuck came up slowly as if he thought he might startle me. "It's been a long couple of days. Maybe—"

"Shush," I said. "I'm thinking."

The detectives backed off, watching me with pensive expressions.

"It was a Saturday afternoon. Dad was gone. I have to check Mom's calendar, but I doubt she was doing anything. No. Wait a minute. There was baking stuff out in the kitchen. She was going to bake."

"I don't see how that's relevant to leaving Carolina alive," said Sydney.

My eyes went to Sydney's face. "It's the most relevant thing. Nothing was happening. I was in Sturgis and not supposed to come back for another day. When Dad's gone, Claire doesn't come. It's not like we have a housekeeper."

Chuck stretched and put his hands behind his head. He started pacing the length of the small room. "So she was alone. He killed Denny and Carolina was alone."

"For the foreseeable future, lying on the bricks with nearly half her brain dying. Every second that goes by, it's more cells dead. Tick. Tick. Tick."

"He wanted her to suffer long-term, for the rest of her life."

"How bad would it have been?" asked Sydney. "I don't know about strokes. She's talking now, isn't she?"

"Only because I came home unexpectedly and found her within the vital window. If I hadn't, she'd be severely impaired."

"We're talking wheelchair?"

"We're talking completely paralyzed on the left side. Her eyesight, breathing, swallow, the whole shebang. If I hadn't found her until the next day, she might have died. It was that bad and the clot wouldn't have cleared itself. Sometimes they do, but that one wouldn't have."

"I think" —Sydney cleared his throat— "I'd rather be dead."

Chuck kept pacing. "That was the point."

"I know Carolina. Goddammit, she's a stunner. Why would anyone hate her that much?"

"It's not Carolina. It's Tommy," said Chuck. "He adores Carolina. You ruin her, you ruin him. He'd never recover." He crossed the room and scooped me up.

"Let go," I said, struggling. "I'm mad at you."

"I don't care," he said into my neck. "I would never recover."

Bark.

"You'd survive just fine. There'd be plenty of women ready to comfort you."

"I'd never recover. I couldn't stand it."

Bark. Bark.

"That's nice, but you suck. Let go!"

"No."

I was about to kick or something, but it turned out not to be necessary. Chuck dropped me like I went vampire on his neck. He jumped back and began a stream of consciousness cussing that would've left Uncle Morty envious, ending with, "What is wrong with that dog?"

Grr.

I picked up Wallace from beside her puddle and kissed her wrinkly head. "Not a thing. She was defending me."

"With pee?"

"That's how she rolls."

Bark.

Sydney sucked in his lips, trying not to laugh, and grabbed a wad of paper towels from above the sink, giving them to Chuck.

"How much water did you feed this dog?" asked Chuck. His right foot was soaked and his jeans weren't looking so good either.

"Not much," I said. "If you give her a fourth cup of water, Wallace can make three cups of pee out of it. She's gifted."

"Gifted? She's a freak."

Grr.

"That's Wallace the Wonder Pug to you." I sashayed past him and whipped open the door. "See ya, loser."

"Hey," called out Sydney.

"Not you. Your partner."

Sydney grinned at me. "I'm living the dream. Chuck Watts is a loser and I'm not."

I blew him a kiss and trotted off toward the elevators, bypassing them in case Chuck stopped cleaning the wee and followed. I ran down the stairs with a smug pug under one arm and my phone in the other.

"What's wrong with you?" yelled Uncle Morty.

"Running down stairs. They found Denny."

"Yeah. I just saw it. That poor son of a bitch. Wrong place. Wrong time."

"Can you get me the autopsy?"

"Nope."

I stopped at the lobby door and bent over, catching my breath. "Why not?"

"Cause Simon called. He wants you out there."

"Who's Simon?" I asked.

"Dr. Grace, ya nitwit. He's got the body and he wants to talk to you."

I straightened up. "I'd really rather not."

"I ain't giving you a choice. Go." He hung up on me. Swell. Off to the morgue, not exactly the happiest place on Earth.

"I hope you have some pee left," I said to Wallace.

Bark.

"If Dr. Grace tries to show me Denny's body, I want you to spray him good."

Bark. Bark.

I called Fats and she was at the front, waiting. I peeked out the door and then ran through the lobby and jumped in her truck.

"What's with the dog?" she asked.

"She's going to pee for me."

"I don't know what that means."

"You will."

Fats merged onto the highway out to St. James and Wallace decided to get comfortable by spinning in a circle on my lap eighty-five times. Her tiny nails dug right through the thin material of my sundress. If I'd known I'd be running around with the pug, I'd have worn jeans.

I texted Tiny and told him I was off to the morgue with Wallace. He said he'd tell Mom and that she had three therapy evaluations that day. I'd try to get back, but I couldn't make any promises.

During the texting a smell came over me. I sniffed Wallace and she smelled like truffles and high-priced meat. I leaned sideways toward Fats and she said, "It's not me."

A hand came up between the front seats, holding a large coffee cup.

"Aaron!" I spun in my seat, dislodging Wallace and causing her to do her eighty-five spins again. "How in the world did you beat me to the truck and get coffee? You were asleep."

He shrugged and jiggled the coffee.

"Thanks," I said gratefully. "What about Fats? Does she get coffee?"

"I don't drink coffee," she said. "Only green tea."

Another large cup came up.

"Thanks, Aaron," said Fats. "But the green tea is a health thing."

He jiggled the cup and she gave me a sidelong glance and I said, "It's probably tea."

She took the cup and gave it an experimental sniff. "Holy crap. It is tea. How did you know?"

Aaron just shrugged and produced a hot dog from somewhere, stuffing half of it in his mouth.

"His gift is food," I said. "He's kind of a savant."

Fats drank half her cup in one go. "How often does that come in handy?"

"More often than you'd think," I said.

"So why are we going to St. James?" she asked. "New patient?"

"In a manner of speaking. Denny Elliot is in the morgue. Dr. Grace wants to talk to me."

Fats shivered and I asked, "Not crazy about the morgue?"

"Not crazy about dead people."

"Really? I would've thought you'd made a few," I said.

She grinned wickedly at me. "That's different. I didn't visit them afterward."

It was my turn to shiver. "You're freaking me out."

"Yeah, I do that." She smiled wider. "It's my gift."

"I thought your gift was the ability to take a bullet," I said.

"That, too." She exited the highway and took the back way to St. James. We made good time since it was still pretty early and the traffic was only starting to heat up.

Fats wasn't keen on coming in with me, but I insisted. Something about our unsub was making me nervous. He sent his minion right up to the ICU. What was he going to do if the security guard hadn't shown up?

We parked and I didn't ask Aaron to come in. I didn't have to. He trotted along behind us, barely keeping up. I did marginally better. Fats was a fast walker, even when going to the morgue.

We took the elevator down and I gripped my cup so hard the top popped off. Aaron reached over and silently put it back on. I leaned on him, feeling oddly comforted by the hot dog stink. So much had changed in the last two days. At least Aaron hadn't.

The doors opened and the morgue feeling was immediately apparent. Fats stepped back. "Oh, that's not good."

Morgues are super sterile and not smelly, but even if you didn't know it was a morgue, you'd still sense the creepy. That was a feeling that everyone got. I put my head up and walked out like it didn't bother me. It so bothered me. The last time I'd been there was when Gavin Flouder was murdered. Goosebumps rose all over my body and the sight of the bruises on Gavin's body appeared in my mind. I could see them like it was happening at that moment.

Fats took my arm. "Mercy? Are you okay?"

I shook my head. "Yeah, I just...bad memories." I walked down to Dr. Grace's office and knocked as fast as I could manage. If I didn't do it fast, I might not do it at all.

"Come in," he called out.

I opened the door and the doctor smiled at me from behind stacks of files. They weren't as high this time and I could see his whole face. He came out from behind the desk and said, "And an entourage. Come in. Come in."

I introduced Fats as my bodyguard and Aaron with no explanation at all. Nobody could explain Aaron. Why try? Dr. Grace didn't care in any case. He was all about the work, like a certain red-headed detective I knew. He ignored Wallace so completely, I wasn't sure he saw her sitting on my right foot.

"Sorry to bring you down here, but I heard Tommy's been detained indefinitely and I wanted to give you what I have before I give it to Chuck and Sydney."

I raised an eyebrow. "Really? Why?"

"As far as I'm concerned, this was meant to be your father's case. Carolina is his wife and Denny died protecting her. The government has decided to block the greatest—in my opinion—detective available and that makes me angry."

"That's not Chuck and Sydney's fault."

"They work for the government," he said as if this answered all my questions.

"Okay. Works for me," I said. "What have you got?"

He squeezed out between Fats and Aaron. "Come with me."

Ah, crap. Please just x-rays. No body. Please, no body.

Fats grabbed my arm as I went past. "Where are we going?"

"To see the body," called out Dr. Grace.

Dammit.

"You don't have to go in," I said to Fats.

"Thank God," she said.

Dr. Grace held the swinging double doors open for me and said, "This won't take long. I've only done the prelim, x-rays, and started the labs."

Wallace scampered through the doors, her nails making quite a clatter in the empty hall.

"You might want to leave the Wonder Dog," he said.

Grr.

"Or not. It's up to you."

Bark.

"I guess the pug is coming." I walked a lot more slowly than Wallace, who wagged with excitement like there were treats on the horizon. What a weirdo!

There was only one body on a slab in the room. Thankfully, it was covered with a sheet. Dr. Grace went to the head, grabbed a chart, and assumed his lecture pose that I remembered so well. I stood back a couple of feet, reluctant to get too close with the feeling of intense dread that was coming over me like a bad case of the stomach flu, nausea and all.

"Subject has been deceased for approximately forty hours. I can only say that because you came upon the scene so close to the incident. Normally, it would be thirty-six to forty-eight hours with the rate of decomp and insect infestation."

Oh, no! Not the insects.

"Swell." I swallowed hard and Wallace ran around my feet, wagging and doing the pug smile. I picked her up and the warmth of her wiggling body allowed me to take a deep breath and actually look at the body before me. "Any insight into the killer?"

"Absolutely," said Dr. Grace.

He said absolutely, but I wasn't so sure. Denny had been shot three times initially, square in the middle of the chest in a good grouping.

That showed both training and experience, but that could describe a lot of people, including me, Mom, and Tiny, for instance.

Denny's death wasn't instantaneous, but it was pretty quick. One shot hit a lung and another severed an artery. Our guy was good with a gun and he meant to kill Denny. He wasn't just firing out of fear. That was consistent with the cold planning of Sturgis.

"What's most interesting is that after death, which I believe happened in your mother's garden, the body was moved without leaving traces of blood anywhere else."

"So he packed the body off. We knew that," I said.

Dr. Grace smiled indulgently. "Have you ever tried to move a body with massive hemorrhaging?"

"Gross. No."

"Think about it."

I thought about it. There would've been a lot of blood and blood was disgusting, sticky. It got everywhere. I'd been in the ER with a gunshot victim where blood got on the inside of a lamp, a good six feet to the left of the patient. Nobody knew how it got up there. He wasn't spurting.

"I don't know how you control blood that way," I said. "It spurts and drips. Denny couldn't have been in the garden very long after death, so the blood wouldn't have congealed."

"Experience," he said.

"A serial killer?"

"Possibly. Or a gun for hire. They know their business very well. Maybe someone who served in law enforcement or perhaps the military."

"Not a newbie."

"Definitely not. He's seen blood. He wasn't shocked or startled by the amount. He knew just what to do."

I'm so afraid to ask…

"What did he do?" I asked, petting Wallace so fast she gave me a lick.

"Okay. The table is the back of your parents' house." Dr. Grace walked me backward to another table. "You're Denny in the hostas and I'm the killer, standing on the left side of the door. I shoot Denny."

"That's a decent distance," I said.

"Fifteen feet."

"So Denny came out the door. The killer put the gun on him and he backed up into the hostas?"

Dr. Grace nodded. "He shot Denny as he was pulling his weapon."

"How in the heck do you know that?" I asked.

"Simple. One of the shots went through Denny's left hand before striking him in the chest. Denny was right-handed. People who are putting up their hands in defense put up both hands. What was the right hand doing?"

"Reaching for his weapon," I said. "Ah, crap! The shot in the door wasn't from the killer's weapon. It was from Denny's. He got a shot off."

"Correct."

"How did nobody hear that?" I asked.

"I'm sure your suspect used a silencer so it was only the one shot on a lazy Saturday afternoon."

"But it was a gunshot."

"Do you know what weapon Denny preferred?" he asked.

I thought about it, but it wasn't like Denny and I hung out. "We were at the range with him one time. He had a Ruger. 22."

Dr. Grace nodded. "Yes. Yes. Those are quiet compared to say, a .38."

"Still, it's a gunshot."

"A few people reported hearing a noise at around three thirty, but they didn't think it was a gunshot until the police told them about your mother's attack."

I rolled my eyes. "Come on."

"Keep in mind. It was one shot on a very hot afternoon with impending rain. Everyone was inside with the air conditioning going strong. One lady thought it was lightning. People talk themselves out of reporting things all the time," said Dr. Grace.

Palfrey. That measly butler.

"So why do you think he bothered to retrieve the bullet then?"

"I wondered about that, too. But I don't think our man expected your mother to be discovered so soon. In fact, I believe he knew her schedule well and he knew where you were, obviously. I think he expected it to be at least twenty-four hours before she was discovered, possibly more. Carolina wasn't going to get up and walk away from the type of stroke she had."

"Still..."

"They were calling for rain on Saturday night, a real gully washer."

I remembered the clouds and the heaviness in the air, but I hadn't thought about it. "But it never rained."

"Weather people are always wrong," said Dr. Grace. "If they'd been right and you hadn't shown up—"

"The blood would've been washed away. But you would've noticed the trampled plants."

"I wish I could guarantee that, but I can't. When I arrived on the scene, the breakage wasn't obvious, far from. There were only a few snapped leaves from where Denny walked and where he fell was well-concealed. We had no reason to think there was a second victim. We weren't looking. The going in theory was that he shot at your mom, striking the door. Then he attacked her, bringing on the stroke."

"How did you find the blood then?"

He tapped his nose. "I smelled it."

"Ew," I said. "If it had rained and you did find the area where Denny fell, what could you have discovered?"

"Very little. He probably thought Denny's disappearance would go unnoticed for a few days at least. A few more to put it together that he'd been with your mother. After that, I might've found traces of blood, but I doubt with our heat and the amount of rain they were calling for that I could've gotten DNA or even a type."

"So he rolled the dice."

"He did, but he handled the whole thing very well." He held up a finger gun. "This is what he did."

Dr. Grace fired his finger at me, came over, and made like he was flipping me over, facedown on the ground.

I went cold and even Wallace shivered. "You mean he put Denny facedown so he could bleed into the ground as he was dying?"

"What better way to control the victim and the blood?" he asked.

"That is so cold."

"Ice cold."

"But if he thought it was going to rain, why bother?" I asked.

Dr. Grace pointed at me, almost with glee. He was so in his element. "Excellent question. Think about it."

"You are such a professor," I said.

"I do teach three days a week," he said. "So Miss Watts, what does your experience tell you? You've killed someone. How did you handle it?"

"I froze." My mind, with perfect clarity, showed me Richard Costilla's face exploding, him tumbling backward down the stairs, and landing in a heap at the bottom. Every instinct I had kept me from going down those stairs. I could never have flipped him over and held him down as he died. Never.

"It was instinct," I said. "He wasn't thinking. He reacted. If he had been thinking, he wouldn't have bothered. He'd have remembered the coming rain and just let Denny bleed wherever."

"Exactly."

"How in the world do you get that instinct? He must've done it before."

"Or have known someone who did," said Dr. Grace.

I walked to Denny's body and stood at his hip. "What else?"

Dr. Grace joined me on the other side. "He's arrogant."

"I guess anybody who could kill like that would be arrogant."

He paused and tapped his chin. "I would say that's more like a sociopath, but this guy has feelings. He's definitely not dead inside." He reached for the sheet. "May I?"

"If you think it's necessary."

Dr. Grace didn't answer. He pulled down the sheet to Denny's waist and I sucked in a breath. The detectives said he'd been shot after death, but that didn't begin to cover it. He had more gunshot wounds and...

"Are those stab wounds?" I asked.

"Yes. Twelve in total and there's damage consistent with kicking. We're looking at a size ten work boot. Men's. New with no wear marks."

"Why in the world would he do that so long after Denny died?" I asked.

"Looks like frustration to me. It was out on the wires that Carolina had been found and was expected to survive. It obviously didn't rain and he changed his plan."

"How long after death?" I asked.

"At least twelve hours and the body was moved."

"How do you know?" I asked.

He pointed at the dirt on the body. "He was originally buried and then placed in the parking lot."

"Parking lot?"

Denny was found in a school bus parking lot. It was the weirdest place to put a body, but it guaranteed he'd be found early. The first drivers arrived at five and found him straight away as he was in no way hidden. The dirt was average Missouri dirt, but it had sheep manure in it and some composted material, possibly from a garden.

"I don't see how this makes him arrogant," I said.

Dr. Grace appeared slightly disappointed in me but quickly brightened up. "I forgot for a moment that however your mind might work like Tommy's, you haven't his experience."

The doctor read the killer as arrogant because he'd been quite careful at the scene. He left nothing for us to find, not a fingerprint, not a hair, and certainly none of his DNA. Then he unburied the body and left the dirt on it.

"That sounds like he got bored to me," I said. "It was too much work to wash the body or find a way to cover the kick marks like burning or something."

He nodded approvingly. "I agree, but he also stopped being careful because he is arrogant and thinks he can change a plan on the fly with no consequences. I don't know why he decided to move the body. It's not a smart move."

"Dad says that killers do that. They get nervous and second-guess themselves," I said.

"They do," said Dr. Grace. "And Denny's being at the house was a wrinkle in his original plan. There's one more thing." He waved me over to a microscope. "Take a look at that."

I peered through the prisms and said, "Um...some kind of powder?"

"Give that girl a gold star. It's cornstarch."

"From the gloves he was wearing?"

Dr. Grace had matched the cornstarch from a certain type of nitrile gloves and he took me back to Denny's body. He'd found the cornstarch on two sections of the body, the head and shoulders area and the lower back and buttocks.

"I get it," I said, feeling pleased with myself for the first time. "He ungloved over the body twice, when he buried it and later when he left it in the parking lot."

The doctor rubbed his hands together. "There was plenty of powder to be found, particularly on the hair and in folds of the clothes."

"He double-gloved," I said. "It's like he's well-trained but not that good at it."

He did a fist pump. "Arrogant!"

"That's good for a profile." It was, but I had no clue how arrogant helped me. Lots of people were like that. Hell, Dad was described as arrogant by people that he out-maneuvered and there were a lot of them. "Let's get back to the gloves. Any way to match them to a batch?"

He smiled at me. "I like your mind, Miss Watts. I certainly do. I can't give you a batch, but I can tell you that they stopped making those gloves in 2005. They had too much cornstarch in them. Your father got the department to stop ordering them in 2003. He thought they could possibly contaminate crime scenes and he was right, of course." He dipped his chin and watched me over the top of his horn-rimmed glasses. "Any questions?"

"Are you testing me?" I asked.

"I am indeed. You are a Watts. To whom much is given, much is expected."

I groaned. "I've been given a bunch of stuff I don't want. Dad should be here doing this, not me."

"You have to take the burdens along with the gifts. Give it some thought. Denny isn't going anywhere for the time being."

"Can we cover him?"

"Of course."

Dr. Grace covered Denny and I paced the length of the room with my nose pressed into Wallace's fur for more reasons than one. I went over everything he had told me. It was a ton and I had to do a mental sift twice before I remembered something, the one question that hadn't been answered. "How did he control the blood leaving the scene?"

The doctor perked up and got sly. "I told you that he rolled him over. There was no flailing and the blood was in a rather small section of ground, considering the extent of Denny's injuries."

"He still had to get him out of the yard without dripping. It would've been messy, but he didn't make a mess."

"Excellent. There is only one thing that I know of that can keep all fluids and fibers contained and is easy to use. A—"

"Body bag," I said with a prolonged shiver. "He brought a bodybag."

"Try not to think what you're thinking."

"Impossible. That bag was intended for my mom. I doubt he expected to find Denny hanging out at our house on a Saturday afternoon. Why would he? When I left for Sturgis, Mom had no protection at all."

"That's what he intended. Again, arrogant. He didn't think things had changed in the days you were in Sturgis and acted with over-confidence."

"Can you buy body bags?" I asked.

"Sure and they're cheap. This was a good one. It left no traces on the body. Thirty bucks or less."

"You said he wore a size ten work boot. He's not a huge guy."

"No, he's not. I say five nine to possibly five eleven."

"How'd he carry Denny out alone? He's not small,' I said.

"One hundred and ninety pounds. It could be done if our guy is exceptionally strong, but my money is on a helper."

I looked at the ceiling. A helper. Of course.

"Mercy?"

"We know he has a helper," I said.

He frowned. "Chuck said nothing about that."

I told him about Blankenship's visitor and the man at the hospital.

"Are you sure you want to trust that man?" asked Dr. Grace. "He could be leading you to places you don't want to go."

I spread my free arm wide. "I'm already there."

He nodded and said, "I understand."

I left him to do the full autopsy and found Fats pacing outside the door. "I hope that was worth it, because I've got the heebie-jeebies something fierce."

"It was." I hesitated. "I think. Our guy is arrogant, good at his job to a point, and cheap."

"Weird. How did you get cheap?" she asked.

"He used gloves that they stopped making in 2005."

"I've got an uncle like that. He never throws anything away if it can still be used."

"A hoarder?"

"Borderline."

I found Aaron squatting by the exit, scribbling away in his recipe notebook. "I don't know what you've been writing in there, but if the morgue inspired it, I'm not interested in eating it."

"You hungry?" he asked, coming to his feet.

"Not yet. Give it a minute."

He trotted off to the elevator, but Fats beat him there. I had too much on my mind to jog. This guy felt...I don't know...familiar and it unsettled me. Could I have met him? Could he be one of the stalkers that followed me and then got over it, except he didn't get over it. The body bag popped into my mind and I hated that I was grateful that Mom didn't end up in it. It felt like being happy that Denny died instead. That was sick and not true. Not exactly anyway. Why did anybody have to go into that bag? Who could hate us that much?

CHAPTER FIFTEEN

Brian Shill was at home. He was always at home since he was on bail for the minor sex act thing and the judge had slapped an ankle monitor on him.

Uncle Morty had given me his address, but I hadn't paid much attention to it. Shill was a one-time janitor and a felon. I assumed it was trailer park city. It wasn't. Shill had hit the lottery or something. His place of residence, as Uncle Morty called it, was in Clayton, a spiffy part of St. Louis, not quite as spiffy as Hawthorne Avenue or as old but pretty damn sweet for a felon.

"You need to double check the address," said Fats. "The dirtbag in your dad's file can't live here. Fate wouldn't do that."

Fate did do that. Uncle Morty told me that Brian Shill was the son of the famed—and now deceased—divorce attorney, Conrad Shill. As the only child, Brian inherited the entire estate, although the rest of the family had been fighting it for going on eight years, using a variety of arguments, but mainly that the parents wouldn't have left him a nickel, if they knew what a perv he was.

"Can you believe this, Aaron?" asked Fats. "Look at that house."

"Huh?" he said, still writing in his notebook.

"Don't bother with him," I said. "He's working. We'll be lucky to get lunch out of him."

Aaron's head jerked up. "You hungry?"

I smiled at my foodie partner. "After I interview this murdering dirtbag, I could eat."

He nodded and went back to scribbling.

We rolled to a stop in front of a Tudor-style house, not a mansion but good sized. It had gorgeous brickwork and lovely black beams with a massive chimney and an ornate front door that outshone my parents' front door and that was saying something.

"This is my dream house," said Fats. "I'm gonna punch that guy in the throat."

I looked back and forth between her and the house. That didn't seem right. "This is your dream house?"

"I love this house." She paused. "What'd you think I'd like?"

"I don't know. Something more modern and cool."

"That house is cool. It has class and I'm a classy girl," said Fats, getting out and cracking her back.

I followed her steel-cut bulk up the beautifully manicured front walk with Wallace straining on her leash. "It's definitely classy."

"But you don't think I'm classy," she said, but not angry, which was a relief. To say Fats could grind me into dust was an understatement.

"You're classy of a sort, but you're more edgy." Actually, I was thinking she was more what Grandad called a broad, but I didn't say it. I valued my life.

"Edgy. I like that."

Thank goodness. I will continue to live.

"I hope he'll talk to us," I said.

Fats scoffed, "Please. He'll talk to us one way or another."

"Please don't, you know, rough him up."

She laughed in a way that made me nervous. If Shill didn't get smacked around, it would be a straight up miracle. Normally, that wouldn't have bothered me much, but Dad and Big Steve weren't around to talk me out of a night in jail and I didn't want to go back to stinking.

"It's still illegal to hit felons," I said.

"Illegal." Fats patted my cheek. "You are so cute."

"Er...Fats, I think we need to talk about how this is going to go."

She pushed the doorbell and numerous chimes went off inside. "We want information. He's going to give it to us. Got it."

"Well, there's a little more nuance to it."

"You are truly adorable. I'm all about the nuance." She popped her knuckles one by one.

"I don't want him to call the police," I said.

She pushed the doorbell again. "Mercy, if I had to hazard a guess, I've gotten a hell of a lot more information out of people than you have."

"Er...probably."

"Good. We understand each other then."

I didn't understand anything other than I had a problem and no clue how to fix it. Come to think of it, this was kind of my usual deal, so I shrugged and went with it. Fats worked for Calpurnia. If she couldn't fix what was about to happen, nobody could.

I rang the doorbell a third time with no result. "He has to be here."

Fats pounded on the door so hard I think I heard the wood cracking. "Open up, shitbag. We're coming in one way or another."

"Who is it?" said an irritated man's voice from the other side of the door.

I kind of expected Fats to say, 'Your worst nightmare," but instead, she said, "Fats Licata. You want to open the door or I will break it down. Look out the peephole. You'll see that I can."

"What do you want?" he said.

Fats responded by pounding on the door and there was some serious cracking that time.

"Wait a minute! Wait a minute!"

Some locks were thrown and a brown eye peeked out a small crack when the door opened. "Okay. Now what do you want?" He said it with insolence and that wasn't a good idea. Fats shoved the door and Shill flew backward across the highly polished hardwood and hit the wrought iron bannister, falling to the floor.

Aaron trotted past Shill and disappeared into the depths of the house.

"Where's he going?" asked Fats.

"Probably the kitchen," I said.

Shill rubbed his head and sat up. He was decidedly older than in the picture in Dad's file. His black hair had turned salt and pepper and he had a sizable gut under the faded Old Navy tee and cutoff khaki pants that showed spindly and incredibly hairy legs. "Get that asshole out of here. I'm calling the police."

Fats stomped up to him and he cowered against the stairs, raising a pasty arm over his face.

"Yeah, you're quite the hero, Shill," she said.

He slowly came to his feet, his face filled with an odd combo of defiance and cowardice. "Get out."

She laughed. "Yeah, right. This is Mercy Watts. She has some questions for you and you will answer her. Understand?"

Watts was apparently the magic word. The minute Fats uttered it, Shill's face formed the Joker smile and he became overly casual, leaning on the bannister. "Another Watts. To what do I owe the pleasure?"

"Tell me about Cassidy Huff," I said.

"I'll tell you about how I bested Tommy Watts at his own game," he said with glee.

I walked past him into the amazingly clean and tidy dining room. Dad's file on Shill seemed to indicate that he thought Shill got lucky. Things went perfectly the night he took Cassidy Huff. No witnesses. Anybody could've seen him in the parking lot with her and no one did. But that dining room said a lot about his mind. A single guy with an unbelievably clean house. How often did that happen? Chuck's apartment usually looked like there had been a recent break-in.

I pulled out a chair and sat with Wallace on my lap, propping my feet on the gleaming table to see what he'd do. Shill's face twitched with irritation, but a glance at Fats' hard face told him not to object and he didn't. He sat opposite me and steepled his fingers in a position of power. Yeah, right.

"It wasn't his game," I said.

Shill frowned. "What?"

"It wasn't my dad's game. He's a detective, not a murderer, and he got you on attempted rape."

He put his chin on his fingers and said, "Tommy Watts is your father. Beautiful."

He doesn't know who I am. Not the unsub.

Fats came over and smoothly popped him on the back of the head. "Sit up and pay attention."

Shill reluctantly sat up and eyed me coolly. "So what are you doing here? Trying to fix one of your father's great failures?"

"You're not one of my father's great failures," I said.

"He has greater failures than me? How nice to hear."

"Grilled chicken."

"What?"

I shrugged. "He can't grill chicken. He either burns it or it's raw."

"Why do I care?" asked Shill.

"That's one of my father's great failures. He also can't do plumbing or sing." I ground my heel in the finish of the table and watched with pleasure as Shill cringed. "You, on the other hand, I've never heard of before yesterday."

"He told you about me yesterday?"

"No. Kent Blankenship did," I said bluntly and was rewarded with a look of shock on Shill's narrow, weasely face.

"Who's that?" he asked, but it was totally fake.

"You know, mass murderer, mental patient, friend of yours."

Shill started chewing on his lower lip and Fats gave him another pop.

"What was that for?" he complained.

"You piss me off," said Fats. "Tell Mercy about Blankenship. I can hit a lot harder than that."

"I'll press charges," he said, looking up at her, haughty and defiant.

She squatted next to his chair and said in a low tone that made the hair come to attention on the back of my neck, "You've been to prison. Have you ever heard the name Calpurnia Fibonacci?"

The defiant look, as well as all the color in Shill's face, drained away. "Yes," he said slowly.

"I work for her and she doesn't like child rapists. Have you heard that?"

"I might've heard something to that effect."

"Then we understand each other. Tell Mercy what she wants to know."

He turned to me and he had a slight hand tremor. Dad had noticed that during interrogations, but he could never break him. Of course, Dad was being videoed and he didn't have Fats in the room.

"Blankenship likes me," I said.

Shill looked doubtful and I could see his point. A sociopath with psychotic features didn't really like people as a general rule.

"No, it's true. He thinks I belong to him and he wants to protect me," I said.

"From who?"

"One of your friends."

"I don't have friends," said Shill.

I laughed. "That I can easily believe. How about accomplices? You have those."

Shill began shifting in his seat. "I don't know what you're talking about."

"Sure, you do. Blankenship told me and the only reason the cops aren't here right now is that I haven't told them what I know."

The color came back up in Shill's cheeks and I informed him that Blankenship confessed to being his accomplice in Cassidy Huff's murder. "When did you meet Blankenship?"

"I'm not going to tell you that."

I shrugged. "Fine. He'll tell me. Let me remind you that he's serving multiple life terms for Tulio with no chance of parole. He has nothing to lose, except me, and he doesn't want to lose me."

Shill muttered "shit" under his breath. "How do I know you won't tell the cops what I say?"

"You don't."

He sneered, "Then why should—"

Fats grabbed his face with one enormous hand and drove his head back against the chair. He scratched at her arm, but the woman was smothering him with one hand. "You want to ask that question again?" she hissed in his ear.

"Let's not kill our lead, Mary Elizabeth," I said, calmer than I felt. I'd seen some stuff, but I'd never seen anyone like Fats Licata.

"He deserves it for Cassidy alone. Who knows who else he's attacked." She let him go and he went facedown on the table, gasping.

"I agree, but for now, let's see what he has for us."

"What do you want to know?" Shill whispered.

"We all know you killed Cassidy, poor girl, but I'm more interested in who you told about it," I said.

Shill looked at me, still breathing hard but genuinely puzzled. "I didn't tell anyone."

"Come on, you told the other Unsubs."

"But that was before—" He clammed up and I smiled. "Before they let you play in their reindeer games?"

"I don't know—"

Fats slapped both hands on the table, making Shill and I jump. "Boy, I'm about to go Fibonacci on your ass."

"Yeah." Shill slumped in the chair. "2002 was before."

"So when did Blankenship let you in?"

"Blankenship? That son of a bitch." Shill jolted out of his chair and began pacing. "That fucking son of a bitch."

Ding. Ding. Ding.

"You didn't know he was in the Unsubs. Interesting," said Fats. "He dicked you around, porkpie."

Shill glared at her. "I didn't need them."

"But you joined," I said. "When?"

He got all shifty-eyed.

"When?" yelled Fats.

"2004," he said reluctantly.

"If Blankenship didn't bring you in, who did?" I asked.

Shill brightened up. "Josef Mayer."

The name sounded vaguely familiar and he came up with it so fast I knew it wasn't important. Just the date. Why the date?

I yawned and then said, "You're boring me. Fats, should we give this to my dad or to Chuck?"

"Give what? Chuck who? I gave you what I have," insisted Shill.

"I doubt that," said Fats.

Shill's face flamed and he glared at me. "You're not better than your father. I bested Tommy Watts. A pair of knockers isn't going to get me."

Fats grabbed him by the throat and threw him into the china cabinet, rattling the dishes and cracking the glass. "Who's in the Unsubs? Name them."

"I don't know their names," he burst out. "If she knows anything, she knows that's true."

I nodded. "It is. But someone in the group is posing as you."

Shill's mouth flew open. "Who?"

I told him about Blankenship's visitor and asked, "So who was that?"

He flopped into his chair. "Son of a bitch."

"Who was it?"

Shill held up his palms. "I don't know. I didn't tell anyone anything. No details."

"Except Blankenship," I said.

"Not even him. You've got to compartmentalize. He's the same."
That's why Dad couldn't break him.

"You don't know where Cassidy's body is," I said.

"Yeah, your father, what a snotty piece of shit he is. Always thought he could get it out of me. Dumb ass. Never, ever knew about Blankenship, did he?"

"No, he didn't," I said. "But you are so going to prison again."

He gripped the table. "So you got Blankenship. He's in Hunt, so he's as crazy as a shit house rat. Waylon said you gotta have a body. You've got no body and Blankenship made sure you'll never find one."
Waylon?

"So you're not worried?" I asked.

"No," he said with his chin tilted up.

I put Wallace on the floor and steepled my fingers. "I suppose we don't have a body, but we do have the guy who disposed of the body. That's good enough to reopen the case."

"You'll never find a trace," he said. "You know what? I don't believe you. Blankenship didn't tell you crap. He wouldn't."

"He wouldn't tell me he put Cassidy through a wood chipper?" I think Shill threw up in his mouth a little and it gave me great pleasure.

I was going to ask him about Waylon when he let out a shriek and jumped sideways. "Your damn dog peed on me."

Fats burst into laughter and I said, "Yeah, she does that. I thought it might be a sign of affection, but I guess not."

"I will fucking kill that dog." Shill drew back his foot and Fats snatched him up by his throat. He danced on his tiptoes and she said in a low voice, "We don't hurt dogs or girls. Didn't your mother teach you anything?"

"Who do you think taught me the value of a scream?" he choked out.

Fats dropped him like he'd sprouted boils and he fell in the pee, slipping around and cursing.

"Just when you think this turd can't get any more disgusting," she said.

"Tell me about it," I said, coming around the table and picking up my favorite incontinent pug, just in case. Wallace had been kicked more than enough. "Who's Waylon?" I asked Shill.

"Waylon?"

"You said 'Waylon said you gotta have a body.' Waylon who?"

Shill didn't answer. He bolted. We were so surprised, it took us a moment to react and that's all it took. Shill ran up the stairs and into a back bedroom. Fats and I got there just in time to see a heavy door close. The turd had a panic room. Just my luck.

Fats pounded on the door. "Dammit! I should've beat him when I had the chance."

"I'd rather you didn't beat information out of people," I said.

"Really?" she said with a bucketful of doubt.

"Most people. If we see this guy again, go ahead and beat him."

She frowned. "See him again? Aren't we going to wait him out?"

"Why bother? He's not going anywhere and we have plenty to go on," I said, leaving the room and jogging down the stairs.

"Wait," she yelled. "What have we got? This Waylon guy?"

"And the dates," I said. "Aaron!"

He didn't answer, but I followed the smell of happiness to a gourmet kitchen that was as spotless as the rest of the house.

Aaron stood at an enormous Blue Star range with three skillets going at once. By the smells, I'd say sausages, bacon, eggs, and oddly, baked beans.

"What the hell are you doing?" I asked.

He flipped an egg without the aid of a spatula. "You're hungry."

"This isn't our house."

Aaron shrugged and shook the sausage pan.

"Not yet," said Fats with a wicked grin.

"What?" I asked.

"It's not our house *yet.*"

I gave her a sideways glance. "You worry me."

"This house was meant for me."

"How much do you make? This sucker's got to be about 1.5 million."

She licked her lips slowly, tasting her future success. "He won't be selling it for that."

"What are you going to do?" I asked and then quickly said, "Never mind. It's better if I don't know."

Fats got out plates and silverware. "Give me some credit."

"I think I am." I sat down and sniffed a glass of orange juice that Fats poured for me.

"He's not going to poison his own orange juice," said Fats. "Paranoid much?"

Aaron began plating a full English breakfast, complete with tomato and bread fried in bacon fat, but no blood pudding. Thank goodness.

Curiosity got the better of me and I asked, "What credit do you think I'm supposed to be giving you?"

"I plan to get this house legally and soon."

I took a deep breath, sucking in the meaty steam. "How will you do that?"

"You know he killed his parents, right?"

I gagged on my first bite of sausage. "Where'd you get that?"

"You think a lawyer would leave his house to his piece of shit raping son?"

"There's no accounting for parents. Mine? Not a chance. But Blankenship's parents are still trying to see him and they don't get much worse."

"I'm telling you. This house? No. He killed them before they could disinherit him and you can't inherit from the people you murdered." Fats inhaled her fry-up as Aaron stood at the island, watching with hands clasped.

"I'm not so sure Shill's parents were as against his crimes as you think. You heard him about the mother," I said.

"She might've been what he implied, but he still killed them. Trust me."

"The family will inherit and sell. They'll want the money."

She snorted. "Yeah, there's a hot market for murder houses. I bet he killed them here and who knows who else."

I shivered but managed to push the murder house thing out of my mind and eat myself into a stupor. Wallace ate so much sausage she passed out and started gassing in the middle of the floor. Fats cleared my place and efficiently cleaned up after Aaron, who was watching me expectantly. I finally gave in and said, "It was fabulous."

Fats started scrubbing the pans while whistling Beethoven's Fifth.

"For crying out loud, Shill can clean that up," I said.

"I'm not leaving my house a mess."

"You are too bizarre."

"True, but I'm right," she said. "I'll make you a deal."

Not a deal. I get screwed on deals.

"What kind of deal?" I asked.

"I'll square you with Calpurnia if you help me get this house."

"I like the idea of not owing her, but don't you think if Shill killed his parents, somebody would've noticed?"

"Not necessarily."

"Where do you suggest we start with an eight-year-old double-murder that isn't thought to be a murder?" I asked.

"You're the brains of our little operation. Figure it out." She dried her hands and put my hat on my head. "Where to next?"

"Hospital," I said. "My mom's got evals to do and I should be there."

"And after that?"

I got up and dragged Aaron away from the Subzero fridge. "Come on, nutter. I've got a job for you."

He tried to return to the fridge. "Still hungry?"

"Not even a little bit, but I want you to make me something I'll hate."

Aaron rubbed his hands together and went up on the balls of his feet. "Crab."

"Worse. Seafood stew."

CHAPTER SIXTEEN

I'd never made Aaron so happy. When we dropped him off at Kronos, he was humming. This didn't bode well for me and I was starting to have some serious second thoughts.

"It's too late," said Fats.

"Well..."

She turned toward the hospital and raised an eyebrow at me. "Why did you ask for it in the first place? Don't you hate seafood?"

"More than I can say."

"So..."

"I have to go back out to Hunt." My stomach twisted in anticipation.

"What for? You said we've got a lot to go on."

"We do, but I don't think it's enough to get my dad out of Homeland Security's clutches."

Fats applied a fresh coat of lip gloss and redid the bun on top of her head during a stoplight, managing to look fresh and fabulous, not like she'd just smacked around a murderer. I didn't look in the mirror. It wouldn't be a good thing.

"You could try it," she said.

"I could, but I don't want to. They're holding onto my father for a reason and it's something to do with Mom's attack. I'm not sure they'll follow the trail if it leads where they don't want to go."

"Makes sense. What do you think Blankenship has that you can trade?"

"More Unsubs. They may have been anonymous, but they showed each other proof."

"Speaking of proof." Fats told the truck to play the news and we were rewarded with a breaking story out of Kansas. An anonymous source was credited with leading the FBI to a serial killer's burial site. Over thirty remains had been recovered so far, men, women, and children. No names were being released to the public. It should've made me feel good. People would be getting answers. Whoever did it would likely be caught. But I didn't feel good. I felt overwhelmingly sad. There were people in that field, lives stolen. Until I heard it on the news, it didn't feel real. The horror of it was far away. Being far away allowed me to think of it as a triumph for me instead of a tragedy for so many others. Not anymore.

"I don't know what to hope for," said Fats.

I whipped off my stupid floppy hat. Who cared if I looked ridiculous? It wouldn't be the first or the last time. "What do you mean?" I asked.

"I was hoping that Blankenship would give you good stuff. Now...I don't know. This is horrible."

I leaned on my door and looked at her. Fats worked for Calpurnia and she was obviously no stranger to violence, receiving and dishing it out, but this disturbed her. I couldn't reconcile the two.

"I know what you're thinking," she said, tucking a wisp of hair back up into her bun.

"Oh, yeah?"

"You're thinking that I, too, know where the bodies are buried and this shouldn't bother me."

"It's occurred to me that you've probably killed people," I said.

She gave me her wicked grin. "In the words of Arnie, 'But they were all bad.'"

"What the what?"

Fats rolled her eyes as she turned into the hospital. "You wound me. *True Lies*. Arnold Schwarzenegger's wife asks him if he's ever killed anyone and he says, 'Yeah, but they were all bad.'"

"I've never seen it," I said.

She gasped. The woman actually gasped over an ancient Arnold movie. "Tell me you've seen Conan the Barbarian."

"The new one or the old one?"

"Either."

"Neither," I said and was rewarded with another gasp.

"What have you been doing with your time?" asked Fats.

I tossed my hat into the backseat. "Chasing psychos, usually. Sometimes, I get to be a nurse."

"Your education is woefully inadequate."

"If you say so." I reached for the door handle to get out and Fats grabbed my arm. "How about *Dune* or *Excalibur*?"

"Are you sure you're not a dude?" I asked.

She punched me in the shoulder, ramming me into the door. "I mastered in movie watching. What does Chuck watch? I hope you're not forcing him to watch girly stuff with petticoats and tea."

"He's into *Hill Street Blues* right now."

"Oh, my god."

"I know. It's kind of a nightmare, but it's been worse," I said.

"How?" she asked in a low, horrified voice.

"He went through a *Kojak* phase and—"

Fats squeezed my arm. "Don't say it."

"*Chips.*"

"You want me to punch him?" she asked.

"Thinking about it," I said. "I'll call after Mom's therapy stuff."

She nodded and I dashed into the hospital. To my dismay, five reporters were there to greet me and security wasn't happy when they pulled out their cameras. There was yelling about filming on hospital property and I ran to the stairs when a guard blocked them. "Thanks!" I yelled over my shoulder. All I heard in response was, "Miss Watts, just a few questions about Kansas."

The door to the stairs slammed behind me. What the hell? Kansas? Somebody leaked that I was the anonymous source? Fan-freaking-tastic.

I ran up the stairs muttering, "I hate the FBI. I hate the FBI."

When I pushed the door to Mom's floor open, I was breathing so hard I needed an oxygen tank. My body wasn't the Stairmaster type and it showed. Big time. Normally, I wouldn't have minded, but I had an audience for my gasping and it wasn't good.

I stumbled onto the floor to find Chuck, Sydney, the FBI agents, and a couple uniforms at the elevators. I tried to lurch past them, but Chuck had the nerve to snag me. "What happened?"

"Let. Go."

"Mercy, what is it?"

I waved a finger around. "All. You. Bastards."

Then I gave him a stinging smack on the hand and he yelled, "Ouch! What is your deal?"

I sucked in a shuddering breath and turned on Hatchet Nose. "You sleazy son of a bitch. First, you renege on our deal, then you leak me to the press."

Hatchet Nose's usually bland face went to shock mode. It was brief, but I caught it.

"You didn't know, did you? I guess you're out of the loop. Feel good? I hope you enjoy it."

Chuck turned me around. "What leak?"

"I just got chased through the lobby by five reporters. They know I gave you Kansas. Thanks a lot. I don't want to be connected to that. I'm just the messenger."

Both agents whipped out their phones and began having tense conversations about leaks while Chuck and Sydney cussed up a storm.

I poked Chuck in his super-hard pec. "You know they're screwing me and us on this. Dad is going to be pissed."

He went silent.

"You're on the task force. Do something!"

Sydney rubbed his bald head, making the sparse hairs on top stand up on end. "Something's going on. We don't know what it is." He cocked his head to the angry agents. "And neither do they."

"Really?" I couldn't have been more sarcastic if I tried.

Chuck sighed. "Really. We were out at the site until three this morning. As soon as it was confirmed that your information was correct, the four of us were put on a helicopter back here. The Bureau claims they have a special team for exhumations and they're on it."

"Maybe they do."

"Yeah, but we're on the task force," said Sydney.

I bit my lip, thinking about Mom in her hospital bed and Dad in custody. "They didn't want you to see what was there."

Hatchet Nose walked up, his face like rolling thunder. "We're supposed to see what's there. It's our case."

I got an idea. Maybe it was his expression or the set of his shoulders. I don't know. He had a Watts kind of thing about him. "What's your reputation?" I asked.

"Huh? I mean, why do you ask?"

"Are you honest? Is the truth the most important thing? Do you ever let go of a lead?"

"Yes. Yes. And no."

I smiled. "And there it is. You might work for the FBI technically, but you're more like my dad, not big on political moves. Am I right?"

He nodded.

The other agent, Toupee, came up. "This could ruin us."

Hatchet Nose turned to his partner. "You're okay with being stonewalled? Watts should be here, not held in Chicago indefinitely without being charged."

"I agree, but we have careers to think of."

"You do," said Chuck. "And so do we, but this isn't right."

"Sounds like you have a choice to make," I said. "And I have therapy to get to."

Sydney grabbed my arm this time. "They leaked it to make it harder for you to move around. What have you got?"

"Something. Not nearly enough."

"Miss Watts, we need what you have," said Hatchet Nose.

"Decide where you stand and we'll talk." I took off down the hall to Mom's room. There was a sleepy uniform outside the door. He barely blinked when I walked past. Great. But inside was a better story. Tiny blocked the entrance with his bulk and he was bright-eyed. "Glad you're back," he said, moving aside for me to squeeze through.

Nana was there, curled up on the bed with Mom. Her green eyes were overflowing and her short, blond pixie cut was still a mess. Not like her at all. She held out a hand. "Mercy, sweetheart, where have you been?"

"Getting information, Nana," I said, sitting on the foot of the bed and taking her small, warm hand.

"About what?"

"Don't worry about it."

She frowned and stroked Mom's hair as she wept into a pillow. "Your place is here."

"I'm here."

"Let the FBI do their job. Don't be like Tommy. Your mother needs you."

I pushed down a seed of anger. "I know what Mom needs. Did something happen? I didn't miss therapy, did I?"

Mom looked up. "No. It's fine. I'm just so...I can't stop crying. I want to, but I can't."

"That's normal," I said. "You've had a trauma and stroke patients often have trouble controlling their emotions." I picked up Wallace and she scampered into Mom's open arms. "Sorry I took her."

"It's okay. You didn't know about the news."

I stiffened. "You mean, about Kansas."

"Kansas?" asked Nana.

Not helping, Mercy. Shut up.

"There was a thing in Kansas, a crime. Nothing to do with us." *Liar. Liar. Pants on fire.* "What are you talking about?"

Mom kissed the top of Wallace's head and said, "Do you remember John Jameson?"

"Not really."

"He worked with your dad. His son died this morning. He was only nineteen."

I breathed out a sigh of relief. I shouldn't have, but I was afraid she'd say Grandad's friend, Robert, who was still recovering from the stabbing in Sturgis, had taken a turn for the worse. "That's terrible. What happened?"

"They're not saying exactly," said Nana. "Sounds like an overdose."

"College student?"

Mom wiped her eyes and said, "Yes. John was so proud. Austin got full tuition for the engineering program at Edwardsville. I can't believe it. He was so young. Everything seems like bad news lately."

No more news for you.

I picked up the remote and switched the channel from CNN to HGTV.

"What are you doing?" asked Mom.

"The news is depressing," said Nana quickly. "You don't need that. Let's stick to happier things."

"That's fine with me, but is everything okay?" Mom looked at me closely. "You asked me about Denny. Have you heard from him yet? I think he was at the house, but he must've left."

Oh, crap. Oh, crap.

"Denny...um..."

Nana checked her watch quickly. "Where is that therapist? They've restricted Carolina's meals. They have to clear her."

"What did you have for breakfast?" I asked Mom.

She made a face. "Oatmeal."

"Blech. They just have to see how your swallow is and then they'll clear you to eat whatever you want."

Before Mom could remember her question about Denny, there was a knock on the door and a voice identified herself as the speech therapist. Tiny said, "I checked the ID and it matches, Mercy."

"Come on in," I said.

A young woman with a tray walked in. She was rattled by Tiny's scrutiny and I was okay with that. Keeping Mom safe was the most important thing.

I stood up and pulled over the tray table. "Sorry. We have to be careful."

"I understand," she said, setting down the tray and shaking my hand. "I'm Jennie Frankel, speech therapy."

She went on to talk to Mom about the effect of her stroke on swallowing and breathing. Nana got emotional and left under the guise of seeing what Pop Pop was up to in the waiting room. I stayed and I can't say it was easy to watch Mom try to swallow a dry cracker and cough her head off. I distracted myself with Wallace and reviewing what I knew. I was playing connect the dots, but all the dots weren't visible yet. The dates were important. I had the weirdest feeling like the knowledge was on the tip of my brain, but I couldn't access it. So frustrating.

Jennie cleared Mom to eat whatever she wanted, but with specific instructions to chew and swallow on the right side of her mouth. Mom had some exercises to do to help with her speech and swallow. Jennie would come every day until Mom was released and we discussed getting her into rehab, which Mom wasn't thrilled with, but Jennie said she was all for it so Mom grumbled and agreed.

When Jennie walked out, physical therapy walked in. They were a pair, Jim and Carol. They talked to Mom and then invited me to leave since they thought Mom would walk better without me as a distraction. I told them about her daring escape from the Cardiac Lab and we had a good laugh.

"You're probably good to walk if you could pull that off," said Carol. "But we have to run you through the gamut to clear you for walks in the hall and showering on your own."

"Let's do it then," said Mom, handing me Wallace. "I need a shower badly."

Jim waved me away. "She'll be fine with us."

"You understand the security situation?" I asked, getting nervous.

"Your grandfather talked to us," he said. "We'll be in this hall and the policeman is welcome to watch."

"And me," said Tiny. "Carolina don't go anywhere without me."

"I'm sure I'll be fine," said Mom.

"I'm sure I'll be making sure that's true," said Tiny.

He was obviously unmovable on the topic, so Mom gave in to being watched by Tiny and I went to the waiting room, where I found Uncle Morty, Grandad, and Pop Pop deep in a conversation about the new Star Trek show. My life was filled with nerds and Trekkie nerds, at that.

"Mercy, sweetheart," said Pop Pop. "How's the therapy going?"

"Fine. Speech is done and she can eat again. Physical therapy's got her now."

Uncle Morty growled, "Why aren't you in there? Ain't that why we have you?"

Grandad and Pop Pop laughed and I said, "They made me leave. Close family is distracting."

"Was it a man?" asked Uncle Morty.

"One was, but I'm telling you it's normal."

"Yeah, right. Like you know normal."

I sneered at him. "I'm more normal than you. Ask anybody."

He grumbled and went back to his laptop. "What'd you get from the doc?"

"Mom doesn't have the heart defect, but they can't rule out Afib."

"Yeah, we know, but I meant Dr. Grace," he said.

I shrugged, not wanting to talk autopsy. "Where's Nana?"

"She went for a walk to clear her head." Pop Pop hugged me. "This is very hard on her."

"She knows to stay inside, right?" I asked. "Did someone go with her?"

Pop Pop's hazel eyes went wide. "You think she's a target?"

"I don't want to take any chances. Where did she go?" I started for the door, but Grandad called after me. "It's fine, sweetheart. I told her the score. She's with Dixie and Tenne. They'll stick together."

I slumped into a chair. "Thank god. You just about gave me a coronary."

Pop Pop sat next to me and patted my hand. "Are you okay?"

"I'm fine. What about you? Nana said you were kinda upset."

"Well, it's upsetting, isn't it?" he said in his lovely Southern accent. Just the sound of his voice soothed me.

"It is, but we'll figure it out," I said.

"You will," said Uncle Morty. His voice was not soothing, quite the opposite, in fact.

"Chuck talked to you; I take it."

"He is pissed as hell that you won't give up your info."

"Serves him right. He was a real jerk and now he has no access," I said.

Grandad eyed me and crossed his arms. "So you have something?"

I glanced at the door and he went to close it without my asking. Nobody else was in the room, so we were relatively safe.

"Do you know anyone named Waylon?" I asked Uncle Morty.

He stopped typing. "Waylon Jennings."

I rolled my eyes. "Someone closer to home and, you know, not dead."

"Waylon Flowers," said Pop Pop.

"He's dead, too," said Grandad.

"Is he? I thought he retired."

"No, he died. AIDS, I think."

"Poor man," said Pop Pop. "Such a talent."

Uncle Morty looked at me. "You want to put a stop to this and tell me what Waylon you're talking about or what?"

I told them about my conversation with Brian Shill, dirtbag extraordinaire, including the dates and mention of the mysterious Waylon.

Uncle Morty typed for ten seconds and had my answer. "Waylon Parks, former DA and current criminal defense attorney."

"Is he defending Shill in his latest case?" asked Grandad.

"Nope, that's a woman, Marissa Milsap. She's filing every kind of motion ever invented. He's getting his money's worth."

Waylon said. Waylon said. Think, Mercy.

"Is Parks on any of Shill's motions?"

Uncle Morty scanned through some things on his laptop. "Doesn't look like he's on anything."

"How about the last case? The attempted rape?"

Pop Pop squeezed my hand. "You interviewed a rapist? I don't think that's a good idea."

Uncle Morty scoffed, "She does it all the time."

"That doesn't make me feel better."

"No? Well, whaddaya gonna do? Anyway, it was this Waylon that prosecuted Shill in 2005. They ain't friends."

"Except they are," I said.

"What the hell you talking about? Parks sent him to prison."

"I read Dad's file. He was pissed about that. Shill got five measly years for attempted rape of a fifteen-year-old and there was another charge of luring a minor for sexual purposes over the internet."

Uncle Morty typed for a minute. "Yeah, that one got dropped."

"Seems light," said Grandad. "Who was the judge?"

"Walter Ellison."

Grandad sat down next to Uncle Morty. "That geezer. He's still on the bench?"

"He was retired in '10 and died six months later. What was the deal with him?"

"Ellison was the kind of judge you want if you're a guy like this Shill," said Grandad. "Not that it mattered. I don't remember the particulars, but Tommy fought like hell with the DA over the case. Tommy wanted to go to trial, but they ended up with a plea bargain. Tommy was sick about it."

Uncle Morty tilted the screen toward Grandad. "You seen a lot of trials. What do you think about the sentence?"

Grandad scratched his two-day-old beard and said, "It's within the judge's discretion. The DA and defense agreed to it."

"The DA went against Tommy. I remember that, too. It happened, but not often," said Uncle Morty.

"Has Parks got anything hinky in his background?" asked Grandad.

Uncle Morty typed for a moment. "Member of the bar in good standing. No arrests. Unmarried. Credit's good. Let's see if he's been sued." He typed and scrolled through some pages. "Several suits. Inadequate counsel. A few were dropped. A couple settled."

I groaned. "This guy's a lot more boring than I hoped."

"Yeah, pretty run-of-the-mill. He was sued by his former partner's wife, but it was dropped, too."

"That could be something. How recent?" I asked.

"'95."

"I thought he was a DA."

"Not until 2003. He was in private practice and not so successful. Didn't help that his partner killed himself," said Uncle Morty.

Please let this be something.

"Are they sure it was a suicide?" I asked.

He did some more typing and said, "No doubt. John Evans shot himself in the office and left a note to his father, saying he couldn't live with the burden. He mentioned shame and some decision. The secretary was there when it happened and Parks was in court. Definitely in the clear."

"Then why did the wife sue him?" I asked.

"Defamation of character. She claimed Parks told people that her husband killed himself because he was gay."

"I take it he wasn't," said Grandad.

"Not according to her, but the judge had a talk with her and she dropped it."

"You're missing the point," I said. "This has nothing to do with anything."

They looked up at me.

"He called the DA by his first name. He said Waylon, like they're friends. DAs don't usually become friends with the people they prosecute, do they?"

Grandad thought about it. "No, not that I've seen. They'll sometimes arrange services if they have sympathy, for some reason. Your father did that occasionally. He visits some of his collars in prison."

"I know and he does call them by their first names, now that I think about it."

"Would you call them friends?" asked Pop Pop.

"Sort of," I said. "I visit Greta at Hunt and I guess she's a friend. She gave me some information. I totally forgot about that."

Uncle Morty sat up and his belly pushed over the edge of his keyboard. "What information? You holding out on me?"

"I told you. I forgot. It's been kinda busy." I told them about Greta and the orderly she overheard, possibly threatening Blankenship.

"Could be something else," said Grandad. "Journalist undercover, trying to get the kind of information that you get out of him."

"Could be," said Uncle Morty. "But it ain't."

"Don't journalists go undercover in prisons and whatnot?" asked Pop Pop.

"Yeah, but the prison's in on it. I'll bet a month's royalties that they don't know a thing about it or this guy would have access to Blankenship."

"And he can't get in," I said.

Uncle Morty nodded. "And he can't get in. I'm gonna run down every damn employee they got."

"Sounds like fun."

"Take me hours, but I got to do it. If you ain't got anything else, beat it."

"Have you got some paper?" I asked.

He jerked a thumb at his laptop bags and Grandad got out a pen and paper. "What have you got?"

"I'm not sure. It's a timeline. I need to see it."

I drew a line across the long legal pad, noting the years that had cropped up. Cassidy in 2002. The gloves being discontinued in 2005, the same year that Shill was convicted. And, of course, the year he didn't want to give me. 2004. The year he was brought into the Unsubs.

"Add 2003 and 2006," said Uncle Morty.

"What for?" I asked.

"Parks started with the DA's office in '03 and left in '06."

"Was he any good?"

"Beats the hell outta me." He gave a laptop to Grandad. "Read his record."

Grandad looked at me and winked. "I guess I'll read his record."

"See if he was easy on all attempted rapes or if Shill was special," I said.

"No problem." Grandad was grinning. "Feels good to be back in the saddle. Maybe I won't go on the road with Double Black Diamond after all."

I stopped writing. "What did you say?"

"Mickey offered me a security job."

"Grandma J will kill you and me. Are you crazy? You're supposed to be retired...again."

"If the last week and a half has taught me anything, it's taught me that I like excitement. How many chances does a man have to go on the road with a world-famous band?'

"How many chances does a man have to get divorced?" I asked. "You promised to retire. Grandma wants to travel and be together."

"We can be together on the road," he said.

"No, you can't. Grandma meant go to Paris, take the Orient Express, stuff like that."

Grandad gazed at me under pale lashes. "Or I can start hanging out with my favorite granddaughter. You're plenty exciting."

Why does this feel like a threat?

"What do you want, Grandad?" I asked.

"Back me up when I put it to Grandma. Tell her that the guys are swell and that she'll have fun."

"I can't and besides, she'd know I was lying. I'm a terrible liar."

"You're a great liar," he said.

Pop Pop looked at me with puppy dog eyes. "You are?"

"But I only lie to the bad people," I said.

He didn't seem comforted.

Grandad was eyeing me. "Besides, I said we need to talk."

"About what? Mom?" I asked.

"Not about Carolina."

Oh, crap.

"What then?"

"Cats and things that go bump in the night," he said.

"Okay." I avoided his eyes and looked back at my paper and marked, for no real reason, that Dad got the department to stop ordering those particular gloves in 2003. "Anyone know who Josef Mayer is?"

Pop Pop and Uncle Morty were blank, but Grandad said, "Sounds familiar. Why?"

"He brought Shill into the Unsubs and he didn't mind telling me who it was."

Grandad pulled out his phone and started searching. "I can see why. Josef Mayer died in prison of a heart attack in 2012, if that's the right guy."

"There has to be a ton of Josef Mayers. What did that one do?"

"Well…"

"Come on, Grandad. How bad can it be? They're digging up shallow graves in Kansas and I just interviewed a guy who put a girl in a wood chipper. Lay it on me."

Never ask anyone, "How bad can it be?" Because it's guaranteed to be worse than you imagine. And Josef Mayer was a case in point. He imprisoned his two daughters for a decade and fathered five children with them. There was more, but I made Grandad stop talking. I'd heard enough depravity for one day.

"Sounds like Shill's kind of guy," I said. "This wasn't here, was it?"

"Montreal, Canada."

"Blankenship said the group was international, but how would those two meet?"

Grandad nodded and looked at Uncle Morty. "Good question."

"I'm gonna have to subcontract some of this shit out." Uncle Morty glared at me. "Anything else you want me to do?"

"Hey, usually, you're complaining that I don't have enough. You should be happy," I said.

"I'm freaking thrilled."

"Good."

"Great."

There was a knock on the door and it opened, revealing an older woman carrying a clipboard. "Is Mercy Watts in here?"

I raised my hand. "Occupational therapy?" I asked.

"No. I'm Diane Przybocki from psychological services and I need to speak to you outside," she said.

I said sure, but I wasn't enthusiastic. It was probably about Mom's attempted rape and I so didn't want to think about that. I gave the timeline to Pop Pop, who looked at it with distaste. "What should I do with this?"

"I don't know. Give it a think. Maybe something will come to you," I said, heading out the door.

I got outside and instead of finding Diane Przybocki on her own, Mr. Snyder, the head of security, was there, and Aunt Miriam, for crying out loud.

"This can't be good news," I said.

"I'd like you to come with me so we can discuss the situation," said Mrs. Przybocki.

"There's a situation? And it's not about my mother?"

"No. This has nothing to do with Mrs. Watts."

I glanced at Mr. Snyder and Aunt Miriam. He was pulling on his collar and avoiding my gaze. Aunt Miriam's thin lower lip was poking out, but her chin was up.

"Just tell me," I said. "What happened?"

"It's better if we go to my office."

"Look. I'm exhausted." I pointed down the hall. "My mother's waiting for me and her next appointment. I've got to get her into rehab. Figure out how to get my father unarrested in Chicago. Interview a psycho at Hunt. Oh, and there's a guy out there who's totally into killing my family. I'd say it can't get any worse, but it totally can. Just tell me."

"It seems that you may have threatened to" —she looked at her clipboard— "eat the feet of a couple of doctors and you sprayed them with a fire extinguisher in the ICU."

"What of it?"

That was not the answer she was expecting. "Miss Watts, I…that is not—"

"Acceptable behavior? Got it. Next."

"We have to decide whether to…"

Mr. Snyder stepped up. "They're talking about barring you from the hospital, Mercy. I'm sorry. I've tried to tell them who you are."

"Mr. Snyder, it hardly matters who she is. She may be an unstable person and she's walking around our hospital."

"Those doctors are unstable," I said. "Talk to them about keying cars and fish in trunks."

"That's immaterial to your behavior."

"What do you want me to say?" I asked. "I did it. I'm sorry those jerks were fighting outside my mother's ICU room and acting like nuts. I'm not sorry I sprayed them."

"I may have to recommend that you and your aunt are banned."

I was on the edge of yelling, but that stopped me. "My aunt? She wasn't even there."

Mr. Snyder swallowed hard and said, "There was another situation."

"With?"

"A couple of candy stripers in an elevator."

I turned on Aunt Miriam. "What did you do?"

"Nothing that wasn't warranted," she said with her trademark stink eye.

"Did you whack them? Did you?" My voice went up three octaves.

"There aren't any witnesses," said Mr. Snyder.

Mrs. Przybocki looked like she wanted to whack him with Aunt Miriam's new cane or her clipboard. Whatever would hurt more. "The girls said she hit them and they have welts."

"Aunt Miriam, hitting me is one thing. I'm family. I have to put up with you," I said, getting more tired by the second.

"What do you mean, 'put up with'?" asked Aunt Miriam with so much stink eye I'm surprised her eyes weren't burning.

"I mean, I put up with you and the rest of this gaggle of nuts we call a family because you're my family. Nobody else has to do it. Especially a couple of spoiled brats that torture disabled people and post it on the internet. Don't make me break your cane again."

"They were saying things about you," said Aunt Miriam with her blue eyes going watery. "I couldn't stand those girls judging you. They're trash and you're...you."

"That's nice, but now we're dealing with all this." I turned back to Mrs. Przybocki. "What do you need from me? I'm not staying out of this hospital. That's not happening."

"They tortured a disabled person?" she asked.

"Why do you think a couple of douches like them are doing community service?"

"I have no idea, but I can't just let this go. The doctors are making a fuss and you know how they are."

"I do and I'll tell you what, I won't tell my godmothers about this." I'd never, ever used the Bled name to get out of trouble before and I wasn't proud of it, but this conversation needed to be over.

"Your godmothers?"

"Millicent and Myrtle Bled. They're generous donors, I believe."

"Yes, they are. What are you saying?" asked Mrs. Przybocki.

"Just that I won't do anything like that again and I have no interest in eating any kind of feet."

She tapped her pen on her clipboard. "Perhaps if I could assure the doctors that you won't be dealing with them anymore and that you'll go to therapy..."

"I'm already in therapy, so you won't even be lying. My grandparents will deal with the doctors." *Until I decide to deal with the doctors.*

"Alright, but what about her?" She indicated Aunt Miriam. "She did assault those girls."

"I have an idea." I whipped open the waiting room door. "Grandad, can you watch Aunt Miriam?"

"I will not be watched like a child," protested Aunt Miriam.

"Then stop hitting people like a four-year-old."

Grandad came out. "What did you say?"

"Mr. Snyder, can you take it from here?" I asked.

"I guess I will."

Mr. Snyder started to explain the elevator incident as I trucked down the hall to Mom's room. All I heard from Grandad was, "Dammit, Miriam!"

I waved to the cop at the door and went in, ramming straight into Tiny's chest.

"Thank God, Mercy," he said. "Where you been? We got a situation."

Fan-freaking-tastic.

CHAPTER SEVENTEEN

Nana, Dixie, and Aunt Tenne stood around Mom's bed, staring down at Wallace. She was making a low growling noise, but other than that, everything seemed fine. I mean, as fine as a stroke room got. Mom had a tissue to the corner of her mouth for the drooling, but she wasn't crying anymore, so that was a plus.

"What's up with Wallace?" I asked when no one said anything.

Nana put her hands on her generous hips and said, "What have you been doing?" She said it like I might've been getting a pedicure or something equally as frivolous.

"Working with Uncle Morty on the crime timeline." *And getting me and Aunt Miriam out of hot water.* "What's the problem?"

Aunt Tenne gripped Mom's side rail like she might rip it off and Dixie still wouldn't look at me. She fussed with Mom's blankets, her delicate hands shaking. Nana clenched her jaw and looked over my head.

On cue, Tiny said, "He called."

"Dad?" I gasped. "Thank god. Wait. What's wrong?"

Mom's shook her head no and her eyes filled again.

"I give up. Who called?"

"Him," spat Nana. "The guy."

I turned to Tiny. He had spots of dusky pink on his cheeks. "The one who attacked Carolina."

People talk about throwing up in their mouths, but I really did. And it was that quick. I heaved and burning liquid almost made it past my lips. I forced it back down and gasped, leaning on Tiny. "How? When?"

"Just now," said Nana. "He hung up a second before you came."

"How do you know it was him and not some crank?" I asked.

Mom began shivering and I automatically pulled the blankets up, giving me a moment to think.

It was simple to get connected to a patient room in a hospital. I should've thought of it, but it never occurred to me that the bastard would reach out. That was a special kind of arrogance. Dr. Grace was right about the personality we were dealing with. I should've paid more attention to what he said. But it was so rare that killers did that, would I have even considered it? No, probably not.

"He knew about our house," said Mom.

I came to her bedside and took her hand. "Lots of people know our house."

"He described her underwear, Mercy," said Aunt Tenne. "The ones she was wearing when it happened."

I didn't throw up again, but my stomach wanted to. "Tell me exactly what happened."

There wasn't much to tell. The phone rang and Dixie answered. The caller said he was a friend of my dad's from the force and he asked how Mom was doing. Dixie gave a cheerful report and asked if he wanted to talk to Mom. He did. Mom was hesitant to talk on the phone with her slur, but the speech therapist said the more she talked the better, so she took the phone.

The conversation started out fine. He asked how she was and she gave the same answer as Dixie. Then Mom asked who he was. His voice was vaguely familiar. He didn't give a name. He described Mom lying on the bricks, so beautiful, so damaged. He said he kissed her. He wanted to know if she remembered his touch, if she was looking forward to the next time he would touch her. He said he'd always wanted to touch her and he knew that she wanted it, too.

Mom was so stunned she didn't say anything. She just listened. The way she described it, her silence got him going. He switched from her to me, saying that he'd touched me in Sturgis and I didn't even know it. He said he would touch me again and asked what Tommy would think.

Mom came alive at that and said, "You stay away from my daughter." She slurred badly and he laughed about it. Aunt Tenne snatched the phone away from Mom and yelled, "Who is this?"

He said, "Tell Mercy hello for me. I'll be seeing her soon."

He hung up and everyone stared at the phone on the bed like it carried the Ebola virus.

"I'm sorry, Mercy," said Tiny. "I'm so sorry."

I patted his enormous bicep. "You didn't know that would happen. Neither did I."

"Why didn't you know?" asked Nana, tearfully sinking into a chair beside Mom's bed.

"It's not her fault, Mom. Mercy can't know everything," said Mom.

"You always say she's just like Tommy."

"She's doing the best she can." Mom looked at me with such generosity, I nearly broke down right there. Instead, I grabbed the phone and ripped it out of the wall. "I'll be right back."

I left the room and leaned on the hall wall, shaking. The young cop watched me with apprehension before saying, "Are you alright?"

"The man who tried to kill my mother just called and threatened her," I said.

"Oh, shit." He fumbled with the radio at his waist. "I'll call it in."

I nodded and went to the desk, plunking the phone down hard on the counter. The nurse looked up in surprise. "Can I help you?"

"No phones in my mother's room," I managed to get out.

"Phones are standard. Is there a problem?"

"Yes." I tried to say it again, but the words wouldn't come out. It was nasty, so hideously cruel, that I started shaking. I wanted to yell, to curse, but Mom would hear and she didn't need that. What she needed was my father. And I needed him, too. That was a new concept. I spent most of my time trying to avoid my dad and his demands. Lucky for me, he worked incessantly and my childhood was mainly just me and Mom. We were a duo. Dad had said many times that he felt like an intruder when he came home because we had such a routine. But when he was home, *I* felt like the intruder. The two of them were so connected, so into each other that they needed no one else. It'd never really been the three of us, just pairs switching out members.

A hand touched my back and I screeched, knocking the phone to the floor. Pete bent down to pick it up. "Are you okay?" he asked. "What's with this phone?"

I threw myself into his arms and sobbed, blubbering about the call and not getting Dad back. I snotted all over his lab coat, but he just asked the nurse for some tissues and let me go on snotting.

"He's evil," I said once I calmed down a bit.

"You've dealt with evil before," said Pete, smoothing my hair. His hand hesitated on the shorn parts, but he didn't say anything. That was so like him.

"Not like this. He taunted Mom. He wants to go on hurting her after what he's already done to her."

"Evil sounds accurate." He held me back by the shoulders. "You're going to figure this out and you'll get your father back, too."

I blew my nose and said, "How?"

He chuckled and pushed his glasses up. "I have no idea, but you have a talent for figuring things out. You would've been great in forensics."

"I don't know if I can do anything. The FBI already screwed me over once."

"I heard about that. Are you going back to Hunt for more information?"

I nodded and blew my nose again. "I have to. I'm going to eat seafood stew."

Pete shuddered. He wasn't a big fan of seafood either. "That's commitment."

"It's disgusting, but I can't think of anything else to do. I have to have something else to trade for Dad and Blankenship likes to torture me for it."

"You'll do great," he said.

"You're so nice," I said. "Why are you so nice to me?"

"I'm that kind of guy."

"You're a great guy."

"I'm seeing someone," Pete blurted out.

It startled me, but I smiled. "Not really a concern for me right now."

"I just thought I should tell you."

"I'm glad. I hope she's nice to you and normal. You should get some normal."

The cop walked up and said, "The detective wants to talk to you."

I looked past Pete's shoulder and saw Chuck hovering by Mom's door, looking like my cat, Skanky, after I was forced to give him a bath. Angry and miserable at the same time.

"I've got to go deal with him," I said.

"By the way, I came up to tell you that I'll be the liaison for your mom's case. It seems Millikan and Nishi don't really want to talk to you."

"I heard. Thanks.

"My pleasure." Pete took off and I faced Chuck. He wouldn't look at me, but Sydney had no problems marching up and demanding to know what happened. I gave him the gist of the call.

Chuck came up reluctantly, still wet cat angry.

"Don't even start with me," I said. "I'm Alexander and this is the terrible, no good, very bad day."

He looked up and his expression changed to the sweet one I'd come to expect over the last few months. "I'm sorry."

"Nothing's going on with Pete. He's seeing someone and he showed up right after the call," I said.

"I know. Are you okay?"

"Not so much, but that doesn't matter, does it?"

"It does to me," said Chuck, extending a long arm and pulling me into his chest.

Sydney slapped his notebook down on the counter. "For Christ's sake, this isn't your honeymoon. We've got shit to do."

I wiped my eyes. "I know. It was just a shock that he called."

"I didn't see that coming," said Sydney.

"Nobody did," said Chuck. "Anything stand out to you? We'll have to talk to Carolina, but your instincts are good."

"What have you decided?" I asked.

The detectives went stock still.

"Hello? The Feds have shut you out, despite my best efforts. Are you with them or me?"

"I thought you wanted us to work with them," said Sydney.

"I did until they screwed me over."

Chuck stepped back and said, "Blankenship gave you something else."

"Ya think?"

"Mercy, please."

"Got anything to trade?" I asked.

"Like what?'

"Like what did you get from Palfry?"

They went blank for a second and then Sydney said, "Oh, that snotty son of a bitch."

"Huh?" asked Chuck.

"You know, that asshat butler from Hawthorne."

I laughed. "That is such a good description of Palfry. What did he say?"

"Wait a minute," said Sydney. "You going to give us something?"

"Are you going to give it to the Feds?" I asked.

They exchanged a look and then shrugged.

"Screw 'em," said Chuck. "Palfry didn't give us anything. Just a bunch of crap about how your family is a stain on the street."

"He's lying," I said.

"Hell, yeah, he's lying."

Sydney raised his arms and interlocked his fingers over his head, revealing the pit stains that went all the way through his jacket. Even my day wasn't that stressful. Ew. "We don't have anything to hold him on and Hawthorne Avenue doesn't exactly buzz with activity. I don't know how Palfry would've seen or heard anything anyway. He works six mansions down."

That was an obvious problem. I rarely saw Palfry, which was no great loss. He wasn't social. At least, not with us.

Aunt Tenne came out of Mom's room with Wallace, holding her at arm's length. "She needs to go out and you got the short straw."

The story of my life.

"Come on, Wallace. Want to go on a road trip?"

Aunt Tenne put her down and she scampered over to me.

"Where were we?" I asked Chuck.

"Palfry not being outside."

Bark.

"I know. I know," I said.

Bark. Bark.

"Hold on. I'm thinking."

Bark. Bark. Bark.

"You'd better go," said Sydney. "The pug has got to pee."

"That's it," I said, picking up Wallace in triumph. "He does go outside. Palfry walks the dogs."

"He didn't mention any dogs," said Sydney, grabbing his notebook off the counter.

"The McCallisters have two Afghan hounds. Palfry walks them." I kissed Wallace on the top of her head. "You are getting to be so useful. Don't pee."

Bark.

All Chuck's muscles went tense. "When does he walk them?"

"Whenever," I said. "I don't think there's a schedule."

"Does anyone walk with him?"

"Not that I've seen, but I think he does the circuit."

Sydney looked up from writing. "The circuit?"

I described what Mom called the circuit. It was the best way through the Central West End's streets, the walk with the most shade and the prettiest houses. At the far end was Ode de Caffeine, a coffee bar specializing in single estate beans and high prices. When Mom did her ill-advised jogging, she stopped there for an espresso shot and to flirt with Johnny and Jim, the owners.

"They have great coffee," said Chuck. "But it costs six bucks for a cup of the house blend."

"That's insane," said Sydney. "Give me some Folger's. I can get a whole can for that."

"Ode de Caffeine is always packed," I said. "You should see if Palfry was there on Saturday."

"The butler pays six bucks for coffee?"

I shrugged. "You met him. What do you think?"

"I think we're going to try out how the other half drinks coffee," said Sydney. "Anything else about Palfry?"

"I'd recanvass Hawthorne. Palfry's a gossip. He stops on his walks to get the dirt from the maids."

"They like that snotty bastard?"

"I guess. I've heard from Joy that he's always in the know."

Sydney wrote furiously on his pad. "Who's that?"

"The Bleds' housekeeper," said Chuck. "Now what have you got for us?"

I gave them everything I'd found out so far, including the years that seemed significant but remained mysterious.

"Parks, eh?" Sydney scratched his chin with his pen, leaving a blue line in the stubble. "I know him."

According to Sydney, Waylon was a mediocre DA and was now representing gangbangers and random thugs. He loved to deal and spent little time in court, which was good for his clients since he had a terrible record in trials.

"Is he sleazy?" I asked.

Sydney shrugged. "He's a lawyer."

"I mean, sleazy sleazy as in Shill sleazy."

Chuck's eyebrows shot up. "You think he's in the Unsubs?"

"I think he might be our guy. Sounds like he went toe-to-toe with my dad. Maybe Dad did something to him that made him leave the DA's office."

Sydney nodded. "I wouldn't put it past Tommy. He's been known to grind the mediocre into the dirt."

"You know, Parks could be in the Unsubs," said Chuck. "If that porn ring taught me anything, it's that guys like that look like everyone else. We got doctors, lawyers, all types. Are you staying here?" he asked me.

"I'm going back out to Hunt," I said without thinking. I should've lied. Chuck hated my going to Hunt, worse than I did, actually.

"What the hell for?"

"I need something to get my dad out of custody unless you've got a better idea," I said. "No? I didn't think so. Hold on. I have an idea." I went to Mom's room and called in, "Hey, Aunt Tenne, can you come out here?"

"I'm not taking that dog!" she called back.

"I know. Come on."

Aunt Tenne came out, eyeing Wallace. "What is it?"

"What did he sound like, the guy on the phone?" I asked.

"Just a man."

"Young? Old?"

She crossed her arms over her bosom. "How would I know?"

"Come on," I said. "Just think about it."

Aunt Tenne leaned against the wall's hand rail and closed her eyes. "Not young, I don't think. Mature. Middle-aged. A little bit grouchy but not like Morty."

"Was the voice gravelly?"

"Not at all." She opened her eyes. "What are you looking for?"

Chuck grinned at us. "Did he sound like a smoker?"

"No. Average white guy."

I hugged Aunt Tenne. "Thanks. That's a big help."

"I don't see how, but okay. You staying?" she asked me.

"I've got to find a way to get Dad out of jail."

"While you're at it, get your hair cut. I don't know what you did to it this time, but your mother's having a fit."

"Good. It'll give her something else to think about," I said and she went back inside.

Sydney continued to write while Chuck mused, "So he knows Tommy personally and hates him."

"And he's not the guy who visited Blankenship."

"Or showed up at the ICU. The volunteer said the voice was distinctive," said Sydney. "I'm thinking Parks is important. He's got to have some guys who'd be willing to do him a little favor."

Chuck kissed me on the forehead. "We'll work him hard. Good luck at Hunt. How's that bodyguard Ace got you?"

"She kinda rocks in a scary way," I said.

"Scary is good as long as she can back it up."

"Don't worry about that. She's good."

They walked away and I took a moment to watch Chuck's rear view. He was a pleasure to view, when I didn't want to wring his neck, that is.

I went in the opposite direction and called Fats. With the press on my tail, it was time to get creative.

And get creative, I did. Sometimes, it's helpful when you know people and even more helpful when people know who you are. I had that kind of face. Unforgettable. Usually, I found it annoying, at best, but that day, when the EMTs all knew exactly who I was and why I had to get out of the hospital unseen, it was a huge help.

I hitched a ride on an ambulance that was supposedly going to get washed, but I think Jason and Ally were just doing me a favor without saying so. Ally let me borrow one of her uniforms. I barely squeezed into it, but where there's a will, there's a safety pin.

A respiratory therapist slapped a Cardinals cap on me and I walked past the reporters clustered around the ER with no problems. Security was threatening to call the cops on them, but like all press, they were willing to take the chance.

I walked past them and got in the back of the ambulance. Jason put a large box labeled "Blue Disposable Underpads" in with me and closed the door. We drove away from the hospital and the press was none the wiser.

Bark.

I opened the box and Wallace looked up at me, smiling her pug smile. "You were very good. Maybe Aaron will have a sausage for you."

Bark.

"I think I'll call him."

She spun in a circle and I texted, requesting a sausage for Wallace and a palate cleanser for me. I got no answer. Typical. Fats, on the other hand, loved my great escape and met us at The Shaved Duck. She'd already gone in the restaurant and bought my co-conspirators an obscene amount of barbecue, so we were on our way to pick up Aaron and then on to Hunt in a mere ten minutes.

Fats used her snazzy radar detector and I found myself standing outside the Fishbowl, holding an adorable mussels pot like the ones they used in Paris, before I could get nervous about it. I'd never actually eaten mussels out of one of those pots, but Millicent and Myrtle did. I stuck to the fries and cheese board. You can live off cheese in Paris. I proved it on a couple of trips when Myrtle and Millicent were in a fishy frame of mind.

"That smells fantastic," said Shelley. "I'm so jealous."

"I sincerely wish you could eat it," I said, taking the smallest breaths possible.

"What did he put in there? Smells like mussels, maybe some kind of fish, and...shrimp. I'm drooling," she said. "Can you see me drooling?"

"Squid," said a voice behind me.

I jumped and spun around, nearly spilling my stew, but I saved it. Dammit. "Don't do that, Aaron."

He held up a glass container with a blue rubbery top.

"If that's crab, you can forget it." I held up the pot. "I'm good."

Shelley leaned over and peered at the container. "Looks like toast."

Toast could be good. Mom gave me toast when I'd been throwing up. But I doubted it was dry toast. I couldn't get that lucky. It was Aaron, after all.

"What's on the toast?" I asked.

Please don't say octopus pâté or anything gross.

"Gremolata butter," he said.

"Really? No squid ink or caviar?"

He peeled off the top and I took a sniff. There wasn't any seafood horror, but it wasn't regular gremolata either. "What'd you put in there?"

He shrugged.

"Am I going to like it?" I asked.

"Yeah."

"Alright then. I'm trusting you. Where's Wallace?"

"Truck." With that, Aaron trotted away.

"Is he usually like that?" asked Shelley.

I stretched out my aching arms. "No. Usually, he's not so chatty."

She was going to inquire further, but her radio squawked, saying that Blankenship was in place.

"I warn you. He's been in a real mood since you were last here," said Shelley.

"Define real mood."

"Demanding a phone to call you. He bit a guard, Herb, and he likes him. I mean, as well as he likes anyone besides you. Doctor had to give him a shot of Thorazine to calm him down. He's been in a strait jacket almost the whole time."

"Weren't the chains and waist belt enough?"

"No," she said stone-faced. "You ready for this?"

"I've got to admit I'm a little freaked."

"Good. I want you on your toes."

A couple of other guards joined us and they unlocked the many locks before escorting me inside. The room was as usual, but Blankenship wasn't.

"What the hell happened to you?" I burst out without thinking.

Blankenship stared at me from his normal spot in a straitjacket and chained to the chair. One eye was swollen shut and a livid purple. He had scratches all over his face, a split lip that hurt to look at, and his right earlobe was torn. His brown hair was greasy and looked like someone had rubbed his head with a balloon.

I put the pot and the toast container on the table and sat down, pulling out the over-sized spoon Aaron insisted I use. "Seriously. What the hell?"

"They wouldn't let me call you." Blankenship's eyes were dead and I mean dead, like in that weird type of animation where the characters can almost fool you, but the dead eyes give it away. Snakes had more warmth than those eyes.

"And you thought beating the crap out of yourself would help?"

"What else have I got?"

"Good point," I said. "Well, I'm here. What's up?"

He opened his mouth slowly, like a crocodile. Inside was what looked like a plastic packet about an inch square.

"What's he doing, Mercy?' Shelley's voice came over the speaker behind me.

"Er...nothing, just being him."

Blankenship closed his mouth and shifted the packet to his cheek. "I missed you."

"Do you miss people? Really?"

A smile flickered on his swollen lips and it was almost as creepy as the crocodile thing. "You do know me."

"Yeah, it's been swell," I said. "Look, I've got a situation."

"Why are you wearing that?" he asked. "I don't like it."

"What?" I looked down. "Oh, the uniform. It was necessary."

"Take it off."

Shelley's voice came out in a panic, "Don't take it off."

"I'm not going to take it off," I said with an eye roll.

"I don't like it," said Blankenship.

"I got that and believe me, it's not my first choice."

He shifted in his straitjacket and eyed me calmly. "Tell me."

So I told him about the press, the FBI, and Shill. He especially liked the part where Fats came close to smothering him.

"You need more information to bribe the Feds to let your father out. Is that it?"

I paused and said, "Yes."

He tilted his head, interest lighting up his eyes for the first time. "What else?"

How do I play this? How do I make him want it?

I looked away. "Nothing. I brought this disgusting stew. It has squid in it. You want me to eat it?"

"What else?"

I ignored that and forced myself to lift the lid. It was as bad as I imagined. God help me. There were tentacles floating around in there in a thin, reddish broth. Tentacles. Why? Weren't mussels and fish bad enough?

I dipped in my spoon. "I've got tentacles. You want me to eat a tentacle?"

"I want you to touch me," he said.

"Don't touch him," said Shelley.

"If you think that's worse than tentacle, you're wrong," I said.

"I want to feel your skin on my skin," he said.

I mouthed, "Why?"

He did the crocodile thing again, showing me the packet. Crap. I was going to have to touch him. Shelley would freak. Everybody would freak. Wilson Cleves didn't look that healthy. He might have a coronary.

I made the smallest air kiss I could and he got the message.

"Tell me what else happened," said Blankenship. "I've got all day."

"I don't."

"I know."

I put the lid on the pot and said, "Your friend showed up at the hospital."

"I don't have friends."

"That's what Shill said. Let's go with accomplice," I said.

"Who came to the hospital?" he asked.

"Your visitor. He was trying to get in the ICU where my mother was."

Blankenship looked over my head and said, "I don't like that."

"Who the hell are you talking to?" I asked.

"He knows."

Okay. This is getting worse and worse.

"And my mother's attacker called her."

Blankenship grimaced, opening the split in his lip. Blood pooled and then ran down his chin to plop on the strait jacket, obscenely red against the pure white. "What did he say?"

"What do you think? He threatened her and me, of course."

"He threatened you? You belong to me."

"I don't think he's heard," I said. "Apparently, he touched me in Sturgis, but I'm trying not to think about that."

"He can't have you."

"I quite agree. Do you have something for me or what?"

Blankenship sat there, blankly watching me. For a minute, I thought he would say no. I didn't know what I'd do if he did. He was my only source.

"How's your memory?" he asked.

Mom lying on the bricks flashed in my mind. "Too good."

"Excellent. Remember this." He tilted his head down to conceal his mouth from the cameras. "G&T Bank and Trust."

I nodded, my stomach in a knot.

He gave me another safe deposit box in Hannibal, but I'd need a court order to get into it. That wouldn't be any help with Dad. The FBI would get whatever was inside and I wouldn't.

"How does that help if I can't get at it?" I asked.

"*You* can."

He could be sending me off to Hannibal to make me look like a fool or maybe it was real. I couldn't tell. The blank expression was back in a big way.

"I guess I don't have to eat this stew then," I said.

"What's in the other container?"

"It's no use to you. I'll like it."

"Open it."

I opened the toast container and he sniffed the air like a hound trailing a fox.

"Lemon?" he asked.

"Looks like it."

"Garlic?"

"Yep, but don't ask me what else. I didn't make it," I said.

He shifted slightly in the restraints. "Eat one."

I eyed him suspiciously but went ahead. I didn't draw it out like one of those stupid Carl's Junior commercials. First of all, it's hard to be sexy in an EMT uniform that's restricting blood flow to the lower half of your body. And second, I didn't want to, not even to get more information out of him.

I just stuffed a whole toast round in my mouth and chewed noisily.

Blankenship fixated on my lips and when I went to wipe away the buttery fabulousness off my lips, he said, "No."

My hand froze. I knew he was up to something. "No?"

"Kiss me," he mouthed.

"Ew. No."

He did the crocodile thing again and the packet was on the tip of his tongue.

"Mercy," Shelley said. "Time's up."

"One more minute, please," I said.

There was a pause where the guards must've been conferring.

"Thirty seconds."

I had to decide. Did I want that packet or not?

"Is it worth it?" I asked, knowing the answer, but I couldn't think what else to do.

"For both of us. Tommy Watts will want it. The FBI will want it," he mouthed.

Shit!

"If it isn't good, I'll never come back."

He smiled and I shivered.

"I'm not worried. You'll definitely be back."

"Fifteen seconds," said Shelley and I heard the door creak.

That cinched it. I didn't think. I just did it. If I had thought, I would've known what would happen. But as it was, I jumped out of my chair and ran around the table and I did it. I laid a kiss on a psycho. The packet slid into my mouth and the bastard bit my lower lip. I screamed, feeling his teeth cut into my flesh and Shelley was there. She tased him and he released me. I fell backward and landed on my rump. Two guards grabbed me and hauled me back toward the door. Blankenship shook violently, but his eyes were on me. My blood ran down his chin and a smear of gremolata butter was on his upper lip. He managed to lick them both, sucking in my blood and the butter with a twisted smile that was more like a grimace.

Out in the hall, the door to the Fishbowl slammed and Shelley screamed. "What the hell was that?"

I put my hand to my lip and came away with a good amount of blood and the packet, which I palmed. "I'm okay," I said.

"You're okay? Shit!"

I struggled to my feet and leaned against the wall, catching my breath and dabbing at my lip with a tissue one of the other guards offered. Shelley paced with wild hand gestures and cussing I didn't think she had in her. Wilson Cleves ran down the hall, his normally jolly face sweaty and red.

"Mercy, are you alright?" He bent over, gasping.

I rubbed his heaving shoulder. "I'm okay."

He stood up. "Why would you do it? This is an incident. We have to write it up. And Tommy, what will he say? He trusted me to keep you safe."

"I am safe and, more importantly, I got what I needed."

"What could be worth kissing that creature?" he asked.

"I'm going to go find out."

He threw up his hands. "You mean, you don't know? Christ, Mercy. He might be playing you for a fool."

"He might, but he wants me back. Anybody can see that."

Cleves and the guards got quiet and nodded.

"He does. God help you," said Shelley. "It's not a good thing."

"But it might do some good." I lowered the tissue. "How bad is it?"

Shelley took a close look. "He got you good. A couple of stitches to close it up."

"We'll probably just butterfly it," I said.

"I think he almost went all the way through."

"Yeah," I said. "I felt it, but a girl's gotta do what a girl's gotta do."

"Who are you?" she asked.

I thought about it. "Right now? Desperate."

"He took advantage of that desperation," said Cleves. "You shouldn't come back. The department may bar you anyway."

"I doubt it," I said.

They walked me out and I had to concentrate to walk a straight line. My head was light and the feeling of exhaustion was overwhelming.

Shelley got me an ice pack and a towel for my lip. She wasn't cussing anymore, but the anger and fear were still written all over her.

"It won't happen again," I said.

"You can't guarantee that," she said.

"I guess not, but I'd only do it if I thought I had to. Eat the stew. I'm sure you'll love it. The toast is fantastic."

She smiled. "I guess there's that."

"Always a bright side."

We high-fived and I joined Aaron in the empty waiting room. He was buzzing with excitement, rubbing his hands and bouncing up and down on the balls of his feet.

A wave of unexpected guilt came over me. I didn't eat the stew. He wanted me to eat it. He lived to make me eat food that I hated in the hopes that I wouldn't hate it. Failure was not a deterrent to Aaron. He just kept trying.

"The toast was amazing," I said through the ice pack.

He stopped bouncing.

"Sorry. I didn't eat the stew."

I expected his shoulders to slump. Instead, he pulled down the ice pack, took one look, and put it back up. Then he hustled me out to the truck, where Fats was leaning on the hood with Wallace sitting on one of her enormous feet. The pug hadn't peed on her. Thank goodness.

She lowered her book and said, "Ah, crap! What happened to you?"

"He bit me." I got in and she stared at me for a second before picking up Wallace and going to the driver's side.

She got in and gave me the pug, who sniffed my face and growled.

"My feelings exactly," said Fats. "Why in the hell were you that close? What about the glass?"

"There's no glass."

"Why isn't there glass?"

"Beats me. But there is a table."

"How did he get over the table without them stopping him? Isn't he chained up or something?"

I looked at the towel. The bleeding had pretty much stopped, but it was starting to hurt. It was kind of like having a sprained ankle on your face. That kind of burning. "He was in a straitjacket and chained to a chair," I said.

"You went to him? What the hell is wrong with you?" she asked. "When Calpurnia hears about this...shit!"

We drove out of Hunt and once we got back on the highway, I held out the packet.

Fats glanced at me. "What is that?"

"What I got bitten for," I said.

Aaron asked from the back, "You hungry?"

"I'm not going to be eating anything solid until the swelling goes down," I said.

Fats took the packet from me and held it up to the light. "There's folded up paper inside with something written on it." She gave it back. "Open it."

"I will when I have tweezers and an evidence bag. We've got other stuff to do."

"There's more?"

"There's always more. How long will it take to get to Hannibal?"

"What's in Hannibal besides Mark Twain stuff?"

I shifted in my seat and smiled before yelping in pain. "A safe deposit box with our names on it."

Fats grinned. "Hannibal, it is."

CHAPTER EIGHTEEN

The bank manager watched me like I might have rabies. Considering who bit me, it wasn't out of the realm of possibility. Hopefully, crazy wasn't catching.

Mr. Thompson walked us back to the safe deposit box area inside the vault and rechecked my signature and passport photo for a third time. I don't know why he bothered. He recognized me the moment I took off my Cardinal's cap and that's with an ice pack on my face.

"Can I get you anything?" he asked me.

"Got any Motrin?"

"I'm sure I do. Can I ask what happened?" Mr. Thompson flicked a glance at Fats, who was standing there, looking menacing, but I don't think she meant to. She couldn't help it.

"Sorry. I can't say," I said. "Where's the box?"

He went down the rows of boxes and surprised me by unlocking a larger one. It was thin but wide, about two feet across. Mr. Thompson set it on the table and hovered.

"Thanks," I said, waiting for him to beat it, but he didn't leave.

"Miss Watts, I don't remember you ever coming in here before," he said.

Fats crossed her arms. "Sometimes, she blends."

He looked doubtful. "No. I don't think so."

"It's my box," I said. Convincingly, I think, because he left to get me some Motrin.

Fats and I gathered around the table and looked at the box.

"What do you suppose is in there?" she asked.

"At this point, I'm just hoping it's not a body part," I said.

"You think that's a possibility?"

"I wouldn't put it past the Unsubs." I put my ice pack on the table and took a deep breath. "Here we go."

There wasn't a body part in the box. There was a laptop and only a laptop. No cord or anything else. I took it out and opened it. Dead, of course. I flipped it over, looking for any clue as to what it contained, but it was just a cheap, run-of-the-mill laptop.

"We need a cord," said Fats. "I don't have this kind. Do you?"

"No, but I know someone with every kind of cord in the world."

She smiled. "Morton Van Der Hoof?"

"He practically collects them." I closed the box as Mr. Thompson came back with Motrin and a cup of water.

He glanced at the laptop, but he was more interested in my face. "You need to go to the ER. It's five minutes away."

"I'm okay," I said, carefully placing the pills in my mouth and taking a sip of water. I dribbled because I couldn't fully close my mouth. Mr. Thompson cringed and Fats gave me my towel and ice pack. "I think he might be right," she said.

"I'll get it looked at when we get back to St. Louis," I said. "Thanks, Mr. Thompson. Have a nice day."

"Please go to the ER," he said.

"Please don't tell anyone I was here."

He shuffled his feet. "The word is already out. My assistant called her mother. She has 20,000 Twitter followers."

"What does she do?" asked Fats.

"Sex therapist."

I looked at the ceiling. "That's what I need. A sex therapist tweeting about me."

Fats laughed. "That is so your life."

"Let's get out of here."

We took off and thanks to the radar detector, we made it to Uncle Morty's apartment before he did. But there was vacuuming happening. Nikki was in residence, sterilizing the joint, as she did weekly. I knocked and she answered, took one look at me and dragged me off to the bathroom, leaving Fats, Wallace, and Aaron in the living room.

"I'll go to the hospital," I said when she pulled my ice pack down.

Nikki snorted. "Hospital. You don't need a hospital. I'll take care of it." She pointed at the toilet. "Sit down."

I obeyed, perching on the toilet lid and enduring Nikki's painful ministrations. She flushed the wound several times and decided to butterfly the outside since I said it was a human bite. She didn't ask how a human bit me on the face. She took it totally in stride, saying, "You'll need antibiotics."

"Are you a nurse?" I asked.

"I was. I left to pursue my real passion." Nikki dug out some steri strips and had me tilt up my chin.

"What's your real passion?"

"Library science."

I thought she might be joking, but she wasn't. Nikki had a passion for the Dewey Decimal System and mourned the demise of microfiche. I'm pretty sure she was the only one. I'd only seen it on reruns of *The X-Files* and it seemed like a huge pain in the ass.

She stood back and admired her handiwork. "You'll still need a strong antibiotic. Get that old boyfriend of yours to write you a script and you'll have to keep flushing it. I'll do it, if you like."

"Thanks. I might take you up on that," I said, happily escaping the bathroom to find Fats in Uncle Morty's second bedroom. At least, I thought it was the second bedroom. It was so neat and organized I wasn't sure.

"What are you looking for?" asked Nikki.

Fats held out the laptop. "A cord for this."

"Ah, a Dell. What year do you think it is?"

Uncle Morty stomped into the room. "It's five years old or maybe six. I got a universal cord that'll work." He looked at me. "You look like crap. What'd you do?"

I tried to frown, but it hurt too much. Instead, I held up the packet. "I got this."

"Who'd you get it from? A shark?"

"Close. Blankenship."

"Jesus. That's just great. Tommy is going to freak."

"Only if we can get him a ticket home with this." I tapped the laptop.

"Blankenship gave it to you?" he asked.

I told him about the trip to Hunt—light on the bite details—and he got more interested in the laptop. "So Blankenship put it in that safe deposit box with your name on it."

"Mine and his."

"The signatures matched?"

"Perfectly, but the manager noted that I'd never been there before. Whoever did the signing for me didn't bother to fake my face."

"Nobody could fake your face," said Fats. "He probably strolled in with another Unsub and did it."

"A female Unsub," I said. That was disturbing. Women didn't usually commit the kind of crimes that the group prided themselves in.

"Did you check the date on the last time it was opened?" asked Nikki.

We all looked at her and she patted her curly hair. "They keep a record of that kind of thing, don't they?"

"They do," I said. "It was only opened on the date rented. December twentieth."

Uncle Morty found the cord and fired up the laptop. "You'll have to go back and interview witnesses. Maybe someone was awake and will remember the Tulio shooter coming in for a box."

"I doubt it. Blankenship is pretty generic and if they recognized him, they probably would've called the cops when Tulio happened."

"You might have to jog their memories." Fats cracked her knuckles and Nikki gave her a wide berth on her way to get me some milk. It was the only thing in the house that wouldn't sting my mouth.

"They might have surveillance footage," said Uncle Morty, staring at the scene as the laptop went through its startup routine.

"That was almost eight months ago," I said. "I doubt they keep it that long, but I'll check."

The screensaver came on and we all recoiled.

"Does anyone else want something?" called out Nikki from the kitchen. "I have Coke and lemonade."

"Don't come in here!" yelled Uncle Morty. "Close the damn door!"

Fats slammed the door and we stared at the screen. The screensaver was a photo of a body, partially nude, on the ground with rocks and tree roots around it.

"I'm going to be sick," I said.

"Don't throw up," said Fats. "Your mouth can't take it."

I stood up and went to Uncle Morty's newly organized bookshelves, leaning on them with my head down.

"Do you know who she is?" asked Uncle Morty.

"Cassidy Huff," said Fats. "There was a picture in the file."

Nikki knocked on the door. "What's wrong?"

"Don't come in here," said Uncle Morty. "I don't want you to see this." Then he muttered under his breath, "I don't want anyone to see this."

"So this is Blankenship's laptop," said Fats.

"Or Shill's," I said.

"No," said Uncle Morty. "It's not."

I reluctantly turned around. The screensaver was down and he was in the computer's files. An encrypted file came up. There was a certain pattern to the encryption. I mean, it was all gobbledygook, but there was symmetry and spacing that was familiar.

"It kinda looks like a chat," I said.

"Yes, it does," said Uncle Morty. "Let's see what else we got."

He pulled up file after file. Most had the look of chats, but some were probably emails or photos. The picture of Cassidy's body was the only thing on it that wasn't encrypted.

Fats sat on the edge of the desk, making it creak. "I think it's Unsub chats and the proof of their victories."

"Can you break it?" I asked.

He snorted. "I'll break it."

"Soon?"

"It's tight, but I'll get it." He pointed to several different parts of one particular file. "He used different encryption on different sections, but he forgot or meant to leave unencrypted the dates that each file was created. What's the last date you gave me?"

"Um...Shill got out of prison in 2010."

"What's the date before that?"

"2006. Waylon Parks left the DA's office."

He nodded, hunching over the keyboard. "That's right. That's right."

Nikki knocked. "Can I come in now?"

"Yeah, yeah."

Nikki came in with a tray. I didn't get milk. I got a milkshake, vanilla, Fats got lemon water, and Uncle Morty held out his hand. She put a Mountain Dew can in it.

She put her arm around me. "Looks like you did well."

"Maybe. Can't really tell yet."

"I can tell." Uncle Morty grabbed another laptop and began transferring files. "I'm going to send this to Novak in Paris. He loves this stuff." He was almost gleeful. Check that. He *was* gleeful, absolutely giddy. It was a puzzle and Uncle Morty loved a puzzle. When he used to babysit me, we had to do the New York Times crossword and heinous 1,000-piece jigsaw puzzles. On the upside, there was always pizza and he read me books that Mom would've considered inappropriate for my age, like *To Kill a Mockingbird* in the second grade. I asked questions and Mom was pissed.

"What can you get right now?" asked Fats.

"I got a date range. 2004 to 2006."

"Weird," I said. "That's after Cassidy. Why the picture?"

Uncle Morty looked up from the screen. "That was for you."

"Blankenship didn't even know me then. You're saying he arranged all this with the hope of what?"

"It's just one of his nuts," said Fats.

Aaron came in with Wallace tucked under his arm. "You want nuts?"

Nikki pointed at him. "Almond cake."

The two cooks left and pots started banging in the kitchen.

"Okay," I said. "What about nuts?"

Fats crossed her arms and tapped her foot. "Blankenship's a squirrel burying nuts. In case he needs them later. This one's for you and he did know you. He said he followed you for that Unsub. That's how he got attached."

"He put Cassidy in there because that's what the guy used to prove he was for real," I said.

"And to horrify you," said Uncle Morty. "He wanted to mess with you and he was betting he'd get the chance. He knew that guy would come after you so he buried a nut. Just in case, he decided to save you."

"I don't know if I should be happy or freaked. A lot of planning went into this."

"I'm both," said Fats. "Have you got specific dates?"

"Hold on," said Uncle Morty. "Novak's on it. He says five hours for portions. Maybe less."

"What about those dates?" I rustled around through his laptop bag and found my timeline. "What's the last date we've got on the laptop?"

"Looks like February 10, 2006." Uncle Morty pulled a laptop out of the bag without looking and handed it to me. "Ace did a synopsis on Parks. Maybe there's a case on that date or something."

I found Grandad's file and scanned it, a chill going through me. "It's not a trial date or a case. It's Parks last day in the DAs office."

"That can't be a coincidence," said Fats. "What's the first day?"

"Well, Parks was already in the office in 2004. What happened in 2004?" I looked back at the timeline. "Shill got into the Unsubs."

"Look up that guy," said Fats as giddy as Uncle Morty.

"What guy?" I asked.

"That guy!"

"There's a lot of guys," I said. "You've got to help me out here."

She clenched her fists. "The one who brought him in. The daughter rapist."

"Oh, Josef Mayer." I'd rather not look up that waste of skin, but I did and found a Wikipedia page dedicated to the scumbag. There were details, gross ones, but not the specific dates I was looking for. "He was arrested in 2004 and sentenced in 2005," I said. "Do you have that date?"

"I got it," said Uncle Morty. "August first."

I found a newspaper article on Mayer with specifics. "Mayer was arrested on July fifteenth. A man moving into the house next door heard screaming and called the police."

Fats looked at me aghast. "You're telling me nobody heard screaming before?"

"Says here that neighbors heard plenty of screaming, but it was known that Mayer beat his wife so they were used to it. The new guy wasn't. He insisted the cops enter the house. They did and found the dungeon."

"Because beating his wife was fine," she said between gritted teeth.

"I'm just telling you what it says." I looked back at the article. "Mayer immediately went on suicide watch and was never released on bond."

"Got something right," muttered Uncle Morty.

"So the first file happens fifteen days after Mayer was arrested. He had to have brought Shill in before that because he was locked down tight."

Fats undid her sock bun and shook her head, giving her a mane. "I don't get it. What's with these dates? It's killing me."

"We'll know in five hours," said Uncle Morty.

I pushed back the laptop and took an icy sip of my milkshake. "I think we know now."

Uncle Morty stopped typing. "We don't know shit. We got dates and dirtbags."

"And...the FBI that doesn't want Tommy Watts anywhere near this."

"So?" burst out Fats.

Uncle Morty smiled at me. "Wait for it."

"They know about the Unsubs. The FBI knows."

Fats threw up her hands and stomped around the room. "Because Mayer got arrested and a DA quit? You're losing it. That bite injured your brain."

I did have a headache, but I wasn't losing it. I was getting it. The dates worked and keeping Dad finally made sense. The FBI said they'd put Chuck and Sydney on the case, but then they blocked them when the burial site was real.

"That has to be it. The FBI loves my dad. He's their golden boy."

"Damn straight they do," said Uncle Morty. "He's like Mulder without the alien obsession."

"Mulder?" asked Fats.

"X-Files," I said. "Chuck likes them, too."

"Oh," she said. "Wait a minute. What are we saying?"

I explained Tommy Watts to Fats Licata, as much as I could, anyway. FBI did love my dad. They'd tried all the way through his police career to bring him in as an agent, but Dad liked being a cop. He said no. They tried again after he retired and it was still no, but he started doing consulting for them. Serial killers, spree killers, rapists. Dad worked on a lot of cases for them. My father considered a ninety-hour work week light, so he was always ready and willing to fit in more cases. He taught classes for them and the media loved the skinny redhead with charm for days. Why would they not want him on his wife's case? A mass grave site that his daughter led them to? That's a no-brainer unless they had something to hide and they thought Tommy Watts could find it. They had to get the cover-up well in place before Dad was back in action. Me? I was just a dingbat that got lucky a few times. My father was the real deal. Everybody said so.

"If they knew about the Unsubs, why didn't they do something?" asked Fats.

Uncle Morty kept typing. "They probably couldn't get in the club. Knowing there's a group and getting in the group are two different things. Probably suspected Blankenship for an Unsub. That's why they wanted Mercy in there talking to him. Then you got Sturgis. They saw some connection and they took the case over, trying to cover up the ball they'd dropped. There's definitely something there that they don't want Tommy to know. The files will tell us." He pointed to the screen. "You see that?"

Fats and I exchanged a look and shrugged. More gobbledygook to us. Uncle Morty groaned in frustration. "I shoulda made you learn coding."

"Yeah, right," I said. "That totally would've happened."

"Look at it!"

"We're looking," said Fats.

Uncle Morty explained in excruciating detail how he could tell that the encryption had changed to a much more sophisticated style on the fifth file. I'm not going to lie. I blanked out and thought about chocolate several times, but the point was that he thought the Unsubs caught on quick and changed up what they were doing, leaving the Feds in the dust.

"So if I'm right and Mayer got the Feds in, it didn't last," I said.

"Right. The Unsubs ain't no idiots." He drummed his stubby fingers on the keyboard. "You go on. You're distracting me. At this damn rate, Novak's gonna beat me on every section. I'll never live it down."

Fats and I left, leaving him muttering about the Feds and idiots in our wake. Aaron and Nikki were in the kitchen, making an Italian almond cake. They shooed us out, along with Wallace, so we left the apartment, slowly walking down the stairs, our minds full.

"You know, even if you're right about the FBI, that doesn't get you any closer to finding out who attacked your mom or getting your dad back."

I lowered my ice pack and gave her the tiniest of smiles while holding up the packet. "But I still have this."

CHAPTER NINETEEN

I sat in the back of another ambulance with Wallace on my lap, gnawing on some sort of Greek sausage that Nikki gave her. It had feta cheese and spinach in it. The feta alone sounded like a bad idea, but Nikki insisted. Wallace had only horked down half the sausage and she was already gassing.

"This is so not working out for me," I said.

Bark.

"You stink. Mom might kick you out."

Grr.

"What was that?" Dan called back, another EMT with the kindness to fake an ambulance washing to pick me up from Forest Park.

"Nothing. The pug is stinky."

He laughed. "Isn't that normal for pugs?"

"It is for this one."

"We're getting close. You're going to want to stow her in five."

I went to put Wallace in the empty blue pad box, but she wasn't having it. I was about to wrestle her in with the sausage when my phone buzzed. A thrill went through me when I saw it was Uncle Morty. It was way too soon for the encryption to be broken, but I couldn't help hoping.

"What took so long?" he bellowed into the phone.

"It just buzzed."

"Yeah, yeah. You want to hear this?"

"I don't know," I said just to bother him. "Do I?"

"You're a pain in my ass. You know I got books to write. I could be doing other stuff."

Wallace snorted. Even the pug knew that was ridiculous.

"Puhlease. You're helping to catch my mother's attacker. You don't want to do anything else."

He grumbled. "Parks is in the clear. He's not the one."

"How do you know?" I asked.

"In court during Sturgis, defending some dirtbag drug dealer."

"The whole time?"

He started typing. "That's what I said."

"Well, there's obviously an accomplice," I said.

"The guy in Sturgis was white. The accomplice is Hispanic. Think, Mercy!"

"You sound like my dad."

"Somebody has to."

I sighed and touched my torn lip. Sound like Dad. I was doing more than that. "How about this? Parks isn't the guy, but he's the connection between the accomplice and the doer. What kind of gangs does Parks represent?"

"All kinds. He ain't particular."

"Well, Blankenship said he saw a tattoo on the neck. That could be gang-related."

Uncle Morty snorted. "Grandmas got tats these days. That don't mean nothing."

"I guess not. Barney didn't say anything about the guy being—"

He cut me off, "Being what? Like a gangbanger? There ain't no mold."

"Isn't there? Barney thought the guy was normal."

"You think gang members can't be well-spoken? You're hanging out with Fats Licata."

"She's not in a gang."

"Ya don't think?" he asked with a juicy snort.

"It's not the same."

"The hell it ain't. I wouldn't let that chick near you if Ace hadn't arranged it."

Thank you, Grandad.

"We're pulling in, Mercy," said Dan.

"What was that?" asked Uncle Morty.

"I'm at the hospital," I said. "Gotta go."

"Find some new connections. Don't be sitting on your ass, eating lime Jell-O."

I stuffed Wallace in the box so fast she didn't have time to growl. Now I knew what worked with the pug—the element of surprise. "First of all, I never eat Jell-O, period. And since when do I sit on my ass? You were just complaining about having too much to do. Now you want more?"

Uncle Morty hung up on me. It was kind of a relief. I'd had about as much crabby as I could stand.

"Hat on," said Dan as he parked. "I'm coming back."

Dan got us out of the ambulance and into the ER with zero problems. It helped that the press was nowhere to be seen. He took me to the staff locker room so I could change.

"I think they gave up," he said.

"They never give up," I said. "Trust me on that."

"I guess you'd know. You want me to walk you up to the floor?"

"Thanks, but my bodyguard will be here in a minute."

"That huge guy?"

I put my ice pack to my face to hide my smile. "She's a girl."

"Oh, sorry. She was just so…"

"Huge? I know," I said. "Can you send her my way when she gets here?"

"Sure. It's not like I can miss her." Dan left and I changed back into my sundress and wished I hadn't left my floppy hat in the truck. I didn't get my hair cut as Aunt Tenne instructed. Who had time for that? Mom wasn't going to be happy and she might try to cut it herself. It wouldn't be the first time. I had some tragic bangs when I was a kid and Mom was too cheap to pay a stylist when she could do 'just fine myself'. It wasn't 'just fine', but that never stopped her.

Wallace finished her sausage and I got her out of the box. "You don't have to pee, right?"

Bark.

The pug had peed four times since we'd left earlier, but there was always more where that came from. Fats came into the locker room, frowning. "Did you clear this area?"

"Er...no."

She smacked her forehead with a hard crack. "You've got to be careful. That EMT could've done it for you."

"I wasn't thinking. Besides, nobody knew I was going to change in here."

"You don't know that. People talk. Even people who are helping you."

I agreed to be more careful in order to stop the lecture, if nothing else, and we headed up to the floor via the stairs, to my dismay. Fats didn't want me in an enclosed space. She had a bad feeling about me being in elevators and wasn't about to let me override her.

I huffed and puffed my way up to Mom's floor. Fats didn't even get winded. I think she would've run up, if I hadn't been holding her back.

She opened the door to the floor, scanned the area, and said, "All clear."

I had my hands on my knees, swaying. "Just. A. Minute."

"You are pathetic. Doesn't that hot body boyfriend take you to the gym?"

"He tries. I keep sneaking off to the juice bar."

"Juice bar," she scoffed. "You need a real gym."

"I really don't." I straightened up. "Okay. I'm better."

She rolled her eyes and we went to Mom's room that now had two cops in front of the door.

"We're getting serious," said Fats.

"I guess so."

They checked our IDs and reluctantly let Fats in. She looked suspicious and only Grandad's intervention got her past them without an altercation.

We walked in and found Tiny eating a flaky chocolate croissant. He took one look at Fats and pushed it away. I tried to go to Mom's bed, but Grandad whispered to me, "You want to tell me what happened to you?"

"I had a thing. It's not a big deal."

He pushed down the ice pack. "Jesus, sweetheart. What was this thing that happened?"

"Mercy," Mom called out.

Grandad tried to stop me, but I pushed past him. There was no hiding my lip. Mom may as well see it straight away.

"What in the world?" she gasped. "Were you in an accident? Honey, come here."

I sat on the edge of the bed and gave her a short rundown on what happened. She had a tissue to her own mouth and with the drooping, it was kind of hard to tell what she was thinking.

"Um...are you mad?" I asked, sounding like I did when I got a C on a pre-calc test in high school. Unlike in high school, Mom wasn't mad.

"What's done is done. I want you to call Pete," she said with a calculating look in her eye.

"Okay."

"You look like a mutant."

"That's fair."

"Did you get it?" she asked.

"Huh?"

"The thing" —Mom shivered— "in his mouth."

"Oh, yeah," I said. "I got it."

"Turn around."

Oh, no!

"I'm good."

"If you won't turn around, you obviously aren't," said Mom. "Ace, can you get me some scissors?"

"No scissors, Mom. My hair is fine."

"Turn around!"

Grandad suppressed a smile and made a little finger sweep. I turned around.

"Ace, I need scissors," said Mom.

I backed away slowly. "You're not cutting my hair. I'll go to a stylist."

"You don't need a stylist when I can do it for free."

Flashback.

"You just had a stroke. I'll pay to have my hair cut."

"You aren't walking around like that. You look like you have mange."

"It's not happening, Mom," I said.

"Think of what this looks like to the public. Your father has a business and a reputation to uphold."

"He's in custody for throwing a hissy fit on a plane. My hair is the least of his worries."

Mom clenched her jaw and Fats said quickly, "I'll cut it."

"Nobody's cutting my hair," I said. "Enough."

There was a knock on the door and a gentle voice said, "Excuse me."

Grandad went to the door and I heard him exclaim, "Avery, my brother, how are you? Good. Good. He's one of us, boys."

He came back into the room with a man I recognized from Dad's days on the force, but his full name escaped me.

Mom sat up and smiled. "Avery, how sweet of you to come."

Avery gave Mom a bunch of glorious, enormous daisies. "Ace called me. Is there anything I can do? I'm all yours."

Tiny pulled up a chair for Mom's visitor and it was a good thing, too. Avery wasn't looking so good. I remembered him as a stocky guy with a full head of curly black hair and a booming laugh. Dad described him as an excellent detective, but they didn't work together that much.

Now Avery's hair was thinning and not so well-kept. He'd lost a ton of weight and I doubted laughing was in his near future.

"You remember my daughter, Mercy?" asked Mom.

"Of course. How could I forget?" Avery shook my hand and Mom went on to introduce the rest of the group. She called Fats Mary Elizabeth and I saw a flicker of recognition in Avery's eyes, but he said nothing.

He and Mom started talking about her condition. Avery's brother had had a similar stroke and recovered very well. His words seemed to fluff Mom up. She needed good news so bad.

Tiny and Fats excused themselves under the guise of getting coffee. From the look in their eyes, I doubted coffee was on the menu.

"Bring me some," I said with a smirk that hurt my mouth.

"Yeah, yeah," said Tiny, rushing out and dragging Fats with him.

I rolled my eyes and found Avery looking at me. "I have to ask. What happened to you?"

Mom told him about Hunt and I put the ice pack on my lip while texting Pete, saying I needed antibiotics. He said he'd be up in a half hour or so.

"It sounds like you're getting closer," said Avery to me.

"I don't know," I said. "Maybe."

"Tommy keeps me up-to-date. I know all about your abilities. I'm sure you're close."

"My dad talks about me?"

Mom crossed her arms. "Of course, he does."

I wasn't sure what to do with that. Dad seemed to think I wasn't very good at anything. Chuck was his favorite child and he wasn't even related.

"Okay," I said. "So how have you been?"

"Mercy! What a thing to ask," said Mom.

Avery patted Mom's hand. "It's fine, Carolina. It's been over three months."

"Dixie still struggles with Gavin's death," said Mom. "And the man is in prison."

That's when I remembered. Avery was Avery Sampson. His wife, Lainie, was killed in a drive-by shooting in College Hill on the North side of St. Louis. She'd been delivering Meals on Wheels to the elderly. My parents went to the funeral and I remembered how upset they were.

"They never caught anyone?" I asked.

"No," said Avery, seeming to shrink in his chair. "It was gang-related. Lainie was in the wrong place at the wrong time. It's a real mess up there and no one will say who it was for fear of retribution."

"They have no leads at all?" asked Mom.

"The detectives, Conn and Bartlett, think it may have been a gang initiation, but of course, they can't prove it."

"I don't understand. I thought it was random."

"They think it was, but whoever did it was out to kill someone. The shots weren't sprayed at the car haphazardly."

Mom took his hand and rubbed it. "It's not over. New leads happen all the time. They get a weapon off a robbery suspect and you're in business."

"That's what I've been praying for," said Avery.

Gang-related. Targeted.

A feeling came over me, a Tommy Watts kind of feeling. Something wasn't right. Who targets a sixty-year-old woman for a gang initiation? Killing Lainie Sampson in her car at a distance would hardly make some young punk a bad ass, which I assumed was what they were going for.

"Excuse me," I said. "I'm going to get my own coffee. Anybody want some?"

Avery said yes, but Mom said she was holding out for Aaron's next delivery and so was Grandad. I went out and found an empty room to call Spidermonkey in. I would've called Uncle Morty, but I wanted him on the encryption. Plus, I didn't want to hear the crabbing. Spidermonkey was usually happy to hear from me and that would be welcome for a change.

"I'm so glad you called," he said in his comforting way and I instantly relaxed. No yelling. Sweet.

"Sorry," I said. "It's been crazy."

"I know. How's the lip?"

"It's fine. Sort of. How did you know?" I asked.

He laughed and said, "I have sources. You know that. Did you read the file?"

I blanked and he could tell. "Dr. Bloom's file."

"Right. Sorry. I didn't, but I will. When did you contact him?"

"After I made sure he was no danger to you and the good Dr. Bloom is exactly what he says he is. I found the police report on the office break-in. His files on WWII were stolen back in the eighties. All was correct. He's very well-respected in the world of military history, particularly with the Resistance in France, Belgium, and The Netherlands."

"Good," I said.

"But that's not what you called about," said Spidermonkey.

"No. I need a little research done. Nothing big."

"On your mother's case?"

"Sort of. On Lainie Sampson."

Spidermonkey remembered the case, but he'd had no reason to look into it. I gave him one. I asked him to see who the detectives interviewed on the case, in particular, gang members. Then I wanted to know if any of them had a connection to Waylon Parks. I explained my theory of the timeline, the FBI, and the Unsubs.

He was quiet for a time. Unlike Uncle Morty, Spidermonkey was more quiet consideration than pounding the keyboard. "You're trying to get to the killer through the back door, so to speak."

"Through his accomplice. Yeah," I said. "You don't like it?"

"Don't take this the wrong way, but I hope you're wrong."

"About the FBI?"

"I want there to be a better explanation for them holding back your father than self-protection," he said.

"This happens all the time. People decide that an institution has to be protected at all costs," I said.

"Like what the Catholic church did."

"Exactly, and I can't think of a better reason." To change the subject that was so obviously disturbing Spidermonkey, I went back to more comfortable territory. "Any idea what Dr. Bloom put in that file for me?"

"No. But I told him about Stella's portrait at the mansion."

"All of it, the flower and its name?"

"Yes. He was very intrigued and said he would go through his files."

Someone down the hall called my name and I told him I had to go. He said he'd see what he could dig up on Lainie Sampson's murder and I had a feeling that wouldn't be the end of it. Like all hackers, Spidermonkey was intensely curious about nearly everything. He wouldn't let the FBI thing go. He couldn't.

I went into the hall and saw Fats charging down toward me. She stopped short and said, "Don't do that."

"I'm fine. I just needed a moment."

Avery Sampson and Grandad left Mom's room and Tiny hurried to take their place. They came over to me and we said goodbye. Grandad said he'd walk him to the elevator.

Fats and I trailed them down the hall, stopping at Mom's door and watching them go. Avery was older than my dad but younger than Grandad, but you wouldn't have thought that from the stoop in his broad shoulders. It was like he was carrying Lainie and could never set her down again.

Grandad clapped him on the back and I heard him say, "I never thought this would happen to the best and the brightest."

"Not so untouchable now," said Avery and then they were out of earshot.

Fats looked down at me. "Are you thinking what I'm thinking?"

"If you're thinking Lainie getting killed by a mysterious gangbanger is an odd coincidence, then yes."

The cops looked at us. "Who got killed?" asked the one on the right. His name tag said *Weiss*.

"Avery Sampson's wife," I said.

"Oh, yeah," said the other one, named Spitz. "You never think something like that could happen to people like them."

Fats raised an eyebrow. "People like them?"

The cops got a little nervous. "You know, top-flight detectives. They seem untouchable."

"Nothing gets to them," said Spitz.

"The wife's dying did," said Weiss. "He's not the same man. How's Tommy doing with this?" He inclined his head toward Mom's room.

"I barely got to talk to him, but he knows what's happened. You know him?"

"Not well, but he was a great cop," said Spitz. "That's why we volunteered for this assignment."

"It's not right what the Feds are doing to him."

"You know about that?" asked Fats.

They nodded. "Everybody knows. Pretty damn obvious," said Weiss. "Have you got a plan? We'd love to help."

"I've got the beginnings of a plan." I turned around. "I have to get something."

"Then I do too," said Fats.

I couldn't shake her, not that I tried that hard. And she turned out to be handy, as usual. Nobody likes to say no to Fats Licata. I asked for a surgical tray with forceps, tweezers, bandage scissors, and a scalpel. Your basic kit.

"You're not going to try and stitch that chin, are you?" asked Daphne, who was a little braver than the rest.

"Nope," I said. "I've got a little project I need to work on."

"Well, we don't usually—"

Fats coughed and I got my tray posthaste. We hurried back to the room and I asked her, "Do you enjoy scaring people?"

"Not always."

The cops were very curious about my tray, but I wasn't ready to let anyone but family in on it. Fats counted as family in my book. I guess I had a lot of my dad in me. Only he would consider Uncle Morty family and make everyone do the same. Fats was a lot easier to absorb.

"What have you got there?" asked Grandad, back from the elevator.

"I'm going to do a little surgery," I said.

"On what?" asked Mom, petting Wallace rather harder than necessary.

"Not you. Don't panic."

"There are scissors. We can fix your hair," she said cheerfully.

"It's not for my stupid hair." I pulled out the packet. "It's for evidence."

I set the packet on the tray, took pictures from every conceivable angle, and then set to work, carefully using the scalpel to slice open the layers of plastic. Then I clipped on the forceps to hold it open and removed the folded piece of paper with the tweezers. With two sets of tweezers, I gently unfolded the paper. The whole thing was about four inches by two inches and had a handwritten message on it in purple ink.

Keep to the path or say goodbye to your girlfriend.

I flipped the paper over and said, "Yes!"

"What is that?" asked Tiny.

"That, my cousin, is the bottom of a prescription pad." I pointed at the *Dispense as Written* block and the *Generic Substitution* block alongside the line for the signature of the Prescriber.

"Too bad it's not signed," said Fats.

"Blankenship didn't write that," said Grandad. "Someone threatened him."

Mom took my hand and pulled me close. "You're the girlfriend."

"I would assume so," I said.

Tiny dropped down in a chair and grabbed a coffee cup, rolling it between his big hands. "But what's the path?"

"Probably some kind of Unsub creed." I told them about Greta's catatonia and the phone call she overheard.

"They're going to kill Blankenship once they get a load of what he handed over today," said Fats.

Tiny looked at my lip, glowering. "Works for me as long as they don't hurt Mercy."

"Fats will take care of Mercy and we need Blankenship alive," said Grandad. "For now."

"What can we do with that scrap?" asked Tiny. "They won't release Tommy for that."

I smiled widely and winced. "They will if they don't know what's on it and we have the laptop. I say we combine the two."

Grandad clapped his hands together and rubbed them furiously. "I like it, but we need more information on the writer."

"Handwriting analysis," said Mom. "Tommy has a guy. His information is at the house."

"Good. Good," said Grandad. "But I want to know whose pad that is."

"Me, too," I said, dialing my phone.

Shelley answered and she wasn't thrilled to hear from me, but she asked, "How's your lip?"

"Hurts like hell. I have a question for you."

She paused and then sighed. Resigned, I guess. "Fine. What is it?"

"Do you know anyone at Hunt that uses a purple pen?"

"That's out of left field."

"Do you?"

She spoke to someone in the background and then came back with Dr. Angelica Rohner, one of the psychiatrists at Hunt. She'd been there two years and was well-liked, if a little idealistic, hence the purple ink.

"Does she have an office?" I asked.

"Yes."

"Prescription pads?"

"What are you getting at?" asked Shelley.

"Bear with me."

Dr. Rohner had a small office, which was always locked. Even the cleaning staff didn't go in unless the doctor was there. It was standard procedure for Hunt with all the sensitive patient information they had. There'd been breaches in the past, journalists getting in and trying to get files on patients. There was always talk about whether certain patients ought to be in prison or in the hospital.

"Could a staff member get into the office if they really wanted to?"

"I suppose. Dr. Rohner leaves her keys around sometimes, but why would anyone want to?"

"I'm not sure. Is Blankenship one of her patients?" I asked.

"Yes," Shelley said slowly.

And there it is.

"Are you still at work?"

"Yep. Twelve-hour shift."

I asked her to find Dr. Rohner, get in the office and see if Blankenship's file looked out of whack. Then I asked her to go through the trash and look for a blank prescription with the bottom cut off. She wasn't keen on digging through trash, but I told her there was a very good reason or I wouldn't ask. She said she'd call me back.

My phone rang. Without thinking, I answered it. But it wasn't Shelley. It was Spidermonkey and everyone was looking at me.

"I've got something," he said.

"Who is it?" asked Grandad.

Say something smart.

"A guy."

Grandad frowned.

Say something better.

"It's Pete," I said. "About the antibiotics."

Yeah, me!

"Did someone say my name?" asked Pete, walking in the room—not holding his phone, I might add.

How can I be this unlucky? Seriously. How?

"Mercy's talking to you on the phone," said Mom, giving me Aunt Miriam-level stink eye.

"She's what?" he asked.

"It's another Pete," I said.

Nobody bought that. It sounded stupid, even to me.

"I'm going to go do something that is not here," I said, dashing out of the room.

"Mercy, I have to look at your face," Pete called after me.

"In a minute. I have diarrhea." That was all I could think of. A new low point in the life of Mercy Watts. Everyone heard, including the cops at the door, Chuck and Sydney, a gaggle of nurses, and normal patient visitors who were anxious to get out of my way.

"Mercy!" called out Chuck.

"Bathroom!" I ran to the closest bathroom, thankfully a single-toilet room with a lock. "What did you find?"

"You have diarrhea?"

"No. What did you find?"

"You're an odd duck," he said. "Did you know that your father and Avery Sampson were on some task forces together?"

I went cold. "Serial killers?"

"Yes. Three, I think."

"Was Waylon Parks involved?"

"No. These were in the '80s, and '90s. One went into the 2000s, but that was before Park's time and he wasn't top-notch anyway. He wouldn't have been on anything high-profile."

"Any connection to Shill?" I asked.

"Not that I've seen, but this just popped up," said Spidermonkey.

"This is interesting. It was really just one task force, known as Collective Inquiry, but everyone called the group The Brain Trust because—"

"They were the best and the brightest," I said.

"Exactly. Have you heard that somewhere?"

"Yes, I have." I flung open the bathroom door to find Chuck, Sydney, and Grandad standing there with amused expressions.

"Get Avery back!"

"What?"

"Get Avery Sampson back here right now."

"Why?" asked Chuck.

"Because he's a member of The Brain Trust."

"That old task force?"

"Yes, get him. He's probably in the garage by now."

"Mercy," Spidermonkey's voice came out of my phone.

"Yeah?" I said. "Can you give me the other detectives' names?"

"Just a second," he said. "Here they are. Keely Stratton, Scott Frame, your dad, Gavin Flouder, and John Jameson."

I froze. John Jameson's son. Avery Sampson's wife. My mom.

"That cannot be a coincidence," I said.

"What?" asked everyone.

"John Jameson's kid died of an overdose this morning."

"I'll get you everything," said Spidermonkey.

"Thanks."

We hung up and I came out of the bathroom.

"Avery's coming back," said Grandad. "What's this about?"

"The Brain Trust."

CHAPTER TWENTY

Avery Sampson sat in Mom's room recounting his time in The Brain Trust. He gripped the arms of his chair and forced himself to talk about murdered women, men, and even some teens. He didn't want to go there and I hated that I asked it of him.

The first Brain Trust was back in the eighties and lasted two and a half years. It was the case that Dr. Capshaw up in Sturgis referred to, Dwayne Davis Smith, a truck driver who murdered prostitutes all over the Midwest. Davis was executed in '95. According to Avery, Smith had no family. Certainly, no one mourned his passing. Also, he confessed in bloody detail and there was absolutely nobody who thought he was innocent. The Brain Trust was commended for catching him so quickly. Davis was only in action for eighteen months and I guess that wasn't long, considering how much he got around.

The next case was a couple, Ronald and Marietta Beck. They, too, got around, killing people in Missouri, Kansas, and Arkansas, but they were different from Davis in that they didn't do it for the pleasure of killing. They murdered for money, taking in elderly lodgers, poisoning them, and cashing their Social Security checks. They moved houses and states to avoid detection. The Brain Trust caught up to them in 1999 and they both committed suicide in jail before trial. There was a fuss about whether such a mild-mannered couple could poison twenty-three men, but when bodies showed up buried under every house they'd lived in, it was pretty hard to deny.

"So Banging Bob was the last case," said Chuck.

If his name was Banging Bob, it must've been a bad one. I vaguely remembered the case, mostly because of the name. I was young and spent most of my time annoyed with my dad, not following what he was up to. "Did he bang people's heads or something?"

Avery shook his head. "No, he was a DJ, working in and around St. Louis through the '90s and into the 2000s. His real name was Robert Horowitz."

Mom asked for her water, took a sip, and said, "He drove Tommy crazy. He was absolutely obsessed with that case."

"When isn't he obsessed?" I asked.

She thought about it and came up empty, as I knew she would. Tommy Watts was all about focus. "Anyway, it went on a long time and that was hard. It was the longest case you all ever worked, unless you count the unsolved ones."

Avery smiled. "So long that I retired before it was solved."

"When did you retire?" I asked.

"2003 and Tommy got Bob six months later in 2004."

I stood up and looked out the window at the afternoon sun glinting off the cars driving by.

"Mercy?" asked Chuck, coming over and gently touching my back.

"If it's anyone, it's Banging Bob?"

"I think he might be dead."

I turned back to the room. "I don't care. It fits the timeline perfectly."

"Timeline?" asked Sydney.

I gave them all the dates I'd gathered and there was a lot of nodding. Avery got a little shaky and Tiny got him some tea. He rolled the cup between his hands, not drinking it.

"That case," he said. "It really got to me. My daughters were the age of some of the victims. I had nightmares that he got them. Still do, if I'm being honest. That case is the reason I retired. I had to step back. Lainie thought I was going crazy. I think I was."

"Why was that one so bad?" asked Fats. "Davis sounds pretty nasty."

"He was, but he had an MO. Prostitutes strangled and dumped by a highway. He even left hair and fibers to test. He wasn't the brightest bulb. It wouldn't have taken even eighteen months if he hadn't been a driver. Interstate cooperation wasn't the greatest back then."

"Banging Bob didn't have an MO?" I asked.

"No, he didn't. I've never seen a killer so random. I heard that Tommy eventually found a pattern, but I never asked what it was. I didn't want to know."

"Will you tell us what you do know?" I asked.

Avery nodded and recounted in detail his time on Banging Bob's case. I could see why that particular serial killer got in Avery's head. He didn't make any sense whatsoever. Bob had male and female victims, ranging in age from thirteen to seventy-eight. There was no continuity in race, religion, employment, or location. Bob nabbed young women who got wasted at the raves where he worked, but he also broke into elderly men's homes. He flagged down unsuspecting motorists, pretending he had car trouble. He lurked in parking lots and got a few when they came to their cars.

Avery stared down into his cup. "You'd have to ask Tommy about the end. Like I said, I didn't want to know."

"We talked about it," said Chuck. "Do you mind if I say what Tommy told me?"

"Go ahead. If this has something to do with what happened to my wife, I need to hear it."

Chuck continued with what my dad told him over some beers three years ago. It took over five years to catch Bob and when they did, he never gave up a motive. He didn't sexually assault his victims, take any trophies, or seem to derive any pleasure from the killing other than he'd gotten away with it for so long. Bob seemed to consider it a job well done, but that was about it. He did confess to even more murders than were originally attributed to him. Dad had said that he knew there was more to the story, but he couldn't get anything out of Bob.

I had such a hard-core Tommy Watts feeling as Chuck spoke that I had to sit down on the bed and pull a snoring Wallace into my lap. "Did Dad think he had a partner?"

"We all thought that," said Avery. "But we never found any evidence of a second killer. It was more about the diversity."

"Tommy did say that," said Chuck. "But Bob said he was a single."

"So it was just the diversity of the crimes?" I asked.

"That and Bob was no genius. He left evidence behind and was only successful at hiding the bodies some of the time. It was the area and when he started repeating crimes, we realized it was one guy and that was pretty late in the game. There's this myth that serial killers are all highly intelligent, but that's not true, in my experience. Davis had an IQ of ninety-two and the Becks were in the 110s."

"What was Bob's IQ?" I asked.

Avery shrugged and Chuck said, "I don't know. Tommy didn't mention it, but he did say that in his interviews, he couldn't believe that guy had evaded him for so long. He wasn't very bright."

"Maybe he was just lucky," said Fats.

"Nobody's that lucky," said Avery. "I figured he had a partner, but hell, maybe he was a loner with a yen for diversity. If Tommy Watts couldn't find a partner, I don't think there was one."

Fats smiled wickedly. "We could send Mercy in to talk to him."

"Thanks," I said. "You're all heart."

"Can't," said Sydney. "Bob is dead. Died in prison. Sleep apnea."

Mom scowled, taking Wallace back from me. "He died peacefully in his sleep. Tommy was so angry about that. He was hoping for a broomstick in the bathroom. It only seemed fair."

"Did anyone think Bob didn't do it?" I asked.

"His mother, Valentina Dwyer, had a hard time accepting it, but she did in the end," said Avery. "Your father knew her better than I did."

"Do you still have your notes on Bob?"

"No. Lainie burned them. I was getting up in the middle of the night and going through them. She couldn't take it anymore and barbe-cued the file when I went to Home Depot. But Tommy was a much better note taker than me. He probably has a whole drawer dedicated to Bob."

"He does," said Mom. "It's in the office."

I stood up. "I'll go check it out."

Sydney shook his head. "I get the timeline, but I don't see how this would be connected to Carolina's attack, much less John Jameson's kid overdosing and a random drive-by."

"Maybe if we had another Brain Trust member attacked," said Chuck.

"Maybe we do," I said. "Do we know how everyone else is doing?"

Avery finally sipped his tea, frowning. "There were a lot of cops involved at one time or another."

"Okay. Who were the main detectives?" asked Chuck. "Tommy, you and..."

"Tommy was the acknowledged lead. His partner, Gavin Flouder, was in it, but he died last year. The rest were John Jameson, Scott Frame, and Keely Stratton."

"What did they do?" I asked.

"Do?" asked Avery.

"Did you have a specialty?"

Avery leaned back and said, "Oh. Of course. It wasn't formal, but we had certain roles that we gravitated to. I was the tech guy." He looked slightly embarrassed. "Nothing like Morty, you understand, but I had an interest."

Chuck nodded. "And Gavin was a ballistics guy."

"Right. Keely was an amazing profiler. Her instincts were only second to Tommy. I'd say she was second in command. Scott was forensics. He was an EMT back in the day. John was statistical analysis. The man loved maps. He's the reason we got Smith—John and his maps."

"And you were the best and the brightest," I said.

"I suppose so," said Avery. There was a lot of hesitation in that sentence.

Chuck heard it, too. "Someone didn't agree?"

"You know how it is."

I leaned forward. "I don't. How is it?"

"Keely was a beautiful woman. People said she got in on looks, which was ridiculous. She was top-notch," said Avery.

"And the rest of you?" asked Chuck.

"We all had our specialties that set us apart."

"You weren't all top-notch then."

Avery sighed and glanced at Grandad. "Scott Frame was average, and John had a closure rate just above his, but they both worked hard and put in the hours."

Grandad nodded. "The hours matter. You've got to put in the time."

"You know it."

"Have you heard anything about them recently?" I asked.

"I haven't talked to any of them," said Avery. "John's around, obviously. I think Keely moved to Mexico or something when she retired. Not sure about Scott. He doesn't come to events, like Cops for Kids, but I think I would've heard if something happened to any of them, especially after Lainie. People came out of the woodwork to tell me about every tragedy that ever happened."

"When my dad died, people did that," said Tiny. "My mother stopped answering the phone."

Mom had closed her eyes. We'd worn her out, but she murmured, "They think they're commiserating. I've had a bunch of people tell me about their family members who've had terrible diseases. Like that's supposed to make me feel better."

"Who?" I asked.

"Nurses, friends..." She trailed off and I signaled that we should clear out.

They all filed out, except for Tiny, who positioned himself between Mom and the door. I leaned over the bed and put my forehead to Mom's forehead. "I'm going to get Dad back."

Her eyes fluttered and then closed. "I'm so tired."

"I know. Just rest. We're going to get it. I have a feeling," I said.

"So like your father." She snuggled down with Wallace and started breathing deeply. Tiny handed me the tray with Blankenship's packet on it. "What are you going to do about that?"

"I'm open to suggestions."

"I got nothing."

I gave him a quick hug. "I don't think the FBI will bite on that, but the laptop…maybe."

He grinned and picked up the TV remote. "Go get 'em."

I went into the hall to find everyone in a cluster. "Do you have a plan?"

Chuck and Sydney had their phones to their ears. Chuck held up his finger and said into his, "Hey, this is Chuck Watts. I've got a job for you."

By the look in his eye, I knew he was talking to Spidermonkey, getting background on the remaining Brain Trust members. Sydney was asking someone if they'd heard from Keely or Frame.

Grandad and Avery were talking in hushed tones about Mom and her accident in June. Avery was getting paler by the moment.

"You're saying this was a multi-family member attack, not just Carolina, but Mercy and you, Ace?" he asked.

"Assuming it's the same person, yes," said Grandad.

"I've got to call my daughters." Avery walked away, dialing his phone.

Grandad patted my arm. "I'm going to stick with him. He's pretty shaken up." Then he pointed at the tray. "Tell Chuck and Sydney about that."

I nodded and Fats drew me away from the detectives saying, "What was that phone call all about?"

"It was my hacker, Spidermonkey," I said. "He found out that my dad and Avery were in The Brain Trust together."

"Well, he's dead useful. I'm going to want his number."

Pete came around the corner with an ice pack and a troubled look on his face. "I see your *diarrhea* has passed."

I smiled and it burned like crazy. "You know me too well."

Pete put the fresh ice pack to my face. "Yes, I do."

Chuck glared at us and I rolled my eyes at him. I never expected Chuck Watts to be the jealous type. He'd always been so cavalier about women.

"I don't think Chuck likes me very much," said Pete with obvious pleasure.

"Yeah, he's a nut," I said. "And speaking of nuts, this is my body-guard, Fats Licata."

"Who are you calling a nut, Scarface?" asked Fats.

I lowered the ice pack. "You think it's going to scar? How bad?"

Pete examined my lip and then said, "You are unbelievable. The nurses said you'd really screwed yourself up, but I didn't expect this."

"Just tell me."

"How did you do it?" he asked, taking a second look. "It's not a... human bite, right?"

"Well..."

"How did you...no, I don't want to know," said Pete, pulling out his script pad. "I'm going to give you some antibiotics and you have to take them religiously. You've already had it cleaned?"

"Yes," I said. "I think I'm good."

"I think you're crazy."

Chuck walked over, his face now smooth and laissez-faire, the big faker. "I agree, but she won't be going out to Hunt again anytime soon."

"I'll go if I have to," I said.

"Mercy, for the love of God."

Pete tore off the script. "I've got to go. Surgery in twenty, but I'll be back around to check on Carolina."

I thanked him and Chuck turned his attention from Pete's retreating back to my tray. "What is that?"

"Can't you tell?" asked Fats. "You're the official detective."

"I'd like to know more about you, officially," said Chuck.

Fats laughed and stuck out her hand. It swallowed Chuck's. He was disconcerted and I so enjoyed that. I got to be smaller than people every day of my life, people who put things on top of refrigerators where I couldn't find them, and it was nice to see the tables turned.

"Mary Elizabeth Licata," said Fats. "Look me up. It'll be a short read."

"I bet," said Chuck with narrowed eyes. "Who hired you again?"

"Grandad," I said quickly. "And this is a clue."

Sydney came over and they peered at the tray.

"Of what?" asked Sydney. "Looks like a prescription or part of one."

I looked around quickly and since the hall was empty, I flipped the paper over to reveal the threat. Chuck's jaw quivered. "Where'd you get that?"

"Blankenship's mouth."

Chuck and Sydney drew back. "Are you saying?"

"That I went mouth-to-mouth with a murderer? Yes, I did," I said.

"Your father is going to have a heart attack," said Sydney.

"My father is the reason I did it." I gave them what I'd found out about the packet so far.

Chuck pulled an evidence bag out of his pocket. He always had a few stashed on him, just like my father. "I'll take that, if you don't mind."

I stepped back. "I need it to get Dad out."

"I'll keep it on the down-low for now," he said. "I've got some favors I can call in, but I want that dusted for prints ASAP."

I took his hand. "I have to get Dad out. You can't let it go up the chain."

He kissed my forehead. "I swear to you it won't." He bagged the slip of paper and the plastic. "Can you call that guard and see if she's got anything new?"

I stared at the evidence bag for a second. It was hard to let it go, but I had to. If for nothing else, I had to for Chuck. He needed me to trust him and I needed to see if I could trust him. Instead of snatching the bag back, I called Shelley.

"I was just about to call you," she said. "I'm with the doctor now. Here she is." Shelley handed over the phone and a tense woman's voice said, "I'm sorry, but I have to report this."

"I've already reported it." I looked at Chuck and he winked at me.

"You have?" asked Dr. Rohner. "Shelley thought you would want to keep this quiet. Something about your father."

"I do and so do the detectives."

"Which detectives?" she was sounding more doubtful by the minute and I was forced to hand the phone to Chuck. He went into charming mode and identified himself. By the end of the conversation, the doctor was eating out of his hand and my eyes hurt from rolling.

"You have no shame," I said. "She practically thinks you're going to ask her out."

"I might if you dump me. I'll need a good therapist," he said.

"You already have a therapist, Dr. Witges."

"I'm not sharing a therapist with you who dumped me."

Fats put a hand between us. "Let's just say nobody's getting dumped. I don't have all day. Tiny and I have a dinner scheduled. I don't want to be chasing Mercy around until midnight. What did the horny doctor say?"

The horny doctor said that she thought Blankenship's file had been gone through. Nothing was missing, but the file wasn't in the right spot. Somebody had taken it out and put it in front of Nathan Black's file. Dr. Rohner noticed immediately because the tabs were lined up wrong. There wasn't a torn prescription in the trash, but she took out the trash every day.

"I'll send one of our guys out there," said Sydney. "Anthony Bell can do the dusting and keep it quiet for a day or so."

"You sure he won't feel obligated to call it in?" asked Chuck.

"Are you kidding? I'll tell him it's for Tommy. He kept Anthony's kid out of the system when he did those smash and grabs a few years ago. The kid's in the army and doing well."

Sydney went off to deal with Hunt and I had second thoughts about the packet. "Mom said Dad has a handwriting guy. He can take a look at the note."

"Are you trying to take it back?" asked Chuck.

Kinda.

"Mercy can just take a picture," said Fats, poised to move between us. "The guy doesn't need the original, does he?"

"It's probably best, but a picture will do." We laid the paper flat and I took several pictures of the note. They weren't fantastic, but good enough to see the particulars of the handwriting. I didn't know stink about handwriting analysis, but the note looked natural to me with no hesitation or choppiness. If somebody was trying to disguise their handwriting, I didn't think it would look like that. "Alright," I said. "I'm going over to my parents' and see if I can find that handwriting guy." I eyed Chuck. "What are you going to do?"

"I'll go back to the station and see if anyone has Frame's number," said Chuck.

Grandad walked up and said, "I can get that for you. Scott is Leo Frame's nephew."

I almost said something but managed to clamp my mouth shut in time. I knew that name sounded familiar. Leo Frame was the lead detective on the Bled Mansion break-in that happened before I was born, but I wasn't supposed to know that.

Grandad gave me a curious look. "I'll give Leo a call. Are you okay, sweetheart?"

"My lip's really stinging. I think I need to fill this prescription before I go to the house," I said.

He took the slip from me. "I'll do it. You go and get that hand-writing analyst's number. I'd never be able to find it."

"And The Brain Trust file," said Fats.

"And that," said Grandad. "Don't be long. I think I just heard a nurse say they want to take Carolina down for another MRI."

I groaned and went to the desk. Mom did need another MRI. She'd moved during the last one and it was blurry. I came back and told Grandad to stay with her. She'd done it before so it shouldn't be a big deal, but I'd try to get back.

Chuck walked me and Fats out. I was ready to make another great escape via ambulance, but Chuck called security and they swore the press had given up. It didn't hurt that there was a police standoff in Kirkwood with a postal employee.

We walked right out the front door and it felt great. "Since you don't have to find Frame, what are you going to do?" I asked Chuck.

"I'm going to check in with the investigation in Kansas, since I'm supposedly on that. They'll stonewall me and then I'll see what our FBI guys have to say," he said.

"Does Spidermonkey have anything on the rest of The Brain Trust?"

He smiled his most charming smile and I very nearly melted before reminding myself that he'd been a jerk. "You knew that was him. Nice."

"I can tell, you big dufus," I said.

"Dufus. I guess that's probably better than whatever you've been calling me."

"Marginally," said Fats. "What did he say?"

Chuck gave Fats the once-over. "How much does she know?"

I sighed and told him about Dr. Bloom's file, including the gas mask incident. Not my finest moment. That got me thinking. I'd never had a finest moment, just the *not* variety, which seemed unfair. The universe kinda owed me. I did look like I had mange.

"You need professional help," said Chuck.

"I've got professional help. Chuck, meet Fats."

"I meant for the hair. I know a girl—"

I held up a hand. "Stop right there. I know all about how you know girls and I'm good."

"You mean that I know her in the biblical sense? Does that bother you?" Chuck was grinning from ear to ear, shades of his old sleazy self and I couldn't resist. "You probably know her the way I knew Marcus Collins in college."

His smile vanished and Fats was beaming. "You don't mean Marcus Collins, the tight end for the Vikings?"

"I do," I said.

"Go on," she said.

Chuck growled. "Do not go on."

"Marcus had this thing for hot tubs and since he was an athlete..."

Chuck threw up his hands and walked away. "Just for that, I'm not telling you what Spidermonkey said."

"You know I can call him, right?" I yelled after him.

He just stalked off.

The valet parking attendant brought the truck and we zoomed off, laughing.

"For someone so handsome, he really is a dufus," said Fats.

"Aren't they all?" I asked.

She thought it over. "Probably, but I still have hope. Tiny is a sweetheart."

"He is, indeed."

"Exactly how are you two related?" she asked.

I explained what happened in New Orleans and our discovery of our mutual ancestor as we drove home. I don't know why, but I had the feeling that her estimation of me went up. I couldn't imagine why. The concept of Plaçage was repugnant to me. Despite what Tiny said, I still thought that contracting Josephine as a kind of bonus wife was sick.

We drove onto Hawthorne Avenue just as dusk was starting to settle. For a second, it became my home again, a place of beauty and elegance, not the place where my mother was attacked and our neighbors behaved badly. We rolled past the big houses, mansions to most people, I guess, but Mom and Dad never made a big deal about where we lived. I knew we didn't have any money, but it never bothered them, so it didn't bother me. We never really fit. I didn't know how much until the neighbors got together, yelling about the inconvenience of the police interrupting their precious lives.

"It's beautiful here," said Fats. "It doesn't look like the same city where I grew up."

"Where did you grow up? The Hill?"

She grinned. "How'd you guess?"

"Just lucky."

"Look," she said. "Somebody cleaned up."

Somebody did clean up, whether it was from guilt or to keep the street looking nice, I couldn't say, but the crime scene tape was gone, the grass pampered back to a lush green, and the flowerbeds replanted.

Fats gave me a sideways glance as we parked. "That's nice."

I grumbled. "Maybe."

"What else do you want?"

I didn't answer. I trotted up the walk, bypassing the front door and going straight to the side yard, fully expecting it to be trashed—after all, you couldn't see it from the street—but it was perfection. No tape. New hostas planted in the bed where Denny died. Only the lingering smell of some kind of cleaner, flowery and sweet.

"Looks better," said Fats.

"It does. Why do I want to bulldoze it?"

Fats turned me around and we went to the front door instead of trying the side door. A wise decision, in retrospect. I might've lost it if I had to walk over where I found Mom. It was different when the cops were there, all busy and finding things. It didn't really seem like my home then. It was a crime scene, strangely impersonal. Now, it was like nothing happened *and* something happened at the same time.

We went in the front door and it was eerily silent. There wasn't a cop on duty anymore since the crime scene stuff was all done. And the Siamese were still at the ASPCA instead of trying to scar me for life. I climbed the stairs to the second floor, aware that I was looking for something. I just didn't know what. There was just this vague feeling that something was waiting for me.

In Dad's office, I found the handwriting guy easily. Claire had made a drawer just for independent contractors. I texted Donald Greenburg with my request and he got back in seconds. He'd heard about Mom and expressed his sympathies. I asked him to do what he could with the note. Mr. Greenburg wasn't thrilled with not having the original, but he'd do what he could. I thanked him and asked him not to tell anyone about the note. That wasn't a problem. He knew the drill.

I looked up and Fats said, "It's gone."

It took me a second. "What?"

Please don't say what I think you're going to say.

"The Brain Trust file," she said. "It's not here."

Dammit.

We went through the cabinets three more times and it was definitely gone. Claire was so organized that we knew exactly what had been taken. She'd arranged Dad's files in a system that was easy to understand, if you understood my dad. There were sections for the contractors, employees, criminals, clients, etc. It was all cross-referenced. So if you went looking for the file on Dwayne Davis Smith, which we did, it had a marker saying his file was in the Brain Trust file in the Major Cases drawers. All the major cases were there, at least as far as I could tell, but The Brain Trust cases were gone.

"Well, that isn't helpful," said Fats. "I wonder if those other detectives kept their files."

I sat down in Dad's chair, feeling so sick it was like I'd just eaten another crab hotdog.

"Mercy? What about that detective who died? What's his name? Your grandfather said your dad and he were partners."

"Gavin Flouder," I said. "He probably does."

Fats wedged herself into the chair opposite me. "So we'll go over there. Will the widow mind?"

"No, but Gavin wasn't the lead. He wouldn't have everything." I frowned.

"What's wrong?"

"Where's my dad's file?" I asked.

She shrugged. "Your dad took it or that Claire. You said she takes work home. Maybe she was color-coding it. She's obviously a freak when it comes to this stuff."

"Yeah, she really whipped my dad into shape." I held up a blue slip.

"What's that?"

Claire loved organization to perhaps an unhealthy level. She'd ordered Dad to place a blue slip in the place of any file he removed so she'd know he'd taken it. All Dad's people had their own slips since they came and went, pulling old files and cases as the need cropped up. Denny's slips were green. I got pink, even though I pointed out that I would not be pulling any files, but Claire insisted. She was a freak that way.

Fats returned to the cabinet and looked again. "You're right. No slip."

"He was in the house. He took the file," I said, the creepy crawly feeling back in a huge way.

"The cops didn't think he got in."

"Because nothing was taken or at least we thought nothing was taken. I was looking at normal stuff people steal. I never thought about files."

"Who would? That stuff happened decades ago," said Fats. "You've got to tell Chuck."

"I will." I spun Dad's chair around to look out the window behind his desk, mentally kicking myself. We'd lost all kinds of time.

"Hey," said Fats. "I thought your mom's cats were in a kennel or something."

Every hair on my body went to attention. "They are."

"Well, somebody brought them back."

Please let it be the Siamese. Please let it be the Siamese.

It wasn't the Siamese.

CHAPTER TWENTY-ONE

I spun around in my chair and watched as Blackie, the cat of doom, slinked into the room. He was silent and unblinking, commanding our attention as he leapt from a chair to a filing cabinet to the mantel, where he sat in the center and wrapped his long, skinny tail around his paws.

"That cat doesn't look Siamese," said Fats.

"He's not," I said.

"Is there another one?"

"God, I hope not."

She frowned. "Why do you say it like that? It's just a cat."

"Uh huh." My phone rang and it was Spidermonkey with an update. Chuck had told him to leave me out of the loop so he immediately called me. I might've met Spidermonkey through Chuck, but he was my guy now. Suck it, boyfriend.

My über hacker had lots of info that seemed useful, but it wasn't immediately apparent how. Lainie Sampson's murder was cold case city. The cops had nothing. There were witnesses, but they were unwilling to say anything. There was one old lady who initially said it was a Hispanic male, but she immediately changed her mind, saying she saw nothing and wasn't wearing her glasses. Her glasses were on her face at the time. Forensics had multiple rounds from the same 9mm Glock, but they'd been unable to match them to anything. Unless new evidence showed up—and no one thought it would—Lainie's case was done.

Austin Jameson's death that morning was a different story. Although it'd been reported in the news as an overdose, behind the scenes, it was classified as suspicious, possibly a murder. Austin had gotten up that morning as usual for his nine o'clock Precalculus class. His roommate said he was fine but tired from studying the night before for a test. Austin left for the coffee shop, where he was going to meet his girlfriend before going to class with her. He arrived on time at eight thirty, but she was late, showing up at ten till nine. She didn't have time for a coffee so she took a sip of his. By the time they got to class, Austin was slurring his words and weaving. She thought he was having a stroke and called 911. By the time the ambulance got there, he was unconscious and she was woozy. Austin never regained consciousness and died an hour later. The girlfriend recovered and blood tests confirmed that they both had the drug known as 25i in their systems. 25i was a kind of synthetic LSD and taking it was like playing Russian Roulette. You might be okay or you might die. The girlfriend insisted that Austin drank and did a little pot, but no acid. She didn't even know what 25i was and the cops believed her, especially after the coffee cup found at the scene came back full of the stuff. If you were going to try 25i, you'd put one of the tiny, colorful tabs under your tongue, not stick an entire strip of the stuff in your morning coffee.

Beer but no drugs were found in Austin's room and his roommate backed up the girlfriend's claim that he didn't do any drugs other than pot. It looked a hell of a lot like murder, but who would want to kill a college student? The kid had no enemies, was well-liked, and a good student.

"It's a totally different MO, but I can't deny the connection," said Spidermonkey.

"They're all different MOs," I said slowly. "Totally different."

Fats kept an eye on Blackie, who continued to sit on the mantel without blinking once. She was starting to squirm in her chair, a sure sign that the so-called cat was getting to her. "How many MOs do we have?" she asked.

"Well, we've got the stuff in Sturgis that was done by manipulating a third party." I quickly told her what happened and then said, "The OD. There's my mom. I assume he was going to shoot her, since he obviously had a weapon with him, but the stroke stopped him. Denny was shot. Lainie got a drive-by that looks Hispanic gang-related. A truck tried to run Mom off the road in June. How many is that?"

"Five, if you count your mom's attack and Denny's death as one crime," said Fats. "Six, if you consider leaving her to die from a stroke as a separate act."

"Seven," said Spidermonkey.

"You found somebody else?" I asked, looking at Blackie, who stared back and then gave out a curly-tongued yawn.

"I'm not sure it's related," he said. "It seems far-fetched, but Scott Frame's ex-wife died in December. It could be a coincidence."

Coincidence. Yeah. Right.

Scott Frame lived in Belleville, Illinois, working low-level security for some company. He was divorced in 1995 and the wife moved to California with their two kids. The divorce wasn't friendly, but it wasn't bitter either. According to Spidermonkey, they had some disagreements about summer visits, but the kids were adults now and saw their father occasionally. More importantly, they were both still alive.

"How did the wife die?" I was ready for anything, but my guess was a stabbing. I was wrong. Allison Frame died of carbon monoxide poisoning from a faulty furnace. She was found by a friend after she failed to show up for work. There were no signs of tampering and it was ruled an accident.

"I don't know," said Fats. "That's kind of left field. If you're killing people that The Brain Trust members love, why would you kill an ex-wife? Guys hate their ex-wives and they've been divorced for forever."

"Maybe he didn't hate her," I said. "Who divorced who?"

"She divorced him," said Spidermonkey. "But your bodyguard is right—killing the ex isn't exactly a body blow."

"I agree, but it's suspicious. Have you found anything on Keely Stratton?"

Spidermonkey had found little on the former detective. Keely was married to Ed Stratton. They had no children. After her husband sold his dental practice, they did move to Mexico, a town near Puerto Vallarta, but they only stayed for a couple years before they moved farther south to Columbia. They stayed there for only a year and had moved to Granada, Nicaragua. That was as far as he got.

"When did they move to Nicaragua?" I asked.

"Almost two years ago," he said.

"I wonder if they moved again. They sound adventurous."

Spidermonkey made a subtle displeased sound, the first I'd ever heard from him.

"I'm sorry," I said. "I know this is a pain."

He chuckled. "They're a pain, not you. I'm happy to help. I need you safe and sound."

"Why?" asked Fats, tearing her gaze from Blackie.

"Mercy has brought a certain mystery into my life," said Spidermonkey. "She's essential to solving it and I like her."

"This would be the thing with The Klinefeld Group?"

He didn't reply.

"She got ahold of Dr. Bloom's file," I said. "And she told me something you might find interesting."

"What would that be?" Spidermonkey sounded stiff and guarded.

"Don't worry. I think our secret's safe with Fats."

"Based on what?"

"Well...based on we don't have any choice," I said. "Go ahead, Fats. Tell him about the board."

Fats told Spidermonkey how The Klinefeld Group got control of the art museum board, getting his attention fast. He hadn't come across anything to do with the board, but he hadn't been looking.

"They're getting more dangerous by the minute," he said. "If we don't find something soon, perhaps we should consider backing off."

"You make it sound like they'll back off if we do," I said. "They've shown no signs of it."

"When this is all over, we need to sit down and map out a strategy. Right now, I have nowhere to go," he said.

"There was information in the Bloom papers," said Fats. "Something about DH8. I don't know what it means."

"That's something, at least."

"Don't get down in the dumps," I said. "I did get a tidbit from Myrtle and Millicent."

"Really?"

I told him about Agatha and Daniel's memorial being in St. Sebastian.

"I can't believe it," he exclaimed. "I assumed the crash was near Jeff City."

"Me, too, but it wasn't. Maybe I should go out there and talk to the local cops. They might know something."

"They might. Let me get my source on it. I'll see if she can get access to the evidence, but first, I'll find the wayward Detective Keely," he said. "Is there anything else?"

I glanced up at Blackie, who continued to stare at me. I could tell him about the cat, but it would only upset him. As far as I could tell, the cat warned of impending doom, but nobody ever managed to avoid what was about to happen, which was just plain obnoxious. I mean, what was the point? "No, nothing."

"Are you going back to the hospital?" asked Spidermonkey.

I stood up and shook off the weight Blackie had put on my shoulders. There was no use worrying about something you couldn't change. "We're going to see a man about a lie."

"That doesn't narrow it down."

I laughed and hung up.

"Where are we going?" asked Fats.

"To see Palfry, but I guess I'd better call my beloved first." I called Chuck, who was in a snit about Spidermonkey choosing me. He crabbed for a minute before I filled him in. He'd only found out that Keely moved to Columbia and that pissed him off further. The news about Scott Frame's wife wasn't impressive, but he said he'd drive over to Belleville and have a talk with Scott to see how upset the detective was about her death. I asked about Palfry and they hadn't had time to re-interview yet, but Chuck had a uniform go over to interview Johnny and Jim. They said Palfry was in Ode to Caffeine on Saturday afternoon sometime around four. More interesting was Palfry's topic of conversation. He did his normal gossip with the add-on that the Watts family was always mucking up the peace of the avenue. Jim asked if my parents were having a barbecue, something Palfry considered very low-class, and he said 'Who knows' with a snotty harrumph. Johnny and Jim knew my parents and liked them. They thought Palfry was, in their words, an amusing old prig and made a mental note to tease Mom about her out-of-control afternoon barbecues when they next saw her.

"So that old buzzard did see or hear something," I said with a thumbs-up. She just gave me an odd look and glanced back at Blackie.

"Yeah. I'll get it out of him one way or another," said Chuck.

"Leave Palfry to us," I said.

"Mercy, what are you going to do?"

"Let's just say a little Licata goes a long way."

"I can't let you assault a witness," he said, sounding a bit panicked.

I chuckled. "We won't assault him. Unless, of course, he doesn't cooperate."

"I'll deal with Palfry. You go to the hospital. Do not—"

"Oh, no. My battery's dying. What did you say?"

"Don't even—"

I hung up, giving Chuck plausible deniability or something like it, if we did happen to beat the snot out of Palfry the weasel. He couldn't stop us if he didn't know what we were about to do. I must admit I wanted to beat Palfry senseless myself.

"Ready?" I asked Fats.

"There's something wrong with that cat," she replied.

"Noticed that, did you?"

"I don't think it's breathing and it definitely hasn't blinked."

"Yeah, well, ya know," I said.

"I don't know. What is up with that cat?"

"I'll tell you on the way to Palfry. I don't suppose you have any brass knuckles?"

She crossed her arms. "As if I'd need them."

"I meant for me."

"You continue to surprise me. So what do we do about the cat?"

"There's nothing we can do about him." I trotted out of the room and down the stairs with Fats hard on my heels, protesting the whole way. I wasn't going to fob her off with some tale that Blackie was just weird. Not Fats Licata. Like me, she was nosy by nature.

By the time we'd walked down to the McCallister mansion, Fats had gone silent. We went around to the servants' entrance and I rang the bell next to the narrow security door.

"You expect me to believe that your family has a two-hundred-year-old ghost cat that warns you of impending doom?" she asked.

I shrugged. "Believe what you want."

"You do have that bruise on your forehead. Do you have a concussion?"

"Probably." I rang the bell again and a maid in an actual French maid-type uniform answered. "Miss Watts," she exclaimed. "How is your mother? We were so sorry to hear what happened."

"She's better. Thanks."

"Why did you come to this door? You're supposed to use the front."

"Because I want to talk to Palfry," I said. "Is he here?"

Her nose twitched ever so slightly. "I wouldn't bother. The police already talked to him."

"I think I'm a little more persuasive than the average cop."

Doubt was written all over her pretty face until Fats stepped into view and gave her a finger wave. "And I'm not half bad at persuading people either."

"I imagine you'd be quite good at it," she said, stepping back. "Would you like to come in?"

"I think we'll stay out here." I wanted Palfry out of his element. He was an indoors kind of guy. Plus, there was less to break outside.

The maid went to get Palfry and Fats said, "I don't believe that cat means anything."

"Suit yourself."

"It's just a cat."

"That doesn't breathe. Got it."

The door opened and Palfry stuck his nose out. "What do you want, Watts?"

Fats didn't hesitate. She grabbed him by the scruff of the neck and dragged him outside before tossing him against the wall. "That's Miss Watts to you."

When I imagined beating the crap out of Palfry, I imagined him taking it like a man or at least like a five-year-old girl. Palfry peed. All it took was a light slap to the jowls and Fats yelling, "What did you see Saturday?"

He flooded his pants and begged, "Please don't hurt me."

Fats stepped back in utter disgust. "I don't even want to touch you."

"I'll touch him," I said.

My bodyguard couldn't believe it, but heck, I touched Blankenship on the lips. This was just a pissy butler. He wasn't nearly so disgusting.

"Go for it," she said with cringe.

I kept my feet from the puddle and stuck a finger in his quivering face. "I know you were out walking at the time my mom was attacked and from what you said in Ode to Caffeine, you heard something."

"I...I..."

I flicked his jowl and he may have let loose again. I didn't care. "Palfry, I'm losing patience with you. Maybe me and my parents aren't your style. Maybe we aren't good enough for the avenue, but that's not the question. The first question is do you want to be charged as an accessory in a rape and murder?"

"But I didn't do anything," Palfry whined.

"Oh yeah? Then why are you helping the guy who did to get away with it?" I asked.

"I don't know who did it."

Fats came in close. She was so big; her breath ruffled the thin hair on the top of his head. "The second question is where do you want me to hit you first, the face or the stomach? I, myself, favor the face. You have a chance of being knocked out and missing what's coming to you. Until you wake up in intensive care, that is."

"Nice," I said.

"You like that?" she asked.

"Very well put."

"Thank you." Fats popped him on the cheek, just hard enough to make the flubber shake. "Head or stomach? The choice is yours."

Palfry put his shaking hands over his face. "I thought your mother was..."

I stepped back and put my hands on my hips. "What?"

"You don't want me to say."

"I assure you, I do."

"She'll hit me," he said, peeking through his sweaty fingers.

Fats shrugged. "Likely, but you can still save yourself."

"I thought she was having sex outside." He shielded his face with his arms.

"What the what?" I pulled his arms down. "Why in the world would you think that?"

Palfry heard something when he walked by my parent's house at four on Saturday. Having a low opinion of my mother, he automatically thought the muffled groans and thumping noise was her, outside, in broad daylight, having sex with someone other than my father. He knew Dad was gone because the maid we'd just talked to had told him he was.

The butler walked on by, went to Ode to Caffeine, complained, and returned about four thirty and this is where he felt guilty. He avoided my eyes and began sweating more, which was saying something, considering that he was already soaked. Palfry saw a man walking down the cross street away from Hawthorne wearing a wrinkled suit and pulling, of all things, a wheeled trash can. It struck him as odd for many reasons, most notably who drags a trash can down Beecher Stowe Boulevard? Where was he going? All trash got picked up in the alleys. The closest business was Ode to Caffeine and that was several blocks away. Also, the can was heavy like it was full to the brim and trash day was Friday.

My chest got tight. "What did he look like?"

A bead of sweat ran down from his sideburn and dripped off his jowl. "I didn't look."

"You were afraid," said Fats.

His chin trembled. "I don't know why. I just felt nervous and it was very odd, a man with a trash can like that."

"What did you see? Anything will help," I said.

"He was a good-sized man, not skinny like your father. He had on some kind of hat, but like I said I didn't look."

"White or Hispanic?"

"White," he said, automatically, then more slowly, "I don't know why. It was just what I thought. He was definitely out of place."

"Aside from the trash can?"

"Yes, he wasn't our sort."

I gritted my teeth. "Like how my parents aren't your sort."

Palfry put his hands down finally and clasped them under his chin. "Is she going to hit me?"

"No," I said quickly. "Just tell me."

Like the feeling that the guy was white, the feeling that he didn't belong was just as instinctual. Palfry was an unbearable snob, but he had a nose for social rank. Oddly, he placed that man below us. He admitted that while my parents didn't have the social graces that came with being born with money—I called it entitlement, he called it breeding—they had a certain style to them. The blue suit the man wore was cheap and heavily wrinkled. Mom and Dad were always acceptably turned out, even when we really didn't have money and Mom drove a 1987 Honda with tremendous hail damage. We had that car until it died on the highway and had to be towed away when I was in high school. My parents had something that said they weren't Palfry's sort but better than most people and that guy didn't have it. Notice that I wasn't included in the better than most or acceptably turned out, just the parents. I was dirt and getting worse, with the leather bikini poster and whatnot.

"Did you smell anything?" I asked.

"Like what?" asked Palfrey, for the first time curious.

"I don't know. Mothballs, for instance."

He shrugged. "I was across the street, but the suit did look like it'd been in storage."

"What happened then?" I asked.

"Nothing," he said, once again avoiding my eyes.

"Come on. You know you want to tell us."

"It might be nothing."

"Spill it."

"The alley gate was ajar. I saw it and pushed it closed. That's it, I swear to you," said Palfry.

Fats patted him on the cheek. "Now, don't you feel better?"

He appeared puzzled for a moment and then said, "I think I do."

"Why didn't you just tell the cops when they interviewed you?" I asked.

"I thought Mr. McCallister might blame me for what happened to your mother. He has a soft spot for her. I didn't want to lose my job and if he thought I should've saved her..."

"To be clear, you didn't hear a gunshot?" I asked.

"No, but I was inside before my walk with the dogs. I don't think anyone else was home that Saturday. All our maids were off. The street was really quiet." He had the good sense to look ashamed. "Are we done?"

"We are but bring out that maid we were talking to earlier," I said.

He vanished inside the house and the maid came out, looking nervous herself. "I don't know anything about what happened."

"I don't think you do, but I'd like to know how you knew my father was out of town."

She relaxed. "Oh, that's easy. Your mother told me. I took my little sister by. She was selling candy bars for her soccer fundraiser. Mrs. Watts is always so good about that. She bought a whole box and said your father was out of town for a while."

"Did anyone ask you about my parents?" I asked.

"No, why would they?"

"Just checking. So you told Palfry that my father was gone and nobody else?"

She shrugged. "It was common knowledge. Nancy down at Mrs. Huff's knew."

"Do you talk about my parents a lot?"

The maid blushed and lowered her voice. "You're a celebrity, singing with DBD, and your father's a world-famous detective. Your mother's so nice and classy. Your family's fun to have around and something's always happening. Palfry hates that, but I think it's exciting."

Exciting was one word for it. I thanked her and we left, heading back for my parents' house, both silent until we reached the truck. Neither of us went for it. Instead, we went up the brick walk, around through the side yard.

"Garage?" asked Fats.

"Yep," I replied.

Just as we both expected, my parents' garbage can was missing. That's how he hauled Denny's body away. He rolled him right out in front of the whole world, but the world, except for Palfry, wasn't paying much attention.

CHAPTER TWENTY-TWO

Fats insisted we stop by my apartment, saying I needed fresh clothes, but I think she was really sick of my mangy hair. Before I knew what was happening, I was draped in a towel and having it snipped. I suppose I could've protested, but I was too tired to fight it. My whole face hurt and I looked like I had a purple slug in place of a lower lip. Of course, I still had the nasty egg from Sturgis on my forehead to match. I'd like to say I'd looked worse, but I hadn't. It was a new low, complete with mangy hair.

My bodyguard/hair stylist stepped back. "Not bad. You look almost normal. From the back, that is."

"Thanks."

"Don't mention it," she said, ponytailing her hair and then sock-bunning it with amazing speed. "How about you put something comfortable on, baggy jeans or sweats?"

"My mother hates jeans. She doesn't even own a pair."

"Do you really care? Your day sucked."

"I think I do. She's hurt and she likes it when I look appropriate."

Fats heaved a sigh and dug into my closet. "Holy crap! You've got Valentino in here."

"It was a gift from Millicent and Myrtle for funerals." I collapsed on my bed. It felt so good I could've gone to sleep for twenty-four hours.

Fats poked me. "How about this?" She held up a pair of Ponte pants that were sort of a cross between yoga pants and regular pants.

"Perfect," I said, throwing them on with a super-soft fitted button-up. "I have to go back to the hospital."

"You don't sound convinced."

"I just want to sleep."

Sleep wasn't in the cards. Fats dragged me out of the apartment, snagging Dr. Bloom's packet as we went.

"What are you doing with that?" I asked.

"You can read it at the hospital and get back to Spidermonkey," said Fats.

"It can wait."

She gave me a glare. "Can it? They kill people."

"So do you," I said.

"Not lately."

"That doesn't make it better."

"Depends on who you ask," said Fats, putting me in the truck and handing me my phone when it started ringing. "Chuck. You've got to tell him."

I groaned and didn't get hello out before he blasted me with, "You made him pee, Mercy. I said I'd handle it."

"So I handled it. Big diff."

"It is a big difference. I wouldn't have made him pee and terrified him."

I snorted. "Oh, really? You'd threaten him with the full weight of state prosecution and possibly federal. That's better? I don't think so. Besides, he's an easy pee. Fats barely touched him."

"I'm sure she didn't."

"You want to hear what we got?"

"I already got it with no urination," said Chuck.

"We softened him up for you and, by the way, our trash can's gone," I said.

"So he hauled Denny out in broad daylight. He must've had a truck stashed somewhere. I can't wait to get my hands on that guy."

"Get in line," I said. "Anything on Scott Frame?"

"We're tracking him down. He's supposed to be pulling a night shift and he wasn't answering the phone. Probably turned off the ringer."

"You might want to send somebody over," I said.

"Already on the way. He's not dead though. Our guy isn't interested in killing the Trust members, just their families." Chuck paused. "You've got Fats with you, right?"

I told him I did and all about the missing Brain Trust file, which sent him into spasms of rage.

"There must be something in that file," he yelled.

"I can hear you and I know," I said.

"Go back to the hospital where you'll be safe," he said.

I said I would and leaned my head on the window, hoping for a five-minute snooze. Not gonna happen. Spidermonkey texted. "They're dead."

Fats glanced over and asked, "Who is it?"

"Spidermonkey." I texted him, "Who's dead?"

"Keely and her husband," he texted back.

We went back and forth. The information was simple and horrifying. Keely Stratton and her husband were selling their house in Nicaragua and had an open house. They got a lot of traffic since the expat community was huge in their area. The local police thought someone stayed behind, possibly hiding in a closet. After the Strattons went to bed, he came out and shot them in their sleep. That was in March and there were no clues whatsoever. Spidermonkey thought the locals had been very diligent in the investigation. Murdered expats were bad for business. Plus, Keely and her husband were well-liked and generous to the local community. No enemies. No one suspicious sniffing around. A few items were taken from the house—jewelry and a pricey watch—but the cops thought it was for show, not a real robbery. Certainly, no one local. Keely had bought quite a few art pieces from Nicaraguan artists. They were worth thousands and would've been easy to hock. Apparently, the population wasn't fussy about the provenance of pieces. The killer could've made a bundle, but he'd left behind the art and plenty of electronics.

"Make sure you stay with Fats," he texted.

I told him that I had Dr. Bloom's file and was headed back to the hospital with her. He said Mom had just gone down to her MRI. I guess he hacked the hospital. He and Uncle Morty couldn't help themselves. Information was addictive.

Spidermonkey tried to get some Brain Trust information for me, but he didn't have much hope of it being useful. There'd been no break-ins at the other detectives' houses, except for Keely, so he assumed that their files didn't have anything important. My dad was the lead so he would naturally have everything and now everything was gone.

When I told Fats what happened, she asked, "I wonder why he'd kill Keely. That's different."

"She was the only female in the group. Maybe that pissed our guy off," I said.

Fats nodded. "It's not easy being the only girl and she was second to your dad. Has anyone heard from your dad yet?"

"Not as far as I know."

"They have to give him a phone call sometime," she said.

"You'd think." I hugged Dr. Bloom's envelope to my chest and found it oddly comforting. For once, The Klinefeld Group seemed like a fascinating puzzle instead of an ever-present threat. At least, they weren't shooting detectives in their sleep or dragging bodies around in trash cans.

Fats pulled into valet parking and we trotted in. There still wasn't any press, thankfully, but a couple of nurses warned us that reporters were sneaking in and roaming the halls, just in case I turned up.

Hopefully, nobody told them Mom had another MRI and we went to radiology instead of Mom's floor. She wouldn't be done yet and it would be nice to be there when she got out.

We stopped in a side hall after spotting a guy skulking around with a video camera and calling security on him.

"I wonder if Aaron's bringing dinner," I said, peeking around the corner to see if the coast was clear. It wasn't. The guy was questioning everyone who came down the hall.

"You know Aaron's cooking, but call him and ask when," said Fats. "I'd like to have dinner with Tiny before midnight."

"You should go back to his apartment. He needs a break and I'll be here."

"Excellent idea." She rubbed her hands together gleefully. "Alone time. You know what I'm going to do first?"

"No and I don't want to."

She opened her mouth and I held up a finger when Aaron answered, "Huh?"

"It's Mercy," I said. "Are you bringing dinner?"

"Yeah."

"When?"

"Tonight," he said.

"Care to be more specific?" I asked.

"No. Here's Morty."

I rolled my eyes at Fats. That was useful. I could've saved my breath and a discussion with Uncle Morty.

"I was just gonna call you," Uncle Morty said. "We got 'em."

"You broke through already? Impressive." I could hear him preening on the other end of the line. For all his grumpiness, he did love a compliment. "So what have you got?"

He and Novak had broken all the encryptions and they were layered, so it was crazy impressive. We'd been right. Josef Mayer had given up the Unsubs to the Canadian version of the FBI. They'd passed the information to our guys, who really screwed the pooch, as my dad would say. The FBI put a small computer hacking task force on it and they had broken through. But despite their hacking skills, they had no ability to blend with the well-informed psychos. Like the guy who showed up to visit Blankenship, they gave up details on crimes the Unsubs knew they didn't do. They strung them along, letting them dig holes before telling them that they'd been made and changing the encryption. Of course, the task force could break through again and they did, but the Unsubs laughed at their attempts and once again changed the encryption. It became a game to them and the Unsubs were nothing if not good at games.

The real problem wasn't that the task force wasn't as good at blending with psychos as Chuck. The problem was that they gave up. The investigation got dropped and the task force disbanded out of sheer frustration. From what Uncle Morty found out, nobody seemed to care that a skilled group of serial murderers, rapists, and child molesters went on doing their thing unbothered by a little thing like law enforcement. Uncle Morty got ahold of internal memos that said the Unsubs couldn't be real, so why bother when they had real terrorists to worry about? Previous memos said the Unsubs were absolutely real and must be stopped. In short, the FBI got beat and talked themselves into thinking they didn't.

"That's fantastic," I said. "Well, I mean, that we have evidence, not—"

"There's more," he said.

"More?"

Just then, a voice came over the speaker system. "Code Silver, Radiology. Code Silver, Radiology."

I froze and Uncle Morty said, "It's about you. The Unsubs—"

Click. I hung up on him. Fats grabbed my arm as a security guard ran past us with his weapon drawn.

"What the hell is a Code Silver?" she asked.

"Active shooter."

"Shit!" Fats grabbed my arm, attempting to shove me behind her. It didn't work. I ran, dragging Fats along behind me and that's no mean feat.

"Stop!" she yelled.

"Let go! My mom's in there!"

She got me in a bear hug. "My job's to keep you alive."

"And mine is to keep my mom alive."

A door to the stairs burst open down the hall and Chuck ran out, weapon drawn with Sidney five steps behind, yelling into a radio, "Man down. Man down! Shooter headed to ER. Lock it down!"

I struggled in Fats' arms. "That's the other way. Let go! He's gone."

A trauma team ran by us with a nurse saying, "I saw that guy. He won't fit on a regular gurney."

"Tiny," Fats whispered.

She let go and we ran to radiology, bursting through the double doors to find the hall crazy crowded. The MRI suites were farther down around the corner. I didn't see a wheelchair. Mom would've been in a wheelchair.

"Where is he?" asked Fats. "I can't see him."

EMTs came running from the other direction with an oversized gurney yelling for everyone to get out of the way and that's when we saw him. Tiny lying on his back with multiple stab wounds to the chest and abdomen. The pool of blood under him grew as we watched. Two nurses were struggling to staunch the bleeding as they tried to figure out how to lift him.

"Oh my god," said Fats.

"Clear an OR," yelled Dr. Calloway.

"We need more guys!" yelled a nurse. "He's too big."

I pushed Fats toward them. "Go. You do it."

She ran through the crowd, shoving people aside and then kneeling in Tiny's blood to single-handedly lift him onto the gurney. She was strong, but I didn't think she was that strong. It must've been like when mothers lift cars off their kids. Love gives you strength. She probably could've lifted a Mack truck.

They strapped Tiny on the gurney and ratcheted it up to pushing height.

"OR five! It's ready!"

"We need five liters of O neg!"

"Pressure's dropping!"

They pushed Tiny down the hall and a doctor turned back to yell at Fats. "Come on! You have to put him on the table."

She looked at me and I yelled, "Go!"

Tiny disappeared with his entourage and I pushed my way through the crowd. People were running this way and that. There was another area of blood. It wasn't all Tiny's. The guy with the video camera stood against a wall with his mouth hanging open and the camera hanging limp at his side. He was going to kick himself later.

I grabbed a nurse as she dashed by with bags of blood. "Where's the other victim?"

"OR," she yelled, pulling away from me and running down the hall.

I went for the MRI suite around the corner and found that hall surprisingly calm. The doors were all locked, presumably because of the Code Silver, but I hadn't heard any shots. Tiny's wound definitely wasn't gun-related.

"Who's in there?" I yelled, banging on a door. "I need to find Carolina Watts!"

Nothing. They were hunkered down. It was no use, so I ran for the elevators. The OR. Somebody would tell me if Mom was in there. I pounded on the up button. "Come on! Come on!"

"Mercy!" Mr. Snyder, head of security, was at the emergency stairs. "Come this way."

I ran to him. "Did he get my mom?"

"Carolina? No. She was in MRI when it happened. Everything's locked down. She's still in there."

I grabbed his arm to steady myself. "Thank god."

"He stabbed her bodyguard and a cop."

"Unbelievable." I cocked my head to the side as a faint sound echoed through the hall. "Did you hear something?"

"What?" asked Mr. Snyder.

We both listened, but nothing happened. I thought it was in my head, but then Mr. Snyder's radio squawked. "Suspect cornered at loading dock. Shots Fired! Shots fired!"

Mr. Snyder yelled obscenities as he ran off full steam, presumably toward the loading dock.

I didn't know where to go, up to the OR or back to Mom. A nurse peeked at me from around the corner by the elevators. "Is it all clear?"

"I guess so," I said. "They've got the guy at the loading dock."

She came out slowly. "Thank God. They make us do all those drills, but I never thought I'd actually have to do it in real life."

"Were you there when it happened?"

"I was in mammography, doing a scan." She shook a little and I eased her against the handrail to steady her. Tricia wasn't a nurse. She was an ultrasound tech and when she heard the commotion in the hall she ran out to see what happened. She saw Tiny and a cop on the floor, blood everywhere. A man ran right past her. She only got a glimpse. The suspect had a bloody knife in his hand and was wearing scrubs with a mask and cap, which she thought was odd. There was no shooting. Tiny and the cop had been stabbed.

Tricia was so shaky I almost had to force her to come back to radiology to make a statement. Chuck and Sydney would want to hear her story.

"I freaked out," she said. "I called a Silver."

"Is there a code for stabbings?"

"No."

"Then you did the right thing."

"You think?"

"Absolutely. It's fine. Just come with me and you can wait in the office."

"What if he got away?" she asked, growing more shaky by the second.

I took her by the shoulders and steered her down the hall. "My boyfriend and his partner were chasing him. There's no way they didn't hit him. Crack shots, both of them." I didn't really know that about Sydney, but it sounded good and calmed Tricia.

We got back to the MRI suites and I put her in the office.

A voice came over the speaker. "Code Silver all clear. Code Silver all clear."

She sank into a chair and put her face into her hands. "Thank God."

Several of her co-workers came over to comfort her and I asked about my mother. She was still in Suite C and they'd be unlocking it now. I went out to find Suite C and had to restrain myself from pounding on the door. My heart was racing, but it could all be over. He made a move in the hospital, not the brightest idea. It was too strange. Something must've happened. Tiny wasn't close to Mom's suite when he was stabbed and he wouldn't leave her. No, something definitely happened.

The suite door clicked and a head poked out. A tech saw me and then visibly relaxed, "Oh, good. You're here. Carolina's been asking what happened and I don't know what to say."

"Did you already do the MRI?" I asked.

"No. I was just going to put her on the board when the Code Silver came down," he said.

"Did you see anything unusual?"

"Like what?"

"A man in scrubs with a mask and a cap on?"

He had seen a man matching Tricia's description. He'd walked by Mom and said something, but he didn't hear what. Then he walked away down the hall.

"He didn't touch her or anything?" I asked.

"Not that I saw. Carolina was smiling. Come in and ask her before we get started," he said, opening the door for me to come in.

"Mercy, what was that code?" asked Mom from her wheelchair. "And where have you been?"

"The code's nothing to worry about. I was out...gathering information," I said.

She gave me a lopsided smile that was oddly charming. My mother could even pull off a stroke. "Anything to get your father home?"

"As a matter of fact, yes. I have the goods."

"Have you talked to the FBI yet?" she asked as the tech put up her foot pedals and prepared to get her out of the chair.

"Not yet. I will as soon as you get going."

Mom waved me away and another tech came in. "We're all set here. Can you step outside, Miss Watts?"

"I can, but what happened to the second cop that was on my mother? She had two."

Mom took my hand. "They're outside, Mercy. They can't come in. Tell Tiny to get a snack. He needs a break."

The techs looked at me, their mouths set. There was no point in telling Mom that Tiny was upstairs fighting for his life and the cop, I had no idea what happened to him. "I will. You just get this done. No squirming."

She frowned. "That thing is the worst and I don't even have claustrophobia."

"Thank goodness for that," said the tech. "Are you sure you don't want a sedative again?"

"No. I'll do it straight this time."

They lifted Mom gingerly and walked her to the board, laying her down slowly. The techs in Radiology are always the nicest. They put headphones on her with the classical music she wanted and gave her a warm neck pillow and blanket. When she was tucked up like a burrito, all warm and cozy, I went for the door.

"Miss Watts?"

I turned and the second tech had Mom's chart in his hands and a strange kinda horrified expression on his face.

"What?"

"Your mom's chart. It was in the pocket on the back of her chair," he said.

The other tech came over, looked, and said, "Ah shit. Call security."

I walked over. I didn't want to, but I made myself do it. There was a note scrawled in black ink in the tech's hand.

I've got your daughter.

"It was just in there." He went stiff. "I touched it. What if it has fingerprints?"

I grabbed a tissue off the desk in the corner and said, "It's fine. They'll just have to exclude you after they dust it."

"Yeah?"

"Sure. Call security and tell them what you found. Let's put this in the control room. I don't want my mom lying there for any longer than necessary."

They agreed and I carried the note into the control room, laying it on a clean surface and then taking several pictures and texting them to the handwriting guy. My phone was buzzing almost non-stop in my pocket. Uncle Morty. Either he'd heard what happened or he was pissed off at me hanging up. Neither would be pleasant.

"You should stay in here," said the tech.

"Thanks, but I've got things to do."

They looked at the note and then me.

"It's fine. I think they got him at the loading dock," I said.

They nodded. "They did. Shot him. He's dead."

"Damn. I was hoping they could question him." I smiled and my lip began stinging anew. "You can't have everything, I guess."

They suggested I get a new ice pack and I left, walking out into the empty hall. The noise around the corner was pretty loud. It sounded like crime scene had arrived, but I didn't hear Chuck's or Sydney's voices. They must have stayed at the loading dock.

I walked the other way, pulling out my phone. I had messages from pretty much everyone from Raptor in Sturgis to Spidermonkey. Uncle Morty was calling every thirty seconds. He'd logged twenty calls in the last ten minutes, a new record. I sighed and pressed *Return Call*.

As I put the phone to my ear, a hand came around my face, covered my nose and mouth, and yanked me back against a hard chest. I scratched at his arm. There was some kind of thin fabric over it and I dug in my nails. His other arm was around my waist. He dragged me backward. I saw a door frame. Alone in a room? No. I kicked and twisted. He grunted and hit the frame. I couldn't breathe. There was a blur of beige and something hit my waist. Hard. Twelve pounds of hard. He screamed in my ear and let go. I fell to my knees and he stumbled over me.

"Help!" I screamed as I landed flat on the floor. I got a glimpse at a man running away down the hall in scrubs. He was stripping them as he ran around the corner.

Someone was at my side. "Oh, my god, Mercy!"

Pete rolled me over and patted me down. "I can't find anything."

"What about the face?" asked someone.

"She had that before."

"It's bleeding."

Pete put a bandage to my chin. "Mercy, can you hear me?"

"I'm okay." I flailed my arm. "He went that way."

Someone ran past us.

Pete looked up. "Someone page Chuck Watts."

The loudspeaker said, "Chuck Watts to Radiology. Chuck Watts to Radiology stat."

"What did he look like?"

I struggled to sit up and Pete got me propped against the wall. "I don't know. I didn't see him. He got me from behind."

"Where the hell is your bodyguard?"

"In the OR, moving Tiny to the table."

"She shouldn't have left you," said Pete.

"I told her to. You've seen Tiny. Nobody else could move him."

A wet something nudged my hand. I looked down and there was Wallace, doing her pug smile with a scrap of white fabric. "You were the blur."

Bark.

I took the scrap from her mouth. Light tee material with some blood.

"Good work, Wallace," I said, gathering her into my lap. "You really are The Wonder Dog."

Chuck came running up with Sydney. They saw me and came skidding to a halt.

"What happened?" asked Sydney.

"Somebody grabbed her," said Pete.

"Wallace saved me," I said.

Chuck didn't move and Sydney pushed past him, squatting next to me. "Tell me exactly what happened."

Before I could get a word out, Mr. Snyder ran up. "Mercy, where's the note? Why are you on the floor?"

I stood up with Pete's help and said, "The note's in the control room. I thought it best to leave it there."

Pete explained what he saw and Chuck sprang into action, running off in the direction that my attacker went. He didn't say a word to me. Sydney whispered, "He's upset."

"It hasn't been a great day for me either."

Sydney took my statement. To nobody's surprise, my guy was nowhere to be found. The other suspect was unidentified, except as a middle-aged Hispanic male. I was right. Something had happened. The something was Tiny. Weiss was the other cop on duty watching Mom. He said that when she was going in, the dead suspect said to her, "Sorry about what happened to you."

Mom replied with, "Thank you."

That was it. The tech rolled Mom inside the MRI suite and the guy walked away. Tiny said to Weiss and his partner, Spitz, "I'll be right back." He went off in the direction the suspect went, turned the corner, and a few seconds later, they heard Tiny scream. They ran to him. The suspect charged them, slashing Spitz's throat and running off. Weiss gave pursuit through the hospital to the loading dock, where he cornered him. Chuck and Sydney arrived. They tried to talk him down, but he pulled a weapon and they shot him. All of them. Twice.

The MRI suite door opened and the tech wheeled Mom out.

"I got it right this time." Then Mom frowned. "Did you call the FBI? Is your father coming home?"

"Er...I got distracted," I said, putting Wallace in her lap.

"By what? For heaven's sake. Give me the information and I'll do it."

"No, no. I've got it."

Mom looked around at the small crowd. "What is everyone doing? Don't you have things to investigate?"

"Yes, ma'am," said Sydney. "We're on it."

"Good. Now if Mercy can get her ducks in a row we'll be all set."

"I will, Mom."

"Now?"

"Absolutely. Let's get you back up to bed. Aaron's coming with dinner."

Mom scratched Wallace's noggin. "I haven't been really hungry since it happened and now all of the sudden I'm starving. This has been such a weird day."

Tell me about it.

CHAPTER TWENTY-THREE

We got Mom back to her room and she was none the wiser. I knew I had to tell her about Tiny, but she was slurring so bad, I just couldn't do it. The more tired she was, the more she slurred.

Aaron hadn't shown up yet, so I gave her milk and applesauce. She ate it with no problem and fell asleep immediately. Two fresh uniforms were on her door and beyond them, pacing like an insane gladiator, was my bodyguard. To say Fats was scaring everyone who saw her was an understatement.

I closed Mom's door behind me and said, "Please stop that. You're freaking people out."

"I almost got you killed," she said, tearing at her sock bun and giving her hair a distinct Medusa vibe.

"No, you didn't. You helped save Tiny."

"I left you. I'm never supposed to leave you."

"I told you to," I said.

"I don't listen to you. I listen to me. What the hell was I thinking?"

I took her arm and steered her toward the waiting room at the end of the hall where Grandad had holed up, feeling just as guilty as Fats, if not more. He'd gone to The Shaved Duck for beers with the respiratory techs and missed the whole thing. He was sitting on the sofa with Uncle Morty, surrounded by laptops.

"I'm so sorry, sweetheart," Grandad said for the tenth time.

"It's not your fault. It's nobody's fault." I sat down, tucking my leg to my chest. I was a little shaky, I'm not gonna lie, but for almost getting kidnapped or whatever he was intending, I felt pretty good.

"You wanna hear this?" asked Uncle Morty gruffly, but I could tell he was shaken.

I didn't, but I said okay. Uncle Morty told me that I was mentioned in the Unsub chats more frequently than was remotely comfortable. There was one guy, Nightmaster, who kept asking about me. He referred to Cassidy Huff and claimed her death as his own work, saying he'd buried her out at Shaw's Arboretum. He gave an exceedingly disgusting rundown of what he did to her, but I asked for the laptop and read it for myself a couple of times. It stopped turning my stomach after the third read.

"That sounds weird."

"No kidding," said Fats. "He's disgusting."

"I mean, it sounds rehearsed. Like he read it in a book or something."

Grandad smiled. "You are getting good. That was my feeling as well. There's no passion in what he's saying. It's a recitation of facts. Nothing more."

"There's plenty of passion when he talks about Mercy, but that ain't the point," said Uncle Morty.

"I'll bite. What's the point? I've got to call the FBI before Mom wakes up or it's going to be ugly."

Uncle Morty crossed his arms over his belly. "Read it again. If you don't get it quick, I'll think you're a moron."

"You already think I'm a moron," I said.

"But now I'll have proof."

I rolled my eyes, put the fresh ice pack to my mouth, and read the kind of stuff that made your eyes want to bleed. I knew there were sick people out there, but this stuff was beyond what I'd seen in Dad's files or my worst imaginings. It was a straight up horror show in print.

It took me about ten minutes and the feeling that came with it was nothing short of nauseating. "I got it," I said.

Fats looked over my shoulder. "All I've got is the urge to vomit."

"That, too, but I've got why the FBI wanted to keep my dad away from the Unsubs at all costs."

She shrugged. "Because they dropped the ball."

"That wasn't enough. Dad works with the FBI. He wouldn't go public and throw them under the bus even if he found out. He'd just go to work catching the Unsubs. It's what he does."

"Unless..." said Uncle Morty.

I pointed to my name on the screen. "Unless he found out that the FBI knew I was a target and said nothing. They were in those initial chats with Nightmaster. He said he wanted to rape me and literally skin me alive. Did they warn Dad, me, the local cops? Hell no, they didn't. If Dad found that out, he'd throw them under the bus so fast, they'd never see it coming."

"And there it is," said Grandad. "Those bastards. They knew what was coming our way and they sat on it."

Uncle Morty muttered curse words and pink tinged his cheeks. "Time to call the FBI."

Hatchet Nose walked in. "No need. We're here. Did you get something from Blankenship?"

"Hell, yeah, she did. Look at her."

"I meant, besides the bite." He walked over to the window and leaned on the sill, crossing his arms. It was an attempt to appear casual and it failed. He was so stiff I was surprised his joints didn't creak. "What possessed you to do that? You know what Blankenship is."

I lowered my ice pack and he winced. "Better than anyone, but it was worth it."

"The consensus is that he passed you something. How about telling me what it was?"

"Oh, I will, but I want my father back and I don't mean in a week. I mean tonight."

Hatchet Nose smiled. "Fine by me, but you should know they've cut me and Harwood from the investigation in Kansas completely.

We've been put on background checks that are supposed to have something to do with it, but they clearly don't."

"Are you asking me to get you back in?" I asked.

"Can you?"

"Possibly. Can you get through to whoever is making the decision to hold my dad?"

"Without a doubt. That is, if you've got something," he said. "Concrete evidence would be a plus."

"Tell your superiors that I've found what they're trying to conceal," I said with a slight smile. It hurt so much more since the whole hand over the mouth thing.

"And what would that be?"

"Oh, no. You get nothing right now. I want my father out of custody and on a spiffy FBI plane tonight. Preferably within two hours. I'm sure they can swing that."

"A private plane? That's a big demand," said Hatchet Nose.

"Not a private plane. An FBI plane."

"What's the difference?"

"Trust me. There's a difference," I said.

"This had better be good," said Hatchet Nose.

"It is. Tell them if Tommy Watts isn't at his wife's bedside tonight, I'm going to call everyone who ever interviewed him, from The New York Times to the Sacramento Bee, and give them my evidence. It's in black and white and shit storm won't begin to describe the fallout. There will be lawsuits."

Hatchet Nose steepled his hands, rhythmically tapping his fingers together. "Why would they believe you?"

"Just tell them that the Nightmaster had plenty to say," I said, putting my ice pack to my chin.

"The Nightmaster?"

"He's an interesting guy. You'd hate him."

The finger tapping got faster. "You've got evidence of more crimes and the Bureau knew about them?"

I just nodded.

"Shit."

We all just looked at him. There would be no freebies.

"I want first crack, me and Harwood. This fiasco has done nothing for my career."

"How much will it hurt you?" asked Grandad.

"I'm on background checks like I screwed something up. I could stay there indefinitely."

Grandad stood up and began pacing. "That's not my granddaughter's concern. It's your people who pulled this crap."

"I'm aware, but if I'm in, really in, I can keep you in the loop. I'm sure that, from his reputation, Mr. Watts will want in."

"If he decides not to drop the dime on your people."

"Assuming that," said Hatchet Nose.

My phone rang and it was Pete calling to say that Tiny was still in surgery. The damage was extensive. They had to resect his colon, remove a lobe of his liver, and inflate a collapsed lung. He lost three liters of blood. Considering it happened in the hospital, he absolutely would've died had he not been. Pete said everyone felt good about his chances.

Then Pete said he'd put in a painkiller prescription for me. I protested, but he said I should take it or sleeping would be difficult. I agreed just because it was easier than arguing. I wasn't the fan of painkillers that the rest of the world seemed to be. I could get by with Motrin.

Everyone watched me, tense and fearful as I hung up. I gave them the update as cheerfully as possible, but it didn't seem to help.

Fats sat down beside me, her face unreadable. "When can I see him?"

"When he comes out of recovery. He'll go to the ICU. You can see him there."

"I'm not family," she said, a glint of tears in her amber eyes.

Uncle Morty looked up from his screen. "This mess is a lawsuit waiting to happen. They'll make a damn exception."

"You think so?"

"I'll make sure," he said, more kindly than I'd ever heard him.

"I guess I'd better call Aunt Willasteen," I said. "She and Tiny's mom might not be on a plane yet."

Aunt Miriam marched in. "I'll call Willasteen. How is Tiny?"

I told her and she dialed her phone, getting the wrong number three times. I knew she couldn't answer the phone half the time, but the dialing problem was new. I got up, dialed the phone, and waited with a wince for Aunt Willasteen to answer. Nothing was easy when it came to Tiny's aunt.

"Willasteen Plaskett," she said stiffly.

"Hi, Aunt Willasteen, it's Mercy. Tiny's doing well in surgery. It's looking good. Here's Aunt Miriam." I pushed the phone at Aunt Miriam as Aunt Willasteen protested, "Don't give me to that old bat."

"Old bat?" asked Aunt Miriam. "You're six months older than me."

She walked into the hall, arguing about how premature Aunt Willasteen really was and how it didn't make a difference in their respective ages in any case.

Fats' eyes had grown large. "Tiny said Aunt Willasteen's his favorite relative, aside from his mother."

"She is," I said.

"But she sounds..."

"Like a nightmare? She is. Think of her as another Aunt Miriam, just with an accent and superior cooking skills."

"Whoa."

"Tell me about it. Having them in the same room again is going to be interesting and possibly bloody."

Hatchet Nose waved at me. "Are you going help us get back on the case or not?"

"Not," said Grandad. "Why should she?"

"Actually," I said, "I don't mind giving him first crack. Somebody has to get the info and I'd rather have him than some douche, who might bury it. I have one condition."

"Your father coming home. I know," he said.

"Yes, but I want Gansa and Gordon on it with you."

He blanched. "They're practically rookies with zero experience. They might be morons."

"The FBI doesn't hire morons and I kinda want to help them."

"Why, for crying out loud?"

I shrugged. "It's a Watts thing. You wouldn't understand, because even I don't."

"Alright. Me, Harwood, and a couple of wet behind the ears rookies," he muttered, leaving the room with his phone to his ear.

Grandad shook a prescription bottle at me. "When do you take these again?"

"I just took it."

"The swelling is worse. Maybe you should take another for good measure."

"That's not how it works, Grandad," I said. "Every six hours will be fine."

He wasn't convinced and looked to Fats for backup. "It is worse, right?"

Fats glanced at me. "I don't know. I guess."

I sat down and asked, "What?"

"You were right and I didn't believe you," she said.

"I don't get to hear that very often. Right about what?"

"The cat. You said something terrible would happen and it did—to Tiny."

I hadn't thought of that, but of course, she was right. Tiny was family, not to mention from New Orleans, the origin of the cat. It made sense that he would be included in the feline warning system.

"What cat?" asked Uncle Morty.

I rolled my eyes and told him about the latest appearance of Blackie, not an hour before Tiny was nearly stabbed to death. Grandad and Uncle Morty claimed it was a coincidence and I was so tired of people denying things that I'd seen with my own two eyes that I didn't bother to argue. The cat wasn't real. Fine. Whatever.

"Aren't you worried that he'll show up again?" asked Fats, ignoring Grandad's and Uncle Morty's denials.

"There's nothing to be done about it. If he does, he does. I'm not as concerned about that as I am about how they knew the exact time Mom would be going in for her MRI and that I would be there," I said.

Fats frowned, but Uncle Morty snorted. "Any thirteen-year-old hacker could get into this hospital's lousy system. It's total crap."

I set my ice pack on the arm on my chair and gave him the stink eye. "And when was Mom scheduled?"

He typed for a second and then looked up. "She wasn't, but there were some blocks open."

I crossed my arms.

Grandad started pacing again. "How did they know she was getting an MRI then?"

"There was a request for Carolina to be transported to Radiology," said Uncle Morty.

"Okay. Maybe. That works for Mom, but how did they know I was rushing back for it? They wrote a note and were ready for me."

"Well, their plan sucked," said Fats. "One's dead and you got away."

"I don't think that was their plan. Tiny noticed something suspicious about the one that dropped the note. He confronted him. I don't think they expected that and when Fats left, the other one took a shot."

"They must've had a plan to get me away from you," said Fats.

Grandad and Uncle Morty said nothing, only looking at her.

"You don't think...I would never have left Mercy, if it wasn't life or death."

"We don't know that," said Uncle Morty.

"I do," I said. "I told her to go. There was no way they could move Tiny without her."

"Perhaps we need another bodyguard," said Grandad.

"We do, but not for me. Mom has nobody and I doubt Calpurnia has anyone else clean enough to get past the cops."

They stayed silent.

"I'm telling you. Fats didn't do anything. Hell, she could've killed me at any time in the last two days. She could've taken me out during what happened today. It was a cluster down there. Instead, she saved Tiny."

Grandad came over to me. "How do you *feel* about it?"

"I feel good. I would know," I said.

Uncle Morty pushed aside his laptop. "You can't listen to Mercy. She gets lost here in her own hometown. She didn't *feel* that Cheryl Morris was the murderer in Sturgis until the woman tried to kill someone under her freaking nose. I'm sorry, but Fats is out."

"No, she isn't," I said. "It's my life and she's in."

"Hell, no."

"Nobody's asking you."

Chuck came in with Sydney. "How about asking me?"

I groaned. "We're full up on opinions."

"How about facts?"

"I'm good."

Chuck eyed Fats. "You want to tell them or should I?"

Fats stayed silent, but she wasn't remotely worried. I knew her well enough to see that.

"Tell us what?" asked Grandad. He wasn't worried either, but my boyfriend didn't pick up on the mood of the room.

"She works for Calpurnia Fibonacci, the mob boss," he said triumphantly.

Uncle Morty put his laptop back on his lap and started typing leisurely. I yawned and Grandad barely suppressed a smile. Fats kicked her heels up on the coffee table and said, "Took you long enough."

Chuck blanched. "You knew? Mercy, your bodyguard is a known felon."

"She's not a felon. Her record's cleaner than mine."

"Only because she's got the Fibonacci luck," he said. "Ace. How could you bring this woman in to watch your granddaughter? We could've hired from an agency."

"You don't bring a knife to a gun fight," said Grandad.

"You don't bring a Fibonacci to protect Tommy Watts' daughter."

Grandad came over and patted my steaming boyfriend on the back. "You do if you want the best. She's the best."

"The best who might've sold Mercy out," said Chuck.

"Mercy says no. I believe her and Calpurnia."

"Calpurnia? Calpurnia? You sound like you know her."

"I do. Now let's think about more practical matters like how they knew where Mercy would be."

"They were following us," said Fats. "And listening in. We spoke about the MRI in Mercy's apartment. She doesn't even have double-paned windows. A parabolic listening device would do it."

"That could be useful, assuming they don't know that we know," I said.

"No," said Chuck. "It's not happening."

"Nobody asked for your opinion."

"I'm in charge of this investigation and you are not going to lure anyone anywhere."

Uncle Morty chuckled. "No, you're not."

"Huh?"

Chuck had been put on desk duty, along with Sydney and Weiss. An officer-involved shooting had to be investigated, even one that was so obviously clean. Chuck fumed and I didn't rub it in. No need. I didn't work for him and I was as bad at following orders as I was at following directions.

"I still say no. I'm thinking of your safety."

We argued about it until my phone rang. It was Pete saying Tiny was going into recovery. He would be awake soon. I told Fats and she practically ran out of the room, dragging me behind her. Chuck chased us to the elevator and pulled me off, holding the door.

"I'm not going to let you put yourself in danger, so just forget it," he said, giving me a kiss next to the bruise on my forehead. "Do you hear me?"

I nodded, but I didn't forget it. A plan was forming in my head and once a plan starts, you've got to follow through. That's just the way plans work.

I stepped on the elevator, giving him a smile and a wave. He watched me as the doors closed with his jaw twitching.

We only saw Tiny for a few minutes before we were ushered out of the ICU, but it was enough to both soothe Fats and fire her up.

"Whatever you're planning, I'm on board," she said.

"I'm sure we can use the listening thing to our advantage."

"The question is how to use it."

"It would help to know who we'd be using it on. I wouldn't like to go in blind," I said.

She nodded. "I'd like to know how much fire power to have on hand."

"We're not going to kill him or them. Apprehend is the goal."

She said nothing and I took that as a bad sign. It was also a bad sign that Chuck hadn't left the hospital. He was in Mom's room along with everyone else. Aaron and Nikki had shown up with dinner, a fabulous Moroccan tagine with preserved lemon and lamb with almond cake for dessert. Mom was able to eat it pretty well if she concentrated on her swallowing.

Chuck got a call during dessert and he was all smiles. "You really don't need to do anything, Mercy. We're almost there."

"Meaning?" asked Grandad.

"We have the identity of our dead suspect. Alfonso Cruz. It's just a matter of time before we get who hired him."

There was something in the way Chuck said it that made me think this wasn't exactly the news he was hoping for, although he sold it well.

"Oh, yeah? Who's Alfonso Cruz?"

"Don't worry about it."

Whenever a man says, 'Don't worry about it.' You definitely should worry. A lot.

"Hey, Uncle Morty," I said. "Can you—"

Uncle Morty choked down an enormous bite of cake and said, "On it."

"Dammit, Mercy," said Chuck. "Can't you take my word for it?"

"Let me think," I said. "Nope."

Uncle Morty started laughing and Grandad joined in.

"He was a dry cleaner with no criminal record. Paid his taxes and was literally a Boy Scout. You got nothing," said Uncle Morty.

"Not nothing. He dropped that note on Carolina for a reason. We'll find it."

"It ain't gonna be soon."

Chuck gritted his teeth and watched me like I might make a break for it right then. He needn't have bothered. I wasn't leaving Mom until Dad got there, especially with Tiny out of the picture.

When we finished eating, the phone call Mom had been praying for came. Dad had been released and was about to get on a plane, private, no less. I gave Mom the phone and her emotions overcame her. I doubt Dad could understand much of what she said. I couldn't and I was in the same room.

While they were on the phone, Hatchet Nose showed up and waved me into the hallway.

"I don't know what you've got, but they were falling all over themselves to get your father on that plane," he said.

"I figured."

Chuck came out and put a protective arm around me. "What else did they discuss?"

"Everything was on the table, including arresting Mercy as a material witness, but I convinced them that you aren't the only one in the know and it would just make them look worse."

"Thanks for that," I said.

He smiled, his sharp eyes boring into mine. "And..."

"And there's an Unsub posing as an orderly at Hunt Hospital for the Criminally Insane. He's trying to get access to Blankenship, most likely to kill him. He used the name Jones on the phone once, but there's no Jones employed there."

The agent's mouth fell open and I enjoyed giving him what I had, including the recently arrived handwriting analysis. The notes were written by two different right-handed individuals, most likely male, and they had completely different personalities. Mr. Greenburg said he was disturbed by the handwriting from the Hunt note because it held almost no hint of a personality. It wasn't copperplate, but it had been perfected to the extent that the author of the note didn't have to think about how to form the letters and they were written with no hesitation. The handwriting had no graphic signs of a schizoid personality. None. Mr. Greenburg felt that the author had in-depth knowledge of handwriting analysis and probably had several perfected styles at his command. He would use one for his real life and the others when needed for criminal purposes. If we were to get handwriting samples from all the employees at Hunt, none would match.

The second sample was totally different. The person was upset when writing it. The ink was light on the page and there was considerable hesitation when forming the letters. There were several signs of a schizoid personality, but this was not definitive. Mr. Greenburg felt the author had written the words under duress and that if he had to guess, the author was not a career criminal.

"That fits with Alfonso Cruz," said Chuck.

"It doesn't give me anything for Hunt," said the agent.

"Recent employees are a place to start."

"What did your people come up with?"

Chuck shook his head. "Not much. Dozens of prints in the doctor's office. Nazir's discreetly interviewing staff about anyone enquiring about Blankenship."

The agent looked at me. "I'm going to have to go out there."

"Don't get any ideas," I said. "I've had enough of Hunt for a while."

"You want to keep Blankenship alive, don't you?" he asked.

"Not that much."

Hatchet Nose took a deep breath. "What else can you give me? What about this catatonic patient?"

"Greta can't give you anything else. If she knew something else, she would've given it to me."

"How about this mysterious Unsub evidence you've got? When can I get a look at that?"

"When my dad is standing at my mother's bedside and not a minute before," I said. "I learned my lesson with you dirtbags."

"Hey, not the dirtbag here," he said.

"We'll see."

The agent took off and we went back inside. Mom's eyes were barely open, but she held out her hand to me. "He's on the plane. You're a good daughter."

I suspected the painkiller they gave Mom for her latest headache had something to do with Mom's unexpected assessment of me, but I didn't care. It was nice to be good. Mom drifted off to sleep and Grandad shooed everyone out of the room. Everyone but me, Fats, and Aaron. My partner had gotten a blanket and was reading a pile of comic books, clearly in for the night.

Pete showed up with the painkillers for me and insisted I take one. He and Fats ganged up on me and I gave in. I took one with a mug of hot chocolate that tasted like Peruvian to me.

I curled up on the foldout bed, ready to sleep, when Fats put Dr. Bloom's file in my lap.

"Are you kidding me?" I asked.

"I've made up my mind."

"About what?"

"I'm going to help you. I owe the family," she said.

I pulled the sheath of paper out of its envelope. The top sheet was a cover letter, saying generally what was contained in the papers, a timeline, etc. I briefly glanced at the timeline. It started in 1938 with Stella Bled meeting Nicolas Lawrence in New York city. 1938. The year that set in motion my great-grandparents' murders a half century later and changed two families forever.

I looked at Fats, who'd decided that ten o'clock at night was the perfect time to do squat thrusts. Freak.

"What family?" I asked. "The Fibonaccis?"

"No, stupid. Your family."

"Oh. I think tomorrow you'll be paying us back plenty."

She did an extra-low squat. "Tomorrow, eh? You have a suspect."

"Not exactly. The timeline's bothering me and the missing file. I think the Brain Trust's last case is key."

"What about the lawyer, Parks?"

"He's a link, but not our guy. I'm missing something. Something obvious."

Fats leapt up, touching the ceiling easily. "So what happens tomorrow?"

"My dad takes over," I said. "You'll get to see how it's really done."

She went into another squat. "I think I've already seen that."

"No, this is driving me crazy. All these dates and people. Cassidy Huff. She's important. Why? Brian Shill's on house arrest. He didn't do it, but he's friends with his prosecutor. None of it makes sense." I rubbed my eyes. "I'm losing it."

"You're fine." She pointed at the papers in my lap. "Think about the past for awhile. It's not trying to kill you."

"For the moment," I said, settling in for a good read.

I read through Dr. Bloom's file in less than an hour. It shouldn't have taken that long, but I could barely keep my eyes open. Aaron's hot chocolate and Pete's painkiller hit me hard. Only Fats' nutty exercise routine kept me from passing out completely. I wished Dr. Bloom had just done bullet statements. Bullet statements would've been so fast, but the historian was a gifted writer in love with his subject. I had to read the prose and I had to admit I was starting to see thin spiderweb-like threads between the people that I hadn't seen before.

He started with Constanza Warnock, Big Steve's mother. I hadn't thought about her at all since he told me that Aleksej Bled had gone to Europe after the war to save her from certain death after she was released from a concentration camp. Dr. Bloom's colleague, Dr. Fritz Broszat, specialized in the Nazi art thefts across Europe and he knew who Constanza was through the art world. That woke me up a little. Big Steve wasn't an art person that I knew of. Then again, I didn't know how he was connected to the Bleds until Dr. Bloom told me, so anything was possible.

I turned the page and Wallace gassed, snuffling deeper into the covers. Mom rolled over, sighing softly. In that moment, she was who she used to be. Her face was so relaxed that it matched and there wasn't any drooling. Her breathing was a bit labored, but her oxygen level was good. Mom would recover as much as anyone could recover from an acute stroke. She was lucky. But the word lucky didn't sit well in my mind. How could you be lucky having suffered what she'd suffered? Did Big Steve think his mother was lucky to have survived the death camp only to die of wounds that would not heal later? What did Mom know about Constanza and the Bleds? What did Big Steve know? And why the hell did it have to be hidden? I'd been to Big Steve's house half a million times. I'd never seen a picture of his mother. Constanza had survived something that was pretty much unsurvivable. I wanted a picture of her on my wall. I wanted to look at her face and see what strength looked like.

I leaned over and tucked the covers in around my own survivor mother, gave Wallace a scratch, and went back to the file. These new puzzle pieces took me away from Mom's injuries and the immediate threat to our family as Fats said they would and I was grateful for the distraction.

Dr. Broszat said that nineteen-year-old Constanza Stern went with Florence Bled to New York in 1947. She sold a collection of jewelry and two small Aubusson 17th century tapestries at Christie's. Dr. Bloom, being super thorough, included a photo of the sale catalog The jewelry ranged from a tiny tiara to earrings, all dating from the Belle Époque era in France. The jewelry sold for $37,000 and the tapestries together, $7,000. That was almost a half million in today's money. Quite a haul for a young woman fresh from the horrors of the Nazis. Dr. Broszat theorized that Stella had smuggled those pieces out of the country for Constanza's family. Since the Bleds were extremely tight-lipped about the pieces they held for survivors, no one knew for sure. But the historian's theory went beyond that. He thought Constanza was in the Resistance and, therefore, her particular fate was known to Stella, who dispatched her family to save the young woman. I thought that was a reach, but he had some compelling reasons. Dr. Broszat had been following The Girls' search for survivors since they took over that duty from their mother, Florence. He was even aware of my going on those trips to Europe, where I did puzzles on the floors of libraries and records offices. In the set of photos was one of me in a graveyard in Prague, sitting on a blanket and eating a pastry. Millicent was behind me, doing a rubbing of a Jewish headstone. The photo was taken with a telephoto lens and I couldn't tell whose gravestone it was and I didn't remember it at all. I looked about six in the photo.

Until I saw that picture, I had no inkling that anyone was aware of The Girls' search. Heck, I only realized what they were up to recently. It's funny how kids accept things. I never thought it was odd that we went to Europe and spent half our time searching through dusty records and talking to local historians. Most of the pictures The Girls had of me were taken in graveyards. It was creepy, now that I thought about it.

Dr. Broszat thought Constanza was in the Resistance because Stella knew what happened to her and the Bleds clearly didn't know what happened to the owners of the other pieces Stella had smuggled out. Occasionally, they were able to track someone's descendants, but that was getting rarer as the years passed. The second reason was the more important one. Constanza Magdalene Stern didn't exist before she turned up in the Red Cross center in 1945. The Nazis had been almost as good at destroying their records as they had been at creating them. Only about ten percent of the records at Auschwitz survived and Constanza was in Auschwitz-Birkenau. Constanza wasn't in any of those records, but that wasn't surprising. What was surprising was that Constanza wasn't in any of the records from France either, where she was supposed to have been deported from. Big Steve had told me that she was deported through Drancy, but Dr. Broszat hadn't found any record that she was or that anyone by that name had been arrested in all of the Third Reich. Of course, the records could've been destroyed or lost, as many were, but there was no wealthy Stern family with a daughter named Constanza or even a daughter her age. Dr. Broszat, who was apparently obsessive, went back a hundred years and couldn't find any family that would match. He believed that Constanza Stern was an alias that she adopted when she was arrested, possibly to hide her involvement in the Resistance, and for some reason, she kept it.

Dr. Bloom and Dr. Broszat could hardly stand it. They wanted to know who she really was and where the pieces she sold came from. I was curious, too, but more interested in the next tidbit Dr. Broszat had for me. He'd already researched Florian and Annika Witold, the Parisian art dealers, but he didn't know that they were personal friends of the Bled family and had attended Stella's small wedding. Dr. Bloom told him about Helmut Peiper being Stella's enemy and he found a fascinating connection.

I turned the page and there was a photograph taken at the Witold gallery in Paris in 1940. The image was familiar to me. I must've seen it somewhere, but I couldn't think when. Hermann Göring, head of the Luftwaffe and an avid art collector, was in the photo, smiling at the art he was confiscating in the name of the Reich. Members of the SS were taking pieces off the wall, but from the angle, I couldn't tell if they were significant.

I yawned and Fats stopped her donkey kicks to ask, "Anything good?"

"More mysteries and a photo that's important."

She came over to look. "Who are they?"

"Nazis."

She punched my shoulder gently. "Even I know that. I mean, *who* are they?"

"That's Göring and the rest are just officers...oh, my god, it's him— it's Peiper."

Helmut Peiper was in the background, looking at a sheath of papers in his hand. I told Fats about the SS officer and Stella. This was a connection. Peiper had been on loan to Göring and Dr. Broszat didn't understand why. He had no background in art. For some reason, Göring put him in charge of cataloging all the objects found in the gallery. Any paper pusher could've done that and Peiper was fairly high-ranked.

"Why would he do it then?" asked Fats.

"It doesn't make any sense unless he was looking for something." I explained The Klinefeld Group's obsession with something we thought Stella had smuggled out of the country in 1938. I thought back to the photo of Stella and Nicky at the cafe with Amelie and Paul. They were in rough shape. Something had happened to them on their honeymoon. Maybe what happened was the Nazis. It'd be just like The Klinefeld Group to spring from that poisoned well.

"Works for me," said Fats. "Does everyone in the art world know each other?"

"Yes, at least to some extent."

"So whatever they're looking for is a piece of art. The Bleds, those art gallery people, and that nut job, Göring. What else could it be?"

"It could be anything, but a piece of art is a good guess." I turned the page to find another picture of Peiper in an over-the-top room that reminded me of the Louvre. He was watching paintings being carted away. He looked distinctly bored, dissatisfied to the extreme. The note on the photo said, "Palais Nathaniel Rothschild, Vienna, Austria."

The next page was another picture of Peiper in Vienna, still unhappy, but this time in the Block-Bauer house of The Woman in Gold fame. There were more pictures of Peiper confiscating Jewish art collections in several countries and, curiously, at a brewery in Germany. Dr. Broszat wanted to know if the Bleds were closely connected with the families and the brewery. The brewery was a no-brainer. I'm sure they were. The Bleds were famous brewers with connections everywhere. They'd helped European brewers get back on their feet after both world wars. As for the families, I didn't know. The Girls had watched Maria Altmann's struggle to reclaim her family's Klimt paintings with keen interest, but it didn't seem like they knew her personally.

Dr. Bloom told Dr. Broszat about Stella's portrait in the breakfast room at the Bled mansion. He told him not because he thought it was a great work of art but because he thought there was a chance he might know the artist, someone who was imprisoned in DH8. He didn't, but he referred Dr. Bloom to Dr. Karina Bock. She specialized in Nazi interrogations and political prisoners. Dr. Bock had the most information on DH8, including extensive interviews with prisoners. Dr. Bloom knew her but not well, so he had Spidermonkey clear her before giving her the information I had.

I dozed off after reading Dr. Bock's credentials. University of Heidelberg, blah, blah, blah. Credentials are a cure for insomnia if there ever was one.

A strange feeling came over me as I snoozed. One of those instinct things where you know something without having to look. Before I opened my eyes, I knew my father was there. No reason. I didn't hear anything or smell anything. Tommy Watts had a presence and I felt it like someone had wrapped me in a warm blanket and sung the knowledge to me.

I forced my heavy lids up and saw him at the foot of Mom's bed, gripping the footboard and staring at her face with a most unusual expression. I'd seen my dad look every which way, mostly frustrated when it came to me, but this wasn't anything I'd have expected from him. It took me a second and then I recognized it. Grief. Overwhelming, paralyzing grief. I'd only seen it once before when his partner, Cora, was murdered. Dad lost his mind, had to take a leave of absence from work, and drank so much the local liquor stores got worried.

There was the look again, etched on his emaciated face and in the death grip he had on her bed. But Mom wasn't dead. She could easily have died, but she was functioning amazingly well. She'd be released on

Thursday to whatever rehab I got her into. We were on the stroke floor. All you had to do was take a walk and you'd know how amazingly blessed she was to be okay.

I should've said that to Dad when we spoke. I should've said something more...I don't know...comforting. I thought he understood. He talked to her. His wife was still there, different but there.

Fats stood at the entrance to the room, her light brown hair loose around her face that held only uncertainty. I kept waiting for Dad to move, come to Mom's side, and speak to her. He didn't. He was barely blinking.

"You can talk to her," I said finally.

He didn't respond and Fats and I exchanged a look. "Perhaps we should go," she said.

"Do you want us to leave, Dad?" I asked. "We can leave."

Instead of saying what I expected—yes, get out—he straightened up slowly like he had rust in his joints and walked out of the room.

"I've never met your father," said Fats. "Is he normally like that?"

"No. Usually, you can't get him to shut up," I said.

"He knows she'll recover pretty well, right?" Fats returned to her chair and did some stretches.

"I thought he did."

"What are you going to do?" she asked.

Aaron sat up in his chair and said, "Go."

"Go where?" I asked.

"After him."

I looked at the door. I so didn't want to go after my father when he looked like that. When Cora died, Mom sent me to live with The Girls for a few weeks because he was so nuts. Mom said she could help him, that she knew what to do and she did. Dad came out of that extreme grief to become more successful than ever, absolutely driven to catch every criminal he came across. Come to think of it, maybe Mom wasn't so successful. We saw less of him than before. We were lucky to eat a whole meal with him. He went to work with the flu. Once, he had a sinus infection so bad that he interviewed a suspect while lying on the floor because of the vertigo. That guy confessed and that never happened. His appeal said Dad used emotional manipulation to an unusual extent with the floor thing and the confession ought to be thrown out. The judge laughed and Dad landed in Newsweek for the first time.

"I don't know what to say," I said.

"He's your father," said Fats.

I put Dr. Bloom's file on the windowsill and forced myself to stand up. "Yeah, but I don't know him that well. It was mostly me and Mom."

"Somebody has to do it."

"I wish Grandad hadn't left."

"Well, he did," said Fats. "Suck it up, buttercup."

"That's what Grandad would say."

"Go," said Aaron.

"Have you got any whiskey?"

My partner shook his head and closed his eyes, immediately snoring. I took a deep breath and left the room. The hall lights were dimmed and I didn't see Dad anywhere. The two cops at Mom's door said he went left.

"Did he say anything to you?" I asked.

They shook their heads and looked like they'd rather get syphilis than question the great Tommy Watts, so I went to the desk. The nurse there said he'd walked past her, but she didn't know where he went. At least, he wasn't headed for the elevators. I didn't fancy chasing my father down and dragging him back up to Mom's room, but I absolutely would if I had to. I only wished I had a taser on me. I had my Mauser, but I wasn't quite prepared to shoot him. Yet. But if he didn't come back and comfort Mom, I might consider it. I'd gotten bitten by a psycho to get him back. He'd better give Mom what she needed. She always gave him what he needed.

The more I thought about it, the angrier I got. I marched around the floor, looking for my damn father. I was supposed to suck it up. How about he suck it up?

I ended back at Mom's room, fuming. Fats came out. "No luck?"

"I can't believe this," I said. "He ran away. My father, a guy who watches full autopsies and chases freaks through dark alleys, ran away. I might kill him."

"I guess you can call Ace," she said.

"It won't do any good if I can't find my scarecrow of a father."

One of the cops cleared his throat and I gave him the stink eye. "What?"

"Did you try the bathroom?" he asked reluctantly.

"No. I didn't think of it," I said. "It's down the hall. Go in there and see."

The cop backed up against the wall like I'd put a gun in his face. "I can't leave my post."

"For crying out loud, I'm a girl. You're a man. It's a man's bathroom. Go look in the bathroom."

Neither cop would budge. Fats rolled her eyes. "I guess I can go."

"You're a girl, too."

"It's three in the morning. I don't think anybody's in there taking a whiz."

I threw up my hands. "Fine. I'll do it." I marched down to the bathroom. I don't know if I wanted him to be in there or not. There didn't seem to be a good choice. The only thing I knew I wanted was for my know-it-all, large and in charge father to make an appearance. I wanted him to be with Mom and look at the evidence I'd gathered and bring his brilliance to the table.

I didn't hear anything, so I opened the door a smidge. "Hello?"

There was something, a little sound, a hint of a presence, and it dawned on me that I couldn't go in there. A bathroom. Alone in the middle of the night. That was a fast way to a quick death.

I looked back at the cops and Fats, who were watching at the end of the hall. The dim lights wreathed them in shadows, so I couldn't tell what they thought. If I had to guess, it was something like better you than me.

"Dad, it's Mercy," I called through the crack. "Are you in there?"

Nothing.

"I can tell someone's in there. If you don't answer, I'm sending cops in. Exhausted cops with guns and no coffee. You seriously don't want them."

"It's me," said Dad in a barely recognizable voice, all strained and deep.

"Are you coming out?"

"No."

I wasn't sure what to do with that. Where was Uncle Morty or Grandad when I needed them? I rubbed my eyes and called to him. "I'm coming in."

"No."

"I'm not asking permission," I said, flinging open the door.

I marched in and surveyed the line of urinals and yes, it smelled, but not as bad as I expected. What I didn't see was my father. I went around a tiled corner and had to peek under the stalls. His feet were in the far stall. I recognized the shoes. Dad wasn't on the toilet, thankfully. He was standing sideways, most likely leaning on the wall. That was the good news. The bad news was that my father was crying.

CHAPTER TWENTY-FOUR

I came out of the bathroom an hour later. Without my father. I don't want to say he was hysterical, but he kinda was, completely torn up about Mom and useless to anyone, including himself. He blamed himself for what happened. He shouldn't have left Mom. He shouldn't have been a cop. He led a criminal to her. He shouldn't have trusted the FBI. He shouldn't have sent me to Hunt where I would eventually get my face bitten to get him out of airport jail. The whole nine yards. I tried to talk him down and get him to eat something. My father, like Grandad, was a terrible eater, but Dad would usually eat when he was away, if only to keep Mom from yelling. This time, he'd been so upset he hadn't eaten since he found out. From the slackness of his pale, freckled skin, I'd say he hadn't been drinking either.

I never expected him to react like that. Sure. I starved myself after Richard Costilla, but I kept functioning, doing the minimum to keep my body going. Dad wasn't doing the minimum. I talked about Mom, trying to focus him. My parents were super tight, the only parents I knew that still adored each other after twenty-seven years of marriage, but that wasn't helping. Talking about catching the one who did this to her didn't help. It was like he short-circuited and I was making it worse.

Outside the bathroom, I leaned on the wall and called Grandad. I didn't know what else to do. If I couldn't move Dad, maybe his father could. Grandad was dead asleep and he wasn't happy when I told him what was going on. Apparently, this had happened before when Dad was in high school and didn't get a perfect score on the SAT. He holed up in the bathroom for three days, hysterical, and Grandma J had to threaten to burn down the house to get him out. I had no idea that my father was so emotional. He always handled things with charm and aplomb, except for Cora's death. Even Gavin's death last year hadn't caused much of a ripple unless you counted excessive whiskey drinking.

Once Grandad agreed to come and handle his nutty kid, I asked a nurse to keep an eye on my father and went back to Mom's room, settling in my chair and pulling my blanket up to my nose. Fats followed me in and raised an eyebrow. "Well?"

"He's out," I said.

"Of his mind?"

"That, too. But more importantly, he's not going to be investigating. We'll be lucky if my grandad can get him out of the bathroom. It's all us."

"Do you have a plan?" she asked.

I yawned. "We're going to interview Banging Bob's mother."

"Why? He's pretty dead."

"That's the only Brain Trust case going on at the right time." I closed my eyes. There wasn't anything else I could do.

I awoke to the smell of croissants and expensive perfume. I was six again, warm and safe. Then I yawned and pain zinged through my lower jaw. Not so much six or safe, for that matter.

My eyes opened slowly and the first thing I saw was the last thing I wanted to see. Millicent's favorite George Hobeika suit, a cream and silver affair with a peplum jacket and a crystal studded Peter Pan collar. It was pretty snazzy for a hospital visit, but that's not what concerned me. Millicent was standing next to me, looking at Dr. Bloom's file that I thoughtlessly left on the windowsill.

The file was open. She was reading it. Didn't take a genius to know I'd been investigating the Bleds, for all intents and purposes, my family. I held my breath and hoped I'd vanish or, at the very least, sink into the floor.

"I know you're awake, Mercy." Millicent looked down at me. Her hair was in Marcel waves with a fascinator hat perched on the left side.

"I'm sorry," I said and I really was, in that moment anyway.

She closed the file firmly. "We'll speak of this later."

Let's don't and say we did.

"Okay."

She gave me a fresh ice pack and I pressed it to my lip.

"That's much worse than I expected," she said.

"How did you know?" I asked.

"Sister Miriam told us."

I glanced up at the clock. Six thirty. Then I looked at Mom. She was still asleep and I wished she could stay that way until Dad got it together, but it could be days. "My dad—"

"Tommy has been admitted," she said, her face growing tender and full of sympathy.

"For what?"

"Severe dehydration and exhaustion. Poor man. Ace says he's quite distraught."

I sat up. "He's not the only one. Why couldn't he hold it together for Mom?"

Millicent bent over and kissed my forehead, so I guess she didn't hate me. That was good.

"Because he couldn't," she said. "There is no why."

"That is so not comforting." I lowered the ice pack. "I did this to get him here."

Instead of answering, she gave me a hot croissant. Aaron poured me hot chocolate that smelled like it was made with half and half and possibly heavy cream. It was heavenly and just one sip made me feel sort of fluffy and light-headed. "Where did you make this?"

Chuck strode in. "The hospital kitchens. I hear he's reorganized their system and they're not happy about it."

"I imagine not." I looked at Aaron and he stared at the wall over my head. Hopeless. "Any new information?"

"Tommy's one floor up."

"I mean, on the case."

"There might be, but it's not your problem," he said.

I gobbled down half the croissant and stood up. "How do you figure that? Somebody tried to kill me yesterday."

"What?" exclaimed Mom.

My mouth fell open and a bit of flaky crust fell out. "Metaphorically. I meant metaphorically."

Mom held a tissue to the corner of her mouth and said, "I don't believe that for a moment." She looked around the room. "Where's your father?"

Yeah. A distraction.

"He came last night while you were asleep," I said. "He didn't want to wake you."

"That's ridiculous." Mom appealed to Chuck. "Where's Tommy? Didn't they release him? Is he on a plane?"

"He's back," said Chuck gently. "And he did come in, but he's sick. They admitted him."

Millicent explained the situation. Myrtle was up with Dad right then, checking on his condition. Mom tried to climb out of bed to go to Dad and it made me so mad, I literally bit my tongue to stop from screaming.

"Carolina, darling," said Millicent. "Tommy's fine. Sister Miriam, Ace, and Myrtle are with him."

"I should be with him," said Mom and it hurt my heart. I gave her a croissant. "Maybe you can go up later, but you need to eat."

"I'm not hungry. Why didn't he wake me up?"

Cause he's a self-involved nut.

"I told him you needed to rest," I said. "Want me to get an update?"

Mom nodded and accepted a cup of hot chocolate from Aaron.

I left the room with Chuck and Fats in tow, quietly closing the door behind me. "Did they find Scott Frame?"

"Aren't you going to see Tommy?" asked Chuck.

"Not just no, but hell no. Did you find Scott or not?"

Chuck pulled me down the hall away from the cops, who were intently listening. "You don't need to worry about it. Tommy's back."

I crossed my arms. "Oh, you mean the guy I found hysterically crying in the bathroom four hours ago? Yeah, I don't think he's going to be doing crap."

Chuck stared at me. "What do you mean?"

"I mean, he freaked out. Tommy Watts freaked out."

"Ace said he's dehydrated."

"From the crying."

My handsome boyfriend went stiff. "Why are you mad? His wife had a massive stroke. He gets to be upset."

"I know. I found her. The worst part's over. I did all the hard stuff. All he has to do is hold her hand and he couldn't even do that," I said. "Did you find Frame or not?"

"I'll handle it."

"You're off the case and frankly" —I pointed to my face— "I think I've earned it."

He sighed. "We found his truck. There was blood, a good amount, but not nearly enough to kill him. But this guy doesn't kill the detectives. He goes after the loved ones."

As far as you know.

"No body?" I asked.

"Not yet."

"Prints?"

"Still processing," said Chuck, giving me the once-over. "What?"

"I don't know. The blood in the truck thing is weird," I said. "Did you find a bullet or a casing?"

"No. They're thinking it was a stabbing, but I know what you mean. Who stabs a fully-grown man in his car? It might've started outside the car and Scott tried to get away."

"Blood trail?"

"A bit."

"He's getting messy, leaving the truck and the trail."

Chuck crossed his arms and I tried not to get distracted by the pecs. It wasn't easy, I can tell you.

"I think our guy is feeling the pressure," said Chuck. "He didn't expect Denny at the house, Blankenship's talking, and you got away."

I put my ice pack on the handrail and ran my hands through my hair. The good news about Fats' haircut was that I didn't have as many tangles as usual. Of course, I didn't have as much hair either. "So...any suspects at all?"

Chuck said nothing. If I didn't know better, I'd have thought he was embarrassed, but Chuck Watts didn't do embarrassed.

"What about that dry cleaner, Alfonso Cruz?"

"Nothing new, but his son, Rafael, is in the wind," he said.

Fats put my ice pack back on my face. "You think he was the one who grabbed Mercy?"

"Possibly. We're running the blood on the scrap of material that Wallace got when she bit him."

"Do they have any connection to my dad or me?"

"Not that we can see," he said. "Morty took a look and found nothing. They must've been hired to do it."

I snorted. "Unless Cruz has a drug or gambling problem, I don't see it."

"He doesn't," said Chuck.

"Then it's something else," said Fats.

"It is, but we don't know what."

"Does the son have an arrest record?" I asked.

Chuck nodded. "Some small-time stuff. Drug possession. The gang unit thinks he's in the DTOs, but they can't prove it."

"Swell. Anybody we know arrest the son?" I hoped for a connection to The Brain Trust.

"No. All routine busts after your dad retired. The same with the other Brain Trust members. If we could find Keely, maybe we could get some answers," said Chuck.

Fats and I exchanged a look.

"What?" he asked.

I told him that Keely and her husband were dead. He wasn't happy with me. I should've told him. Some crap like that. I didn't really care. He wasn't all that forthcoming and I paid for my info.

"So all we've got from the Trust is Avery and his wife torched his files. We should try Gavin's files."

"If our guy thought there was something in Gavin's files, he would've taken it already. He didn't bother, so I'm guessing that only Dad had whatever it is."

"That's just great."

"Ask my dad. He'll remember," I said.

"Minute details about cases that happened over a decade ago? I don't think so."

"Ask him and find out."

Chuck gritted his teeth. "I tried. They gave him something. He'll be sleeping most of the day. We've got nothing. No motive and no suspects."

"Was the dry cleaner's son prosecuted?" asked Fats.

"Plea bargain."

I gave my bodyguard a little smile. "Who defended him?"

Chuck's blue eyes lit up. "I didn't think to ask. They handed the case to Nazir. He'll tell me."

"If it's Parks, we've got something."

"If not, nothing."

"Check the juvenile record," said Fats. "He might've been arrested when The Brain Trust was operating."

"Nazir has probably tried. It'll be sealed."

"Not to Morty," I said.

"That's not how we operate," said Chuck.

Fats and I smiled at each other. Thank goodness we had no such issues. "We'll take care of that," I said.

"You're off this."

"Somebody tried to kill me and my mother. What do you suggest? I sit around and wait?"

"Exactly. Nazir's good. He'll get it."

"Detectives are dropping left and right. Speaking of detectives, have you looked at Avery?" I asked.

"Avery Sampson? Are you crazy?" asked Chuck. "His wife was murdered."

"And he looks broken up about it. Are we sure he is?"

"Yes. And Avery doesn't have any connection to the Cruzes or Nicaragua. Are you suggesting that he flew down to Central America to kill his former co-worker and her husband?"

"Somebody did," said Fats. "Why not him?"

"Because he's a good guy, one of the best." Chuck pointed at me. "He's your father's friend."

"We think. Maybe Lainie was divorcing him."

"She wasn't."

"Because he said so?"

"Because she wasn't," said Chuck. "That kinda thing gets around."

I rolled my eyes. "Whatever. Why don't you go check that out?"

"What are you going to do?"

"Take a shower. Slurp down coffee before Mom's therapy appointments."

He stared at me. "Go on then."

"I will."

"You're up to something. I can tell."

"Nope."

"You know I can do whatever you're planning," said Chuck.

I smiled and winced, touching my lip. The swelling was down, but I wouldn't be looking in a mirror soon. "You can't interview people for a case you're not on."

"Who are you going to interview?"

"Don't you worry about it. Fats and I know what we're doing."

He turned me around. "At least go say goodbye to your mom."

I sighed and agreed, but Chuck wasn't taking my word for it. He walked me down to the room and appeared to stand guard. Fan-freaking-tastic.

Mom was sitting up, using a straw to drink coffee to prevent spillage and letting Millicent brush her hair.

"Only Carolina could look this beautiful in the hospital," said Millicent.

Tears filled Mom's eyes.

"What, darling, what?" asked my godmother.

"I'll never look the same," slurred Mom.

I came to her side with a box of tissues, my chest constricted and burning. I didn't care what Chuck said. I was getting out of that hospital and getting it done. Grandma Fontaine was right. I couldn't lay down the load and I didn't want to. Let Dad have his breakdown. Let Chuck get kicked off the case. I was still there. Mom could count on me, whether she knew it or not.

"In a few months, nobody will be able to tell," I said.

She blew her nose. "You really think so?"

"Without a doubt. I'm going to call the rehab places and see where we can get you in."

Mom made a face. "Rehab."

"Rehab is an excellent idea. Myrtle and I will bring it up with the director today. I'm sure he will be able to pull some strings and get you in wherever Mercy thinks is best," said Millicent.

"The director of what?" I asked.

"The hospital, my dear."

"Is that why you're dressed to the nines?"

Millicent took a sip of her coffee. "One must dress if one wishes to impress."

"Why do you have to impress?" asked Mom.

My godmother flicked a glance at me and then said, "There seems to have been an incident with Sister Miriam and she does make enemies, you know. There are some who would like to make it an issue. Myrtle and I will take care of it."

Mom looked at me. "Did you know about this?"

"Actually, I thought I already took care of it." I was so relieved Millicent hadn't mentioned me and my fire extinguisher that I got a little weak in the knees. Or maybe it was just exhaustion. I needed a coffee IV.

"I'm sure you tried. Miriam is...difficult," said Mom.

"Speaking of difficult, I'm going to go visit Dad and see what's going on there," I said.

She narrowed her eyes at me. My mother knew I was lying and I held my breath, waiting to see what she would do.

"Very good," she said, her eyes locking onto mine. "Tell him I expect this case to be solved within twelve hours. With the best mind on it, there should be nothing to stop progress."

I just stood there for a second. She knew Dad was admitted, so was I the best mind? That couldn't be. I was me, the daughter dufus. "I'll tell him."

"Excellent."

Chuck stepped up. "You know what? I just thought of something."

"What?" I asked.

Before I could blink, he snapped a handcuff on me and attached it to Mom's bed rail.

"Are you out of your damn mind?" I yelled, yanking on the cuff.

He pointed at me. "You aren't going anywhere. I'll get myself back on the case."

"And I'll take this bed apart if I have to."

"Good luck with that."

I rattled my chain, literally. "Mom, can't you do something?"

Mom shook her head. "You are a target, Mercy. Perhaps you should let Chuck deal with it. He is a professional."

What the... You just said.

I suppressed a scream and started looking at the railing. The screws were in all the wrong places. I needed a hacksaw. I glanced at Fats and she gave me a pirate smile. She probably had a hacksaw in the truck. She was that kinda girl.

Mom held out her good hand to Chuck. "I know you're doing your best to protect Mercy and I appreciate that."

"I'm glad you understand, even if she doesn't."

"The women of our family are stubborn and independent. We don't like to be told what to do by anyone."

"I know that," said Chuck with a pointed glance at me. I wanted to toss Mom's coffee at him, but it would hit her.

"Soon, you'll understand how deep the independent streak runs," she said. "Give me a hug and get out of here."

Chuck gave her a good hug and said, "I hope therapy goes well today."

"I'm sure everything will go well today. Now go on."

He left, tossing over his broad shoulder to me, "Someday, you'll thank me."

Why do people say that? It's so snotty. He might as well say *I'm smarter than you, ya nitwit.*

"Remind me to smack the crap out of him," I said to Fats. "He'll thank me later."

Fats chuckled. "I'll get you out of that in no time. A trip to the hardware store and we're good."

Mom sat up in her bed and said, "No need."

I looked at her, so disappointed I could've cried. "I have to do this, Mom. I want to."

"I know." She held up a small key ring with two little silver keys dangling from it. "You're not the only one who got lessons from Tommy Watts."

My mouth fell open and Fats laughed. "You picked his pocket. Nice one, Mrs. Watts."

"Call me Carolina," she said, tossing me the keys. "Honestly, that was too easy. Mercy, your man is a sucker."

"You can't have everything. Thank goodness." I unlocked the cuffs and tossed them aside. "Now I just have to get past the cops."

Mom smiled at me, lopsided but with plenty of warmth. "Leave that to me."

"You can't get out of bed. Seriously."

"No problem." She picked up Wallace and jiggled the pug awake. "I have a job for you, my little pee pot."

Bark.

"Can you do it?"

Bark. Bark. Bark.

"Mom," I said. "Come on. She pees on me. That's not so useful."

Aaron came over, took Wallace from Mom, and silently walked out.

"Holy shit!" yelled one of the cops.

"She's peeing all over!"

"What is wrong with that dog?"

Fats grabbed me and we went to the door behind Millicent, who had a large handkerchief out and ready. She went to the right and said, "I have this. Let me help you."

My bodyguard peeked out the door and, a second later, we were sprinting down the hall. I looked back as we turned the corner and saw that Millicent had them facing the other way. Remarkably, Wallace was still peeing. She was running around their feet and spraying away. She *was* three-fourths bladder, maybe more. Aaron looked at us and did a thumbs-up. No expression, of course. My partner—always odd, always useful.

We bypassed the elevator and ran down the stairs. Fats was on the phone, asking someone to bring a car around to the ER ASAP.

"Who was that?" I asked.

"My brother. We'll take The Girls' car. They won't mind." Fats already knew my godmothers quite well.

"Can he stick to my mom while we're gone?" I barely got that out I was so breathless.

"We already discussed it. He'll go up after we're away."

Fats and I dashed through the ER and burst out the double doors into the lobby that happily held no reporters. We ran through the exit just as a vintage powder blue car rolled up.

"You have got to be kidding," said Fats as she skidded to a halt.

Rocco got out and leaned over the convertible top with a grin very reminiscent of his sister. "Hey, Fatasaurus Rex. Problem?"

"You little douchebag, what the hell is this?" she said.

He caressed the mint condition top. "This is a 1954 Borgwald Isabella."

"It belongs in a museum. What are you doing driving it?"

"The Bled Mansion is like a museum and The Girls let me pick the car I want to drive. I drove a '45 Jag yesterday. It was like heaven with wheels."

"I can't drive that," said Fats.

"I didn't know you would be driving it," Rocco pointed out. "It's not my fault you ate your Wheaties...and everything else."

"I hate you sometimes."

He grinned. "Right back at you, but today, being your brother is suddenly worth it. Let's see you cram yourself behind the wheel, Princess Porks-a-lot."

I always wanted a sibling. I begged Mom for a brother, in particular, but now it seemed I owed my mother a card for making me an only child. I might be the only egg in my parents' basket, but at least no one ever called me Princess Porks-a-lot.

I whipped opened the passenger door. "Get in. I'll drive."

"You can't drive. I'm better," said Fats.

"She always thinks she's better. Ask her who went to the Olympics," said Rocco.

I ran around the driver's side. "I really don't care. We have to go before those cops notice I've gone and tell Chuck."

"Badminton," said Fats, attempting to wedge herself in the passenger seat. It was safe to say the Borgwald designers didn't imagine a man as big as Fats, much less a woman. "I bet you didn't even know that was an Olympic sport."

I didn't, but I wasn't about to say that. "Can you close the door?"

Fats sniffed. "Of course, I can."

She couldn't. In what was probably one of the least favorite moments of her life, Fats' brother—also known as Skinny McSwizzle Stick—had to shove the door closed. I'm not sure the Isabella was mint anymore, but it was best not to think about it too much.

Rocco called in the window. "There's a jack in the trunk. You can use the bar to pry her out."

I hit the gas and Fats narrowly missed grabbing her brother by the throat. I could see him laughing in the rearview mirror.

"Remind me to pound him later," said Fats with her knees up to her chest.

"I thought you two got along."

"We do," she said. "If I didn't love him, I wouldn't bother to pound him. I'd kill him and dump the body."

There was a possibility that she was serious, so I left that alone and drove around the hospital. Perfect timing. There was my lanky boyfriend, walking across the street to a parking garage, exuding confidence.

"Look at him," said Fats. "Reminds me of Rocco. All piss and wind."

"I wouldn't say that," I said.

"You're running rings around him." She grinned at me. "I have to do it."

"Oh, no. What?"

Fats reached over and laid on the horn. Chuck glanced up and gasped. So sweet. We gave him finger waves and sped off.

CHAPTER TWENTY-FIVE

We laughed all the way out of the Central West End. My stomach hurt and it felt great.

"This is a great morning," said Fats. "Working for you is entertaining. I like it. Where are we going?"

I had no idea, so I had Fats call Spidermonkey for Banging Bob's mother's address. I couldn't chance asking Uncle Morty. You never knew which side he'd come down on and he did enjoy thwarting me for some perverse reason.

Fats put the address in my phone and sat back to discuss The Klinefeld Group with Spidermonkey.

I poked her and said, "Ask him about Alfonso and Rafael Cruz."

The über hacker's inquisitive mind had already looked into the dry cleaner and his son. He repeated what we already knew and one tidbit that we didn't. Waylon Parks defended Rafael Cruz on his drug charge. Finally, a connection. Cassidy Huff's murderer, Brian Shill, was friendly with his prosecutor, Waylon Parks, who ended up defending Rafael Cruz, who probably attacked me yesterday.

"My head hurts," I said.

"I wonder if Shill knows Rafael Cruz," said Fats.

My head hurt a little less as an intense feeling of hope came over me. "Let's find out."

Fats asked Spidermonkey to see if Cruz knew Shill. But as soon as she said it, I knew it wasn't right. Shill wouldn't have Cruz pose as Cassidy's killer. Blankenship would know he was lying. What would be the point? My head hurt again. "Ask him to send me Rafael Cruz's mugshot and a picture of his father, if he can find one."

He already had them and texted them over as we arrived on Manderly Drive in Brentwood. Nice and close. I pulled up in front of a tiny bungalow with an immaculate yard and freshly painted trim a few minutes later.

"When's she coming?" asked Fats, still holding the phone.

I opened my door, trying to judge whether I'd really have to pry Fats out. "We're here."

"Not us."

"Who?" I asked.

"I thought you read the file," said Fats.

"I did."

She pulled on her door handle and the door burst open. "She's clueless," said Fats. "Yeah, I'll tell her."

I went around to see if I could help, but Fats managed to squeeze out on her own. "Who are you talking about?"

"Dr. Karina Bock." Fats trotted up the driveway past a line of older sedans.

"Hey, wait."

She didn't wait. They never wait. It's like people can't hear me. I texted the Cruz pictures to Shelley at Hunt and asked if she could show them to Blankenship. She didn't answer.

Fats pressed the doorbell as I ran up beside her, gasping. "I said wait. Why didn't you wait?"

"What for? I'm ready." She did look ready. Ready to rumble. Valentina Dwyer was probably in her seventies. Unless she pulled a gun, we were probably good.

"I'm not. We don't have a plan."

"Do you ever have a plan?" she scoffed.

"Maybe." I would've poked out my lower lip if wasn't already as poked as a lip can get.

"No, you don't. You're flying by the seat of your thong. I know because half the world has seen it."

I groaned. "Don't remind me."

"How about you stop wearing thongs?" she said.

"Like you're not wearing a thong under those skintight yoga pants."

She rang the bell again. "The important part of that sentence is pants. You know how many men I'd have to kill if I wore thongs with skirts?"

"How many?" I asked stubbornly.

"Twenty-three."

"That's oddly specific."

"Men," she said. "I remember the bad ones."

There was a clang inside the house and someone yelled, "I'm coming!"

"Hey, what was that about Dr. Bock?" I asked.

The door opened and a woman, younger than I expected, was standing there. "Can I help you?"

"Valentina Dwyer?" I asked.

She looked at my face and shrank back a bit. She was a big raw-boned woman, almost six feet, with a mannish demeanor and spiky black hair with a hint of gray at the temples. "Yes. I'm Valentina."

"Hi, I'm—"

"Mercy Watts," she said. "Yes, I know. You're here about my Bobby, aren't you?"

"Yes, I am," I said. "This is Mary Elizabeth Licata. She's helping me."

"Are you some sort of bodyguard?" asked Valentina.

Fats stuck out a hip and struck a pose. "How'd you guess?"

Valentina smiled in spite of herself. "I think it's obvious."

"We'd like to ask you a few questions, if you don't mind," I said.

She pushed open the glass storm door and said, "You can ask, but I don't know how I can help you."

We walked into a small living room, neat and clean, stuffed with antiques ranging from a Victorian sideboard to a fainting couch. There was barely enough room to breathe.

"Come this way," said Valentina. "My stitching group is here, so you'll have to come back to my sunroom.

"What kind of stitching?" asked Fats eagerly.

"Are you a stitcher?"

"I embroider and my grandmother's teaching me to quilt."

"How lovely. It's nice to hear that young people are learning the old skills."

I squeezed past Fats in the narrow hall and asked, "Who are you?"

"What?" asked Fats. "I can like needlework. At least it's not badminton."

We walked into Valentina's sunroom and were instantly greeted with a dozen warm smiles. The ladies and two men were quilting, knitting, or embroidering. There were scraps of fabric everywhere, Cyndi Lauper on the stereo, and a small table covered with pastries, fruit, and an enormous coffee urn.

"Are you coming to join us?" asked one lady, patting a seat next to her.

"No, Janice," said Valentina. "Go ahead, ladies. Find a seat."

I didn't expect that. "Er...don't you want to go talk in private?"

Valentina picked up a quilting hoop with an ornate star in it and sat down. "I have no secrets here. They all know about my Bobby."

The group nodded sagely.

"Alright then." I sat down and one of the men offered me coffee and a donut. It made me feel guilty. I don't know why. Nobody looked nearly as uncomfortable as I felt. "I'm sorry I have to ask these questions."

"Don't worry about it," said Valentina. "I think I've been interviewed a thousand times. There's nothing you can ask that I haven't already heard. Go ahead."

"You seem like you were expecting me," I said.

One of the men, whose name was Carl, said, "We all were. Your poor mother. A tragedy. Such a beautiful woman. And that man who was murdered. It got our attention, I can tell you."

"Why exactly?" I asked. "Bob was a long time ago."

"Not to me," said Valentina. "It seems like yesterday that I found out. I think about what he did every day and try to atone. I know I can't, but I try."

"But why would you think my mother had anything to do with Bob?"

It was simple. Valentina and her group were avid news watchers. They'd been keeping track of the detectives that put Bob away as a serial killer, following their careers. The events in Sturgis piqued their interest and they watched in horror as my mother's attack was covered. Valentina already knew that Avery's wife got killed and she thought that was quite a coincidence. Then it was on the news that morning that blood had been found in Scott Frame's truck. Valentina knew someone would be coming. She just didn't know it would be me.

I would've expected some malice toward The Brain Trust for locking up her only child, but there wasn't any. She seemed resigned to it. Valentina had Bob at seventeen, too young to have a child, she said, and way too young to marry the father. The first Bob Horowitz. He was a drunk and a gambler. He smacked Valentina around, but lucky for her and her son, Big Bob went out for cigarettes one night when Bob was three and never came back. She raised her son herself, working like a man, she said, out at the Chrysler plant, installing stereos. She was one of the few women on the line and she made a nice living, although it was hard, exhausting work and she did all the overtime she could get. It all sounded pretty normal, except her son turned out to be a notorious serial killer.

"Sounds good. What happened?" asked Fats, looking up from a quilt block.

"So many people have asked me that and the answer is I don't know," said Valentina. "I never hit Bobby. I didn't have to. He was sweet and easygoing. He gave me almost no trouble at all."

One of the women spoke up. "I can attest to that. My own boy, Sean, was hell on wheels, drinking and skipping school. I was so jealous of Valentina. Bob never did any of that."

They all nodded.

"None of you saw this coming?" I asked.

They shook their heads.

"Did you ever doubt his guilt?"

"The evidence was overwhelming and he confessed," said Carl. "We didn't want to believe it, but there it was."

"Did he ever confess to any of you, personally?" I asked.

Valentina sighed and stuck her needle in her star. "To me, he did. I'll never forget it. You can't forget the moment your life changes forever. He called me from jail and I went down to see him. He told me he'd been charged with murder, but I thought there must be a mistake. He'd never raised a hand to anyone that I knew of."

"What did he say?"

Valentina looked away into the distance, but she kept talking. "I went into this room, where he was shackled to a chair. It seems like a dream now, but it happened. I have to remind myself of that sometimes. I asked what happened and he told me he killed people. Lots of people. I was so shocked I think I stopped breathing and passed out." She looked at me. "Then your father was there. He got me into a chair and asked me if I wanted to go. I didn't know what to do, so I stayed. Bobby wanted to tell me exactly what he did, but I didn't let him. I couldn't listen to that. I asked him why and he seemed confused. All he said was that he had to. I asked him if someone made him do it."

I leaned forward.

"I'm sorry to disappoint you, Miss Watts, but he said no. He was sort of insulted that I asked. Bobby was sensitive about his intelligence. He only ever got Cs in school and that was with the teachers helping."

"It didn't seem odd to you that he was able to carry on murdering people for years and evading the police?"

"Of course, it seemed odd. More than odd. My Bobby never had an original idea in his life," she said.

"I thought he was a DJ. That's creative," said Fats.

"Oh, he was, but never a very good one. He just loved the music and was good at imitating the other DJs that had style."

One of the ladies said, "My son did the party scene for a while. He helped Bob with playlists and what to say. As long as my Tom wrote it down, Bob could do it fine."

I sipped my coffee and let warmth roll down into my chest. No wonder Dad thought he had an accomplice. Serial killers aren't necessarily original, but it takes some creativity not to get caught. How in the heck did a C student who needed help with his playlists manage to evade my dad, much less the rest of The Brain Trust?

"Did you or Bob know the detectives that caught him?" I asked.

"No, but I remember your father. He was so kind to me." For the first time, Valentina showed emotion. The tears bubbled up inside her and overflowed at the memory of kindness. I was often proud of my father but never more than at that moment.

"The others weren't so kind?" I asked to have something to say.

"They weren't nasty, if that's what you're asking. They were angry at what Bobby had done. Of course they were. I was. It was the worst time in my life." She reached for Carl's hand. "If I hadn't had my friends, I don't know what I would've done."

"Do you remember anything about the detectives in particular?" I asked.

"The lady detective, Keely Stratton, was kind, too. She wanted to know why he'd done it. You see, everyone thought I must've abused him, sexually or something else disgusting. I took a lie detector test."

"What for?" asked Fats. "You didn't do anything."

"Detective Stratton said it would clear me of any wrongdoing and they could get on with figuring out what happened to make Bobby kill people."

"And?"

"Nothing. They never understood it. He wasn't abused or picked on at school. I taught him how bad it was to hurt women and I never thought he'd hurt anyone. At least he didn't rape anyone. I taught him that much."

I pressed the warm cup against my lip and said, "You talked to Bobby about rape?"

Valentina had discussed sexual assault with her son. She thought she was doing the right thing. Maybe she was. Bobby didn't do anything sexual to his victims. Rape was common with serial killers. Sometimes it was the whole point with murder being the cover-up. Maybe Bob didn't because Valentina told him that she'd been raped by her father's friend when she was twelve. The experience had been so horrible that she was institutionalized for a time. She impressed the need for consent and respect on her son.

"I guess I should've talked to him about killing people, but I thought that went without saying. Obviously, you don't kill people," she said.

"What about Avery Sampson?" I asked. "How well did you know him?"

"He wasn't mean, but he would hardly look at me. He interviewed me once with your father. In the middle, he just got up and left. I don't know what I said. I was crying. Maybe that did it."

"What about the others in the task force?"

"Well, there was Gavin Flouder. He was kind, too, but we had little contact. I heard you solved his murder last year. You're an unusual person."

"That's one way to put it. So it was mostly my father and Detective Stratton? What about Scott Frame?"

"I saw him a couple times, mostly in court. He was fine. Distant, like most of the police. I think they didn't know what to do with me. I didn't know what to do with me either."

My phone buzzed and it was Shelley, confirming that Alfonso Cruz was Blankenship's visitor. I was texting her back when Spidermonkey called.

"You're getting close," he said.

"Oh, yeah, to what? Another murder?" I asked and the stitching group gasped. I whispered an apology to them.

"To figuring this out. You're on to something. Your Mr. Shill was in prison with young Mr. Cruz and they had issues. Mr. Shill was a regular victim of Mr. Cruz and his gang."

"Yes!" I exclaimed. "Wait, I don't know how that helps me."

"I don't either, but I'm sure—"

"What?"

"Nothing," Spidermonkey said in an odd voice.

"Are you okay?"

"Fine. I'll call you back. It's Loretta. She wants to redo the kitchen. I'm in hell." He hung up without saying goodbye. That was odd, but I set my phone in my lap and asked Valentina, "Do you have some paper

I could use? I have to draw this out. I'm missing something. I have to see it."

The stitching group sprang into action. Carl got printer paper and colored pencils they used for drawing their quilt designs. Lydia insisted they move the table into the center of the room so they could all see what I would write. "We're solving a crime. Right now," she said. "It's so exciting."

No pressure.

I spread out the paper and drew my timeline. I hated to put Bob's name on there, but I did. There was no use in pretending he wasn't in this up to his now dead eyeballs. Then I wrote Rafael Cruz, Brian Shill, and Waylon Parks, connecting them with arrows. I wrote a column of the Brain Trust members and connected them to Bob. My dad got an arrow to Brian Shill and Cassidy Huff, who I set off in a corner.

"Are any of these other names familiar to you?" I asked. "Any of you?"

They shook their heads while staring intently at the names. I kept looking at Waylon Parks' name, something about that guy. Wait. He was a defense lawyer before.

"Valentina, you said that Bobby was no problem until he was arrested by my dad, but someone told me he had no record."

"Right," she said.

"What about as a juvenile?" I asked.

She gave out a soft laugh. "Oh, that. Your father and Detective Sampson said it had nothing to do with the murders. Kid stuff."

"What did he do?" asked Fats.

"Nothing violent," she said quickly. "He and a couple of friends broke into a house and rearranged the furniture. They thought it was funny and they got caught. The judge gave them a stern talking to. He was sixteen."

"It only happened one time?"

She laughed again. "Such idiots. No. They did it three times and got caught every single time."

I looked down at the names again. Petty crimes. Banging Bob never got away with anything until he started killing people. Weird.

"Did he ever go to jail?" I asked.

Fats' phone rang and she walked away from the table.

"No. Two warnings and community service," said Valentina.

I got all tingly and pointed to Waylon Parks' name. "I know it was a long time ago, but was he Bobby's lawyer?"

"Waylon Parks? No. I'd remember a name like that."

Dammit.

"But he had a lawyer," I said.

"Yes. My father hired him. I can't remember the name. It was a run-of-the-mill name, not like Waylon."

Carl raised his hand like a schoolboy. "I remember it, if it helps."

Fats ran over with her finger to her lips, stopping Carl as he took a breath. We all stared as she wrote on the paper. "Make up a name."

"What?" mouthed Carl.

She pointed to him. "Make up a name," she mouthed.

"I...think it was Gerald...Smith."

"Gerald Smith," said Valentina, eyeing Fats with suspicion. "Yes, that sounds about right."

Fats pointed at my phone and wrote, "Someone's using it as a listening device."

The stitching group's eyes went wide. Solving a murder just got real in a hurry.

"Carl," said Fats. "How did you come up with that star design for the quilt? It's gorgeous."

"Well, I...uh...drew a simple star to start." Carl started talking about the star and I prodded the rest of the group to talk about stitching and then said, "Oh, let me get my phone out of the way." I took it out of the room to Valentina's kitchen and put it under a heavy glass bowl and covered it in tea towels for good measure.

I returned to the sunroom and Lydia exclaimed, "That was exciting. We had an eavesdropper."

"At least we know how he knew where I was going to be," I said, then explained our theory that someone had been listening before. "How'd you know?"

"Your friend" —Fats held up her phone— "called me. He said that he heard something during your conversation and was able to track a sophisticated bit of spyware that had been snuck onto your phone, turning it into a listening device when triggered."

"I never noticed any weird sounds," I said.

"It was lucky that he triggered it when you were talking to your friend. Most people wouldn't notice the sound and it probably wasn't triggered during a conversation very often. You like to text."

"This could be useful," I said. "Now who was the real lawyer?"

Carl jumped. "Oh, right. John Evans was the name. I went with Valentina's father to the office once to drop off a check."

I would've let out a shriek of joy if my mouth didn't hurt so much. Instead, I picked up a red pencil, wrote John Evans, and drew lines to both Waylon Parks and Bob. I thought I might cry for a moment. What a wuss! But there it was—finally, a connection between Bob and the dirtbag brigade.

I told them John Evans was Waylon Parks' law partner, the one that killed himself.

"How does this help?" asked Valentina.

"Give me a second." I asked for Fats' unbugged phone and called Uncle Morty.

"I got nothing," he grumbled. "Your damn father's still asleep and I poked him. I poked him hard."

"Stop poking my dad and listen. We don't need him," I said.

"The hell we don't. You ain't got shit."

"Banging Bob had a juvie record. I'm with his mother right now."

Uncle Morty started cursing and typing, two things he did very well. "I got it," he said. "This ain't no smoking gun. It was a stupid prank."

"I know that." I told him who was Bob's lawyer. More cursing.

"Who arrested Bob?" I asked.

More cursing. "Nobody," he said.

"Define nobody."

"Nobody we give a crap about."

"Uncle Morty!" I yelled and everyone got still like zebras when they sense a lioness.

He grumbled and said, "Laurie Gavrieli. Got married and left the force in '99. Before you freaking ask, no, she never worked on The Brain Trust."

"Did she have any partners?"

"They partnered her with other chicks. They used to do that. Thought it stopped *problems* from cropping up."

This has to be it. It has to be.

"Okay. Who was her supervisor during Bob's arrests?" I asked.

There was a drawn-out pause and then a yell. "Son of a bitch!"

"Avery?"

"Hell, no. Scott Frame."

"Find Laurie Gavrieli."

"On it."

We hung up and I wrote Laurie's name and connected it with Scott Frame and then to Bob. Fats clapped me on the back, ramming me into the table. "Finally. I knew you'd get it."

"But Scott Frame's dead," said Carl. "It was on the news."

"Like Mark Twain, reports of his death are greatly exaggerated," I said.

"What about the blood?" asked Valentina.

"He was an EMT. He could draw his own blood and splash it around his car to throw us off the track."

Valentina traced the line between her son and Detective Scott Frame. "You think Frame made Bobby do it? He's the reason he got away with it so long?"

"Bobby's lack of an MO supports it. He was all over the place, leaving no clues, always a step ahead. How do you stay ahead of The Brain Trust if you're not the brightest bulb? You have somebody on the inside."

"But why?" asked Carl. "Why would a detective want to kill all those people?"

"I don't know. I'll ask him when we catch him," I said with a grin.

"You should call the police," said Valentina.

"I'm considering it, but they're not going to be jazzed about this idea."

Fats phone rang and she answered. "It's your Grandad and he is pissed."

I held up my hands and backed away. "I'm good."

"He's your grandfather," said Valentina.

"I'm aware."

She took the phone from Fats and put it in my hands. "He's a very experienced detective. He'll know what to do."

Is there no one who won't bother me?

"Er...Hello?" I said.

"You are not doing this! The Frame family is absolutely frantic! They know Scott is probably dead, but they're still hoping! I won't have you implying that Scott did this to us!"

"Grandad—"

"No. Leo Frame is my friend."

"I know, but—"

"You think Leo wouldn't know if Scott colluded with a serial killer?"

"It fits." I was strangely calm, especially since Grandad was yelling at me. It was a little shocking, but it didn't matter. This was a lead. I had to follow it.

"Leo was the best detective I ever worked with. He was the only one who came close to Tommy. He was beyond excellent."

Beyond excellent.

"But Scott wasn't," I said.

"What?" Grandad was still yelling and the whole room could hear him.

"Scott wasn't beyond excellent. He wasn't even excellent. Avery said he was average."

Grandad sucked in a breath. "Scott was an expert in forensics."

"Putting him in a great position to manipulate evidence in Banging Bob's case."

"You don't know what you're saying. Leo was the best. He was better than me."

Better than you. Better than you.

"Did Scott resent that?" I asked.

"Resent what? There was nothing to resent."

"Yes, there was. You were on the Bled Mansion break-in back in the day. Leo was the lead, but you got picked to investigate the break-ins at Prie Dieu and Josiah's house. You got invited to dinner. Not Leo."

Grandad's voice went low. "How do you know that? Mercy, what have you been doing?"

"Your granddaughter became The Girls' goddaughter. I was born in the Bled Mansion. Millicent and Myrtle gave Mom a house worth hundreds of thousands of dollars even back then. There's plenty to resent."

"Leo never resented anything. He never married. He doesn't have children."

"But he had Scott. Why didn't he get our house if Leo was better than you? Why didn't his kids get sent to Whitmore Academy?"

"I don't know what you think you know, but I want you to stop. Stop right now and leave it alone," said Grandad with a hint of fear. Something I'd never heard in him before.

"You went to investigate The Girls' break-in and our lives changed forever. Why you? Why not Leo?"

"Mercy."

"No. Think about it. Not only was Scott robbed of a privileged life, then he gets to work for your kid. Tommy Watts, the acknowledged best ever, outshining Leo. Avery said Scott was average. He's a nice man, so I'm guessing Scott was actually mediocre. How'd he get on The Brain Trust?"

"I'm not going to discuss this. You're wrong."

"Leo got him on, didn't he? He helped his nephew, as any good uncle would do, or perhaps a surrogate father. Did Scott like my dad? Or was the anger just under the surface? Did you see it?"

"Scott is dead, Mercy."

"He's not," I said. "That blood in the car. That's not right. I can feel it. Can't you feel it?"

"I don't. I can't. He wouldn't do this to Leo," he said softly. "He loves Leo."

"But he hates us more."

"What about Keely, Avery, and John? Why would he hurt them? They have nothing to do with the Bleds."

I took a sip of coffee and let that roll around in my head along with the plan that was forming. "They deserved to be on The Brain Trust. They were the best. They didn't need anyone's help to get there."

"Mercy, sweetheart, Scott is dead. He's a victim," said Grandad.

"No, he's not and I'll prove it to you."

"What? No!"

"Gotta go." I hung up and turned to Fats. "I have a plan."

"I don't think I'm going to like this," she said as her phone rang again. We looked at it and I swiped Grandad away.

"I think you're going to hate it, but we're putting an end to this today. Right now." I ran and got my phone, covering the microphone.

"He's listening," I said. "We're going to give him what he wants."

"What does he want?" asked Carl.

"Me."

CHAPTER TWENTY-SIX

Fifteen minutes later, I was in the Isabella alone and talking to myself. Well, not exactly. I was talking to Scott Frame. With any luck, he didn't know it.

"So I'll find that file," I said. "Where would Dad hide it?"

Scott was a lousy detective. He should buy a secret Brain Trust file.

"Not the office. He wouldn't put it in the office."

I glanced in the rearview mirror, but I didn't see Fats. She was supposed to tail me to my parents' house in Carl's ancient Impala and nab Scott when he showed up. We'd planted the idea that I'd gone rogue and run off, trying to prove that I could do it on my own. I figured he wouldn't try to take me if she was by my side. He wasn't that crazy.

I would park in front and dash inside alone, just in case he was watching, leaving the door unlocked. Hopefully, she'd get him before he went inside, but if she didn't, I had my Mauser and the will to use it.

Mr. Knox was waiting at his pagoda at the entrance to Hawthorne Avenue. I rolled down the window slowly because the crank was so stiff. Nobody ever rolled down the windows in the Isabella.

"Where's your bodyguard, Miss Mercy?" asked Mr. Knox.

"She's coming in her truck," I said. "Please let her in."

"Of course. Why do you have the Isabella? Rocco had it this morning."

"Long story. Let's just say I enjoy annoying Chuck."

A smile flickered on his lips, but his voice was stern. "You shouldn't torment that man. He's loved you all his life."

"He's a huge pain in the butt."

"As all good men are. Ask your mother," he said. "How is she?"

"Better and my dad's back." *Sort of.*

Mr. Knox heaved a sigh of relief. "Thank goodness. It's as good as solved then."

I bit back the truth. The great Tommy Watts back to save the day? Not.

"It'll be solved any minute," I said. "I just need evidence from the house."

"That's so good to hear. There's nothing you Watts can't do." He went to open the gate and I drove through, glancing at my phone. "All I have to do is get that file and we're all good." I said it happily, without a hint of the nerves I felt.

Nothing the Watts can't do. No wonder Scott hates us. Ace Watts. Tommy Watts. Mercy Watts. Blah. Blah. Blah.

I parked the Isabella in front of the house, nice and obvious. I looked back and didn't see Fats. She was supposed to be far enough behind so Scott wouldn't spot her, so I wasn't worried. I got out and trotted up the walk, unlocking the front door and keying in my code.

I pulled the door to, but I left it cracked like I was in a hurry.

Where should I wait? Office? Bedroom? Kitchen. There's coffee in the kitchen. Yes!

Carl's phone buzzed in my pocket as I headed for the hall.

"Lock the door. I broke down," texted Fats."

"Shit!" I said.

"Something wrong?" a man's voice said behind me.

I spun around and gasped. Standing inside the door was a man, pale and bloated, casually pointing a Glock at me. He closed the door and armed the alarm with my code. Dammit.

"Who the hell are you?" I knew who he was, but I had to say something.

"Oh, no." He tilted his head sideways and stuck out his lower lip. "You don't know? So sad. Tommy Watts' daughter is as stupid as she looks."

"Judging a book by its cover is always a smart move." The stairs were to my left. Scott looked like hell and obese to boot. I could make it and maybe not get shot.

"If you don't recognize me, you are an idiot. Where do you think he hid that file you've been chatting about like a moron?"

Stall. Stall.

"What file?"

Scott crept forward, his gun arm going stiff. "The one your father so unhelpfully tucked away."

This is good.

"I'm not going to give it to you," I said. "And I know who you are. Scott, the mediocre detective, Frame."

He fired, shattering the glass of a framed lithograph. I shrieked but held my ground.

"Mediocre!" he screamed.

Don't poke the crazy guy.

"Not my words," I said, trying not to shake.

"Whose words then?"

"Someone is going to hear you."

"Whose?"

I made a quick judgment call. What would make him less angry? "Avery Sampson."

His gun arm relaxed a smidgen. "That fool. He was so close so many times and he never saw it."

"What? That you're a serial murderer?" I asked automatically.

"I'm not a murderer!" he screamed.

Dammit, Mercy. Shut up!

"Seriously. Someone will hear you."

Scott pushed a lock of long, greasy hair out of his face. "On this street? Forget it. Your mother cried for help and not a damn thing happened."

"Why her? Mom never did anything to you," I said.

"I want that file."

"I want to know why you attacked my mother and tried to rape her. For that matter, if nobody came to save her, why'd you stop?"

Beads of sweat broke out on his clammy face. "I was interrupted by that Judas, Denny."

He was lying I could see it in his face. Denny was already dead or dying when he went after my mother.

Come on, Fats! Fix the car!

"Judas? What did Denny ever do to you?" I asked.

"He was my friend and then he went to work for your asshole father," he said. "Where's the file?"

"I don't know. There are dozens of hiding places in this house," I said.

"You better figure it out quick or I'll shoot you like a dog."

"Shoot dogs regularly, do you?" I asked.

He fired again and shattered a second lithograph.

Dammit. What is my problem? Oh, yeah. I hate him.

"If you shoot me, you'll never find it. My dad's at the hospital right now, talking to the FBI. Time's a wasting," I said.

"You're full of crap. That arrogant bastard's stuck in Chicago for being a dickhead, as usual."

"Nope."

"He is."

"Not."

"How the fuck did he get out?" Scott screamed.

Come on. Somebody has to hear that.

"I got him out. A little Unsub goes a long way."

He blanched and I ran, dashing to the left and up the long stairs to the landing, cornering on a dime to run for the second floor. I went as fast as my short legs could go, but it wasn't fast enough. Scott got me by the ankle. I fell, whacking my face on a step. The pain stunned me for a second and he yanked me down the stairs.

"Blackie!" I screamed. There was an ungodly shriek like a woman on fire and Scott yelled, letting me go. I glanced back as I scrambled up the stairs. The black cat was on Scott's face. He yanked Blackie off, leaving shreds of skin hanging from his cheeks.

I got to the top of the stairs and hung a right to Dad's office. I slammed the door and turned the old brass key. Scott rammed the door a second later and I went for my purse. It wasn't on my shoulder. Must've lost it on the stairs. I ran around Dad's desk to the safe that I left open on the day of Mom's attack. I grabbed a Beretta 92 off the top shelf and rammed its clip in, turning just in time to see Scott burst through the door, spraying wood fragments across the room.

"Stop!" I yelled, chambering a round.

He aimed his weapon at me and screamed. "I want that file!"

"There's no file, you moron!" I flipped off the safety. That was kinda important. "I said that to lure you here. You're dumber than my dad thought and that's saying something."

He stared at me blankly. I could see his trigger finger itching to pull and I got ready to drop behind the desk, but he just looked at me. "You couldn't have."

"Hello, I found the spyware on my phone."

"But you're an idiot."

"Apparently, I know people who aren't," I said. "Now get out while the getting's good."

He shook his head violently and blood from his cheeks splattered the wallpaper. "No. I'm going to kill you. I'll never get away now."

Agreed, so I'll be shooting you.

Blackie slinked in behind Scott, silent as usual, and I smiled.

"I will kill you," he said, but something about my smile made him nervous.

"Yeah, I don't think so," I said, inclining my head toward the cat.

"That fucking cat." He pointed his weapon at Blackie, who did a curly-tongued yawn and sat on his skinny rump, completely unperturbed. "I'll shoot your cat. How about that?"

I shrugged. "Go ahead."

"What the fuck is wrong with you?" he asked.

"He's not alive, so you can't kill him."

"What the—"

"But *I* can kill *you*." I fired, pegging Scott in his beefy shoulder. He spun around, firing a shot into the ceiling. I'd hoped to bring him down without killing him, but he ran out the door. I dashed around the desk past Blackie, who was cleaning his toes. I slipped around in Scott's blood for a second before running down the hall. I caught a glimpse of Scott as he turned to the stairs, bouncing off the newel post before going down.

I made it five feet before three shots rang out. I skidded to a halt. My first thought was that Scott shot himself, but I knew instantly that wasn't right. I eased down the hall, Dad's Beretta ready. The silence was like a presence in the house, pressing on me and pushing the air out of my lungs. I came around the corner and pointed my weapon down the stairs.

At the bottom on the landing was Valentina, holding a revolver on Scott. He lay on his back, halfway down the stairs with three bullets in the center of his chest.

"She let me in," said Valentina, her voice steady and totally calm.

"Who?" I said after it sank in.

There was movement to the right and Claire, Dad's secretary, crept into view. "She said she was a client."

I lowered the Beretta, flipped on the safety, and took a deep breath, willing myself not to shake. I failed. Go figure. "Okay. Good. Um...can you call 911?"

"Me?" asked Claire.

"Since you're not holding a gun, let's go with yes."

Claire got out her phone and backed down the stairs. There were sirens in the distance. "I think they're already coming."

"Call anyway," I said. "Valentina, can you lower your weapon? He's pretty dead."

Valentina looked at the gun in her hands. She seemed surprised at it being there and she dropped it. "My father taught me to shoot."

"You're obviously a good student, but what are you doing here?" I asked.

"Mary Elizabeth told me to stay home. I didn't."

I wanted to come down the stairs, but Scott's body was so wide I'd have to step on him. Not going to happen. "But why?" I asked. "We had a plan. It didn't work, but we had a plan."

"20/20," she said.

"Huh?" I asked.

"There was a profile of your father and you on 20/20. Remember?"

Oh, I remembered all right. I kinda hated 20/20 for that show. "So?"

"They made you seem like an idiot."

"Thanks."

"They said your plans never work, but you're lucky."

Insulting, but sadly accurate.

"So you thought my plan wouldn't work," I said.

"I looked at your mind map, all those arrows, and I thought of my Bobby." She pointed at Scott. "He killed my boy and those other people. I wasn't going to let him kill you."

"That might be the nicest thing anyone's ever done for me."

"You're welcome," Valentina said with a wan smile. "Will they arrest me?"

"Not a chance, but you'll probably be on 20/20," I said.

"I hope they don't make me look like an idiot, too."

"You have a better chance than me."

Claire came up again. "That's the cops. Mr. Knox called them, I guess."

"Who's Mr. Knox?" asked Valentina.

"The guard who let us on the street," said Claire. "Should I let the cops in? You don't want to hide the body or anything?"

"Since when do I hide bodies?" I asked.

Claire shrugged. "With your family, I never know. I'm coming back from vacation to a shootout on the stairs."

I rolled my eyes. "Let them in."

Claire opened the door. The first one through was Fats, weapon drawn and sweating so hard she looked like she'd been through a car wash. She'd run four miles to try to get there before Scott.

Right behind her was Chuck and Sydney. Chuck took one look at me, got something in his eyes and started pacing, muttering about the house being dusty and dust was a terrible thing by all accounts. Sydney was so relieved I wasn't dead that he sat on the floor and had to do yoga breathing.

I still couldn't make myself climb over Scott, so I turned around and came down the servant stairs by the kitchen. Instead of going out to face the muttering, moist-eyed boyfriend, I made a latte and sat down, staring at Mom's shoes, right where she left them on Saturday.

Saturday seemed like a million years ago instead of just three days. As I sat there, I smelled a smell. A smell Mom wouldn't like. Rotting food. I kicked off my bloodied Vans and put on Mom's Tom's. They were a bit tight but felt good, like my mother, not quite comfortable. I got up and started cleaning. There were vegetables in the sink that Mom must've been washing. They'd gone way bad. The trash was gross, too. I took it all out before I started scrubbing. Valentina came in with Claire and they automatically started helping. We scrubbed every surface, washing all the bad down the drain.

Cops were swarming over the house with the crime scene techs, but we ignored the activity and made sugar cookies. There's nothing a good sugar cookie can't fix.

While we were baking, a marginally calmer Chuck came in with Nazir, the new detective on the case. He took our statements at the kitchen table. At some point, Grandad came with Avery Sampson and John Jameson. The latter was so filled with grief over his son that he couldn't speak. He and Valentina sat at the table and cried until I thought it wasn't possible to cry anymore and then they cried some more. There was no anger in that room, only cookies and sorrow.

Grandad and Avery went over Bob's case in minute detail. I didn't listen. I didn't want to know. I just cleaned. Claire and I decided we should go to a spa, get weird seaweed wraps, and sneak in food because spa food sucks. We didn't talk about Scott Frame other than our theories of how to get blood out of carpet and off wallpaper. Claire was all for calling a service, but I wanted to do it myself. I think there might be something wrong about that, but Aunt Miriam came with Millicent and Myrtle. They agreed. If you pay someone to clean up your mess and make it like it never happened, the mess is still there, just in your head. We'd do it together.

Fats said little. She sat in the corner, fuming over the breakdown. I think she was really mad that she didn't get to kill Scott. That's what she'd been planning. I wouldn't have killed him if I could avoid it, but with Fats, there was no way he'd have made it out alive. As it was, it didn't matter. He was dead and it would take a good while to scrub him off all the people in that room.

CHAPTER TWENTY-SEVEN

A week and a half later, Mom was in a swanky rehab, doing three hours of therapy a day and sleeping fourteen. Valentina was on 20/20 and I was once again deemed not-quite-bright and extraordinarily lucky. My lip had healed well, but every picture the press decided to use was taken right after Blankenship bit me. I looked like Marilyn Monroe crossed with a mutant. Mickey Stix freaked and flew in a Beverly Hills plastic surgeon to fix my lip, but oily bastard hit on me and I decided I'd heal fine on my own. To apologize for picking Dr. Dirtbag, Mickey decided to hold a charity concert for the American Stroke Association. The press Double Black Diamond got for the Sturgis event was huge and he was one to spot an opportunity from a thousand miles away. Since my lip had healed so well, Mickey wanted me on stage. I wanted to get out of town and was plotting my escape as I stood at the drop-off entrance at the rehab center. Tiny was arriving in a few minutes. He was still in rough shape and his stay was sure to be longer than Mom's.

"I'm telling you, she's not ready to go home." Grandad looked at me and I shrugged. He'd been arguing with the insurance company on and off for three days, trying to do what my dad wanted. My father had stopped crying long ago and had devoted himself to my mom. He tried to check into the rehab, but they said no. So he stuck to Mom, making sure she ate, slept, and did her myriad of exercises. He was exactly the way I hoped, except there was a problem. Dad was driving Mom crazy.

He wouldn't leave her alone and he'd taken to apologizing for everything all the time. He apologized for missing anniversaries, birthdays, and graduations. He apologized for leaving toenail clippings on the bathroom floor and coming home smelling like a corpse. He researched every aspect of strokes known to mankind and tried to make her read studies. Dad wanted to fly her to Sweden for some oxygen chamber treatment. Mom suggested he go and check it out in advance, but he didn't fall for it.

Since Mom was cleared to walk on her own now, she'd taken to dodging him. Once, when he went to get coffee, she hid in the library for a bit of peace. He called 911. Not the nurses. 911. To be honest, I missed the crying. It was less annoying. The whole family tried to step in and distract Dad, but like when he was on a case, he was undistractable.

That morning when Dad went to the bathroom—he didn't try to take Mom with him, but I think he considered it—she sat up in bed and said, "I know you went through hell to get him here and I love him, but you've got to get him out of here or I'm going to stab him with a fork."

Unfortunately, Pete's parents had come back from vacation and reclaimed Wallace the Wonder Dog. Wallace was the only thing keeping Mom sane, so I did what I swore I wouldn't do. I called Chuck. My boyfriend had had his own dad-like crisis after the case was over. He'd gotten himself all worked up about me getting out of his handcuffs and luring Scott to the house. He ran around and yelled. Not at me. It was unfocused yelling. I could tell he was terrified. He never thought I'd do something like that, but honestly, all the signs were there. You are who you are and I'm a Watts. Asking me not to do what I do is like asking Chuck to not flirt with every woman within a fifty-foot radius. Not going to work. He can't help it and neither could I.

I pointed that out and it was a big mistake. He felt guilty and what does Chuck Watts do when he feels guilty? He buys me stuff. So far, I'd gotten an automatic self-scooping litter box for Skanky and furniture from IKEA—it was still in the flat packs in middle of my living room. I had to climb over it to get to my bedroom. He bought me multiple new razors. I guess my legs are hairy. Next came a bunch of hats, presumably to cover my Fats haircut. All this and I'd barely seen him. He'd been cleared of any wrongdoing in the Alfonso Cruz shooting and was back in action. The Unsub case was kinda huge and getting bigger. When Nazir was at Hunt gathering evidence on the threat to Blankenship's life, a man named Vince Spotnitz left work in the middle of his shift and never returned. Vince Spotnitz was an alias that was so well-orchestrated that he passed his background check with no problems. The FBI and local PD had formed a new task force to investigate the Unsubs. My guys were on it and I didn't even have to eat crab to make it happen. Chuck, Sydney, and Nazir were invited. No blackmail or bribery necessary.

This time, the task force name, Collective Inquiry, stuck. Mostly since The Brain Trust was now considered bad luck. Collective Inquiry was trying to find Vince Spotnitz but had little hope. Somehow, he faked his prints and, on closer examination, his ID picture looked like he might've been wearing facial prosthetics. The FBI had turned up forty-two bodies in Kansas and a 1972 Beetle. That's right. Somebody buried an entire car in that field and nobody noticed. I was starting to understand why eyewitness accounts are so unreliable.

The Scott Frame case was going better. Nazir had found a storage unit that Frame rented in one of his daughters' names and it was crammed full of evidence he'd nicked from the Brain Trust cases and plenty of other ones, including Rafael Cruz. He was blackmailing the gangbanger with evidence from a murder he'd done when he was a teen. Cruz's father ended up getting blackmailed too. Since they hadn't caught Cruz yet, they didn't know why.

I'd been right about Banging Bob. Scott had heard about him from Laurie Gavrieli and he had a perfect mark. He planted evidence in Bob's apartment and car and then arrested the hapless young man. The evidence was that Bob was a rapist of women and young children. In Bob's mind, that was the worst thing you could be. He'd rather kill than have Valentina think he'd committed rape, so he agreed to murder someone for Scott. Once. He killed a vagrant, thinking he could get Scott off him. But then Scott had real evidence of murder. He blackmailed Bob into killing for the next six years. Scott ran the entire operation. He knew exactly what The Brain Trust was thinking, so it was easy to lead them astray.

Scott left rambling letters to my dad, saying how smart he was for fooling him. Scott had planned to let Bob off the hook at a certain point, but then Dad had caught him—with math, of all things. He went to the Wash U engineering department and had the super-nerds program him some sort of probability algorithm. Because even random things aren't really random, especially when you're trying to make them look like they are. Dad said when he saw all the dots on the screen plotted and predicted so accurately, he knew where to go. To be fair, it took a couple of murders to nail it. But Dad ended up in an elderly man's apartment in Ferguson. He sat on the sofa for two nights, having put the old guy in a Motel 6. Bob jimmied the bathroom window on the second night and Dad had him. The secret to Dad's success was that he didn't tell anyone his idea. No one in The Brain Trust knew, so Scott couldn't change course.

Dad didn't know why Scott stole his Brain Trust file. He'd had a feeling that something wasn't right with Bob's case and that's why he kept his algorithm secret, but he never had anything on Scott. Maybe Scott wanted to see what Dad said about him. If he did, he wouldn't have been happy. Dad thought he was mediocre and riding the coat-tails of his gifted uncle. Dad never planned on doing anything about that. He told me that it was hard to reach for excellence when you have no hope of attaining it. He felt sorry for Scott Frame and Scott hated him for it. In his letters, Scott said he'd planned on letting it all go after retirement. He thought my father would fade into obscurity like Leo had done, taking up woodworking and fly fishing. But that's not what happened. Dad went on to national fame, making serious money. The other members of the Brain Trust basked in the reflected glow. They got interviewed about Dad and were sometimes asked to give their insights on new cases. Keely was interviewed via satellite more than anyone else. She was living the dream in beach towns with plenty of money. She was asked to do profiles in her spare time.

Nobody interviewed Scott and his resentment built until they all had to pay.

All those intersecting cases were kind of overwhelming and that gave me an idea. Chuck was the lead of Collective Inquiry and I asked him—no, begged him—to call on Dad for help. Chuck agreed to get him out of the rehab hospital for at least four hours and I agreed that I needed new lamps. I don't know what was wrong with my lamps, but Chuck was getting me new ones, by God.

"I can't do it," said Grandad, pocketing his phone. "They won't let Carolina stay past tomorrow."

"Don't worry about it," I said. "She really is ready to go home."

"Tommy says no."

I hugged Grandad's bony arm. "He's just afraid to bring her home. He still won't sleep there."

He grinned. "How do you like having a slumber party with your father?"

"Swell and there's very little slumber. He paces all night and just catnaps on the sofa."

"Well, Carolina might be ready, but Tommy isn't. Maybe she can go to The Girls? They'd spoil her rotten and there's no bad memories."

"That could work. I was thinking I could take her to Cairngorms Castle for a spa week, no men allowed."

"Tommy won't agree to that. I think he might need medication." He looked over. "There they are. Finally."

Tiny's ambulance turned the corner and drove slowly up the long driveway. The doctors said he was ready to go to rehab, but I wasn't so sure. I would've preferred a couple more days, but the insurance insisted.

"Oh, no," said Grandad.

"What?"

"There's Chuck."

I slumped. Three hours. That's all Mom got.

The ambulance rolled to a very careful stop and the EMTs got out and opened the back. Fats jumped out. She was so nervous about the move that she was sweating and wringing her hands as the EMTs slowly eased Tiny out at a snail's pace.

"How was the drive?" I asked.

"Every bump hurt him," she said with tears in her eyes. "He shouldn't have been moved."

I patted her beefy shoulder. "Once he's in, it'll be fine. Aaron's in the kitchen, making his favorite shrimp and grits. And his mom filled his room with quilts and family pictures. Where's Aunt Willasteen?"

"On her way with Aunt Miriam."

"Together? I'm not sure they'll both survive."

The EMTs rolled Tiny up to me and I took his hand. "They're all ready for you."

Tiny's normally rosy brown skin was a disturbing ashy grey. "Okay," he whispered. "Take away their canes."

I looked at Fats. "I thought you took the canes."

"They bought new ones in the gift shop."

"For crying out loud." I kissed Tiny's forehead. "We'll take care of it."

They rolled him slowly into the building with Fats in pursuit.

"Maybe you can get Tommy on it," said Grandad. "Give him something to do. Getting those canes off Willasteen and Miriam will take some effort."

Maybe. The canes were a real problem. Both aunts liked to whack people and each other. They almost got barred from the hospital twice. Only The Girls' intervention saved them, but they had to lose the canes. The old ladies considered that more of a suggestion than a hard and fast rule.

"Aunt Miriam's your sister. Can't you talk to her?" I asked.

"I'd rather cane her."

"Go for it. Nothing else works."

Dad trotted around the building in a panic with Chuck reluctantly trailing him.

"I'm back," announced Dad. "How is she? Why are you out here? Is she alone? She can't be alone."

I swallowed a groan. "Mom can be alone." I gave Chuck the stink eye. "Why are you back so early?"

"Early?" asked Dad. "It's been three hours. My God! You left her alone. I shouldn't have trusted you." Dad dashed inside, barely hesitating to get around Tiny's gurney.

Chuck flushed with guilt. "I tried. I really did. I think he might be crazy. Do they have a pill for that?"

"Depends on the crazy. I think we'll start with therapy," I said.

"I suggested that. He said he couldn't be away from Carolina."

"She's going to hurt him," said Grandad.

"I'm really sorry," said Chuck, giving me a wonderfully warm hug. "Want to go shopping?"

Dear lord, no.

"I think I have to go do something," I said. "I have no idea what."

Chuck held up his phone. "Actually, you have to go to The Girls. They called. When are you going to get a new phone?"

"When I stop being freaked out about the whole listening device thing."

"So...never." Grandad gave me a pat and went inside to try and calm down his son.

"Not never," I said. "Just not now. It was unsettling."

"Anyway, I have some time. I'll take you over," he said smoothly and I knew what that meant. Shopping.

He's a good guy. He really is.

I threw my arms around his neck—it was quite a jump—and kissed him. "Okay, but The Girls first."

"First before what?" Chuck asked with a hint of his old self.

"Whatever," I replied with a grin.

We never got to the whatever because we went to the Bled Mansion. Chuck parked in the alley by the garage, where a shirtless Rocco had all the bays open while he polished the Maybach to a shine heretofore never achieved.

"Hey there," he said, picking an invisible speck of dust off the swoop of chrome on the driver's side. "This is the best job I've ever had. You think I can keep it? The Girls said Tiny wouldn't have stayed forever anyway."

Normally, I would've said no way in hell, but Rocco Licata was in. For some reason, The Girls loved him despite his dubious connections to the Fibonacci family.

"I guess," I said. "You don't mind the food?"

He threw back his head and gave out a hearty laugh, making his six-pack pop out hard. "Not a chance. The ladies can throw it down. We're making my grandpa's Sicilian gravy tonight. They don't do the Italian so much."

"You're cooking with them?"

"Hell ya. We made puff pastry this morning. Morty's girlfriend, the Greek, she's coming over and we're making something. I don't know what, but it will be amazing."

"You like laminating dough?" I asked.

"What's not to like? Good for the biceps. Good for the belly."

Hallelujah.

Chuck grinned. "Works for me."

"Puhlease," I said. "The last fat I've seen you eat was a tiny bit of butter on that corn-on-the-cob Aaron made and that was a week ago."

"But it was real butter."

"Impressive." I rolled my eyes and Rocco looked straight-up confused. He was a huge eater and liked fish, so Aaron was trying out new crab recipes on him before he tried to sneak them onto my plate. I might've been stressed and sleepless, but I could still spot crab at ten paces, not that that was any kind of deterrent to Aaron.

We left Rocco and went through the garage and I keyed in my code to the backyard. Chuck opened the door and Rocco called out to us, "Hey, Mercy. I almost forgot. Calpurnia wanted me to tell you she put the word out."

Chuck looked at me, his expression suddenly all tense and flinty.

Please don't say I worked for her. Please don't say I worked for her.

"Er...what kind of word?"

"You know, the word," said Rocco.

I looked up at Chuck and he just glared.

"You have to help me here," I said. "What's the word?"

"You know, that The Girls aren't to be touched and if anybody comes sniffing around again, you'll know about it. Tiny and my sister got a good thing going. You're gonna be family before we know it." Rocco went back to the Maybach, whistling what sounded like an aria.

"Thanks," I said and Chuck pushed me through the door, closing it firmly behind us. "I am so screwed."

"Well...maybe she's just being nice," I said before breathing deep the heavenly scent of fresh-cut grass.

"I'm a cop and I'm connected to a mob family."

I walked toward the house, feeling surprisingly good. Rocco hadn't said anything about me and Calpurnia. He'd probably been ordered not to. It was all good. "You're not connected. He doesn't work for you."

"He works for my girlfriend's godmothers. It's like six degrees of Kevin Bacon, except it's Calpurnia and I've got one degree. I'm so screwed."

I grabbed his hand and tugged him toward the back door of the mansion. "It's fine. Everything's fine."

"You're only saying that because Tommy's too freaked to pay attention. Eventually, he's going to look up and see the Licatas have moved in."

"Grandad's taking the bullet on that one," I said. "It's a beautiful day. My mother's in the one percent of stroke recovery patients. You're going to get the bad guys." I opened the back door and he grumbled, "Because my girlfriend got me evidence from a psycho."

"Let's not start that again. I feel good. I want to keep feeling good." I turned to walk into the house. Myrtle stepped into the hall with a blonde woman at her side. "Mercy, we've been waiting for you. This is Dr. Karina Bock, as I'm sure you know."

Good feeling gone.

We sat in the breakfast room and I tried not to panic. I vaguely remembered Fats saying something about Dr. Bock on the day Scott Frame got killed, but it was kind of a blur. There was insurance to deal with, my dad, getting blood out of the carpet, and worst of all, bringing the Siamese home. They bit me. A lot. I didn't have a phone and Dr. Bloom's information fell by the wayside. How I wished it had stayed there.

"This painting is extraordinary," said Dr. Bock.

She'd taken Stella's portrait from the wall and was examining it with a magnifying glass, Sherlock Holmes-style.

The Girls were perfectly pleasant. They'd never been mad at me in my entire life, not even when I nearly burnt down the garage when I was seven. So I didn't really know what their mad looked like. So far, it included coffee and donuts, but that didn't seem like the end of it.

With The Girls' permission, Dr. Bock took pictures of the portrait, front and back, and then put it gingerly back on the wall. Myrtle offered her a latte, which she accepted but barely touched. "Thank you so very much for allowing me to see the portrait." Her Austrian accent was softer than German and musical. She tucked her bobbed blond hair behind her ears and said, "When Dr. Bloom said that he knew a member of the Bled family, it was like a miracle to me."

I glanced at Millicent and Myrtle when she said 'member of the Bled family', but they had no reaction.

"Why would it be a miracle?" I asked. "I thought you specialize in interrogations and political prisoners. You didn't know that Stella was in prison until Dr. Bloom told you about the portrait, right?"

Dr. Bock's dark blue eyes glowed with excitement. "Ah, but I did. Stella Bled Lawrence is of intense interest for many historians like myself. I have eyewitness accounts of a young woman matching Stella's general description being arrested, but I couldn't prove it was her. Stella's covers were very well done indeed." She turned to The Girls. "The recent accusations against her are a travesty. She was nothing of what they said."

Millicent and Myrtle nodded, their eyes growing moist, but they said nothing, taking sips of coffee instead.

"How many witnesses do you have?" asked Chuck.

"Several eyewitnesses and many second-hand accounts. Stella was very active during the war and memorable when she chose to be. Usually, the witness didn't know their contact's true identity. Stella spoke many languages and changed her appearance, but some things remain the same."

Chuck looked up at the portrait and I could see the detective in him. "Her eyes. Height."

"Yes," said Dr. Bock. "Stella had lovely blue eyes and that cupid bow mouth. They were all used in the Nazi wanted posters. I can get you a copy of one. There are four in existence."

"Did you know that?" I asked The Girls.

"No, I never imagined she had wanted posters," said Millicent.

"They did little good," said Dr. Bock. "Stella was an adept spy, but one thing I would like to ask you is why?"

The Girls went blank.

"Why what?" asked Myrtle, pouring me more coffee.

"Why did she do it?" asked Dr. Bock. "She was a young woman. My first evidence of her involvement was at nineteen. Your country wasn't in the war yet. She didn't need to be involved and I can't overstate how dangerous her activities were. Women were burned alive for doing less. She must have known that."

"Burned alive?" asked Chuck with a shudder.

"There were several instances of such barbaric behavior." Dr. Bock held her delicate cup so tightly I thought it might shatter. "It has long been thought that you two, her closest family, must know why."

"I'm sorry to disappoint you, but her precise reason remains a mystery," said Myrtle.

Precise.

Words meant a lot to my godmothers and I knew what that one meant. They knew something, probably quite a lot, but short of Stella telling them point-blank, they would never speculate.

Dr. Bock slumped with disappointment. "I suppose it was too much to hope for. Stella was quite secretive, as I'm sure you know."

A kind of sadness flickered over my godmothers' faces and then they looked at me. "Perhaps Mercy can tell you more."

"Me?" I gasped.

They tilted their chins down and identical smiles formed on their lipsticked lips. "Come now, dear. It's alright to say."

This feels like a trap.

"I don't know anything, really." There wasn't any reason to hide. My godmothers knew I'd been snooping already. "I did talk to Marie in Paris."

Dr. Bock unslumped instantly. "*The* Marie?"

"I don't know. There's probably a lot of Maries," I said and The Girls laughed. "There's only one Marie. *The Marie*."

"Marie Galloway Laurence Morris Huntley Huntley Smith?" Dr. Bock asked.

"The very same."

"What did she tell you?"

I told her about the Jewish tour guide, Abel, that Stella was trying to find. Marie thought he'd been arrested, but she didn't know any specifics.

"A Jewish tour guide," said Dr. Bock. "When was this?"

"November 1938."

She looked up from the notepad she'd gotten out. "That's rather specific."

"I know Stella and her husband were there on their honeymoon. I'm guessing he was their guide."

"No last name?"

"Sorry, no. I really don't know anything about Stella's spying except that Marie thought she had an enemy in the SS, Helmut Peiper."

Dr. Bock scowled. "Ah, yes, Peiper. Dr. Bloom mentioned him."

"You know of this man?" asked Millicent, her interest growing.

"Yes, I do. He is what you Americans might call an odd duck. SS that worked for Göring."

I took a big gulp of coffee and asked, "Did he do interrogations?"

"Not as a rule, but he did a few that came to my attention," she said, reaching down into her briefcase. "I have an interview taken by my father in 1962. Is the name Augustus Gröber familiar to you?

The Girls sat up straight. "Oh, yes. Of course."

"Who is he?" asked Chuck.

Dr. Bock placed her information on the table. "A Catholic priest arrested for being a suspected spy for the Allies in Freiburg."

"Was he?"

She smiled. "No. He was something much better and he was in number eight Prinz-Albrecht-Straße in 1940. Peiper interrogated him."

"1940, not '43?" I asked.

"No. I believe the date on the back of the portrait refers to something else. Stella was in number eight in 1940. It is possible she was there more than once, but I am certain about 1940.

Dr. Bock's father, also a noted historian, interviewed Father Gröber when he was declared Righteous Among the Nations by Israel for his work smuggling Jewish children out of Germany and Austria during the war. The Nazi suspected him of spying and only his fervent pro-Nazi sermons saved him from being sent to a concentration camp. While he was in the prison, he recalled a young English woman in an adjoining cell. She had beautiful blue eyes and strawberry blonde hair. Her name was Charlotte Sedgwick and she claimed to be a nanny for an aristocratic French family of Barbier. She was also arrested for spying in Paris. They spoke several times during the four days that their stays overlapped. Father Gröber liked the young woman. He said she seemed frightened and confused about why she was there. She believed that the Barbier family would secure her release and then she would go home to London. The good father believed she was British, but there was something in her eyes, a sharpness, a raw intelligence that made him doubt that she was a nanny. That and she casually asked questions about him and Freiburg. They were subtle, but she got tidbits out of him with ease. Father Gröber came to believe that she was exactly who the Nazis thought she was and he was saddened to think that she would soon go to her death. She had been brutally interrogated. He had heard her screaming and he was certain she would confess. But that didn't happen. The Barbier family somehow secured her release. When the guards came to get Stella, she took the father's hand and said, "I wish you luck and Godspeed in your endeavors. I do love children."

Father Gröber was shocked to hear that and believed Charlotte Sedgwick knew what his true activities were. He might've forgotten her eyes and words if it weren't for what happened next. The father was told he was being released three days later. Instead, he was interrogated about Charlotte Sedgwick, what she said and her accent. The man doing the interrogation was someone new, Helmut Peiper, and he was furious that Charlotte had been released. He and a young man, only in his teens, beat the Father into unconsciousness. He was released a week later, blind in one eye and barely able to walk out on his own. Father Gröber never gave Peiper anything on Charlotte, not that he had anything other than suspicions. Suspicions that he felt were confirmed by Peiper's desperation to find out about Charlotte.

Dr. Bock pushed the transcript of her father's interview over to me. It was originally in German, but it'd been translated into English. She'd highlighted the Father's description of Charlotte that sounded a whole lot like Stella. "I believe that Stella was Charlotte. No trace of her was ever found. She simply walked out of prison and disappeared. The Barbier family did exist and exists to this day. They never had an English nanny or anyone working for them named Charlotte Sedgwick."

Chuck leaned over and picked up the photo Dr. Bock had of an elderly Father Gröber with an eyepatch over his right eye and a proud smile. He died only six months after the interview. The senior Bock was lucky to get it.

"Who was the young man with Peiper?" asked Chuck.

"The Father thought the two men resembled each other. They may have been related. The only name he heard was Peiper. Before you ask, Peiper had no children that we know of and he was an only child himself."

I scanned the page. "How old was this kid?"

Chuck pointed to the page. "The Father thought maybe fifteen."

"Fifteen and nearly beating a Catholic priest to death. I don't know what to do with that," I said. "You don't have anything on him?"

"I have never come across him other than that one interrogation. But I do have this." She passed me photocopy of some sort of Nazi document. It had a swastika at the top and everything. I had a little German, but all I could make out was that it transferred Helmet Peiper to Hermann Göring.

"October 1938," I said.

"Yes. Peiper was to answer to Göring for the duration of the project," said Dr. Bock.

"What project?" asked Millicent.

"I have nothing on that, but I do have this." She slid over another document. "It authorizes all necessary travel expenses for Peiper and his assistant."

"Gerhard Müller," said Chuck. "No rank."

"A civilian, like the boy Father Gröber described," said Dr. Bock. "It could be the same person or perhaps not."

"You haven't researched him?" I asked, looking at the date. January 10, 1939.

"I had no reason to."

"Can you tell us anything else about the portrait?" I asked.

"The clothes and hat Stella is wearing are consistent with prisoners at that time," said Dr. Bock.

I looked at the portrait. We were on to something, but Father Gröber wasn't a link to the portrait. "Why would she be wearing that stuff?"

"Excuse me?" asked Dr. Bock.

"The House Prison wasn't a long-term facility, right?"

"No. What are you getting at?"

Chuck kicked back and hooked his fingers behind his head. "I get it. That's a picture of a long-term prisoner, not a nanny who got held for a few days. She'd have her own clothes. While we're at it, her hair is brown, not strawberry blonde."

Dr. Bock threw up her hands. "I have wasted your time. I apologize."

"Not at all," said Millicent.

"Your information is fascinating and I'm certain the young woman Father Gröber met was Stella," said Myrtle.

"I'm terribly sorry. Perhaps I can find more on the flower and date."

Millicent rose from the table. "Perhaps you can. So you don't feel your efforts are wasted, perhaps you'd like to see our Klimt."

Dr. Bock jumped up. "I would be honored. Dr. Broszat will be quite jealous."

"We also have an Olère, that you might be interested in," said Myrtle.

"I'd love to see them both and I will do my best to find out if Stella was in a long-term camp."

The Girls left the room, smiling and chatting about Klimt.

"That was good," said Chuck. "Spidermonkey will be all over that Gerhard Müller."

Joy came in with a bucket of cleaning supplies and a sly smile. "Hello, Mercy. Chuck."

"Hi, Joy," I said. "We'll get out of your way."

"And go upstairs," she said, still smiling.

"Upstairs?"

"Your room." She took out a feather duster and flitted it at us. "Good things come to those who wait."

"What are you up to?" I asked.

"It's what you've been up to. Now go upstairs." Joy began dusting the dust-free room.

Chuck took my hand and we went through the house, passing The Girls and Dr. Bock in the library. Millicent saw us and blew me a kiss. Not in trouble, I guess, but I had a feeling something was about to happen.

We dashed up the long curving staircase past paintings, etchings, and photos. The Bled family was interspersed among the masterpieces and miniatures. Snapshots of Stella as a bride, Myrtle cuddling baby Lawton, and Josiah in uniform. And I was there. Me sitting on the edge of Baudelaire's tomb, gnawing on a chocolate babka with ratty pigtails, no more than two. Me on the wall with the Bled family. I ran up those stairs, suddenly aware of how much I wanted to be one of them, not only the cherished goddaughter, but a real Bled. Now that would be beyond special. Josiah would be my uncle, too. Stella, my cousin.

The door to my room was open, warm light spilling into the hall. I stopped short and said, "What do you think it is?"

Chuck turned and took me in his arms, kissing me like he hadn't since New Orleans. His heat flooded me and I lost track of where we were and what we were supposed to be doing. Lips on mine. Lips on my earlobe and neck.

"I don't care," whispered Chuck. "If it comes from The Girls, it will be wonderful, like you."

"I do love you," I said.

"Not as much as I love you."

"Not true."

"It is," he said. "I don't mind."

"But—"

He gave me another toe-curling kiss and said, "Let's see what they've left for you."

"Us," I said, leading him in the bedroom. I didn't see it at first. The bed was turned down and new set of silk pajamas were laid across the plump pillows. It was the red that finally caught my eye. I ran to the bed and saw the last thing I expected. Stella's book. The hand-stitched leather scrapbook embossed with the word *Tarragon* was just as I remembered from the one time I was allowed to see it in the bank vault. What had Millicent said? Something about my needing the knowledge it contained.

I didn't pick it up. I did as my godmothers intended. I put on the pajamas and slid under the covers. They always said the best place to read a good book was cozy in bed. Chuck kicked off his shoes and we cuddled up together with the book between us.

I opened the heavy cover and saw the photo I remembered so well. It was of Stella at a garden party in Newport, New York. She was leaning precariously over a ledge to sniff a riot of blossoms just out of reach. In the background was Nicky, her future husband, with an expression of dazzled awe on his handsome face. The photographer had managed to catch the first moment Nicky ever laid eyes on Stella. The moment when multitudes of lives would change forever. Nicky wasn't supposed to be at that party, a ladies-only tea at his mother's cottage, but, on a whim, he'd driven up from New York to give her a birthday present a week early. If he hadn't, he never would've seen Stella. She was supposed to leave for St. Louis the following morning. A whim can change the world.

"Are you ready?" asked Chuck.

I kissed his cheek. "Turn the page."

The End

Down and Dirty (Mercy Watts Mysteries Book Nine

My life as a nurse had two settings, holy crap and snooze. It was late October and I'd been on the snooze setting for nearly two months. That's a long time for someone like me. I don't do quiet, as a general rule, so you'd think I'd appreciate a steady diet of flu shots and sports physicals, but I didn't. I'm kind of an idiot that way.

And because I lack even a modicum of sense, I sat slumped over in the Columbia Clinic's break room, finishing a bland turkey sandwich and wishing for a little holy crap. Not a lot. Just a little. A mysterious rash or a sudden onset of labor wouldn't have gone amiss, but that's not how my life works. It was go big or go home and I definitely wasn't going home.

Then, like she sensed my boredom, Shawna the nurse practitioner stuck her head into the break room and said, "Done? Someone special needs to see you."

I glared at her and crumbled my brown paper bag super slow because when Shawna says "someone special" she doesn't mean the Pope wants to give me his blessing. Channing Tatum didn't want to try out his new strip routine for little old me and I sure wasn't being awarded Nurse of the Year. "Someone special" meant someone bad because I'm Mercy Watts and that's how I roll.

"Mercy?" she said.

"I heard you."

She walked in, poured a cup of coffee, and gave me the once over, frowning slightly. I don't know what the problem was, since for once I was stain-free and I even had on makeup, if Blistex and a smudge of mascara counts.

"That's not going to work," she said.

"What?"

"Do you have some stuff?"

I screwed the top on my Thermos and wished it had been filled with hot chocolate instead of herbal tea. I was going to need it. "What kind of stuff?"

"Stuff to make you look like her."

I groaned. Her was Marilyn Monroe and I hardly needed stuff to look like the long dead starlet. I was a dead ringer.

"And why, pray tell, do I need to look like her?" I asked.

Shawna sipped her coffee and avoided eye contact.

"If it's Mr. Cadell, you can forget it. I wouldn't blow my nose for that old buzzard."

She chuckled. "No, not him. He's impervious to pretty and everything else that's possibly pleasant."

"I don't have him today?"

"He's your two o'clock."

Dammit.

"So, you found another surly diabetic amputee to torture me?"

"Not today."

I crossed my arms.

"This is a gimme, I swear," said Shawna.

"I'm waiting."

"It's a slow pitch. Put on a little lip gloss and you're golden."

"If this patient is so easy, why don't you take him? I assume it's a him," I said.

Shawna drained her cup and eyed the receptionist's birthday cake on the counter. "Because I'm a mom of four and need to lose twenty pounds and you're...you."

Shawna didn't need to lose twenty pounds and if her kids and husband would stop driving her halfway to crazy town, she'd look a good five years younger, maybe more.

"I say you take him," I said. "If I've got Mr. Cadell at two, I need to save my strength."

"Alright. Fine. You were requested."

"By?"

"Joanna Smart."

I'd seen Joanna a few times. Nothing major. Certainly nothing memorable. A flu shot here, a throat swab there.

"Joanna wants me?"

"For her son, Patrick."

Now it was coming together. Shawna was pimping me out so to speak.

"What am I supposed to do? Bat my eyelashes so he'll get his sports physical?" I know that sounds stupid, but it wouldn't be the first time.

"There's something going on and neither Joanna or I can get a word out of him."

Steve the receptionist ambled in. "Patrick Smart's waiting."

"From what I remember, Patrick couldn't have cared less when I gave him his meningococcal booster last year. What makes you think I'll have any influence?" I asked.

"Because you're sex in scrubs," said Steve.

"Steve!" Shawna blushed.

"You think she doesn't know." He grinned at me. "If I wasn't playing for the other team, I'd be deeply in love. I kinda am anyway."

I went over and hugged him. "You're my favorite."

"Because I don't try to feel you up?"

"That helps."

"Alright you two. Steve, check and see if senior services has been successful in loading up Mr. Cadell. Mercy, go work your magic and charm the truth out of Patrick."

Steve grumbled his way out of the break room and I asked, "What am I looking for? Depression? Drug use?"

"Joanna says he's surly, skipping school, and spending inordinate amounts of time in the bathroom."

"He's a teenage boy."

"She thought she heard him crying in there a couple of times."

"Broke up with a girlfriend?"

"Joanna says no. Girlfriend is Sara and she's over all the time. They searched his room and found no evidence of drugs."

I wrinkled my nose. My dad had searched my room more than once and I wasn't a fan. "No wonder he won't talk to them."

"You'll understand when you have kids."

"People say that about everything. You'll understand when... My mom's been saying I'll like raw onions when I'm an adult. Hell, she still says that. Hello, I'm an adult and I hate raw onions."

"Kids change everything."

"I hope not."

"It's inevitable."

"Swell," I said. "What else ya got?"

Shawna got more coffee and shrugged. "That's it. Joanna's worried. She has a feeling."

Now that I understood. I'd been known to have a few feelings and I was never wrong when I felt something wasn't right.

"Okay. Fine. I'll slap on some gloss and see what I can do."

"Maybe...you know, fluff the hair, put on some mascara and blush."

"The whole shebang."

"You're going to need it. Patrick is...well...sixteen and he's feeling it," said Shawna.

"Awesome."

"I have every faith."

"Glad somebody does." I got my purse out of my locker and the whole shebang wasn't happening. Since the clinic reopened after the flood during the summer and my exploits in August—catching ex-cop serial killer, Scott Frame, and getting him killed in my parents' house— the Columbia Clinic had been all over the news as my workplace. Business was better than ever, if boring, and makeup wasn't a priority. I had a compact, Burt's Bees tinted gloss, and a stick of deodorant. The last one had gotten the most use.

I slathered on the gloss and used a dab to give my cheeks some color. My hair wasn't happy about being yanked out of its ponytail and I wasn't completely sure I should leave it down. I'd gotten a rather unfortunate haircut on the fly from my then bodyguard, Fats Licata, and my hair was growing out in the weirdest way possible, getting curly in spots and straight in others. It wasn't at all the full Marilyn that Shawna was looking for, but what are you going to do.

When I walked into Room 3, Patrick wasn't sitting on the exam table. He sat jammed into the corner on the rolling chair that usually sat at the computer. His arms were tightly folded and his jaw clenched. It can never be easy. Absolutely never.

"Hi. I'm Mercy and I'll be your nurse today."

"Nice get up."

"Get up?"

"Your face."

I yawned. "It's my face. Nothing to be done."

"My girlfriend says you had surgery to look like that."

"Does she?"

"Yeah. Pretty stupid. Marilyn Monroe was a twat."

Nice.

"I wouldn't know. Never met her."

"All that makeup sucks. You should go natural like my girlfriend. She's really hot. You're just sad."

Breathe. No smacking.

"And you're kinda fat. You should go on a diet."

Maybe a little smack.

"You think I'm lame. Got it." I leaned on the door and crossed my arms. "What do you want to do?"

"About what? Your face?" Patrick snickered and I rolled my eyes.

"What are you going to do about you?" I asked.

The malicious joy left his face in an instant. "Nothing. I'm okay."

"If you're okay then you can stop being surly, skipping school, and crying in the bathroom."

Patrick's shoulders went up to his ears. "What the fuck? I don't cry in the bathroom."

"Because you're okay," I said.

"Yeah."

I pulled the gloss out of my scrub pocket and put on another layer. "So we're all good here. Your mom won't be back with you next week or the week after that. I've met Joanna. She *does* seem like the type that gives up easily."

He stared at the floor and shifted in his seat like it was suddenly covered with red ants. "Why can't people leave me alone?"

"I get paid to bother you. And after this, I get to bother an old man with diabetes. He's in danger of getting *another* foot chopped off because he won't stop eating Twinkies."

"Gross."

"Tell me about it."

Patrick met my eyes and defiantly said, "I want to go home."

I stepped aside. "Fine with me. See you next week."

"I'm not coming back."

"Are you self-sufficient?" I asked.

Patrick scowled at me.

"Then you're coming back. What's your co-pay?"

"Co-pay?"

I smiled. Ah the young and financially ignorant. "The amount your parents are paying for each visit."

"I don't give a crap."

"In my experience, dad's care. Mom's not so much. Joanna will want to fix you no matter the cost. Your dad probably yells about turning off lights and tries to put the thermostat down to sixty-three in the dead of winter."

Patrick was back to staring at the floor. "I don't want to come back."

"Got it."

"So...did you get surgery?" he asked, peeking up at me.

"Nope. I was born this way. I look like my mom."

He straightened up and relaxed a tiny bit. "That's weird."

"I say that about my life all the time," I said.

"At least you're hot."

I went over and perched on the exam table. Somebody might as well sit on it. "My current stalker thinks so."

"You have stalkers?" More relaxing. Good.

"Just one at the moment."

His arms unclenched and he said, "Can't you have him arrested?"

"He's new and hasn't actually done anything too crazy yet," I said.

"Like what?"

"Sending me dead animals in the mail, threatening to kidnap me, or breaking into my apartment building."

"That's fucked. Did that stuff happen before you were on the news?"

"A few times. My good intentions often have bad consequences," I said.

He went back to staring at the floor. "Yeah."

"Did you have good intentions?"

"My mom won't think so."

"It doesn't matter what she thinks, it matters what you intended. Did you have good intentions?"

"Yeah."

"And bad consequences?"

"I don't know. Maybe."

I shifted on the table and the paper crinkled and ripped, making me think that Patrick's weight loss idea wasn't totally off the mark. "I could start guessing, but I've got to go be berated and likely have a Twinkie shoved up my nose so let's have it."

"Are you going to tell my mom?" asked Patrick.

"Yes."

Patrick jumped to his feet. "Holy crap. You could've lied."

I laid back on the table with its raised back and put my arms behind my head. "Because you enjoy being lied to."

"She's going to freak."

"It's not as bad as she imagines," I said.

Patrick reached for the door knob, but stopped. "How do you know?"

"Joanna's a mom. She's imagining the worst. She thinks you're hurting yourself or not going to college."

"That's stupid. I'm totally going to college," he said.

"Hurting yourself?"

"Hell no."

"But something's hurting?"

"Yeah."

Before I could ask another question there was yelling outside the exam room. Must've been in the waiting room because I couldn't quite make it out.

"That's probably my diabetic," I said.

"Is he a total asshat?"

"Big time and he *is* hurting himself."

"I'm not."

"Glad to hear it. What's going on, Patrick?"

The kid put his head so far down into his chest I could barely hear him. In short, Patrick Smart had an STD. If I had to guess a screaming case of chlamydia. He was crying in the bathroom because his penis was on fire when he peed and there was something coming out that was definitely not pee. To make things worse, he was in love with the one and only girl he'd had sex with, Sara, and she'd given it to him. In Patrick's hormone-laden brain, the only thing worse than telling his mom that he had an STD was telling Sara that she gave it to him. I could see his point.

"You have to tell her. She needs treatment," I said.

"Maybe it will go away."

"It's not going away. It's—" More screaming erupted from the waiting room and this time I could identify a woman's voice. Something about bastards and appointments. I wasn't taking her. I didn't care who she was. "Patrick, it's not something that runs its course and disappears."

"It might."

"It won't."

Patrick snuffled and I gave him a tissue. "I'll tell her if you want me to."

"Yeah?"

"Sure, but you'll have to talk to her eventually."

"She'll break up with me. She'll think I gave it to her," said Patrick.

Another good point.

"We'll work on the timeline. I'm sure she has symptoms. She'll realize the truth and we'll find out who gave it to her. He's probably infecting half your high school."

He cringed. "You think?"

"Absolutely."

"It's Barrett Smith. He's a total douche. Sara went out with him for six months before me."

"Who's he dating now?" I asked.

"Like you said, half the school."

There was a loud banging and glass shattering. I put Patrick in the chair. "Stay here and don't come out until I tell you to."

"Don't do it," he said. "You'll get more stalkers."

Dammit.

"I know." I ran out and the screaming was recognizable. It was Beth Babcock of the Mission Hill Babcocks, not to be confused with the Babcocks of Conway's Fork. Beth was a long-time patient and a long-time pain in the butt. Shawna had said something about laying down the law with Beth at some point and I guess today was that point.

"Beth, I'm going to have to call the police," said Steve as I rounded the corner and got a load of Beth the Berserker standing in front of the desk, holding a chair aloft.

"Call 'em, you gay motherfucker," yelled Beth. "I've got rights."

Shawna picked up the phone. "You have no right to insult my staff and wreck the clinic. Leave."

"Health care is a right! You have to see me!"

"Pay your co-pay."

"That's bullshit!"

"You owe 700 dollars, Beth," said Steve. "We're asking you to pay fifty."

Beth lifted the chair higher, revealing her bellybutton ring with its diamond stud. "I have a sore throat. You have to test for strep."

"You have to make a payment on your account," said Steve.

"I have bills to pay!" she screamed.

"So do I!" Shawna yelled back and began dialing 911.

Beth hauled back to crash the chair over the desk onto Steve's head. She was a tall woman. She could've done it, but I dashed over and wrenched the chair out of her grasp.

"Take a hike, Beth," I said, slamming the chair to the floor.

"I'll burn this fucker down!" With that, Beth of the Mission Hill Babcocks marched out.

"Good job, Mercy," said Mr. DeCandido, waiting patiently for his stitches to be removed. "But you haven't heard the last of her. Tobin Babcock just got arrested for taking pot shots at Jerry Ford's truck after he tried to collect on a plumbing job. That Mission Hill bunch thinks everything should be free."

Shawna was still holding the phone. "You think I should still call?"

"Mr. DeCandido is right. Call and get it over with," I said.

Steve smiled at me. "Maybe Chuck will take the call. I wouldn't mind saying hello."

"He's got a girlfriend," I said, grinning back. "Me."

"Minds have been known to change."

"Trust me. His won't."

Steve sighed. His dating prospects in rural Illinois weren't lively. "If you know anyone?"

"I'll keep an eye out."

Shawna put her hand over the phone. "Do you hear something?"

"Oh crap," said Steve. "That's a truck revving."

We ran to the window and I gasped before yelling at our waiting patients. "Get out the back. She's going to ram us. Go! Go! Go!"

Steve sprang into action, picking up a pair of toddlers and pushing Mrs. McGinty's wheelchair with one hand. Shawna gathered up a couple of pregnant moms and I ran out the door. They didn't need me. Shawna was nothing if not good in a crisis.

Beth Babcock was crazy in a crisis and getting crazier by the moment. She pulled her brand-new enormous Ram 4WD Crew Cab around, sideswiping two Nissans and Shawna's decrepit minivan and was now facing our front steps, revving her engine and screaming about health care rights.

I ran down the steps, waving my arms and screaming, "We've got kids in there! Stop!"

Robert Babcock of the Conway's Fork Babcocks ran across the Jiffy Stop parking lot, yelling, "God dammit, Beth! You're making us look bad!"

"You want to pay my bill?" she screamed at him.

"Shut up and pay your own bill, you crazy bitch!"

Now you don't say the B-word to a Mission Hill Babcock or the C-word, F-word, D-word. Really, it's best to say no words at all, especially if you happen to be a Conway's Fork Babcock, they of the nicely mowed lawns and paid bills.

Beth howled in rage and, for a moment, just one blissful moment, I thought she might get out and try to beat up Robert. She'd beat up men before, but none ever pressed charges. It wasn't cool to be beat up by a woman, even if it was Beth the Berserker Babcock.

Robert was more than a match for Beth. I could see her calculating the odds and she chose me. Robert launched himself at her open window as she stomped on the gas. I dove out of the way. I felt the bumper brush my toe before I face-planted into Shawna's beloved fall squash display. There was a huge crash, splinters and God knows what rained down on me. So much screaming pierced the air, for a second, I thought I was screaming. I wasn't, but everyone within a mile radius was.

Beth's truck was rammed halfway in our lobby and she was still gunning the engine. The tires were spinning and spewing vile smoke that billowed out like there was a four-alarm fire going on.

I sat up in a daze and watched Beth screaming until she kicked open her door, yelling, "You ruined my truck!" Then she ran to the back and flipped herself over the side into the bed. I probably should've done something, but honestly, I wanted to see what was going to happen. She had a gun rack, but it was in the cab. That's right. Beth the Berserker had a license. Apparently, everyone in the tri-state area knowing you're batshit crazy isn't a deterrent to gun ownership.

But Beth, probably because she's barking mad, didn't go for the semi-auto she had displayed. She went for the gas can she had in the truck bed.

"I'll burn this fucker down!" she screamed and leapt out of the truck like a lynx, pulled out a lighter, and ran up to the clinic.

Fan-freaking-tastic!

I jumped up and tackled the nut job as she was unscrewing the lid of the gas can. When I hit her, it popped off, spewing gas everywhere as we rolled off the porch, down the decorative embankment into the drainage ditch. Beth screamed the entire time and kept trying to light the lighter. I guess it didn't dawn on her that she was covered in gas. Or maybe it did. It's hard to say with the insane.

"Stop that!" I yelled.

"I'm burning this fucker down!" She kept flicking that lighter and I swear I heard a spark. So I bit her and not a little nip either. I chomped down like she was one of my friend Aaron's butter and herb-basted steaks. She screamed bloody murder and when the cops dove into the ditch, they had to pry my jaws apart.

I want to say it wasn't my finest moment, but I can't. I bit a Mission Hill Babcock and lived to tell the tale. I was kinda bad ass. At least, I felt bad ass until I looked up and found more than a dozen cellphones recording. One of them was held by none other than my latest stalker, Jimmy Elbert. He was recording and yelling, "I love you." Half the cameras were recording him. I was so getting on the evening news.

"Mercy Watts, my God," said Jordan Alsop, local cop and pizzeria owner. "Why?"

"I didn't do it," I said, spitting out a glob of something best left unnamed.

He sighed and gave me a hand up. "You're in this ditch."

"Tackling Beth. Didn't you hear? She's going to burn this fucker down."

The other cop, Carrie King, was struggling to cuff Beth and getting spit on in the process.

"You know, I was a half hour to the end of my shift. Now I've got to write a report and book Beth. I'll be late for the afternoon shift."

"My heart bleeds for you," I said.

Beth hawked a loogie at Carrie's face and it spattered her cheek.

"You want to help your partner?" I asked.

"Are you kidding?" asked Jordan. "Carrie'll spit on me. Besides, she's been aching to cuff Beth for six months."

"Any particular reason, I mean, other than the obvious?"

"Beth keyed her husband's car after he parked in the handicapped spot she wanted," said John.

"Isn't Carrie's husband a paraplegic?" I asked.

"He is, but Beth thought she ought to park there being that she likes the extra space for that behemoth of hers."

"I'm thinking about biting her again."

"Word to the wise. I'd watch your back. The Mission Hill Babcocks don't take kindly to anyone fighting back. Tobin's out on bail."

Swell.

"I'll remember that."

Carrie finally got Beth cuffed. Excessive force may or may not have been used. I saw nothing that I'm willing to remember.

Helpful bystanders hauled Beth out of the ditch, but only after she was cuffed. Wusses. Then two pairs of feet walked up and a young man's hand reached down for me.

"I didn't wait for you," said Patrick.

"I see that and you're forgiven."

He hauled me out and then we helped Jordan, who looked like a wet cat and was just as mad. "I'm off to a huge hassle. If any of *those* Babcocks show their face in your vicinity, give me a call."

I said I would, but I wouldn't. What was Jordan going to do? Give them a ticket? I'd rather hire Fats Licata to follow me around and beat up Babcocks.

"So..." said Joanna Smart, wringing her hands. "I hate to bother you."

Why? Everyone else does.

"No problem," I said.

"Patrick says you have something to tell me."

I took a breath and pushed my smelly, wet hair out of my face. "Yes, and given what just occurred here, I hope you'll be calm about it."

"Oh my God," she said. "Oh my God."

"That's not calm, Joanna."

"Sorry. He's just my boy. My beautiful baby boy." Joanna got all teary-eyed. Motherhood. It was a disease of the heartstrings.

"He's fine. Absolutely fine. Only you can make it really bad."

"Me?"

"You."

Joanna promised to stay calm and to my amazement, she did. She found out in one fell swoop that her beautiful baby boy was both having sex and had an STD. She took it well, probably because he kept saying he was going to college and thought she was the best mom in the world.

"He has to get a test, right?" she asked

"Yes, but, at least, we can avoid the bad one these days. It will take a couple of days to get the results."

Patrick gasped. "A couple of days? I can't wait that long. It freaking hurts."

"Shawna might be willing to write you a script since your symptoms are consistent. You still have to test though."

Joanna ran off between EMTs and newly arrived cops, calling for Shawna.

"I can do the bad test," said Patrick, puffing up and looking almost tough.

"You don't want that test."

"I did this and I can take that test."

"It involves me sticking a Q-tip up your penis," I said.

"Never mind."

"That's what I thought," I said, wringing out my scrub top.

Patrick took off his hoodie and handed it to me. "You better put this on."

"It's not that cold."

"You're wearing a polka-dot bra."

I put on the hoodie, but it was already too late. Me and my non-matching underwear was up on YouTube getting views. I could feel the humiliation.

"Your life really sucks," said Patrick.

"Not all the time," I said, smiling for the local news crew. Grin and bear it. It's a motto for a reason.

"Is your stalker here?"

I pointed at Jimmy Elbert. He looked up from his phone and gave me a finger wave.

"What a loser. He didn't even help you."

"They never help. Well, there's been a notable exception here and there, but mostly never."

Patrick yelled at Jimmy, "Hey, you're a douchebag!"

Jimmy went stiff and then turned tail and ran. He really was a douchebag.

**Read the rest in
Down and Dirty (Mercy Watts Mysteries Book Nine)**

ABOUT THE AUTHOR

USA Today bestselling author A.W. Hartoin grew up in rural Missouri, but her grandmother lived in the Central West End area of St. Louis. The CWE fascinated her with its enormous houses, every one unique. She was sure there was a story behind each ornate door. Going to Grandma's house was a treat and an adventure. As the only grandchild around for many years, A.W. spent her visits exploring the many rooms with their many secrets. That's how Mercy Watts and the fairies of Whipplethorn came to be.

As an adult, A.W. Hartoin decided she needed a whole lot more life experience if she was going to write good characters so she joined the Air Force. It was the best education she could've hoped for. She met her husband and traveled the world, living in Alaska, Italy, and Germany before settling in Colorado for nearly eleven years. Now A.W. has returned to Germany and lives in picturesque Waldenbuch with her family and two spoiled cats, who absolutely believe they should be allowed to escape and roam the village freely.

www.ingramcontent.com/pod-product-compliance
Lightning Source LLC
Chambersburg PA
CBHW020859060726
47591CB00004B/1002